MW00914780

ABRA CADAVER

By JEROLD LAST

Copyright © 2017 Jerold Last

1

This novel is a work of fiction. Names, characters, and incidents are products of the author's imagination. Real places and locations are used fictitiously, and the incidents described are not to be construed of as having really occurred. Winters, Davis, and Yolo County are real places, physically very much as I have described the area. I've visited all the places and restaurants described and recommend them highly. However, any resemblance of specific scenes in the novel to actual events, locales, organizations, or persons, living or dead, is entirely coincidental.

Copyright © 2017 Jerold Last

Cover Copyright © 2016 Caitlin Harley

All rights reserved. No part of this book may be used or reproduced in any manner whatsoever without written permission of the author, except in the case of brief quotations embodied in critical articles and reviews.

ACKNOWLEDGEMENTS

We live in Yolo County, California, so the geography, wineries, and wildfires are all based on realities we know or have lived through. The roots of this novel go back more than a decade ago, when I took a trip to Mendoza and Salta, Argentina with a wine expert who was a friend of a friend, and who is now a good friend of mine in his own right. Jim Lapsley is an international wine competition judge, a former owner of his own winery in Yolo County (California), and a historian whose Ph.D. dissertation, on the history of the Napa Valley wine industry, was the source material for a very readable book available from Amazon entitled "Bottled Poetry". We did a bunch of private winery tours while in Argentina, which planted the seeds that sprouted into this book. Jim also made several helpful suggestions and comments about an early version of this book.

Thanks are due to my wife Elaine who read and critically edited several drafts of this book and contributed her considerable expertise to training Juliet in various drafts of the novel, as well as suggesting several specific scenes. I was fortunate to also have expert input from Margaret Norris, a friend of Elaine's who actually trains and works search and rescue dogs, who helped critique Bruce's training and working of Juliet in an early draft of the novel. Melissa Ribley, owner of Rango (one of Jolie's grand-puppies), also read an advance copy and made several helpful suggestions. Caitlin Harley, owner of Bruce (one of Jolie's puppies), designed and created the book cover.

And special thanks to our own Jolie, aka Grand Champion V.D. Nacht's Classic Beaujolais, MH, CGC, the inspiration and the model for Juliet in what are now three novels in this series, who taught us just how versatile and loveable the German shorthaired pointer breed is and can be in real life.

The Roger and Suzanne series is deliberately written so the books can be read in any order; each story is complete and designed to be read on its own. If you'd like to learn more of the backstory about Juliet, she was introduced in an earlier novel in this series entitled *The Deadly Dog Show* and was also featured in *Hunter Down*. Among the recurring human series characters in this book, we first met Vincent Romero in *The Surreal Killer* and Bruce the nanny in *The Matador Murders*. Both have played significant roles in several of the other books, especially *The Deadly Dog Show*, which also introduced Sherry Wyne. Jason Culpepper made his series debut in *Unbearably Deadly*. Gretchen and Barbara Kaufman debuted in *The Origin of Murder*, and we first met Connie Sherman in *Rum, Cigars, and Corpses*.

TABLE OF CONTENTS

Prologue

They walked hand-in-hand through the vast sprawling vineyard, the dark hulking shapes of the house and winery behind them intruding on the bucolic pastoral scene. Or the scene would have been bucolic were it not for the thick pall of smoke and ash in the air around them coming from the raging wildfire perilously nearby.

"Do you think the fire is going to interfere with our wedding plans?" Sherry asked.

Wally squeezed her hand reassuringly. "No, these wildfires have happened frequently enough since the drought began several years ago that people around here are getting used to them. The big ones can burn for weeks, or even months, but they usually stay on the other side of the coastal mountains so this area should be safe."

"Look at the sun, Wally. I've never seen it those colors before. It's red, yellow, pink, beige, and all the other soft colors of the artist's palette. It's weird looking but oddly beautiful through all the muck in the air. Like an abstract painting of how the sun should appear.

"But, despite all that beauty, standing here today surrounded by smoke, ash, and fire everything feels wrong. Can you sense the menace I'm feeling? It's almost like the fire is the embodiment of all that's evil trying to consume us."

Wally looked directly at his fiancé. "I think your imagination may be telling your subconscious mind you're nervous about the wedding. That's normal, Sherry, but you can't let it ruin the moment, or even more importantly the wedding itself for you. Enjoy the colors and ignore the wildfire as best you can."

They stared up at the concentric circles of color around the partially obscured sun in silence for several moments.

"Are you ready for all the fuss of a big wedding this weekend now, dear?" Wally broke the silence.

"I've haven't been more ready for anything in a very long time," she replied with a squeeze of his hand.

Wally kissed her gently. "After all the fuss is over and things settle down I've got lots of things to tell you about the business and my family. It seems like we've both been too busy to find time to just sit and talk about those kinds of things. It's going to be a lot of fun to spend a little time together after we're married and away from here on our honeymoon when both of us aren't just too busy working."

"Are you worried about this fire damaging the grapes or the winery?" she asked.

"A little bit," he admitted grudgingly, "but only if it jumps the mountains. It hasn't shown any indications of coming directly this way yet. But these big wildfires are completely unpredictable and can keep burning for months, so we can't take them for granted. Clay and the winery crew know what to do if it does come this way. We have plenty of water to defend the house and winery from this fire."

Sherry looked up at her fiancé adoringly. "After we get back from our honeymoon I'd like to build some dog runs behind the house and move all my shorthairs over here. Then maybe sell the Carmichael house and live here full time. Do you think you can stand having lots of dogs and new puppies around all the time?"

"Of course I can," he answered. "I understood that would be part of the package when I first proposed to you."

Chapter 1. Searching for a backyard cadaver

It was a beautiful southern California day in June. The sky was cloudless and mostly blue, with little or no smog here in the far west of Los Angeles thanks to the winds of the previous days that had blown most of the gunk east to go-away land. It was warm, not hot, and the sun was shining brightly with a gentle breeze blowing.

Today was a weekday, so we would both usually be working. The normal routine was for Suzanne to come home from her research laboratory at UCLA, where she was now a full professor, to meet me for dinner in the early evening. I'm Roger Bowman, 6'2" and 190 pounds, 36 years old, have blue eyes, and work out of an office in Century City as a private detective. Before becoming a private eye I'd had successful careers as a patent lawyer and a Los Angeles police detective, but the P.I. lifestyle was the right choice for me.

Suzanne Foster is Mrs. Bowman. At 5'8", normally with a lean athletic body and long blond hair, she's worthy of a long look or two. One of my greatest delights in life is giving her those long looks. She's presently very obviously pregnant, but I enjoy looking at her even more these days. Our nanny, Bruce, who looks after our almost 3-year-old son Robert, keeps house and cooks for us. Rounding out the Bowman household are Juliet and Romeo, our two champion German shorthaired pointers.

Juliet lay on her side on the couch cushions to Bruce's left, head dangling over the front end. Her stomach, throat, and all the other vulnerable parts were fully exposed, seemingly shouting, "Scratch me, rub me!" Ancient wild wolf ancestors would have been ashamed of her for violating the wolf credo to never leave your vulnerable parts open to attack. As Bruce absent-mindedly reached over to scratch her flank, the brazen hussy that was Juliet rolled all the way over on her back to demand her tummy needed rubbing too.

Bruce was updating us on today's adventures featuring Robert and Juliet. Wanting to show us her newest accomplishment, Bruce led Juliet outside to the back yard, gesturing we were to follow. In a moment or two all of us, including Juliet, stood in a clump near the northern fence enclosing our large backyard. "Watch this," he announced, gesturing to Suzanne and me.

Bruce called Juliet in, giving her a "heel" command to bring her in beside him.

He gently tapped the back of Juliet's head twice while she was standing to his side, her tail wagging at full German shorthaired pointer speed. "Find," he commanded, in a firm but gentle tone. Our dog sniffed the air a few times before loping out into the large expanse of backyard, carefully quartering into a light breeze.

It took less than thirty seconds for her to stop, alerting by establishing a point and holding her position. She barked twice to announce her find. The imaginary line running from the dog's tail to nose continued directly to the dirt at the base of an orange tree. Juliet remained on alert in her original pointing position, taking great care not to disturb what might have been a crime scene, as I soon learned.

Bruce clipped a leash onto Juliet's collar to begin the process of actively removing her from the would-be crime scene. He walked her several yards back from where she had established her point. Reversing her direction away from her find, he removed her leash and tapped Juliet twice on the back of her head to release the dog from her task. She looked to him for further instructions, receiving a small handful of kibble as a reward. She proudly pranced off away from the direction she'd pointed, obviously very pleased with her new skills, before switching into full blown play mode as she loped around the yard, head high, nose actively testing the breeze for any other interesting scents.

Bruce turned back to Suzanne and me, standing some distance behind him. "It's critically important for police work to protect the integrity of the crime scene, so we can't let the dog or her handler contaminate it. Sometimes the dog will want to mark the spot. That's a big No-No. Sometimes they'll want to dig up whatever they've smelled, and that's another big No-No. Juliet's been trained not only to find the body, but also to hold her point until I get her securely leashed and away from her find to avoid contaminating any evidence that might have been left behind at the crime scene.

"Why don't you do a little digging over where she pointed, Roger?" Bruce requested, handing me a small trowel from his back pocket.

It took me a while and a lot of digging around the spot I estimated Juliet was pointing toward. Eventually I found a jar with several narrow holes punched into its tight-fitting lid lying on its side about six inches down in the hole I'd dug into the well-packed dirt. The jar contained a gauze pad with a dark spot soaked into it.

"I've been working on a new skill with Juliet," Bruce announced proudly. "I thought she might be ready for some training as a cadaver dog. She's taken to it like a duck to water. I guess we shouldn't be surprised. After all, she's Juliet!"

We stood in companionable silence watching Juliet continue to quarter into the light breeze as she followed her nose searching for more concealed scents of human remains. I could readily imagine her doing the same things in large open spaces as she searched dozens or hundreds of acres for a hidden corpse. It was amazing to see a trained dog focus on what seemed to be an impossible task and make success look easy.

"What have you actually had to train her to do while you were converting her from a bird hunter to a cadaver finder?" asked Suzanne.

"Training a cadaver dog is a mix of nose training, hunting, and obedience work. Juliet knows and understands all three things from her previous work in hunt tests. We're just applying the same skills to something different than bird finding. Now she's finding things that smell like dead and decomposing human bodies and alerting us to them."

Suzanne mulled over Bruce's description, then asked, "We all know she has a great nose. That's how she qualified as a Master Hunter. What did you actually have to do to train her to do the little stunt we just saw?"

"Not all that much as it turned out," he replied. "Like any German shorthaired pointer she has an incredibly sensitive and sophisticated sense of smell. She also likes to please her people. So mostly I trained her to find buried or hidden objects that smelled like a dead body by giving her a lot of scent work. Juliet got a food reward every time she found something with the right smells I'd buried or hidden out there for her and held her point until I picked her up. An experienced hunting dog like Juliet already has a lot of the skills she needs. She can find birds by air scent. She can establish and hold her point. Best of all, she knows how to work with her handler. It was just a matter of transferring these skills from pheasant and chukar to cadavers and decaying body parts."

"What would you need to have done differently if you started training her for cadaver work as a puppy?" asked Suzanne.

"Juliet was much easier to work with than a novice puppy. She'd already had all the elements of the essential training when we took her to the Master Hunter level in hunt tests. If she were an untrained dog starting from scratch I'd have treated a few of her favorite toys and some tennis balls with things that smelled of death and decay to introduce her to a new game, finding things I'd hidden that smelled dead. That would have taken a long time and a lot of effort. But we already had the foundation of hunting by scent established."

Bruce paused for a moment to scratch Juliet behind her ears and give her a little love. "I introduced her to the specific scent we were looking for using gauze pads with added scent I hid or buried for her to find. We started by using synthetic corpse scent we bought from a supplier. That got her through most of the early training and is still good for work here in our back yard.

Juliet had heard her name. She pranced up to Bruce eagerly wagging her tail. He slipped her a small dog biscuit, which she happily chewed. "Those placentas and outdated blood samples Suzanne brings home for me from her lab were the buried goodies when we could get out into a large area like a farm or park I could use for more realistic training. After a few days underground the placentas and blood rot nicely into the real smells she's being trained to find."

"At first Juliet just had to find the right object with the right scent I'd buried to get the reward. Then we added several buried objects with the wrong scents like hamburger or decaying hot dogs. That made the job harder, but more realistic. And I've had to find places we can work over an area of several acres to find a single buried sample to make this realistic. She's very good at this game and learns fast, but it still has taken a while to get this far."

I thought I saw the end game here, so asked the obvious question. "How do you see her using these new skills? Just for a fun game where she gets some mental exercise along with the physical part or something more useful, like finding dead bodies?"

"Both," Bruce replied. "Sometime or other you're going to need help finding out whether a missing person is a fugitive or a corpse. Now we have a very highly skilled dog we can use to find out. And, I suspect the Los Angeles County Sheriff's Department might like access to a trained cadaver dog with a certified handler from time to time. You can add the skills and the dog to the list of services provided by your detective agency. I don't know if I ever told you, but I got certified while I was training dogs for the military in Iraq so they should be interested in us and our dogs."

"Hey, Suzanne," I asked. "Where do you get placentas and blood from?"

Suzanne smiled. "That turns out to be surprisingly easy, Roger. One of my colleagues, Tom Goldsmith, whose lab is just down the hall from mine, turned out to be the perfect source. He does a lot of analytical work supporting clinical trials where he assays fats in blood and tissues from human donors. He usually uses less than a milliliter for his assays and stores the samples for later use if they need to check something. The rest of the collected blood has to be disposed of as hazardous waste, which costs him quite a bit of money. He's more than happy to give it to Bruce to use it any way he wants so he doesn't have to worry about disposal fees.

"He also gets placentas sent to him periodically for a study they're doing on how much of a certain chemical a fetus is exposed to if the mother is smoking e-cigarettes during her pregnancy. All of the donors' samples are screened to be free of viruses or any pathogens, and their identity is never included in Tom's samples so there's no way for me to identify the source. This is all perfectly safe as well as permissible and legal thanks to Bruce's certification as a handler."

Juliet trotted up to us, sitting down beside Bruce and barking twice. I think she was thanking Suzanne for her contributions to this new game. Bruce slipped her a couple of dog biscuits, the standard compensation according to canine actors equity for a performance such as the one we'd just witnessed. She followed Bruce back into the house for a well-earned doggie dinner.

Chapter 2. Matchmaking at a backyard barbecue

Today was an unusual day for us. Suzanne and I were home early, at least an hour before we normally ate dinner. We had both cleared our calendars for a backyard barbecue with a carefully selected guest list and several ulterior motives.

Suzanne delighted in matchmaking among our circle of friends. If a likely looking single male appeared on the horizon she immediately paired them off mentally with her single female friends. Tonight's barbecue featured such a potential pairing for the first time. Suzanne's best friend Connie was scheduled to meet one of my colleagues from work, Jason.

Suzanne and I first met Connie Sherman while we were investigating the murder of her husband Delbert in Havana, Cuba several months previously. The two women shared similar professional lives and similar due dates for their expected babies. More importantly, the two hit it off immediately from their first meeting. They were currently spending as much time together as two busy and very pregnant professional women who lived in different cities more than two hours apart could. Suzanne comfortably assumed the role of friend and mentor to her junior colleague at the University of California Medical School in Irvine.

Jason Culpepper, a long-time bachelor who didn't particularly enjoy cooking, lived close to us in Westwood. He was a frequent dinner and barbeque guest when we felt like entertaining. Suzanne had introduced him to a few likely prospects, but nothing had come of her romantic efforts thus far. About 6 feet tall, mid-30s, his blond hair cut short in the traditional military style, looking like he smiled every now and then, Jason very much appeared the part of an eligible bachelor. Suzanne seemed committed to trying to pair him off, and he hadn't shown any signs of objecting to the game thus far.

Suzanne explained to me, "He's exactly what Connie needs now, a potential friend about her age who's handy with tools, fixes things, and doesn't seem to be in any hurry to find a wife. Connie is still grieving for Delbert, but she's making real progress getting back to normal. At least as normal as anyone who's seven months pregnant can be. Right now she's totally focused on impending motherhood, and needs all the friends she can find to help her adjust to her new life. And except for me, she doesn't seem to have any real friends besides a few co-workers who are more acquaintances than friends."

We deliberately hadn't invited any of my colleagues to the barbecue besides Jason so he'd have to mix with people he didn't already know. The rest of the guests were from Suzanne's colleagues in the biochemistry department at UCLA's Medical School. Corey Scott, the chair of her department, and his wife Loretta were coming, as were Annette Bridger and Maria Perez with their plus ones. Annette was Suzanne's closest colleague at work, who filled in for her when she needed someone to teach her classes while we travelled. Maria was the newest faculty member in the department, in her first year on the job. Corey Scott made all the final hiring decisions. And Suzanne had another long-term plan.

"Connie and I are getting very tired of that two and a half hour trip through heavy traffic to get between here and her house. She'd be a perfect addition to our faculty," Suzanne gushed to me. "We have a couple of retirements coming up in the next year or two that will need filling. Connie would be a perfect fit. She's an excellent teacher and her research is a perfect complement to what I do. And, according to the diversity gurus at the university, we need to hire one or two more women for our faculty. Tonight I want to plant a few seeds in the minds of my most likely allies if we're going to try to recruit Connie from Irvine to UCLA. She could move at any time. Her position at Irvine is completely funded by her own NIH grants, and they would move with her to another school."

Connie, as usual, arrived on time. In Southern California, where everybody was habitually late to everything, that made her the first guest to get here by a pretty large margin. The first time I met Connie I was struck by how much she reminded me of Suzanne several years ago when we'd first met. About five foot seven, early 30s, a runner's build, with long blond hair, she was a real beauty. Currently some seven months pregnant, she was even more beautiful. She and Suzanne disappeared somewhere to talk about babies or biochemistry. With Suzanne I couldn't ever be sure which topic was going to get priority but it was sure to be one or the other.

Jason was the next guest to arrive. The former FBI agent and army ranger was the newest addition to my detective agency and was fitting in perfectly. He handed me a bottle of wine before heading out to the back yard to help set up the barbeque. I wandered back with him to check whether Bruce wanted any help from me. Of course he didn't, and of course he was perfectly organized, as he stood by the grill sipping a beer and checking once again that he had everything out there he'd need to cook dinner when all the guests had arrived. He was also keeping a watchful eye on Robert, who was playing in the yard with Juliet and her son Romeo.

Bruce fits the Hollywood stereotype of a flamboyant, flaming gay male perfectly, perhaps because that's exactly what he is. He's from West Hollywood, slim and wiry, has dark hair with a cowlick, and is 30-ish, good looking, with an infectious smile. He likes working as a live-in nanny, a job with excellent pay, easy work in the physical sense, and free travel if you pick the right family. Bruce was great with Robert and was available 24/7 if needed. Before becoming a nanny, he served twice as a Navy SEAL in combat zones, once in Iraq and once in Afghanistan, so is a very good choice to have along in tough situations.

Suzanne and Connie joined us a few minutes later. Connie greeted Bruce and Robert, both of whom she had already met several times. I introduced her to Jason as a colleague of mine. We talked about Bruce's plans for feeding us: steaks, grilled vegetables, grilled corn, a couple of salads, Veggie Burgers just in case they were needed, and a surprise for dessert. Beer, wine, and a pitcher of Mojitos were available for the drinking crowd, as well as juices and other non-alcoholic choices for Suzanne, Connie and designated drivers.

By then the other invited guests started to arrive so Bruce got to work. I introduced the various UCLA people to Connie, Jason, and Bruce while Suzanne put Robert to bed, feeding and crating the dogs inside the house so the barbeque could be an adult occasion. As was typical for a social occasion such as this party, like attracted like. The UCLA contingent clumped together over their beverages of choice discussing Medical School gossip and departmental trivia. That left Connie and Jason little choice except to make a second small clump and talk to each other while we waited for Suzanne to rejoin us and for the food to cook.

Standing near Bruce, I discretely eavesdropped on Jason and Connie's conversation. They were making small talk, the usual what do you do and where did you come from starters that men and women have used since the beginning of time.

"I know all about what happened in Havana, Connie," Jason was saying. "Roger filled us in on the details after he got back from his tour with Suzanne. But I really don't know anything about you. Where did you grow up and what do you do now?"

He looked at her belly, blushed, and continued, "Besides the baby, I mean."

Connie smiled, graciously letting him off the hook. "My short biography: I was born and raised in Madison, Wisconsin, where Dad was a professor of chemistry at the University there. Growing up I was a combination of a math and science nerd and a tomboy. My dad and I did a lot of outdoors stuff, hunting, fishing, and sailing small boats on Lake Mendota. Eventually I graduated from the University of Wisconsin with a BS degree in chemistry. By then I realized I hated ice fishing and cold weather.

"So I came to California for graduate work at UC San Diego where I got my Ph.D. in Molecular Biology. I moved on to UC Irvine for my postdoctoral research training. The rest of it is I married my boss and had three good years with him, half of them as his wife, before he was killed in Havana. While we were in Cuba having a vacation and making a baby, he was murdered, as you know. Now I'm a faculty researcher at UC Irvine expecting a baby girl in a couple of months."

She paused, so Jason decided it was his turn. "Let's see. I was born and raised in Anchorage, Alaska. I did lots of hunting and fishing while I was growing up too. Went to the University of Alaska in Fairbanks on a football scholarship and went through four years of ROTC. Majored in accounting. Then I joined the army as a second lieutenant in the rangers, who were big on taking ex-jocks into their elite training program. I did a couple of tours as a ranger.

"I probably would have stayed in the army but the FBI made me an offer I couldn't refuse. They thought a born and bred Alaskan might stay in Anchorage for more than a single term, so fast-tracked me through Quantico for FBI training. I became a Special Agent in Anchorage and might have lived happily ever after. But I made an error in judgment that meant my career was going nowhere. That's about the time I met Roger. He offered me a job as a private eye here in Los Angeles. It seemed like a perfect opportunity to live someplace else than Alaska, so here I am, still getting settled into my new life."

Bruce called out that dinner was ready about the same time Suzanne rejoined the group. She checked out Connie and Jason chatting with each other, smiled, and manipulated both of them into the food line in a position where they'd end up sharing a table with us, Corey Scott, and his wife Loretta.

Scott was a distinguished appearing gentleman in his late 40s or early 50s. His choice of casual wear was a starched white shirt paired with dress slacks. At least he skipped the tie and jacket for this occasion. Tall, turning to pudgy if not outright fat, professionally styled hair turning gray at the edges, he very much looked the part of the successful professional on his way up the administrative ladder. Loretta, about the same age as Corey, very carefully made-up and tailored, looked the part of the successful professional-on-his-way-up's wife.

The six of us sat at our table. I was amused to see Corey and Loretta were drinking Mojitos, the Cuban national cocktail and the perfect lead in to the discussion Suzanne planned to happen. "I'm glad to see you enjoying the Mojitos, Corey. I'm afraid rum is off limits for Connie and me for another year or so. It may interest you to know we met Connie as a result of the Cuban tour Roger and I took with your help. Unfortunately, Connie became a widow about that time but she and I turned out to have a lot in common, including our research interests and training background as well as our impending children."

"Really," replied Loretta, a veteran of many such conversations as her husband had climbed the academic ladder with her help as a recruiter. "What are your plans for the future, Connie?"

Connie sipped fruit juice from her wine glass as she framed her answer. "My department chair approached me about taking a non-tenure track faculty position to continue the cancer research my husband, Del, was doing. He knew that most of the basic research was mine and that a lot of what went into our papers were my ideas and my experiments. Del focused on the clinical problems. I accepted the job. The nicest part of staying on at UC Irvine as a research faculty member was I could keep my old research group intact so I could continue to be productive while the baby is being born and starting out. After that, I don't know. I haven't really thought about it."

Suzanne jumped into the vacuum. "You know what, Corey? We really should have Connie up to visit one day soon, before her baby is born, to give us a seminar on her research."

"Good idea," he replied. "Annette Bridger is arranging the seminar schedule for this summer. Maybe we could arrange something after we finish eating dinner if Connie feels up to driving to Westwood in the next week or two. I take it we don't have a lot more time than that before her obstetrician will be grounding her."

Even I could see the wheels going around In Scott's head. It looked like Suzanne's Plans A and B had both been well launched. I hadn't told Suzanne yet, but I had a Plan C to start working on this evening, which I'd begin as soon as Bruce served dessert.

Ten minutes later Corey, Suzanne, and Connie moved their chairs over to the other table and went into a huddle with Annette, a middle-aged woman who smiled a lot. She was Suzanne's closest friend and colleague in the department. They came back a few minutes later with everybody still smiling: So far, so good.

After dessert I managed to get Connie and Bruce into a private conversation under the shade of a tree in the yard.

"Connie, you told me you were reasonably well off financially for the next few years, didn't you?"

Connie looked confused but answered my question. "Yes, I did."

"Bruce," I asked, "Do you have contacts back at the nanny school where you trained or in the community where you could find someone with the training and temperament to take on a live-in nanny arrangement with Connie down in Irvine?"

"Sure, there are always good people looking for that kind of long-term, stable arrangement."

"What would it cost Connie?" I asked.

"Newborn to kindergarten, maybe longer?" he asked.

"Yes, I think so," I answered as Connie nodded affirmatively.

"What would it cost?" I continued.

Bruce named a number.

My next question was "What do you think, Connie?"

She thought a moment. "It sounds like a great idea and would cost less than daycare if I'm working fulltime. But I don't know where I'll find the time to go through the process between now and the baby's due date."

I looked over at Bruce. "Can you find three or four possible job candidates over the next week or two, vet them for knowledge and reliability, and arrange for them to drive down to Irvine so Connie can interview them?"

He thought to himself for a bit. "Yes, I think I can. You'd have to pay their expenses for driving back and forth for the interviews, but I should be able to make all the other arrangements for you."

Connie nodded her agreement.

"Thanks, Bruce," I said sincerely. "That's definitely the way to go for Connie if she's going to juggle a professional career with being a single Mom for the next few years."

We rejoined the party. Plan C was now commencing.

Looking up a few minutes later I was delighted to see Connie and Jason sitting at an otherwise empty table chatting back and forth like old friends. The jury was still out, but maybe Plan A was going to work too.

Chapter 3. Prelude to a wedding

We drove about 400 miles north and west from our home in Beverly Hills to Sacramento, with stops at what seemed to be every rest area on I-5 to relieve the pressure on my wife's bladder, a constant preview of our coming attraction. The trip to our hotel was uneventful.

The next day we took I-5 from our hotel to the Hood-Franklin Road exit out in the countryside south of Sacramento. The GPS unit spoke, "Turn right here".

In a short time we were crossing the river on an old two-lane bridge. "Turn left on River Road," was the next command. About two miles further south we heard "You are at your destination."

We looked up to see the back of a hulking building across the narrow levee road beside the river with a large parking lot visible at the front of the building on the inland side. Once a working facility for refining sugar from beets grown in the region, the long unused sprawling brick building housing the mill had been converted into a tourist destination, a showcase for a dozen of the local wineries. Some day a major housing development was planned for an adjacent site in the small town of Clarksburg along the west bank of the Sacramento River.

The semi-rural area south of the Sacramento city limits was visible across the wide, rapidly flowing, river. The two-lane road winding south from Clarksburg on this side of the river led into the fascinating historical delta area where the Sacramento and San Joaquin rivers joined to flow into the southern tip of San Francisco Bay.

The occasion was a wedding. Sherry Wyne, the dog breeder who gave us Juliet a couple of years ago, was getting married. Sherry, who lived in Sacramento, had remained a good friend, especially of Suzanne's. Today we were west of the city, just across the river from Sacramento in Yolo County, with the other guests from afar who had come to watch Sherry marry A. Wallace Fortune, the owner of a large vineyard and winery in Yolo County. The wedding ceremony and festivities would take place tomorrow at the winery Wally owned about 40 miles from here just outside the city limits of the small town of Winters, California.

The venue for the rehearsal dinner was the Old Sugar Mill. As venues go, this one was very special. The rehearsal dinner would be held in the large garden area behind the massive old building. Twelve different wine tasting rooms, some with finger food to complement their wines, in the mill building itself welcomed the out of town guests who arrived throughout the afternoon. One of the tasting rooms actually featured barrel tastings of future wines that hadn't yet been released for sale, a preview of coming attractions if you wanted to think in those terms. Music, dancing, and the sit-down dinner would be in the Mill's garden area.

An obviously pregnant Suzanne turned out to be an even stronger attraction than our dogs usually are. Just about everybody from the out of town contingent, the groom-to-be and his family, and Sherry's wedding party cohort introduced themselves to us before or during the rehearsal dinner. They all seemed to be very nice people and wine was freely available (except to Suzanne) as a social lubricant, so everyone had a good time.

We wandered in and out of tasting rooms, some spacious and elaborate with tables and bars to sit at, others in smaller cramped and crowded rooms where visitors stood at makeshift bars for service. The wine tasting was free if we showed our wedding invitations, a creative and generous wedding gift from the close-knit community of Yolo County winery owners to one of their own, the groom. The wines ranged in quality from OK to drink with pizza or spaghetti with meat sauce to far better wines suitable to drink by themselves before or after dinner, as well as with more elegant meals.

A couple called us over to taste the wines at one of the less crowded rooms near the end of the building. "I'm Susan, Susan Crawford," said an average-sized redhead built heavier than, and about the same age as, the non-pregnant version of Suzanne. "And this handsome gentleman here is my husband Fraser. We're part of the group from Washington State, where they also make some pretty good wines, especially the Rieslings."

We introduced ourselves. Looking discretely at my wife's baby bump, Susan Crawford asked, "When are you expecting?"

"In a couple of months," Suzanne replied.

Susan Crawford absent-mindedly twirled a few of her reddish-brown curls. "Will this be your first?" she asked.

Suzanne hauled out the iPhone full of pictures as she answered, "No, Junior here will have an older brother Robert who's almost three now. Would you like to see a picture?"

Susan Crawford smiled, lighting up her entire face. "I'd love to see your three year old son. I have one just about the same age staying back home with my mother now and I'm missing him terribly."

The two mothers walked off somewhere to discuss three-year-olds as Fraser and I started to compare notes with each other about the wines we were being offered to taste. I tried a very nice local Syrah while Fraser opted for a Chardonnay as his first choice.

"Which of these wines would you recommend we start with?" asked another man's voice from my left.

Fraser waved his glass. "They usually suggest starting with the whites and working your way into the reds, which tend to have much stronger flavors," he said helpfully. "I started with this Chardonnay and like it very much."

"Thanks for the suggestion. I'm Harold Greenway and this is my wife Betsy," he introduced himself and his wife before turning to one of the attractive ladies pouring wines into glasses for the tastings and requesting the Chardonnay for both of them. The Greenways were a couple in their mid-sixties who told us they bred and showed German shorthaired pointers. Fraser and I introduced ourselves as we moved over a bit to make room for the couple at the crowded bar.

"Where are you two from?" Fraser asked as he settled into a new position in front of the bar.

"Bend, Oregon," replied Betsy, reaching for the glass in front of her, which still contained about a half ounce of white wine. "And you two?"

We introduced ourselves and chatted about the wines we tasted as we tried a few different selections suggested by the helpful wine pourer. A stocky middle-aged woman to our left pushed her way to the front of the line and thrust her empty glass in front of the server, who poured her a tasting portion of an ounce or two of their Chardonnay.

The neophyte wine taster took a gulp of her wine, swallowing it quickly. With a strange expression on her face, she carefully examined the small amount of wine remaining in her glass.

"Don't drink any of this wine," she urgently warned all of us at the tasting room bar in a loud voice that carried. "It has ground glass in it!"

The helpful woman pouring the wine laughed briefly. "It's perfectly safe to drink, folks. Those are tartaric acid crystals. Tartaric acid occurs naturally in grapes. Cream of tartar, the potassium salt, develops during winemaking and often settles out of chilled wines like this Chardonnay you're drinking or from older bottles of wine. Sometimes if I try to pour too much wine out of the bottle after the tartrate precipitates and settles to the bottom you can get a bonus."

By mutual consent we moved on together to several different winery stalls and started the ritual again at each one. All of us tried the same varietals we'd liked at the first tasting to compare and contrast the same wines made by different winemakers at different locations, so there were a lot of different wines for us to discuss.

Many of the wine bars included crackers or chocolates as palette cleansers to chew on between wines to enhance the overall experience. The wine pourers were knowledgeable about their wines so we all learned a lot about the similarities and difference between different varieties of grape and different growth conditions in the Central Valley and the Sierra foothills. The time passed quickly.

Wandering aimlessly through the winetasting area of the Sugar Mill with Fraser Crawford I spotted a small tasting room sandwiched between two of the larger ones labeled "Fortune Winery, Winters, California". I dragged Fraser in with me for a chance to taste Sherry's new wines-in-law. This particular tasting bar wasn't particularly crowded. A man I would later be introduced to as Clay Bedford was pouring wines and sharing knowledge with a small cluster of wedding guests around the groom to be, Wallace Fortune.

Without asking, Bedford, a good-looking man in work clothes befitting a winery manger, poured us a generous portion of Syrah wine. "This is the signature wine of the Fortune Winery," he announced. "Let it sit on your tongue a bit before you swallow it. Then tell me what you tasted."

The wine was quite nice, very much the big flavorful red wine I expected from a good Syrah.

Fraser Crawford ostentatiously demonstrated his mastery of winetasting nomenclature. "I'm getting a lot of fruit on my nose—cherry, plum, some kind of berries. It tastes very jammy, with hints of leather and chocolate. It's a nice wine. Maybe a bit more alcohol than I might like. What, 14 or 14.5% percent?"

"Let's ask the guy who made it," Bedford replied with a smile. "Hey, Wally, what's the alcohol content and flavor profile on this batch of Syrah?"

"A little bit above 14% alcohol, a typical big Syrah with lots of fruit. It's one of our better years for this wine varietal because of the drought, which made everything more concentrated and the flavors more intense."

The circle opened up a bit to let Fraser and me into the group. The groom-to-be was talking about his plans to expand the winery. "Several of the local farmers are getting old and don't have sons who want to live the rural farming lifestyle. We have a chance to buy some additional land adjacent to our current holdings at a good price. We can probably increase our own homegrown grape supply by about 50% over the next few years, which would increase total wine production by about the same percentage.

"If my brother Francis' arithmetic is correct we'll recover the cost of the land purchase back in three or four years and it'll be almost pure profit for us in the years to follow. Right now we own most of our farm and the winery outright so financing the land purchase should be simple."

Fraser and I eased our way out and continued wandering aimlessly toward the back of the Mill. As we walked from tasting room to tasting room we picked up and disengaged from other couples here for the wedding. Since most of Sherry's friends were dog owners, breeders, and/or show people, it wasn't a surprise when conversations were dominated by doggie topics, especially German shorthaired pointers. There were a few champions out of distinguished pedigrees with litters in the oven whose humans were hinting about availability of show-quality puppies to come. Thanks to Fraser, that led to inevitable tongue-in-cheek jokes about how many puppies Suzanne was expecting in her litter.

The conversation came back to wines when Elliot and Consuela Barwood joined our little scrum. We discovered that the Barwoods, from Washington State, bred German shorthairs and also owned their own small winery. Consuela explained a few of the more important differences between making wines in Washington, with a moderate climate, and in the hot Central Valley of California.

"Different grapes grow best in different climates and soils," Consuela, a small heavyset woman with dark graying hair cut short in a utilitarian style was saying. "That's why Washington and Oregon are famous for their Rieslings and California's Napa Valley for its Chardonnays and Cabernet Sauvignons. And some of the best Pinot Noirs come from down around Santa Barbara and San Luis Obispo, near the Southern California coast.

"But California's Central Valley, where the grapes these wines were made from are grown, is different. The typical summer day usually goes over 100 degrees, the sun is out full blast every day, and the grapes just want to grow and make lots of sugar. If you like sweet table wines, this is the place to grow your grapes. But if you want to make premium varietals it can be a challenge to bring out the varietal's flavor while you keep the sugar and alcohol levels down so you don't kill all the taste, not to mention also killing the yeast. Wally Fortune makes pretty good wines. You might want to ask him or Clay Bedford how they accomplish this during tomorrow's winery tour."

After a few hours of wine tasting and schmoozing among the out of town attendees, the bride-to-be appeared as if by magic to start leading the guests to dinner in the large courtyard in back of the wine tasting area. Sherry, with the groom-to-be tagging along with her, found me in the herd and gave me a big hello hug. I looked directly at her, a well-dressed brunette in her mid-forties, very attractive with a suntan and an outdoorsy appearance.

"Roger, I'd like you to meet my fiancé Wallace Fortune. Wally, this is Roger Bowman from Los Angeles. He's Suzanne's husband. They're the current owners of Juliet, one of my most successful former show dogs," Sherry introduced us.

Fortune was a big man, about my height at six foot two but at least sixty or seventy pounds, none of which were fat, heavier than my 190. I'd guess him to be in his late forties or early fifties. He had dark hair with an expensive haircut, graying at the edges, with the deep suntan of someone who worked out of doors on a regular basis. His large hands had the calloused palms and fingers of a man who worked in the fields and with heavy equipment. Today he was dressed casually in western wear, jeans and a shirt, but he looked like a businessman who'd also dress up well in a suit and tie on occasion.

He had the firm handshake that went with the big hands, or with being a successful salesman. "It's good to finally meet you, Roger. Sherry has mentioned you and Suzanne quite a bit, especially with regard to how you came to become Juliet's owners. I'm glad you two could make it to the wedding. You'll have to excuse us while we herd all of you cats back to the dinner area, but we'll have a chance to talk again and get to know each other better after the wedding tomorrow."

And off he and Sherry went to find some more wedding guests tasting wines or being tourists in the vast hall. I assumed Suzanne would already be back in the area where the dinner table was set up discussing babies and toddlers since she wasn't tasting wine today, so I wandered back in that general direction, catching up with Fraser Crawford along the way.

"What was the best wine you found today, Fraser?" I asked just to make conversation.

Fraser hesitated as he ran through an invisible card file in his head. "That Chardonnay I started with when we first met," he replied. "In general I'm finding I have a strong preference for the red wines here, but the Chardonnay was a very nice exception to that rule. How about you?"

That was easy. I had a strong preference among the many wines I'd sipped today. "I agree with you about the red wines being better in most of the tasting rooms here. I think the big reds like the Syrahs and Petite Syrahs, and a few of the Old Vine Zinfandels, were my favorites."

By then we were in the back courtyard. There were several tables for six set up, with place cards directing us where to sit. Fraser and I found our settings easily as Suzanne and Susan Crawford were already sitting together at our table just off to the right of the doorway we walked through to enter the courtyard. The two other settings at our table would be Elliot and Consuela Barwood, the other couple from Washington State I'd already met tasting wines.

The Barwoods arrived right behind us. I introduced them to Suzanne. The dinner table conversation quickly turned to how each of us knew the bride or groom. All of us were from Sherry's guest list and shared an interest in showing, hunting, and breeding German shorthaired pointers.

"What made you choose German shorthairs when you first got into dog breeding?" Suzanne asked.

Susan Crawford, unfolding her cloth napkin and spreading it on her lap, responded. "All the usual reasons people choose shorthairs. Fraser wanted dogs he could take out in the field and hunt with, not just show dogs, which was my thing. We planned on having a family, so we wanted a breed that was good around children. I love showing the dogs when I can, but I have a lot of other things to do so didn't want to spend a lot of time brushing, combing, and caring for a long coat on the dogs. And both of us prefer mid-size dogs, which ruled out some of the other possibilities. To me, shorthairs are the ideal balance between working dog, family pet, and minimal care show dog.

"How about you, Consuela?"

Putting down her fork, Consuela Barwood considered the question for a bit. "Almost exactly the same thought process, Suzanne. In addition, we'd had shorthairs at home when I was growing up, so I never really considered anything else."

"Don't forget we were hoping to eventually buy another winery somewhere in California so we could get into a lot of additional varietals that don't do as well in Washington State," Elliot Barwood added. "The shorthairs are a whole lot more comfortable in a hot climate like they have around here in the summer than the double-coated retrievers tend to be. How about you, Suzanne?"

Suzanne told the story, in shortened form, of how we met Sherry and came to know and fall in love with Juliet, who in turn brought us into the worlds of dog shows and bird hunting.

After appetizers and salad, the discussion turned to the venue for the rehearsal dinner, where we'd spent a few hours tasting wines and were soon to taste their catered dinner main course. We'd been offered a choice of beef tri-tip roast, a local favorite, or a vegetarian option. All six of us had opted for the beef.

I tasted the tri-tip, which was tender and full of flavor. "This is an amazing location for a wedding reception," I observed. "It's incredible to me we can be just a few miles outside of Sacramento and be in a part of California that's so different from the traffic and urban feel of the state capital."

"If you think this place is different you need to go exploring further south along the river," suggested Fraser Crawford. "We had an hour to kill so kept going after we found this place. We could have been in Louisiana except for the lack of humidity. Lots of bayous they call sloughs around here, lots of islands overgrown with trees that look like jungles, a lot of swampy areas between the islands, old wooden bridges crossing the sloughs, and we even saw restaurants and shacks selling crawfish alongside the road."

Dessert was a decadently rich riff on brownies a la mode, accompanied by an amusing tongue-in-cheek discussion by Elliot and Consuela of the difficulties of owning a winery in Tacoma, Washington, a city that preferred microbrewery beers by a large margin. While they'd apparently had several very difficult years before they were able to make a comfortable living from the winery, both of them seemed to have come away from the experience comfortable making jokes about the hard times.

After dinner we had toasts to the bride and groom accompanied by more wine for four of us, and grape juice for Susan and Suzanne. We heard from the best man, Wally's brother Francis, that the groom had been owner and winemaker at the winery since he graduated with a degree in Viticulture and Enology from the University of California at Davis. This was going to be his first marriage to a person after having been married to the winery for the last few decades. Insults disguised as wedding toasts were proposed by current and former friends of Wally and Sherry.

Before we left, Wally handed each of us a map of Yolo County with driving directions to his winery, situated in a rural area near the small town of Winters. We were expected to be there for the wedding ceremony at 3 PM. If we could arrive by 1:30, we'd get a tour of the vineyards and winery. At this time none of us had any idea how abruptly and dramatically Sherry's lifestyle was destined to change.

Chapter 4. The wedding

Today's drive took us west from the hotel to an I-80 exit just past Davis, the college town where Suzanne had been born and raised. She knew the back roads that took us north and west past large orchards growing fruits and nuts to Winters, a small town of less than 7,000 people, mostly noted for the cooperative that processed the large amounts of walnuts grown in and around the town. GPS navigation took us the rest of the way to Wally's winery a few miles west of Winters, nestled in the foothills of the Blue Ridge mountains, part of Northern California's coastal range, where the wedding was scheduled to take place later in the afternoon.

We arrived shortly before 1:30, when we had been promised a tour of the winery as an enticement to come early for the wedding. Suzanne parked beside more than a dozen other cars just off the paved driveway, several with out of state license plates, which we assumed belonged to other wedding guests. Sherry and Wally were nowhere in sight, probably preparing for the wedding. I recognized a tall man in his late 40s who greeted us from yesterday's rehearsal dinner. From his permanent tan and weathered look, he obviously spent a lot of time outdoors.

"Welcome to the Fortune Winery," he said, bowing to Suzanne and shaking my hand. "I'm Clay Bedford, the winery manager. Wally asked me to show you folks around today. Don't worry. I'll have you back here in plenty of time for the ceremony. Why don't you just walk over and join the group assembling by the winery buildings. I'll give everybody ten more minutes to get here, then we'll start the tour."

I looked around. Vast vineyards sprawled over hundreds of acres of sloping land. A large modern mansion stood directly beyond the parking area. Several other buildings comprising the winery itself were located about 100 yards to the left of the main house, at the end of the wide driveway designed to accommodate large trucks we'd driven in on.

While waiting for our host, we milled around in the back of the parking area, just in front of the mansion. We were a small group of Sherry's friends from Southern California, Oregon, and Washington, all dog people, talking about dog shows, German shorthaired pointers, and how much Sherry's lifestyle would change with marriage. And babies.

"Hello, everybody," Clay Bedford's voice broke into the discussion. "It's time to start our tour if we want to be back to the main house in time for the ceremony. I think we all met when you arrived, but just in case, I'm Clay and I manage the winery on a day-to-day basis. Wally is the owner and our winemaker. My job is to grow the grapes and get the grapes and the employees to wherever they have to be on very tight schedules. I'm also responsible for being sure that all the equipment is in working order whenever we need it. Wally's job is to select the varietals we plant, prune the grapes, make the wine, and sell it. His brother Francis handles the business side of the winery.

"Look around. You'll see grapes growing just about everywhere we have room to plant them. We grow most of the grapes we use to make our wines here on this property. There are several varietals we grow here, both for red and white wines. A lot of the work is still done by hand, especially the pruning techniques. If you look carefully as we walk around, you can see the different styles of pruning we use for different grape varieties. Some handle direct sun on the fruit better than others. But you can also see leaves we keep on top of all the plants when we prune them to provide some shade for the growing grapes."

Bedford turned toward the winery building itself. "Follow me. We'll walk over, go into the main building, and assemble in front of the equipment we use for the first step in making wines from the grapes we pick from our fields. Then we'll follow the process through the winery all the way to shipping the wines to the customers."

We walked down the path to the winery surrounded by vineyards on either side of the road. Neat rows of meticulously pruned plants ran parallel to the section of road we were currently walking on. Stakes and wires supported vertical stalks and horizontal vines, with most of the vines carrying small clumps of grapes at intervals along the trellis. Narrow rubber drip irrigation hoses were visible running the length of the rows on top of the ground at the base of the plants.

Suzanne studied the vineyard on our right. "It's funny, Roger. I've seen plenty of vineyards before so nothing's new here. But I'm getting vibes from this field I'm not used to feeling when I look at grapes growing. I don't know how to describe it. A little scary, like maybe there are monsters hiding out there concealed by the grapes. I've been having a lot of these kinds of weird feelings during the last trimester, and a lot of scary dreams. I guess we can blame them on the hormones."

I squeezed her hand, stopped to kiss her, and promptly forgot about her weird vibes.

The group entered the winery via the large doors at the front of the relatively new modern building. The first thing I noticed was everything was sparkling clean, with floors and walls designed for efficient washing with high-pressure hoses to keep it scrupulously free of wild yeasts and other contaminants that could spoil a batch of wine. Clay assembled the group in front of a shiny large stainless steel trough with a central rotating rod with projecting blades sticking out from the rod.

"The grapes come in here after picking," he began. "They're dumped into the trough where they're washed, then removed from the stems and crushed by the device in front of you. If we're making a white wine, the juice from the grapes is removed from the skins immediately and the grape juice is pumped into one of the stainless steel tanks we'll see next for fermentation. If we're making a red wine the juice and crushed pieces of skin and seeds are combined to make what we call a 'must', which is what gets pumped over to the fermentation tank for the next step."

He led us to a long row of large stainless steel tanks in the middle of the building. "These are the fermentation tanks, where we change grape juice into wine with the help of some handy yeast we add to the tanks. Note the coils around the outside of the tanks. We can pump cold water through those coils to control the temperature of the primary yeast fermentation while it's occurring over a period of days or weeks. Most of our white wines are fermented at fairly cool temperatures to slow the process down to encourage the flavor profile to develop. The lower temperature also keeps the wine in the tank rather than all over the building by slowing down the fermentation so the gas pressure from the carbon dioxide the yeast makes has plenty of time to vent from the tank.

"Does anybody have any questions so far?"

Consuela Barwood asked, "What kind of wines do you make here at your winery?"

Clay was clearly expecting someone to ask this and answered quickly and precisely. "We make commercial amounts of Viogner, Chardonnay, and Albarino among the whites. Our reds are mostly Cabernet Sauvignon, Syrah, Petite Syrah, Merlot, Zinfandel, and Pinot Noir. We sell all of these wines either as varietals or as generic red or white wine blends if we have extra grapes left over after we make what we estimate the market will bear for a specific varietal. We also make Special Reserves from other grape varieties we've planted on an experimental basis or when we get an especially good vintage year with any of the regular grape varieties."

"Where do you get your grapes from?" someone else asked.

"We grow almost all of the grapes we use for winemaking right here on our own ranch," he answered. "We've got several hundred acres of vineyards under cultivation on the land surrounding the winery here."

It was my turn for a question. "Somebody suggested I ask you what special problems you have growing wine grapes in the Central Valley's hot and sunny climate as compared to Washington State, Oregon, or the Napa Valley."

"Good question," Clay responded, scratching his head while he thought of the best reply for this group. "I'll give you the short answer here since we have a lot to see and I'm sure none of you want to miss the wedding. Feel free to check back with me after the festivities if you want more details. It's a topic I can talk about for an hour or two.

"Most of the world's famous wine growing regions feature moderate climates with sunny days and cool nights, which gives the grapes plenty of time to grow and develop their characteristic flavors. Here in the Central Valley we have hot days and intense sunlight, which makes the grapes produce a lot of sugar in a hurry--too much sugar to make good wines from many of the grape varieties we grow to make the wines. So, unless your viticulturist knows exactly what he's doing when he prunes the grapes, you're likely to get wines you have to pick too early for them to develop their full flavor profile. And with all that sugar you get a very high alcohol concentration after fermentation. It's a lot easier to grow great grapes in the Napa Valley, which gets a lot of morning and evening fog to cool things down."

We moved on. Clay Bedford showed us the barrel room where wines were aged and stored after fermentation, the bottling line where bottles and labels met wine and corks, and the stacks of cartons where bottled wine waited to be shipped to customers.

"We have a few minutes left before we have to get back. Would anyone like to taste some very new wine before it has aged to get an idea of what goes into aging wines to create the final product."

Lots of hands went up.

Bedford picked up a wine thief, a device that looked like a long turkey baster, removed a cork to gain access to the liquid, and withdrew several ounces of what looked like wine from a barrel lying in a rack on its side. He squirted some of the wine into tiny paper cups and offered tastes to anyone who was curious. That was most of us. Several people sniffed, swirled, tasted, and made an unpleasant face.

Bedford laughed. "It has a way to go before you'll see it in the market. But it has a chance to mature into one of the best vintages we've ever made of this particular Pinot Noir wine. This is where Wally earns the big bucks he makes as an enologist. How he ages the wine will determine whether it ever reaches its potential. And on that note I think it's time we all head on over to the mansion where the wedding is scheduled to get started in about fifteen minutes," he declared after a quick glance at his watch.

We thanked Clay for the tour and wandered over to the main house in a scraggly bunch. The front lawn area had been converted to a suitable location for a wedding by the addition of about a hundred seats distributed across several rows in a broad arc surrounding the front of a stage with an aisle bisecting the middle. Most of the seats were already occupied.

Like most weddings I've been to, this one featured discrete clusters of people who already knew one anther. I spotted Wally's brother, Francis, sitting in a more formally dressed group across from us on the other side of our arc of chairs. Next to him was an older couple I guessed to be the groom's parents or an aunt and uncle.

Sitting close to them were people of various ages who had a resemblance, probably the rest of the family.

Another group sat between where we were and the family members. Based on their ages, these were probably Wally's friends and their spouses.

Our cluster included a third group, Sherry's friends and family. About half of us knew each other very casually from yesterday's wine tasting and today's tour.

The wedding ceremony was short, sweet, and simple. A string quartet sitting to one side of the minster provided the music. To the familiar sounds of "Here Comes The Bride", Sherry, in a white wedding dress, walked down the aisle escorted by an older gentleman, possibly her father. Wally, looking very suave and comfortable in a dark tuxedo, was already standing with his brother Francis, the best man, by the minister to greet his soon-to-be bride. A friend of the family, apparently an ordained but not practicing Unitarian minister, performed a simple ceremony that took less than fifteen minutes from 'Dearly Beloved' to 'you may kiss the bride'. Wally and Sherry did so, long and enthusiastically. The sermon, which took another five minutes to deliver, recounted a few key moments in the history of the couple.

The minister ended by noting the smoke in the air and the occasional layer of ash covering the few empty seats. He commented about the pall over the wedding ceremony on what should have been a bright sunny afternoon, which was marred by a gray haze partially obscuring the sun. "Don't worry about all that junk in the air from the wildfire, folks. It'll take a lot more than a little smoke and ash to make our bride and groom miss this party to celebrate their finally getting together."

After the ceremony the newlyweds made the rounds of the guests. Sherry introduced us formally to her new husband, then less formally as 'Juliet's human parents'.

After sizing us up Wally relaxed noticeably, saying "If you two were good enough friends for Sherry to trust you with Juliet, you're obviously special. I know you're from L.A. and it's obvious you're expecting, but that's about all I can remember about the two of you. Tell me more."

We told him a little about us and our family, and a few Sherry stories from several years ago when we'd first met her. Given Sherry was in her mid-40s and Wally almost a decade older, they made an awfully cute couple holding hands in a tuxedo and wedding gown and acting like teenagers on prom night.

Then it was party time. I got to see a side of the bride I'd never seen before, Sherry the ultimate party animal. I found myself thinking the groom, Wally, was going to have to get into even better shape fast if he planned to try to keep up with his younger bride. Late in the afternoon I got to dance with the bride.

Suzanne caught up with me immediately afterward. "What were those sweet nothings Sherry was whispering into your ear, Roger?"

We didn't keep any secrets from one another so I told her the truth. "Actually, she was asking me about Juliet and Romeo, especially what kind of chow you were feeding them now and when we planned to breed her again."

Suzanne looked concerned. "What did you tell her?"

I laughed. "Nothing. I told her to check with you."

Our host from the winery tour, Clay Bedford, came by just then to ask Suzanne for a dance. He was at the wedding without a plus one and I'd just danced with Sherry, so Suzanne accepted his invitation and danced off.

"I saw you at the tour earlier today, didn't I?" he asked Suzanne.

"Yes, you did," she replied politely. "Thank you very much for the experience. I learned a lot."

They were doing a slow dance, appropriate for her condition. It was easy to talk. "Do you have any more questions about how our winery works?" he asked.

"Actually, I do have one as I look around here. How much of a risk do you have of the wildfire coming close enough to destroy your crop in the field?"

Bedford chuckled. "None, or close to it. Vineyards don't burn. The canes are pruned every year so there isn't a lot of wood built up and the grapes are full of water. It would be like trying to burn a field of lettuce. Do you by any chance remember a movie from the 1990s with Keanu Reeves and Anthony Quinn called 'A Walk in the Clouds'?"

Suzanne demonstrated her memory for trivia. "Yes, I do. It was a real tearjerker set in a Napa Valley winery just after World War II, wasn't it? If I remember correctly, they had a big scene with a fire in the grape fields near the end."

Bedford looked impressed. "Very good. Most people your age wouldn't have seen or heard of that movie. That big fire scene was filmed at the Duckhorn winery in St. Helena. But there's a story that goes with that. They had a vineyard that was dying from phylloxera and needed to be replanted. Duckhorn sold the rights to the movie producer to film the burning, so made a few bucks out of what would otherwise have been a financial disaster for them. The movie people found out pretty quickly they couldn't get the vineyard to burn, and had to use propane as the fuel to film the scenes. Every winemaker around here knows that story. That's why we don't worry too much about the fields burning.

"The real problem with wildfires is smoke taint when the grapes pick up unpleasant flavors from the smoke. As long as the winds are blowing to the west, keeping the worst of the smoke away from us, our vineyard will be OK. If the smoke decides to blow this way and the weather conditions favor it staying here, then we'd still have the grapes to harvest but some of the wines wouldn't be drinkable. This actually happened in 2010. There was a July when a lot of the Central Valley was full of smoke and some of the grapes had odd flavors."

With perfect timing the music stopped just as Bedford finished, thanking Suzanne for the dance and returning her to me. He walked off to find another partner.

"He's a good dancer and an interesting partner to talk to," commented Suzanne before she shared her new knowledge about vineyards and fires with me.

Lots of dancing, schmoozing, and dinner later, Suzanne suggested she was tired and it was time we headed back to our hotel. We planned to head directly back to L.A. as early as we could get on the road tomorrow morning, preferably by 6 o'clock so we would miss the local commuter traffic on I-5 around Sacramento and Stockton.

We said good night to the bride and groom and all of the dog people we'd met over the last two days, little realizing how soon I'd be seeing Sherry again. As we walked back toward our car Suzanne murmured, "It was too bad we had all that ash and air pollution marring a perfect setting today. But I also have a bad gut feeling about the day. I don't know why, Roger, but there's something about this place that bothers me and it isn't just the ash in the punchbowl. It just feels wrong to me in some way."

As if to emphasize Suzanne's comment as we drove back to the freeway, we noticed a small herd of fire trucks driving along Route 128 toward Lake Berryessa on their way to relieve the crews fighting the wildfire. There would be a similar convoy later tonight coming back with exhausted and dirty firefighters getting some rest and a break in the workload. The central command post was the United States Forest Service compound just off I-80 east of Davis, which was their likely destination.

Chapter 5. Training Juliet in the wide open spaces

The next few days passed quietly. I caught up on my paperwork during a lull between cases.

Wednesday was a beautiful day, blue skies, a light breeze from the west so no smog, bright sunlight, and temperatures in the mid-70s. It was a perfect day to take an afternoon off, so I did. Connie's seminar to Suzanne's department was scheduled for mid-afternoon today so Suzanne wasn't home today.

A couple of minutes after I got home Bruce asked, "Would you like to see Juliet in action over an area a lot larger than your backyard?"

"Sure," I replied. "Is Robert ready to go?"

"Ready and eager," Bruce said as he directed Robert and Juliet into my car. In another moment he gave me some quick directions and we were off for today's adventure.

Bruce directed me to drive to a large county park about twenty minutes from the house. We parked in a lot at the east end of the facility and climbed out. Bruce guided Juliet on a heel command while I followed beside Robert holding his hand as we walked to the edge of the flat grassy area where we'd begin this demonstration. Juliet looked to Bruce for release from her heel position, which she received via a subtle hand signal. She and Robert chased each other around for a couple of minutes while they both ran off a little excess energy and Bruce explained to me what was going to happen next.

There were a lot of families here near the parking lot. Several were having picnics. There was a large, chaotic, pediatric soccer game underway, and some people were just hanging out. Several of the younger kids started running after Robert and Juliet. A young mother asked "Is your dog safe around our children?"

An evil little voice in my head suggested the perfect answer, *"You know your kids far better than I do, Madam. Are any of them budding little sociopaths?"*

But common sense prevailed. "She loves children," I answered her and the other mothers listening in. "She's been very well socialized with kids from infants to teenagers. She'll enjoy playing with as many of them as want to run around with her."

"This is a lot different from your backyard, Roger," Bruce commented. "You've got a huge lot and a big yard. I'd guess your property occupies something like an acre all told. But that's shooting fish in a barrel for a dog with Juliet's nose. She can smell anything, anywhere above the ground in that small of an area if she's downwind of it. And she can find anything buried in that yard in less than 2 minutes. So it's not much of a challenge for her to find anything that smells like dead human in your yard.

"This area here is a bigger and better challenge. This park is a bit larger than 300 acres, so it's about half a square mile of woods and grassy meadows. And for variety, there's a small lake. Even for Juliet, that's a lot of ground to cover. Several days ago I buried a chunk of one of Suzanne's placentas two or two and a half feet deep in a place I can locate again in the park. That's long enough that my scent trail on the ground should have dissipated by now so she can't just track me to find it. The placenta should be pretty well decomposed and putting off a scent like a real cadaver. Let's see if she can find it."

"Has Juliet searched an area this large before?" I asked.

Bruce smiled. "I've done a good bit of her training here just to make things a lot more realistic than your backyard. She's been here before and knows what we expect her to do. I've worked her over buried scent and air scent. She'll be looking for either or both. It wouldn't do us a whole lot of good if she found human blood in the ground while she ignored a 'victim' hanging from a tree fifty yards away in the woods. It's not only Juliet who had to learn new tricks. I've been learning to read her reactions to this game so I can understand what's going on from her point of view."

"What should I be looking for as we follow her around?" I asked.

"You want to watch for her to go on alert. We should try to keep her in sight, but she's a lot faster than we are and has a lot of ground to cover. When she goes on alert she'll establish a point at the source like she did in your backyard. But, since we might not see her, I've also trained her to bark when she finds something as she alerts when we're looking for a cadaver out in a big, open space like this park."

"Do you always find her when she barks? If she's a few hundred yards away, or even further, that must be very hard to do."

Bruce smiled at me again. "Good question. I cheat. There's a GPS collar on her transmitting a signal so I can tell where she is just by checking the screen on my remote device. Whenever she's out of sight we're following her electronically. The satellite locates her within a few feet and tells me whether she's still moving or stationary on a point.

"I should also mention we'll have to cross a bridle path a couple of times as we go toward the place I buried the tissue so Juliet is going to have to deal with the potential distraction of some very strong smells along the way to find the one I want her to find."

Robert and his now considerable entourage had slowed down a bit so I called out to him while Bruce gave Juliet her recall command. Half a dozen other kids found their way back to the proper parents.

Juliet stood patiently beside Bruce while I explained what we'd be doing next to Robert. We negotiated that he'd walk with us until he felt tired, at which point he'd travel the rest of the way piggyback on my shoulders. Bruce tapped Juliet twice on her head as her "let's go" signal and off we went almost directly west into the light breeze.

For Juliet, this was just another hunt, and she had a lifetime of instinct, experience, and bird hunt training. She quartered into the breeze, head up and nose seeking the right scent in the air flowing by, covering about 50 feet to our left and 50 feet to our right as she loped over huge areas of ground while continually moving forward into the wind. Robert could easily keep up with her as we walked a straight line while she covered at least five times the amount of ground we did as she casted in each direction.

I did a quick calculation. "Hey, Bruce. If she's completely searching 100 feet on either side of us and there's about 43,000 square feet in an acre, for every 430 feet we walk she's searched two acres. That means if we walk a mile, which I'd guess would be Robert's limit, we'll have covered almost 25 acres. Does that sound about right?"

"Plus or minus a bit, yes," Bruce replied.

"Will she find our 'corpse' by then?" I asked.

"Plus or minus a bit, she should," Bruce replied again.

We continued walking while I explained what was happening to Robert. "Keep an eye on Juliet, Robert. We'll know she's found what Bruce hid in the ground a few days ago when she stops and points at it."

This was a new game for Robert. He was fascinated, at least for now.

We passed a young couple with a daughter Robert's age as we walked on. The father called out, "That's a nice looking dog you're with. Is that a Dalmation?"

"No," I responded, "It's a German shorthaired pointer."

"Is it hunting birds now?" asked the mother.

It seemed a good time for the path of least resistance. "Yes," I answered.

Robert was discussing things with the little girl. "Juliet's a pointer," I heard him tell her.

We continued walking, a little faster now so we could catch up with Juliet.

The terrain changed gradually from flat grassland to a bit more up and down, which didn't seem to bother boy or dog. There was a small lake on our left.

"How about searching a lake like this one, Bruce? Can Juliet do that?"

"No, it's a different skill set than I've been training her for, Roger. They use different dogs for land and water searches. The water dogs have to understand currents, different kinds of smells, and a whole bunch of other nuances to searching in a totally different environment."

We continued on past the lake before crossing over the bridle path. Juliet had no detours or interruptions despite the strong odor of recent horse droppings as we crossed the path.

Eventually we came to a wooded area. Bruce continued walking in a more or less straight line through the trees while Juliet continued casting to either side, darting in and out of visibility as we walked. He glanced occasionally at his GPS tracker, but didn't seem concerned about becoming separated from the dog. Robert squeezed my hand so I didn't have to worry about losing him.

We came to a small clearing surrounded by more trees on all sides. I had a good look at Juliet casting to our right just before we got to the end of the cleared area. She suddenly turned to her left, out of her normal cast directly toward the breeze, and continued a short distance into the wooded area in front of us. She halted abruptly, barked twice, and stood on the ground patiently waiting for us to catch up. I realized she was on a hard point.

Bruce had a big smile on his face. I didn't have to ask.

Robert was following the action. "Juliet found something, Daddy."

"I think so, Robert. Let's see what happens now to make sure."

Bruce carefully followed the invisible line from tail to nose straight out from the dog for about ten feet, taking care to minimize any impact he might have on the "crime scene", before marking the spot with a small flag he planted in the ground. Walking back to Juliet, still on point, he reached into his pocket, pulled out her lead, and clipped it on her collar. Walking her about ten yards off to the side, he attached the leash to a convenient tree to prevent her moving back into the "crime scene".

He gave Juliet a small handful of dog treats as a reward for a job well done and a rawhide bone to chew on while he came back to the flag he'd planted to mark the spot. "If this were the real thing, at this point I'd take her back to our car so she couldn't contaminate the crime scene with a call of nature or by digging into the ground. But it's not real this time so this should be good enough for now.

He pulled a small collapsible shovel out of his backpack and dug in the soft dirt under a tree. In a few minutes he had recovered a jar containing a reddish-brown mass that he held up for Juliet and us to see. He walked over to the dog, showed her the jar as he gave her a few more liver treats, and praised her effusively as he removed her leash and gave her a 'heel' command.

We started back in the direction we'd come from, Juliet trotting proudly beside Bruce keeping an eye on the jar he carried as a trophy from this hunt.

"That was amazing!" I exclaimed. "She went right to it."

"Well, not exactly," Bruce replied. "Notice that I defined the search pattern for her by the direction we walked. This is a team effort. I can set up the area of the grid for her to search then it's up to Juliet and her nose to figure out where the bodies are buried, so to speak. My part of the job is figuring out the most efficient search pattern for a given area for her to cast over to get complete coverage and a favorable wind direction."

Robert thought this over for a bit before asking Bruce. "Could Daddy do this with Juliet?"

Bruce was obviously amused. "Not right now Robert. He'd have to practice a whole lot with Juliet first so she knew what he wanted her to do before she could find something like this without me being there."

"How many times, Bruce?" Robert asked.

"Think about how many times you've seen me do the same thing with Juliet in the back yard. At least that many times."

"Wow. That's a lot," said Robert thoughtfully.

Chapter 6. A phone call from Winters

Sherry called several days after the wedding, early Friday night. "I didn't know who else to call, Roger. I need your help."

"What's happening?" I responded.

"Wally's missing and the police aren't doing anything about it," she replied. "He disappeared the day before yesterday, a few days after the wedding. The sheriff is treating it like a routine missing person case and assumes he freaked out about the wedding and just took off. So far, the only thing the sheriff did after I complained was to send a deputy out to the winery. The deputy walked around the grounds between the house and the winery for less than ten minutes before he left.

"The sheriff called that a search of the property that didn't come up with any clues. I don't believe Wally would ever take off without telling me about it. Can I ask you to come back up here to find out what happened to him? In your professional capacity, of course."

"My schedule is clear for the next few days. I can fly up to Sacramento tomorrow morning. I don't want to leave Suzanne for more than a couple of days, so let's see what I can learn in the next day or two."

"Call or text me with your flight information and I'll meet your plane," she replied. "And plan on staying with me out at the winery until you fly back."

My 7:30 flight on Southwest landed in Sacramento before 9. It was my first visit since the new modern terminal had opened. The busy airport was definitely growing up. I texted Sherry who was waiting in the cell phone parking lot that I'd arrived. Her car picked me up five minutes later from the front of the terminal. She gave me a quick hug as a greeting and immediately sat back down at the wheel of the car as I stuck my bag in the back seat and sat next to her in front.

Physically Sherry reminds me in a few ways of Suzanne. She has the same tall, athletic build and quick and graceful movements. On the other hand, she is about a decade older than Suzanne and dark haired where Suzanne is blond. Her voice suggested Western Canadian ancestry left far behind. I could hear it mainly as a hint of something different in her speech cadence, which is slower than typical for Los Angeles and includes an occasional British usage.

After a minute or two of polite welcome we drove off toward the winery while she filled me in on the details of her husband's disappearance. "Everything to do with the wedding went off without a hitch. Wally seemed perfectly normal. He spent most of the next two days working in the vineyards.

"We'd decided to put off our formal honeymoon because of the potential threat of the big wildfire burning now just across the mountain from us. There's always the possibility of a big fire like that changing its direction and hitting the winery. We usually get a few major fires in the forest preserves around Lake Berryessa, just across the mountains from Winters, every summer and fall. Putah Creek runs on our property right by the vineyard. That's the source of water for irrigation and the winery so there's plenty of water and backup generators for the pumps. If Wally and the crew had to defend the winery from a fire that jumped over the ridge and came our way, they could do a pretty good job of it."

"Did you see a lot of Wally while he was working in the vineyard?"

"No, not really. I was doing a lot of my work for the next few dog shows out of my old house in Sacramento, so we didn't have much occasion to see one another during the day. But we had quality time together the next few nights. Everything seemed normal, or even better than normal."

She paused for a moment in her narrative as we joined the heavy traffic onto I-5 over the bridge and causeway. "The third day we had breakfast together, which was our usual routine. Wally said something about planning on going out to dinner together to celebrate, so I didn't have any premonition that would be the last time I'd see him. But sometime during that day he disappeared. Just poof, into thin air! I assumed he had some sort of business or family emergency, so didn't worry about his not meeting me for dinner or being gone overnight. When he didn't call me or show up the next day I got worried and contacted the local sheriff."

She paused to collect her thoughts and regain her composure.

"What happened then?" I asked.

"Lots of stuff, none of it good," she replied. "Bear with me through this part. I can already feel myself getting very, very angry. I've had to deal with a few very unpleasant jerks these past few days."

"Don't tell me, let me guess. Jerk number one was the sheriff, who told you something like new grooms disappear all the time and you just have to be patient with your new husband while he adjusts to a different lifestyle."

Sherry stole a glance at me before turning back to the busy highway. "Bullseye! Am I really that much of a cliché?"

"No, I'd say the sheriff is that much of a jerk, but that's not unusual when you're dealing with small town law enforcement. And, of course, he could be right. But he should have considered the alternatives and made sure that Wally was OK before he assumed this wasn't a case for investigation.

"Let's think about the obvious. Wally is, I assume, a wealthy man since he owns a large and apparently successful winery. He could, at least hypothetically, have been kidnapped. Has there been any contact with you about a possible ransom?"

"No, I haven't heard a word from either Wally or anyone else about where he might be."

"I assume you've talked to his brother Francis, or should I be calling him Frank?"

"Yes, I have talked to Francis, who is definitely jerk number two in this story. I've seen him twice. The first time was the day after my husband disappeared. I asked if he'd heard from Wally or knew where he was. He said no, but I'm not sure whether I believed him. He said something like, 'you don't need to worry your pretty little head, Missy. New husbands decide to take off all the time. Especially confirmed bachelors like Wally who get married late in life.' And yes, he really called me Missy!"

She paused, perhaps for dramatic emphasis. "And the second time was worse. Yesterday I asked him whether Wally had taken any money from the winery corporate accounts on the day he disappeared, or in the days just before then. He told me not to worry about the business side of things, which were 'men's work' and that he handled the finances for the winery and they were all in order. I'm not sure I trust Frank, especially with regard to the financial side of the winery and Wally's estate. I'd appreciate your looking into what kind of shape the winery and I are in if Wally stays disappeared."

"Did you sign any kind of prenuptial agreement before the wedding, Sherry?"

"That's right, Roger. I'd forgotten you were a lawyer before you became a detective. No, I didn't. I assume that thanks to California's community property laws, as of the time we both said 'I do' I became the owner of half a winery and half of Wally's net value."

"It's not quite that simple, but it's a reasonable assumption if Wally owns the winery outright as an individual and there isn't a corporation with a whole lot of stock shares floating around as the true owner of the property."

Sherry glanced over at me fleetingly. "There's something else about Francis that's bothering me. When Wally first told me about owning a winery he said something strange to me that I've not forgotten. He talked about the business side of wine making and selling being largely done in cash, and how it would be very easy to make a lot of tax-free money by selling a lot more wine than showed on the books. And how it would be just as simple to go the other direction, to launder crooked cash by selling less wine than showed on the books. And how glad he was

43

that Frank handled everything legal and financial for the business and he didn't have to worry about that part of things.

"He also told me there have been rumors about organized crime infiltration of the larger wineries in Yolo County, around Lodi, and the Napa Valley, especially the ones that are still privately owned. He's heard rumors about bank and teamster union connections and rumors about money laundering on a large scale. Making wine is an expensive business, with a lot of amateurs finding that out the hard way. There's been an epidemic of merger mania among many of the smaller wineries over the past couple of years. So there are a lot of medium and large sized wineries with financial problems who might be tempted to cheat a bit to survive."

I mulled over what Sherry had told me thus far. "Has there been a jerk number three yet?" I enquired

"Yes and no," she answered. "So far Clay Bedford, the winery manager, has been a perfect gentleman around me. But he's been a little evasive whenever I asked him any questions about winery business."

"So, Sherry, where do you think Wally is?"

"I don't know, Roger. That's what I'm asking you to find out for me. I can't stand the not knowing part. Whatever the answer actually is I'd be a lot happier knowing it than I would be living in the limbo world I find myself in now."

I casually and inconspicuously looked over at Sherry as she concentrated on her driving in freeway traffic. She angrily brushed away a tear rolling down her cheek as she struggled to maintain her composure. I looked the other way at the scenery we were passing, mostly irrigated farmland, so as not to embarrass her.

We turned off I-5 at Woodland, drove south on route 113 most of the way to Davis, and headed west toward Winters in companionable silence. I thought about what Sherry had told me so far, and about one or two potentially significant things she hadn't told me.

As we approached the turn for the winery I noticed my eyes were becoming irritated. "The air looks kind of polluted over there, toward the coastal range. And my eyes are a little irritated. Where do you get all that pollution in the air way out here in the country?"

"That's smoke from some of the wildfires around here, probably mostly from the big one called the Cold Canyon fire, burning through the wilderness area just over the mountains near Lake Berryessa. We've always had the wildfires back there but since we started the drought six years ago we've had a lot more big fires than in the old days. Sometimes the smoke can get thick enough that you can't really see the mountains through all the junk in the air."

"How far is the winery from the fire?"

"During the wedding, it was probably about 10 or 12 miles as the crow flies. But it has gotten a lot closer since then. Parts of rural Winters less than a mile from the winery were evacuated Tuesday. The fire was only a mile or two from the winery the day Wally disappeared."

"Is it still headed this way toward the town and winery? Is this something I should be worrying about?"

"No, not as long as the prevailing winds aren't coming from a different direction than they're blowing now. The fire may be fairly close to us, but it would have to jump over those mountains to get to us and that doesn't happen very often. And a lot of the local fire brigades are out there with water trucks making sure that a stray spark or ember doesn't start anything burning on this side of the coastal range like what happened on Tuesday."

Sherry paused momentarily to pass a slow-moving truck. "On the other hand, we've got constant reminders there's a big wildfire burning out there near us. There's a lot of smoke and ash in the air, and a lot of the vineyard has a coating of ash we'll have to wash off as soon as the fire burns out or moves far enough away from us.

"Yesterday evening a U.S. Forest Service helicopter ran into some nasty air turbulence during what was intended to be a routine water drop on the fire. The fire is big enough, and intense enough, to create locally severe weather conditions over a radius of many miles from its epicenter. In this case the helicopter encountered severe updrafts coming up from the coastal range as it tried to fly over the mountains to drop its load over a local hotspot. The pilot followed the usual protocol for this situation by dropping his load of water over a local farm, which turned out to be our vineyard, and returning to his base to wait for safer conditions. We were lucky he missed the house."

I thought about how much water a big helicopter could lift. "What does a ton or so of water do to your grapes out in the field?"

"Do you know the old saying 'It's an ill wind that blows no good'?" Sherry asked. "In this case that helicopter dropped its bucket of water directly on our vineyard, just missing the winery itself. We got the grapes irrigated and a lot of the ash from the fire washed off the fruit at a good time in their growth cycle---early enough that we're not worried about mold, late enough to help them grow a bit faster while they're developing fruitiness. And the best part is we don't have to pay for the water. We seem to have lucked out in this episode!"

I recalled scenes from the 11 o'clock news on our local TV when the Angeles National Forest caught fire, as it did frequently during the hot, dry summer and autumn months. "What do people around here do about fires like that, way out away from where the towns and cities are?"

"The State has a couple of hundred men out there digging firebreaks and several planes with water tanks dropping water and fire suppressants on the blaze. It may take a few weeks, but they'll get it under control. And, in the meantime, they'll try to protect any ranch or farm buildings that might be in the fire's path. But thousands of acres of wilderness habitat will burn and the watershed for the reservoir up there will get messed up in the process."

I thought about whether Wally could be out there in the fire-ravaged wilderness area. "Do hikers or people who live out there in the wilderness on the other side of the coastal range ever get caught in an isolated area on the wrong side of a fire and disappear until they can safely hike out or get their cell phones to work?"

"Yes, it can happen if you're in the wrong place at the wrong time," answered Sherry. "Are you thinking about whether Wally might be lost out there?"

"The idea crossed my mind," I replied. "Do you think it's a possibility?"

Sherry pondered the possibilities for a while. "No, I don't think so. His four-wheel drive truck is still sitting back of the winery, so there's no way he could have driven over the mountains on his own. And, this is the beginning of the winery's busy season. Wally wouldn't have gone anywhere on his own without telling someone how to reach him."

"Have you thought about what exactly you want me to do for you, Sherry? There may be things we find out about Wally that you don't want to know."

Sherry glanced quickly at me. "Yes, Roger, I have. I want you to find Wally, dead or alive. If there's a ransom, I'll pay it. If he was killed, I want you to find Wally's murderer and see that he's brought to justice. I'll settle for the truth no matter how it makes him look."

I looked directly at my client. "I'll need you to formally hire me so we have a client-detective relationship. That will make my demanding to see winery records and financial papers legal and give me a little more clout than I might have as just a friend. I have a contract you can sign when we get to the winery and I can unpack my bag. We can discuss this a little more while you're looking at the contract. In the meantime I need to think about the logistics of what we need to be doing, who should be doing it, and when it needs to be done."

An hour later Sherry was signing a contract and I'd formulated a game plan. "OK, Sherry, I think I have an idea how to proceed. Wally's been missing for three days. There hasn't been any ransom demand. Usually the police won't do anything in these circumstances for at least a week unless there's been a ransom demand. So there's three more days before we can expect any real action by the sheriff. I think we can do a few things during the next couple of days without needlessly upsetting the sheriff and burning our bridges to that resource."

With a pensive look Sherry asked me, "What are you thinking about?"

"We need to know a lot more about Wally's finances and how the winery is doing to really understand his state of mind. One of my associates, Jason Culpepper, is an expert in investigating the financial details of complex organizations. I think we need to get him up here and working on that end of things as soon as we can. While he's doing that I think I can at least alert the FBI to the possibility of a kidnapping. Maybe we can get their resources started finding out if there are any records of Wally traveling anywhere after he disappeared.

"I'll fly back to L.A. after I talk to my contacts in the FBI, hopefully later today. I'll also check in with the sheriff, who needs to be notified you've hired a private detective who'll be investigating on your behalf. Jason should be here tomorrow. If we haven't found anything more about Wally's whereabouts by day seven, I'll come back up here with some additional resources that might help. We'll also put some serious pressure on the sheriff's department then to do a real investigation."

I excused myself to make the next few phone calls. Former FBI agent, now private detective, Jason Culpepper had worked for my detective agency since transferring from the FBI a year or so ago. He liked following paper trails and was very good at it, so he assisted us in all of our cases that had a strong financial component. Jason was, therefore, our go-to guy for all the long boring paper chases that went with financial investigations. He had a great deal of experience in the FBI on cases where organized crime involvement was suspected, so he also collaborated with me on those kinds of cases.

Given Sherry's doubts about her new brother-in-law Frank's honesty and integrity, especially in regard to all things financial with respect to Wally's estate and what was now her winery operation, this definitely looked like a job for Jason.

He answered on the first ring. "Can you free up your calendar for a week or so of work here in the wine country? There's a financial angle on a case I've gotten involved in that looks like we need your kind of expertise to check it out."

I could imagine him nodding at the other end of the line. "I'm not doing anything here that I couldn't do from your end on a computer if you can find me a WiFi hotspot," he replied.

"Why don't you catch a Southwest flight to Sacramento this evening or tomorrow, Jason. You can give our new client a call when you're ready to board your flight and she'll meet your plane at this end. There are a couple of extra cars here at the winery, so you don't have to worry about a rental. And there's fast Internet access all over the winery. There's also a pretty good possibility this will eventually turn into an FBI case so I'll see if I can convince the Kaufman sisters we may have a kidnapping or an organized crime connection here for them to investigate."

I gave him my contact information for Sherry. "The winery is about an hour's drive from the Sacramento Airport in rush hour. If you call her just before your flight takes off from LAX or Burbank the timing should be perfect.

"I'll try for an 8 AM flight tomorrow morning, Roger, but tell her not to make any plans she can't change until I call her from the airport."

We said our good-byes and hung up.

My next call was to Gretchen Kaufman, the Special Agent-in-Charge at the FBI's San Francisco offices, on her personal cell phone.

"Hi Gretchen. I just got a new case in the Sacramento area. It feels like it might have a strong FBI connection. I hoped you might be able to check out whether a missing person might have appeared somewhere else before I start a full-blown investigation."

I told her the skimpy details I had, and my gut feeling there could be an organized crime connection to Wally's disappearance.

"If you find any trace of him please phone me and I'll call off the dogs. At the moment the dog is Jason, who'll be checking out the winery's finances and the missing husband's true net worth starting tomorrow. If you don't find any trace of A. Wallace Fortune of Winters, California I'll be back and treating this like a possible homicide case in a few days."

"If I do come back up here I thought you might like to get together for dinner. Jason will probably be able to join us if you and Barbara can meet us somewhere between Sacramento and The City," I continued.

"Aren't you lucky? Barbara and I are due in Sacramento to testify in a trial next week and have all the time in the world to meet you after the trial recesses at 4 o'clock any day you'd like. Where will you be staying?"

"I'll be staying with the client, who's the old friend who gave us Juliet a few years ago. We'll be at a nice little winery just outside of Winters, if you know where that is. One of Winters' main tourist attractions is one of the best steak houses in the region, a place called The Buckhorn, if you'd like to meet us there. How about 7 PM for dinner Thursday night if you haven't solved my case for me before then? That should be late enough to keep you out of the worst of the local traffic. Figure it should be about a 45-minute drive from downtown Sacramento."

Chapter 7. Beginning an investigation

I visited the sheriff's office in the new courthouse located in Woodland, the county seat of Yolo County, to officially notify the local law enforcement agency that I'd be performing an investigation in their territory. After being allowed to sit around for most of an hour learning how busy they were and how humble I should be when they finally saw me, I was pointed toward Deputy Fletcher's office.

He was sitting at his desk trying to look busy and pointedly not standing up to greet me. "Sit," he commanded, pointing to a chair in front of his desk. The chair was a nice touch, with brackets for attaching handcuffs or shackles at each arm and leg. I sat. He continued to pretend to be working. After two minutes I'd had enough.

I got up and started to walk out of his office. "This was intended to be a courtesy visit. You've had it."

"Now wait just a minute here. Who do you think you are?" he blustered.

"A former fellow cop. One who worked on a real police force," I answered as I walked out of the door and slammed it shut. I kept going to Sherry's car, which I drove back to Winters.

The wind had shifted again, reminding me there was still a huge wildfire burning out there somewhere just over the Blue Ridge Mountains. There was a trace of ash in the air, but mostly my eyes and nose were irritated and the air seemed a little hazy. The radio and TV news media announced the fire was now more than 80% contained and not currently posing a threat to any populated areas. However, the remainder of the fire burning in some of the most inaccessible wilderness areas most probably wouldn't be completely extinguished until the first heavy rainfall, which might not occur for several months.

I decided to try my luck at the local sheriff's substation. Another office and another deputy were available there. This time I was greeted politely and asked why I was there. I explained the nature of my business. The deputy asked to see my license, which I showed him. He copied the pertinent information down.

He looked up at me from the form he was filling out. "Are you carrying a weapon, Mr. Bowman?" he asked politely.

"No," I replied politely.

"Do you intend to carry a weapon while you're in our jurisdiction?" he continued.

"I don't know," I answered.

"Please let me see your concealed weapon permit."

I passed it to him. He copied some more pertinent information then returned it to me.

"Can I help you with anything else today, Mr. Bowman?" he asked.

"I don't know," I replied. "Can you tell me anything about what your office has done to try to locate a missing person reported to you several days ago, A. Wallace Fortune, a local winery owner?"

"I'm afraid I can't really answer that question since I'm not involved with that case, Mr. Bowman," he answered politely. "We usually don't do much of anything until an adult who has been reported missing has stayed missing for longer than a week. Usually they sober up and come home sooner than that."

"Thank you very much," I said and took my leave. I appreciated the sheriff's department protocols for being polite to citizens here in this small town, even if I thought their law enforcement skills weren't completely up to date.

I returned her car to Sherry and arranged to fly home later that evening. She looked worried, but maintained a brave front as she drove me to the airport to catch my flight. Suzanne collected me at the airport, greeting me with a big kiss and a bigger smile.

"Guess who phoned today?" she quizzed me as I threw my overnight bag onto the back seat and sat down in the front seat of the car. Hearing no answer she continued, "Connie Sherman. She wanted to tell me she had her first interview with an applicant for the nanny job this afternoon and that Jason volunteered to drive down to Irvine as soon as he came back from a case he's working on to help her set up a crib and a few other necessities for the nursery."

"Do you remember our hidden agendas for the barbecue last week, Suzanne? Score one for Plan A and one for Plan C," I replied with a smile.

She checked the rearview mirror before pulling the car into the traffic lane leading to the airport exit, asking. "How was your trip to Winters?"

Out of force of habit I checked my side mirror to see if anyone was following us. I didn't see any likely looking vehicles behind our car. "Wally is still missing. Sherry's worried sick about him but the local sheriff doesn't seem to be doing anything to help. Sherry hired me to investigate his disappearance. I'm still trying to think of where to begin. Can you give me a little background about my new client, please, Suzanne?"

Suzanne switched lanes to get over to the 405 Freeway. "Sure, Roger. Sherry and I aren't all that close but I've spent enough time with her to know some of her history."

"Francis' toast at the dinner the night before the wedding made it pretty clear this was Wally's first marriage. How about Sherry? Has she ever been married before the wedding to Wally?"

"I don't know all the details, but yes she was married and she didn't make the right choices. There was a young daughter and a husband in jail who she divorced. Apparently he was driving drunk at a high rate of speed when he killed an entire family in a car he broadsided. He had a history of previous convictions for driving under the influence and other alcohol-related trouble so the judge threw the book at him and sentenced him to something like twenty years in jail for vehicular homicide.

"The daughter is an adult now, very much following in her mother's footsteps as far as dog breeding and showing. She lives somewhere back east, Ohio I think. She and Sherry stay in touch but aren't very close. I'm pretty sure I saw the daughter at the wedding but she didn't stay around for the wedding party so I didn't get a chance to talk to her. I'd guess the first husband might have been released from prison in the last year or so if he behaved himself while he was in jail."

"*Hmmm*," I thought.

Later that night I had a call from Gretchen Kaufman. "We struck out, Roger. No traces of anyone named Wallace Fortune or A. Wallace Fortune showed up on planes, trains, or buses anywhere in the western United States this past week. No phone usage, no Internet hits, and no credit card usage. Of course, we can't rule out he's traveling around under another identity, but so far there's no sign of him running away."

Papers rustled in the background as Gretchen continued. "I guess that means we're on for dinner 7 o'clock Thursday night at the Buckhorn. We'll see you then and you'll fill us in on this case, OK?"

We agreed to meet then.

Later that night over dinner I asked Bruce if he felt Juliet the cadaver dog was ready for the real thing.

"Ready, willing, and able!" he exclaimed. "She's a lot better than any dog I ever worked with in Iraq or Afghanistan."

"How about you, Suzanne? Can you handle Robert on your own for three or four days while I put Bruce and Juliet to work up in Winters?"

"Sure, it would be a lot of fun for me," she replied. "I can work from home for the week."

I put down my fork to emphasize what I was going to say next. "Do you remember that bad feeling you had at the winery during the wedding, Suzanne? I trust your instincts. Now I have a very bad feeling about what happened to Wally. And I think somehow it's all tied up with the winery. I'm guessing, and it's only a guess based on my gut instinct, that Wally is dead and his body is hidden somewhere on the winery grounds or in the vineyard. I'm hoping Juliet and Bruce can either find his body or reassure me he might still be alive by searching the entire farm and not finding his body."

Which is how Bruce and I came to be driving back to Sacramento with Juliet happily lying in her crate in the back of the family 'dogmobile' after a very early start. We left Romeo at home to minimize the disruption of Sherry's house for the time we'd be searching.

We beat the worst of the commuter traffic in L.A. and Sacramento and made it to the winery before 5. Fortunately, Sherry was a dog person who had also been Juliet's owner before giving her to us. Bruce didn't have to ask. Off came the leash as soon as we entered the house and Juliet had free rein to wander around as she pleased. Like a good German shorthaired pointer she naturally gravitated toward her favorite people to feel contact and live up to the breed description as 'Velcro dogs'. As we sat down in the family room Juliet wandered over to Bruce where she could lie across his feet on the floor and look adoringly up at him.

I'd called Jason and asked him to meet us at the house. The four of us, including Sherry, went to dinner at a very good sushi restaurant recommended by Sherry. Most of the other customers in the restaurant, hidden in a small shopping mall in South Davis, were Asian families with well-behaved children. Over some very tasty rolls and a tempura dinner for Jason, who wasn't yet acclimated enough to California to eat raw fish or pick up his food with chopsticks like the rest of us, we discussed our progress, or lack thereof, on the case.

There wasn't any way to put a positive spin on what I had to tell Sherry next. "Gretchen checked out all the possible methods of travel Wally might have used. Nothing showed up. Unless he's changed identities, which is a lot harder to do than it used to be thanks to Homeland Security, or he's doing everything from a car he's borrowed somewhere, using only cash for gas, food, and motels, he's not out in the wind. It's probably time we looked for him here in Winters. And if that's the case, I'm not feeling any too good about the answers we're likely to find."

Sherry sucked in her breath sharply, but that was her only immediate reaction. Her body language was a little more honest as she struggled to come to grips with what might be the worst possible news while maintaining her usual outward facade of stoic strength.

I looked around. The restaurant was small, but the tables were well separated and nobody at any of the other tables seemed to be paying any attention to our discussion. "I brought Bruce and Juliet with me to help us look. That's the first item on my agenda for tomorrow morning. How about you, Jason? Have you had a chance to look things over yet?"

Jason ate a forkful of deep fried shrimp and a mystery vegetable, probably a coated sliced sweet potato from the size and shape. "Yes, I have. Sherry and I stopped off at the winery. Sherry asked Clay Bedford, the winery manager, to show us all the paperwork. He refused, saying everything to do with winery business had to be approved by Wally's brother, Francis.

"Sherry politely, but firmly, explained to Clay Bedford that when push came to shove he only had three real choices: He could refuse any demand by her, he could call Francis to ask for guidance, or he could do as she asked. Sherry then pointed out that she was the owner's wife, which meant she either owned half the winery as his wife or the whole thing as his widow. She suggested doing what she asked was the prudent choice if he wanted to keep his job."

Jason paused a moment to heighten the drama. "It took him the better part of three seconds to decide on the prudent choice."

Sherry, who had been acting distracted and lost in thought throughout Jason's narrative, absent-mindedly picked up a piece of sushi roll containing rice, freshly sliced fish, and avocado wrapped in seaweed and covered with a flavorful sauce in her chopsticks, dipped it into a small dish of wasabi, a spicy Japanese mustard, in soy sauce, and continued the narrative. "They apparently keep a couple of years of paperwork at the winery, with the older records ending up in Francis' files for tax and legal purposes. Clay showed us where the paperwork was kept and explained the system to me. Then he excused himself to get back to work and left us alone to look the material over. Jason started reviewing the files immediately."

Jason put down his knife and fork on a still half-full plate of deep fried goodies before he resumed answering. "The files were simple and looked like what you'd expect in a medium-sized business. Every bill and receipt was there in a paper copy, with most of it except the most recent bills and receipts backed up onto a business software program on the computer's hard drive. Everything looked good and all the numbers balanced. It was a textbook example of how to keep track of the day to day cash flow for the business."

"Why do I think there's a 'but' coming, Jason?" I asked.

Jason paused a moment to eat a bit more shrimp, this time with a long narrow breaded, fried green bean. "Because there's a 'but' coming, and you know me too well not to pick up on things like that. My dad trained me if I was doing a job

I should do it right. So Sherry and I went out to the area where the different varieties of wine were aging in barrels and bottles. We estimated the total amount of each type of wine made in the last two years from the records and compared it with how much of the wine was currently in the aging rooms.

"We knew how much of each variety had been sold from the paperwork; the numbers should have matched what was in storage for the varietals that were being aged a year or two before they were shipped. Sherry confirmed with Clay which wines were sold quickly and which ones were kept to age. Long story short, there was a lot less of the more expensive red wines than the paper trail indicated there should have been, so some of the wine sales they were showing as incoming money they could pay taxes on and could be spent, at least on paper, for nonexistent items like consultants, bottles, labels, corks, and you name it. And that, Roger, is what we call money laundering."

I considered what I was hearing. "Can you estimate how much money went through the laundry every year?"

Finishing the last of the food on his plate, Jason replied thoughtfully, "At least a few hundred thousand dollars. And if a dozen wineries were doing this it would be in the millions."

Jason pushed his plate aside before continuing, "After we finished studying wine finances 101 we drove over to Francis' office, which was locked and empty. So the direct approach didn't work. I spent the rest of my day on the Internet looking for everything I could find out about the winery from public records. Typically for a closely held private corporation like this one, that turned out to be very little information. And here we are."

Chapter 8: Juliet the cadaver dog

"We have to start somewhere, Bruce," I said. "According to our client, the last time anyone reported seeing Wally alive was at the winery the same day he disappeared. Let's assume he was killed here at the winery or on the grounds outside of it somewhere, and they hid or buried his body in the vineyard."

Bruce made a crude sketch of the winery grounds, more than 300 acres, on the table in front of him. "This is a lot of ground for Juliet to cover, especially if she has to search the entire property completely at random. Let's make a few assumptions to make the odds better of finding Wally's body if it's laying somewhere out there. How big is he, Roger?"

"About my height. He's big, I'd guess he weighs about 250 or 260."

Bruce pointed his pencil at the shapes of the buildings near the front of his sketch. "If he was killed at the house or the winery and someone wanted to hide his body, he'd be quite a load to carry any distance. Let's set up our first search grid by assuming the body is hidden somewhere near the buildings. There's some open space around the buildings and paved drive where he could have been buried that I'll have to run Juliet over to get to the fields that need to be searched. But my best guess is that if there's a body out there it's concealed by a couple of rows of grapes or some kind of structure."

He picked up a ruler and drew several straight vertical lines through the buildings that passed through the sketched areas of grape vines in front of and behind the buildings. Then he drew a series of horizontal lines a few inches apart, perpendicular to, and passing through, the first set of lines. The result was a regular grid with the house and winery at the center and several acres of grapes on all four sides of the buildings within the area covered by the grid.

"I drew this sketch roughly to scale," Bruce explained. "I'll be working Juliet over this entire area today to see if she can find a dead body that nobody, especially the deputy sheriff, turned up when they did a casual look around the open area between the winery and house, and along the driveway. I'd guess Juliet and I should end up walking a couple of miles through the grapevines and cover something like 20-30 acres of this grid this morning. It's going to be a lot slower going than what you saw in the park. Would you like to join us?"

"Sure," I replied. "I love watching her hunt."

Bruce explained what we'd do first. "We'll start with the cleared area between the house and winery. I don't think we'll find anything there. The Sheriff would have checked out any areas that looked freshly dug up. But, just in case, we'll let Juliet's nose confirm that for us. I don't think it will take more than ten minutes to rule out that possibility. Then we'll start searching the grid."

We'd been walking back and forth with Juliet between the house and the winery for less than five minutes when we were accosted by the tall thin man I'd been introduced to at the wedding as Wally's brother Francis. I didn't think we'd exchanged more than half a dozen words during the wedding or after.

"What's going on out here? You know you're trespassing, don't you?" Sherry's irate brother-in-law asked in a demanding tone.

"The owner of this property gave us permission to exercise our dog out here in the fields," I replied quickly and pointedly. Bruce caught on immediately that I was going to take the lead in this conversation.

"I'm the owner of this property and I didn't give you any such permission," he huffed. "Wait a minute. I saw you at the wedding, didn't I? Who are you and what are you doing here?"

"You're not the owner of this property and I don't need your permission," I replied curtly. Sometimes people make mistakes when they're angry so I thought I'd deliberately irritate Fortune and see what happened.

He was too smart to fall into that trap. "I'm sorry, I should have recognized you sooner. You're Sherry's friend from Los Angeles, aren't you? She told me you'd be staying here at the house with her. Perhaps you can introduce me to your friend here."

"Bruce, this is Sherry's brother-in-law Francis. Francis, meet my friend Bruce."

"Call me Frank, please. All my friends do," he said heartily. "I handle all of Wally's legal affairs." We all shook hands.

"I guess I'll get back to work now. I was just bringing the monthly accounts up to date." He headed back into the winery. Bruce, Juliet, and I continued walking out into the vineyard with Juliet.

Bruce took the lead. He had entered GPS co-ordinates onto his search grid sketch and used them to guide us as we walked back and forth through the vineyard. Juliet bounded ahead of us casting right and left through the gaps between the grape vines on either side of the paths we walked on. It was easy walking for us on the narrow aisles between the rows on either side. Narrow paths to facilitate pruning and picking the grapes ran parallel to each row, with the long dimension of the rows broken up by perpendicular paths between groups of rows to further facilitate inspection, pruning, and harvest of the grapes during the growing and harvesting seasons.

Large thick trunks of mature grapevines emerged from mounded earth along each row. Coming off each of the trunks at regular intervals were branches that had been trained along wire trellises. The ripening grapes hung in clusters from the neat lateral branches, which were partially shaded in regular patterns by systematically pruned leaves at the top of each plant. Drip irrigation systems of rubber tubing went from end to end of each mound to save precious water in drought-conscious California.

Juliet checked back with Bruce every five minutes, so we had a very good idea of where she was at all times. She was amazingly quiet as she ran through the grapes, so the frequent check-ins were an essential part of the dog's routine to keep us near her at all times.

We could look down whatever row we were walking through to see most or all of the way to the end of the row. However, the rows were close enough together and the grape leaves thick and abundant enough to make visibility to the sides of the rows we walked past practically impossible. The dense canopy of leaves atop the grapevines would have made an aerial search of the property fruitless, both literally and figuratively.

We were walking along a row running parallel to the winery and perhaps eight or ten rows deep into the crosshatched grid of growing grapes. I could feel myself being watched from the winery, most likely by brother Francis. There wasn't anything I could do about being visible from the winery as I was a couple of feet taller than any of the grapevines.

We'd been searching with Juliet for almost an hour. Bruce looked up from his sketch and checked his GPS co-ordinates again. "If I had the body of someone I'd killed in the winery to get rid of, my best guess is we'd find it out here some time in the next half hour or so."

It actually took exactly 34 minutes by my watch. Juliet barked twice and went on alert about twenty feet to our left. We were there less than a minute later. A freshly dug patch of earth broke up the regularity of the mound directly in front of the imaginary line from Juliet's tail to her nose, which was about six feet away from the freshly turned dirt.

It probably didn't matter to Juliet's nose that the water drop by the helicopter in distress had not only washed the grapevines in this row but had also flushed enough of the soil from the base of the vine to expose the freshly dug earth and a couple of human fingers so we knew precisely where the police would have to dig for the body. The next few steps would wait until the technicians who would collect samples from the crime scene arrived, but there was clearly a cadaver under there to be dug up. It was an odds-on bet we'd found the remains of A. Wallace Fortune.

"I'll make sure we can find this spot again," said Bruce as he walked over to the exact spot Juliet was pointing toward, taking great care to try to avoid further disturbing the soil to the best of his ability.

Out came his little flag, which he planted just in front of the tips of two human fingers visible under the grapevine where the full force of the water drop had washed away much of the soil covering the mound. Bruce walked back to Juliet exactly the way he'd come over to the disturbed soil to mark the spot, snapped on her leash, released her from her point with two gentle taps on her head, and walked her at a heel all the way back to where I was standing a safe distance from the presumptive crime scene. He attached Juliet's leash firmly to the nearest substantial stake. I called 911 on my cell phone to report the body and we sat down on the ground to wait for the cops and make sure nobody disturbed the crime scene before they got here.

I'd told the 911 call operator to have the first deputy dispatched to the scene phone my cell when he arrived so I could escort him to the scene, which was quite literally in the middle of nowhere. I borrowed Bruce's GPS device so I could find my way back to him in the featureless maze that was the vineyard. Juliet and I carefully walked to the house, taking a circuitous route that concealed us from any observers in the winery, to meet the arriving cops.

Ten minutes after I got back to the house the first deputy arrived. Two more Sheriff's cars pulled into the driveway while we were exchanging pleasantries. I explained to the first deputy we were friends of Sherry's, which didn't impress him very much. Then I tried my private detective credentials. Big mistake; he went from not caring to openly antagonistic. My third set of credentials, a deputy Sheriff's badge from San Bernardino County, was the charm.

"Why didn't you show me the badge right away?" he asked. Without waiting for an answer he asked for details about the alleged body I'd reported.

"So far it's just some disturbed soil and a couple of fingers sticking out of the ground, but I'll bet we just found Wallace Fortune's remains. Do you want to wait for the Coroner and the CSI types or go take a look?" I asked.

By then his two buddies had caught up to us. One of them laughed and said, "You've been watching too much TV. It's just us until we call the Highway Patrol out of Woodland. Let's make sure you've got a fresh body before I make those calls."

I led them out to where Bruce and Juliet were waiting patiently. Along the way I explained that Juliet was a trained cadaver dog and Bruce a certified handler. They were clearly starting to take me much more seriously by the time we arrived at the body.

The first deputy looked at the scene, looked closely at the two fingers from a human hand Juliet had found, and started the process. Speaking with a slight twang of Oklahoma in his voice, typical of many of the third generation Californians who end up in Central Valley law enforcement agencies, he took charge. "Hang some crime scene tape all around the area," he instructed the deputy who'd thought I watched too much TV. "Then guard this area till the technicians get here. Nobody comes closer than the outside of the crime tape or arrest them. Especially any reporters who might show up!"

He turned to the third deputy. "I'll take care of interviewing these two." He paused, smiled, and continued. "I mean these three," he said with a nod toward Juliet. Start making all the phone calls. We need the Highway Patrol, CSI, and the Sheriff notified. Let's hold off on family until we get a positive ID. Ask the Sheriff to figure out what to do about the media and ask him if he wants to handle media relations personally."

He turned toward me. "OK, let's all walk over to the house. Then I'll need to see I.D. from both of you."

His hand went down to his gun butt. "Is anyone carrying?"

"No," I replied. Bruce nodded agreement.

We all walked the circuitous route to the front of the house, the deputy trailing behind Bruce and me so he could watch us both. He obviously wasn't ready to completely trust us yet even after seeing my deputy's badge. At this point he probably didn't fully trust Juliet either. I felt Francis watching from the winery, but he hadn't chosen to make an appearance as yet. That was fine by me.

"OK," said the deputy, stopping us beside the road in front of the house where two of the deputies had parked their cars. "Let me see some I.D."

We went through the ritual. He scribbled notes from our Driver's licenses before returning them. The deputy treated both of us with some respect so this was painless thus far. No handcuffs, no threats, just three adults and a dog having a conversation.

"OK," he said again, "now tell me again what you were doing when you found the alleged body."

I thought quickly about what he already must have known or guessed and tried to only tell him that much. "Sherry is a good friend. We were here last week for the wedding. As a matter of fact, unless I'm mistaken I saw you at the wedding, sitting across from us with Wally's family and friends. Sherry was worried about her husband, who seems to have disappeared. So she called and hired me to come up here to investigate. I brought Bruce and Juliet along because she's trained to do

61

exactly what she seems to have done, and Bruce is a certified trainer and handler for cadaver dogs."

The deputy visibly relaxed. He knew I was telling him the truth. "Yes, I was at the wedding. Wally and I go back a long way. We were teammates for a couple of years playing football for the local high school and this is the kind of small town where everybody knows everybody else. Now that you mention it I remember seeing you at the wedding too."

The deputy looked around, making sure nobody could hear what he was saying in our interview. "Is there anyone here in Northern California who can vouch for your honesty and integrity?" the deputy asked. "I don't know you and you've got to admit there's a lot of ways I can interpret your magically finding a well hidden body."

I thought about the best way to answer his question. "I've discussed this case with the senior FBI agents from San Francisco since we initially thought Fortune might have been kidnapped. The Special Agent-in-Charge knows me personally and will vouch for me. If you want to call her I can give you her phone number."

The deputy was on the line to Gretchen Kaufman in a minute or two, told her I'd suggested her as a reference, listened for a bit, and hung up. "OK, she told me how lucky I was to have you working on a case with me and I should watch and learn. How come you didn't tell me you'd been a homicide detective in L.A.?"

I tried to look sincere. I never really had a chance to get to know Wally, so at this point I was just feeling badly for Sherry. "It didn't seem important at the time. Sherry is a close friend. I'm still a little shook up about finding her husband's body a week after their wedding."

The deputy turned back to Bruce. "The killer or killers chose a good place to bury the body, you know," the deputy commented thoughtfully. "Those vines weren't going to be disturbed for 15 or 20 years, which means the body wouldn't have been found for at least that long if it hadn't been for your dog."

Juliet knew when she was being praised. She maneuvered her head in front of the deputy's hand. He absent-mindedly scratched Juliet behind her ears. "She's a very nice dog. Have you ever hunted her?"

"Yes," answered Bruce. "She's good at that, too."

The deputy took a long look at Juliet before turning back toward Bruce. Putting away his notebook, he switched from deputy mode to being our colleague. "I've never seen a dog find a body like this before. How in heck did you train her to do that?"

Bruce patted Juliet's head before he answered. "The short answer is practice, practice, and more practice. Juliet is a German shorthaired pointer. She sees the world through her nose. Tell her what scent you want her to find and she'll find it. And, when she does find it, her instinct is to stop and point at it."

Slipping a few more treats to Juliet as a reward for a job well done, Bruce continued, "Do you want the long answer?"

"I don't think that's necessary," the deputy replied. "But I will say I'm impressed. We might never have found Wally's body if you and Juliet hadn't spent all that time practicing, as you put it."

The deputy paused thoughtfully before continuing to speak. "I'm the ranking deputy on this force. I don't have any real experience with homicide investigations. Normally, we turn those over to the Highway Patrol. If you're planning to investigate this killing on behalf of your client I'd like to have you cooperating with us."

With everything to gain and nothing to lose I nodded. "I'll be glad to share information with you on this case if Sherry wants me to continue the investigation. And if the sheriff decides to take this case a lot more seriously than he seems to have done thus far."

"Sounds good to me," replied the deputy. "It would be nice if we could get access to the FBI and its laboratory on a friendly basis for a change!"

Chapter 9. It's officially a murder case

The deputy called me early the next day while an obviously distressed Sherry and I were sitting at the breakfast table sipping coffee and discussing the case. "The preliminary autopsy results are consistent with a time of death corresponding to the day the victim disappeared. His widow will have to come to the morgue to formally identify the body, preferably some time today. There's no doubt its Fortune. I didn't have any trouble recognizing him and it's obvious he was murdered. There are two bullet holes in his chest. Either wound would have killed him instantly.

"Our search of the burial scene didn't turn up anything of interest except the body. Given the flood almost exactly on top of the area where the victim was buried, any clues that might have been left by the killer or killers would have been washed away when the helicopter dropped its load of water. At this point in time that's all we know."

He hung up as I noted he didn't ask me whether we had found out anything he should know. That wasn't exactly a ringing endorsement of his (or maybe it was the sheriff's?) faith in me as a former homicide detective. It was probably just as well. I didn't have any new information for him.

"I'm sorry to have to tell you this Sherry, but the deputy just confirmed the body we found was Wally's and he'd been shot. Later on today you'll have to go in to the Coroner's office and formally identify the body. I'll be glad to drive you there when you feel ready to do that."

Sherry finally let her emotions show as she stood up and began to cry. I walked over to her and put my arm around her shoulders. We stood that way for a long time as she sobbed into my shoulder. Finally, she pulled herself together, wiping her eyes with a napkin, and stepped back from me.

"I'm sorry I lost control like that, Roger," she said. "It won't happen again. Now, what are we going to do to catch whoever did this?"

I refilled both our cups with coffee. We sat down at the table to resume our discussion of the case. Now that we'd confirmed the body was Wally's, we had a murderer to find. "Up until now, Sherry, we had a missing person case, so our total focus has been on your husband. It's likely the motive for his murder is something he did or didn't do, but we don't want to rule out any other possibilities yet. One remote possibility I'd like to rule out is that someone killed Wally to punish you for something you did. Do you have any enemies who might have done something that drastic to get even with you?"

"No, Roger, I don't have any enemies at all that I know of. Unless I picked up an enemy who hates me that much because of the small roles I played in a couple of your other murder cases, the killings at the dog shows here in Northern California and at the hunt test in Southern California."

'*Hmmm*,' I thought. "Possible, but unlikely, Sherry. Are there any hunt tests happening around here these days?"

"As a matter of fact, yes. There's a test today at the Hastings Island preserve."

I sipped my now cool, if not actually cold, coffee while I considered the possibilities. "Perfect, Sherry," I said. "Let's get you, Juliet, and Bruce over there in time to check everybody out and talk to some of the regulars this morning. Among the hunt test crowd you're looking for someone who lost money because of our investigation in Southern California. You should look for anyone who had a big investment in the hunt test venues near Sacramento. I remember the group that owned the facility where our client's husband was killed in the south also owned one of the big pheasant hunting clubs near Sacramento. Somebody gossipy would know if anyone around here was upset with us last year when that case took place.

"The other possibility is someone who got burned when we figured out who was doing the cheating at the local dog shows. Maybe it was one of the crooked judges the AKC fired or maybe it was someone who got hurt when the AKC cleaned house in New York. You and Bruce should check out the faces and the gossip at the hunt test and see if anyone looks familiar, or whether anyone complained too much when it all went down. Let's try to rule out the revenge against you motive so we can get back to concentrating on Wally here."

Bruce and Juliet were staying at Sherry's old house in an eastern Sacramento suburb called Carmichael. There were dog runs in back, dog tolerant furniture throughout the house, and mostly Juliet's extended family in the backyard to play with. Bruce called with just about perfect timing asking, "What do you want Juliet and me to do today, Roger?'

Sherry and I had just decided we had to rule out revenge against Sherry as a possible motive for Wally's murder. This seemed to be a good job for Sherry to do without me, as long as she had Bruce with her for protection. "Why don't you head over to Hastings Island with Sherry and Juliet, Bruce? There's a hunt test today. Maybe you can sneak Juliet in as a bye-dog so we can show her off to some of the Northern California hunt test crowd. Remember, Sherry and Juliet both grew up here. I suspect Sherry would love to have a few of the locals realize she's breeding all-around show dogs who are also great hunters, not just pretty faces. And, Sherry can also explain to you what she and I decided she'll do while she's at the hunt test and how you can help out in that area as well.

"When the hunt tests are over why don't you come back here to join us for dinner? I don't think you've seen the Kaufman sisters since you met them in Quito on our Galapagos Islands tour. I'm sure they'll enjoy hearing about some of your many adventures since then, especially how you trained Juliet as a cadaver dog."

****

Bruce and Jason had gotten to the restaurant ahead of me. It was crowded, so we took the table offered us and ordered beers to tide us over until the rest of our party arrived. Bruce was obviously feeling good about his day.

"Tell us about Juliet, Bruce. From your mood she obviously had a very good outing at the hunt test."

"Yep!" Bruce smiled as he remembered the scene. "They had just one brace entered for the Master Hunter competition and only one of the two dogs showed up. One of the club officers made the rounds of the spectators asking if anyone had a Master Hunter they could borrow as a bye-dog to run in the brace with the dog actually trying to pass the test. I volunteered Juliet's services, with me as the handler. Nobody knew me, and Juliet was back in her crate in the car, so I got looked at kind of funny, but they were desperate so told me to get my dog to the starting line immediately. I did. A few of the old timers there recognized Juliet from the conformation show days so the gossip mill kicked into high gear. We got a big audience to see if Juliet was just a pretty face or whether she could hunt, too.

"We went out, and as luck would have it the other dog, Max, got the first point. Juliet honored properly and everything went just fine until the handler flushed the bird. There were four shots from the gunners, with zero hits. It's hard to retrieve a bird that's flown away, so off we went to try again. This time I let Max get the point. Max did everything right. The gunners messed up again. The third bird was Juliet's. She did a perfect point. I guess Max and his handler were pretty frustrated by that time, but Max dissed Juliet and tried to steal her point. The judges told the handler to pick up his dog and that was that. Just for chuckles I kicked up the bird. The gunners kept their perfect record intact---four shots, no hits. As we walked in one of the judges asked me if I could shoot as well as my dog could hunt and whether I had a hunting license."

Bruce paused to sip some beer before he got to the punch line. "Obviously they needed some help. There were only three braces of Senior Hunter candidates registered. I figured it shouldn't take more than another hour and a half or two hours, so I told him I shot as well as she hunted or better. It was a perfect day, no wind, just a steady gentle breeze. I shot about a dozen birds. The other gunner missed exactly that many birds. Fortunately they don't shoot birds for Junior Hunter tests so I was done on time.

"There were a lot of questions about Juliet so I hung around for about half an hour longer. I answered a few, referred them to Sherry for the rest. And, Sherry and I both agreed there isn't anyone in the GSP or hunt test world who isn't a big fan of

67

Sherry's, so you can rule out revenge against her as a motive in her husband's murder."

Just then Gretchen and Barbara Kaufman walked into the restaurant from the street. The hostess led them directly to our table. Jason switched over to our side of the table. Bruce and I scrunched together to make room in the booth. The two FBI agents sat down across from us. Gretchen looked to be less than thirty years old, a couple of years older than her sister. Both women were quite attractive and wore the standard uniform of FBI agents testifying in court, business formal attire. In this case it was skirts, blouses, and jackets. They looked enough alike, sharing dark hair and brown eyes, as well as being the same size at about five foot five, to make it easy to see they were sisters. Barbara wore her hair longer and entirely skipped any makeup other than lipstick, while Gretchen used both lipstick and something or other around her eyes.

But appearances could deceive as we'd learned the first time we met the Kaufman sisters. Based on how far she'd advanced at the FBI, Gretchen had to be well over thirty, which would make Barbara at least thirty. I'd spent a couple of hours in Mexico on a small sailboat with Gretchen, who was wearing only a skimpy bikini at the time, so I could vouch for the fact that she had the toned body of a serious athlete and really did look a lot younger than she was.

The waitress appeared with menus, which were studied for a moment or two. Jason turned to me to ask, "What's good here?"

I laughed and pointed at the walls and at the tables of other customers, practically all of them cutting or chewing steaks of various types. The walls were decorated with hunting trophies---heads of deer, elk, moose, and buffalo. "Meat, Jason, mostly steaks. If you want a change of pace, they also have rack of lamb or baby back ribs. And the best genuine sourdough bread this side of San Francisco."

The waitress returned and took our orders for four steaks and one prime rib while delivering large rounds of sourdough bread and butter in napkin-wrapped baskets, then salads, to the table to tide us over while we waited.

"OK, Roger," said Gretchen, "How's Suzanne doing? We need to hear all about the baby. When is it due and do you know whether it's a boy or girl?"

"Suzanne is fine. She drove here with me last week for the wedding that led to our involvement in this case. The baby is due in about six or seven weeks. And Robert will be getting a new sister. He's already got big plans for teaching all kinds of things to his younger sibling."

Bruce added, with a big grin, "I can hardly wait to teach him how to change diapers. Unless you want to do that part, Roger?"

I decided it was time to change the subject, turning to Barbara. "Tell us about your case in Sacramento while we wait for dinner to be served. Then we can tell you all about ours here."

She buttered a slice of bread, took a bite, and nodded appreciatively. "This is real sourdough rye, much better than what we usually get in Sacramento. There's not much to tell about our case. It's about another so-called public servant who was serving herself from the travel expense funds she embezzled from the Federal agency she worked for. It's going to be a long trial while the lawyers posture in the courtroom and negotiate in the back rooms. I'll be surprised if we don't get a last-minute plea bargain so it never gets to a jury. The public mood isn't too generous these days about forgiving government corruption."

We all turned to the bread and butter. A few moments later, large portions of beef appeared and were served, along with baked potatoes and vegetables.

Between bites of food I picked up the narrative. "The wedding was between our client, Sherry, who is the dog breeder who gave us Juliet, and the owner of a good-sized winery here in Winters, Wallace Fortune. A few days after the wedding, Fortune disappeared. Sherry wasn't too happy about the local sheriff's office. They treated it as a new groom with buyer's remorse rather than a crime and didn't do much of anything to investigate. So she hired me to try to find the missing husband. Unfortunately, we did. I'll let Bruce tell you that part."

Bruce explained how he had been training Juliet as a cadaver dog and the way she did her thing in the vineyard behind the winery. He also mentioned the effect of the wildfire and the incident with the helicopter dumping its load of water so there was a complete lack of clues around the area where the body was found.

I picked up the narrative and told everybody about the preliminary findings from the autopsy. "The groom was shot twice, probably with a rifle at fairly close range."

Turning to Jason I said "Your turn," cheerfully as I got back to a very good rib eye steak.

He leaned forward, looking Gretchen directly in the eye to emphasize the importance of what he had to say. "We were stonewalled when Sherry and I tried to get a look at the books and financials for the winery. First it was the winery manager then it was the victim's brother, who is also the winery's lawyer and accountant that refused to cooperate. I think there might be some hanky-panky going on there, maybe enough for you to throw some weight around with a possible RICO case as our justification."

Her slightly furrowed brow indicated Gretchen thought briefly about this suggestion. "From what you've told me thus far, Jason, that would be a real stretch.

The underlying murder case is out of our jurisdiction. You might want to plan on a late night winery visit with the widow, which would be completely legal since she's probably the winery owner now, to see if you can find me some probable cause for the FBI to get officially involved. And maybe also look for any guns that might be laying around to see if you can start trying to get a ballistics match."

Jason leaned back, ate another couple of bites of his roast beef while he thought her suggestion over. "Sure, why not? It sounds like a good idea. I assume everything starts early around here, like just after dawn while it's still cool. The motto is probably 'early to bed, early to rise'. So a late night visit in Winters is probably after 9 or 10 o'clock. I'm sure Sherry and I can handle that."

The waitress was back clearing mostly or completely empty plates and suggesting dessert for us. That was easy---a double shot of espresso coffee for our would-be burglar, Jason, and a couple of teas and a couple of regular coffees for the rest of us. A huge tray of goodies for dessert was offered and refused. Did I say the beef portions were huge?

I picked up the check.

Gretchen nodded her thanks. "We'll help you as much as we can, Roger, Jason. If you can get me something financial that looks like a RICO case we can legitimately take over the entire investigation with all of our resources. If it's just a local murder case all of our cooperation has to stay informal."

Chapter 10. The winery after dark

"Ssshh," Jason whispered to Sherry as he pulled the keys she'd given him out of his pocket. They both winced as the lock made a loud click, or at least it sounded loud to them in the darkness of the isolated building. Jason pushed hard against the large door, which opened reluctantly as it squeaked on its hinges. A moment later they were inside the winery with the door closed, his LED flashlight leading them past barrels stacked in racks to the high ceiling and the loading area. The narrow beam of light illuminated the narrow tunnel between shadowy barrels and less well defined objects.

"There could be an army waiting to jump out of those shadows," whispered Sherry urgently. "This is one spooky place after dark!"

"Sssh," Jason reminded her. "I think we're alone in here, but let's not press our luck."

Passing the hulking shapes of the fermenters, visible only as darker shadows against the blackness of unseen walls, they walked through the winery itself. After a substantial fraction of eternity had passed, they came to the office. The building felt empty to Jason who couldn't see or hear anybody else there. But the shadows were still deep, dark, and menacing beyond the narrow cone of light his flashlight beam illuminated.

"We can talk now. I think it'll be safe to turn on the lights. They shouldn't be visible from the road."

Sherry walked over to flip the switch turning on a bank of fluorescent lights over the desk that illuminated the rest of the small office as well. Jason, and especially Sherry, embraced the comfort from the office lights, which afforded a most welcome change from the darkness and shadows of the main winery. The walls, bare of adornment, had been pressure washed like the walls in the fermentation area. A single straight-backed chair sat in front of the desk's top, cluttered with stacks of paper seemingly in random piles. Drawers on both sides of the desk probably held more papers.

The only adornment on the desktop was a calendar, with various random looking dates encircled with a black Magic Marker. Absent were any personal or family photos. Various tools, especially large wrenches of different sizes, were lying on the floor against the otherwise bare walls.

"I'll take the desk, Jason. Can you crack a safe?" Sherry asked teasingly, pointing to a large floor safe in a back corner of the office.

"As a matter of fact, I can," he replied, walking back to the dull black safe and squatting in front of it.

Sherry shook her head in amazement before starting to go through papers, folders, and books on top of the desk and in the drawers. Jason pulled a small electronic device out of his pocket, stuck it magnetically to the door just above the large combination lock, and started rotating the dial clockwise.

The first two rotations were rapid and the third slow while he paid attention to the output of the electronic device, a needle and gauge backlit for ready visibility. The needle jumped forward as he ever so slowly crossed the number 12. He immediately reversed the rotation to counter-clockwise, one rapid and one slow rotation until the needle jumped again at 34. The third and last slow rotation clockwise ended at 5. There was a loud click, which alerted Sherry to the opening safe door.

"What was the combination, Jason?"

"12, 34, 5," he answered.

"Of course!" she exclaimed. "Simple to remember. How typically pragmatic of Wally!"

Jason quickly checked the contents of the safe, finding a substantial amount of money, other personal papers belonging to Wally including his passport, and a set of ledgers that looked like the winery's books. He returned everything except the ledgers to where he'd found them.

"Have you found anything interesting, Sherry?" he asked.

"Not especially," she answered. "A lot of routine paperwork, mostly related to specific tests of different batches of wine in the fermenters or stored in barrels. There are also stacks of paid and unpaid bills. How about you, Jason?"

He carefully closed the safe door, pocketed his electronic device, and spun the combination lock away from the final number. "I think I found the ledgers we're looking for, Sherry. It's probably time to get out of here."

She turned out the office lights, following Jason and his flashlight beam across the dark, shadowy, but still seemingly empty, winery.

When they got to the front door he turned off his flashlight before opening the large front door a crack to check outside. All clear! Turning back to Sherry he whispered, "I think we're OK now. I feel a lot safer leaving the place than I did when we came into it. This winery is one spooky building in the dark!"

They went out into the dim light provided by a half moon, Jason pausing to lock the door behind them. The night was filled with shadows and blackness as their eyes slowly adapted to the darkness with the flashlight off. Suddenly Jason pitched forward as if propelled by a strong push in the back.

Several seconds later, Sherry heard a shot, the sound of the powerful rifle muffled by distance. She'd been around guns and hunters all her life, so knew enough to dive to the ground, just in time to avoid a second bullet whizzing by overhead that buried itself in the winery wall. The muffled sound of this shot followed a few seconds later.

Sherry had the wits to pull out her cell phone and dial 911. She knew the operator could locate the call and would assume someone was in distress and dispatch a deputy, so she turned off the sound and put the live phone back in her pocket.

The next problem was the tough one. Should she play dead and gamble the shooter would flee from the scene rather than coming over to the two bodies to confirm his kills? Or should she try to make a break for it? The unseen rifleman was obviously hundreds of yards away with some kind of night vision scope on his rifle, and he was obviously a very good marksman. The odds favored lying real still faking she'd been mortally wounded while she hoped and silently prayed something would make him choose to get away as fast as possible. Sherry continued lying motionless, scared stiff, literally and figuratively. Time slowed down, making the wait seem endless. She was amazed how clearly she could think.

Good choice! In the distance she heard the sound of the approaching siren on a deputy's car. That should force the unseen shooter's hand. A minute or so later she heard the sound of a car engine starting, and a car driving away. She cautiously lifted her head and looked in that direction. No headlights. Obviously the gunman was fleeing the scene.

She withdrew her phone, hanging up and speed dialing Roger's number. He answered on the first ring. "Things went wrong here, Roger. Jason's been shot. I don't know how badly he's been hurt. I'm OK, just shaken up a bit. I heard the gunman drive away. I've already called the sheriff's office and they're almost here. You probably want to come down to the winery and see what's happening for yourself," Sherry said quickly.

Then she hung up. There were still a few things she had to do before the deputy arrived. The first was to check how Jason was doing. He was unconscious, but there was still a pulse, as well as a lot of blood pooling under his upper body. The deputy was almost here and would be better at first aid than she was, so she moved to her second task, picking up the ledgers from where they'd fallen and looking around in the dim moonlight for a place to conceal them before the deputy arrived.

Making a snap decision, she concealed the four bound books behind and partially beneath one of the large rocks that delineated the side of the driveway leading up to the winery. The ledgers were invisible from just a few feet away in the shadowy darkness. She was back at Jason's side just before the deputy drove up.

As he got out of the car she waved her hand and loudly called out, "I need some help here. This man's been shot. The shooter drove away a few minutes ago."

The deputy approached cautiously. "Let me see your hands, Mrs. Fortune."

She raised her hands into the air. The deputy surveyed the scene, made a quick decision, and bent down to quickly examine Jason's body, lying still by the front entrance to the winery. He checked for a pulse and looked closely at the widening pool of blood before keying the portable microphone on his shoulder.

"I need an ambulance and some EMTs here at the Fortune winery immediately. The situation seems stable, but we've got a badly wounded man down, so I'll need some crime scene help here as well. Over and out."

Bruce and I ran up from the house, immediately recognizing the deputy as one of those that had responded when Bruce and Juliet found Wally's body, the one with the faint trace of Oklahoma in his speech patterns. Perhaps more importantly, the officer recognized us, waving his hand in greeting.

"Can I look more closely at Jason?" Bruce asked quietly. "I've had EMT and Medic training in the navy. If you have a medical emergency kit in your car, this would be a good time to get it for him."

The deputy nodded before running over to his car, returning with a white box with a large red cross on the top, which he handed to Bruce, now kneeling beside the downed detective. The scene, harshly illuminated by the deputy's car headlights, didn't look good for Jason. Looking at the expanding pool of blood under Jason's body, the officer keyed his microphone, saying, "We can use those EMTs here as quickly as possible. Please order a Life-Flight helicopter for evacuation immediately. We've got a gunshot victim here bleeding profusely. We'll try putting pressure on the wound while we wait. Over and out."

Bruce cut away most of the clothing covering the actual wound, carefully turning Jason's unconscious body over onto his back while asking me to open the emergency medical kit. The large exit wound was obvious at the intersection of shoulder and chest. Bruce took several gauze pads from the kit, placing them directly over the wound and applying pressure to staunch the flow of blood.

"We can ignore the entry wound for now," Bruce declared. "This is the big hole he's losing most of that blood from. Now we wait for help. How long do you think they'll be?"

The deputy did a quick mental calculation. "Five to ten minutes longer for the ambulance, maybe fifteen or twenty for the chopper to get here."

"Can you take my place here, please, Roger?" Bruce asked. "I'd like to get something on that entry wound while we're waiting."

I switched places with Bruce, kneeling down and getting a hand directly on top of the gauze pack to press down and maintain the pressure on the wound.

"You'll need both hands for this next step Roger. Put your free hand on Jason's back so you have something to push against so you can maintain the pressure while I move him around a bit."

I did as he asked. Surprisingly quickly, Jason was on his side with Bruce using his ever-present Swiss army knife to cut away the remaining clothing blocking access to his back to expose the entry wound.

Bruce assembled another, smaller, gauze pack, which he pressed firmly on the entry wound. "Can you tape this down, real tightly?" he asked the deputy.

The entire process was completed quickly. "I'd guess the shooter used a 30.06 or something about that caliber," Bruce mused out loud. "From the size of the exit wound he was using some kind of older hunting ammo, probably with a lead bullet."

I took a long look at Jason. He was now lying on his side, completely unconscious, very pale, breathing shallowly but regularly.

Bruce removed his jacket, which he placed over Jason. "Now we wait. We need to keep him warm and try to delay shock until the EMTs get here with the right equipment. Just keep some pressure on that bandage, Roger."

Glancing over my shoulder I'd seen Sherry taking advantage of all the confusion to recover the ledgers she'd hidden in the darkness beside the road. She continued on to the house with them, presumably to safely conceal them until we could look the books over carefully. Given the price Jason had paid to obtain the ledgers, that seemed a prudent thing to do. I tipped an imaginary cap to Sherry, who could easily have completely fallen apart, for keeping her eyes on the prize in the middle of all the chaos.

It seemed to take forever, but was less than fifteen minutes until the EMTs arrived in a Fire Department emergency ambulance. They took over, rapidly and efficiently checking vital signs before starting an intravenous line to get some fluids into Jason.

"Nice field dressing," commented the senior EMT looking at Bruce's handiwork. "Were you a military medic?"

Bruce nodded.

The EMT turned to the deputy. "Have you already ordered the Life Flight chopper from the Medical Center?" he asked.

"Yeah," replied the deputy.

"What's the ETA?"

"Any minute now," answered the deputy, checking his watch.

On cue, we heard the "thwack, thwack" of the rotors as the helicopter arrived, descending to land alongside the EMT vehicle a few yards away from us, further illuminating the scene with its bright spotlight.

A highly skilled team of nurses jumped out of the helicopter, retrieved a stretcher, and trotted over to us. "Have you got him stabilized, Fred?" the first nurse asked the senior EMT.

"He should be ready to go," answered Fred.

Quickly, carefully, and efficiently they lifted Jason onto the stretcher. In a minute or two he was on the helicopter beginning the short trip by air to the trauma center at the University Hospital in Sacramento. The deputy asked me several questions about Jason's identity as he filled out a form, radioing the pertinent facts to his dispatcher who would relay them to the hospital before Jason's arrival.

Now it was time for deputy Quentin Flowers to get the story for his investigation. Sherry had returned to the group, so I told Flowers, "Bruce and I didn't see anything, we just responded to Sherry's call for help after Jason was shot. You probably saw us running over from the house as you arrived on the scene."

Flowers nodded. Turning to Sherry he politely asked, "Can you walk over to my car with me, please? I need to get some details about what happened here and what you saw tonight."

Sherry nodded and walked over to his car with him.

"Can you just tell me what happened from the beginning, please? Take your time and tell me everything you remember. I'll ask you any questions I might have after you finish your story, Mrs. Fortune," said Flowers, pulling a notebook and small recording device out of a bag on the front seat of his car.

As unobtrusively as possible, I followed them to within earshot of the car so I could listen to Sherry's story as she told Deputy Flowers about the night's events.

Leaning against the deputy's car for support, Sherry began speaking slowly and carefully. "I'll do the best I can to tell you what I remember, but you'll have to excuse me if I'm a little shaky here. Nobody ever tried to kill me before. You've already met Roger and Bruce, who are staying with me here at the winery while they investigate the circumstances surrounding Wally's murder. Jason Culpepper is a private detective working with Roger. We got bored with watching TV, so I brought Jason over here with me to see what a real winery looked like. We walked through the production part, where I explained the fermentation process to Jason. We turned out the lights and came out the front door. Jason had a flashlight, so I gave him the keys.

"He was locking the door when he suddenly fell against the building, exactly where you first saw him on the ground when you arrived here. I heard the shot a couple of seconds after he fell. I've done a lot of bird hunting in my life and know a gunshot when I hear one. I didn't even stop to think but dove at the ground as fast as I could. I was lucky; I heard the bullet hit the wall just about where I had been standing, followed by the sound of the shot about two or three seconds later. I played dead while I prayed the shooter wouldn't come over and check whether I really was dead. That's when I got my cell phone out and called 911, then called Roger for help."

Sherry paused in her narrative as she decided what else to say. I'd already told her, "Less is better, but tell the truth. Forget about the whole truth and nothing but the truth, just answer the questions the police ask you."

She paused again in her narrative to gather her thoughts before continuing, "That's about when I first heard your siren. I think it, and you, saved my life. You must have scared the shooter into fleeing rather than coming down here to check his marksmanship. You probably saved my life. I heard the sound of someone starting a car from right near where the shooter had to have been and the sound of the car leaving the ranch right after I heard your siren. I didn't see any headlights in the direction the car was going. Within a few minutes after that you, Roger, and Bruce all got here at almost the same time."

Flowers read over his notes. "Did Culpepper say anything to you after he was shot?"

"No," replied Sherry. "I thought he was dead until Roger and Bruce started checking him out."

Writing something down, the deputy continued, "Did the victim say anything while you were together before the shooting that made you think he or you might be in danger?"

Sherry made a show of carefully replaying those last moments before the shooting in her mind before answering. "No, all we talked about was how we made wine and what the different pieces of equipment were for."

Flowers asked Sherry questions for another five minutes or so, mostly clarifying details of where exactly she and Jason were when the shots were fired, and what exactly Jason's position had been when he was shot.

The deputy looked up at me. "Was Culpepper working on any other cases that might have upset somebody enough to try to kill him?"

It was my turn to appear to stop and think before replying. "No," I answered. "This is the only case he was presently working on."

The deputy scribbled something in his pad. "Did he have any enemies who hated him enough to want him dead?" continued Flowers.

I touched the hood of the deputy's car, noting it was still very hot. He'd obviously just responded to the 911 call at high speed from quite a distance away. Not that I actually suspected him of being the shooter, but it's always nice to rule out any possible suspects when you can. "Not that I know of. Everybody liked Jason. He's a good guy."

Flowers scribbled a bit more in his pad. "OK, I think I have what I need. You can go home to bed, Mrs. Fortune. I'll hang some crime scene tape around the scene and wait until daylight to send the crew out here to collect evidence. It sounds like we have a couple of bullets to find and some shells to look for. I assume I don't have to tell you to stay away from here until we clear the scene."

The deputy turned back to speak to me again. "Mrs. Fortune can give you the details of where your man was taken and how you can get to the hospital if you want to be there. It's the best trauma center in Northern California, so he's in good hands medically. Give me your phone number so I can reach you if I have any other questions, please."

I gave him the number, which he wrote down in his notebook, closing and pocketing it at the same time as he turned off his recorder. We shook hands.

After Flowers had turned away from me I turned to Bruce. "Why don't you stay here and make sure nobody tries to kill Sherry again tonight, Bruce. I'll drive over to the hospital and make sure I'm there when Jason wakes up."

He nodded.

"We'll have a car driving by here every now and then to keep an eye out for anything suspicious," Flowers added. "She should be safe until you get back."

Chapter 11. Inside the ledgers

The University of California Hospital in Sacramento, part of the Medical School at UC Davis, is a sprawling complex of high-rise modern buildings spreading over several blocks in the heart of the city. At this late hour there wasn't any traffic on the freeways so I made good time and found the hospital easily. Parking in a large garage directly across from the main entrance, I checked in at the front desk. A bored, but polite, clerk directed me to the trauma surgery department in a huge brand new building attached to the front of the main hospital. I found a waiting room and another clerk, Bridget from her I.D. badge, who got enough information to know who I was and which patient I was there for.

Bridget clicked a few keys on her computer before looking up at me. "Mr. Culpepper is still in surgery. One of the doctors will come out here and update you on the case as soon as the surgery is over. If you want some coffee while you wait there's a service Kiosk just past the lobby you came through to get here. You should have plenty of time to get there and back while you're waiting. In the meantime, you can expedite things if you have medical insurance information for your friend. I can take those details from you now."

Fortunately my detective agency supplied group coverage for employee health insurance as part of our benefits package, so I had all the required information in my wallet. After discovering Jason had hospitalization insurance that covered emergency care anywhere, Bridget had a refreshingly positive opinion of the new patient.

"Your friend was only admitted to the hospital a few minutes before midnight Mr. Bowman. My best guess is you'll hear some news around 1:30 or 2 at the earliest. Leave me your cell phone number and I'll call you if you aren't here when he comes out of surgery."

I wandered off to find a caffeine fix. A 24/7 kiosk was open in the lobby, selling good freshly ground coffee. I got a 'Grande', the largest cup available, and went exploring. At this hour of the night there were still staff members at the nursing stations and standing around the lobby sipping coffee and talking in small groups. The corridors were mainly deserted and visitors waiting for news about loved ones were few and far between. The sound of my footsteps echoed and reechoed through the late night silence. There were people accompanying patients and several uniformed cops waiting around the Emergency Department entrance, but the streets around the hospital were empty.

Two coffees later my cell phone buzzed. Bridget, or a Bridget clone, told me it was time to return to the trauma surgery waiting room. I was back and sitting on an uncomfortable chair when a tired looking doctor in green scrubs walked into the waiting area through a different door than I'd been using. Bridget nodded as he walked toward me, stethoscope dangling from around his neck.

"I'm Dr. Curtis," he introduced himself. "You're here for Mr. Culpepper?"

Standing up I replied, "Yes."

He gave me a long look, appraising what information I could handle. "His surgery went very well. He got a through and through wound, entering from the back and exiting from the front shoulder area. The bullet expanded when it hit him, so was almost certainly lead and most probably from a batch of good quality ammunition manufactured a long time ago. It mushroomed and increased in diameter on impact with the bone, so it did a lot of damage, mostly to soft tissue in the left shoulder area. It also broke the bone in a couple of places and damaged some blood vessels before it exited through his shoulder. I was able to fix all that. He'll have some interesting scars and a lot of rehab, but I think he'll regain all of the function he started with in a matter of months."

"That sounds good," I said cautiously. "Is there anything else I need to know about?"

"Yes, there is. He's having some problems breathing without mechanical ventilation. With the extensive trauma and blood loss he suffered there's the risk of Acute Respiratory Distress Syndrome, ARDS, or what we used to call 'shock lung'. The good news is we're one of the best centers in the country for pulmonary intensive care, and we'll be starting the treatment early just in case he's going in this direction. I'm transferring him to our medical intensive care unit, what we call the MICU. He'll get excellent care there."

"When can I see him?" I asked.

"It'll be a while," answered Curtis. "I'd suggest you go home for now. We won't know his long-term lung condition for another day or two. In the meantime he'll be on a mechanical ventilator so he won't be able to talk to anyone and you won't be able to visit with him. Bridget will give you the phone number so you can call the MICU for updates on his condition, and she'll list you on his electronic medical record as his next of kin so they'll actually talk to you. I'd wait until after noon-ish tomorrow so they have a chance to evaluate him completely. If there are any close family members, you should contact them and let them know what's going on."

I thanked Dr. Curtis. We shook hands before I drove back to Winters and a most inviting bed. Everyone else had gone to sleep long before my arrival.

I finally got to bed, looking forward to a good night's sleep. Ah yes, for just a moment I got to live out the rich fantasy life of the German shorthaired pointer owner, which involved sleeping alone on my bed. Lying across the top of my bed, head on one pillow and rump on the other, was Juliet. She gently and firmly was making the statement decisively, 'my master, so my bed!'

I tried to reason with her. "Please move over, Juliet. I can use some sleep too."

For a breed that can hear a pheasant exhale 100 yards away, she was having a lot of trouble hearing me tonight.

"OK, Juliet, move!" I demanded, pushing her on the rump.

Nothing happened. I decided strategy was necessary here.

I grabbed the nearest pillow and plunked myself down on my side of the bed, using the dog as an extra pillow under the normal pillow I'd picked up. I closed my eyes, congratulating myself on the triumph of human intellect over canine instinct.

Drifting into the twilight zone between sleep and wakefulness, I became aware of Juliet standing on my head, no longer part of a pillow sandwich. No, not standing, more like dancing. Then lying down in full Velcro mode planting big sloppy doggy kisses on my face.

Enough! Grabbing her by the collar I staggered up, dragging Juliet behind me to the door to Bruce's bedroom. I opened the door quietly, pushing the dog into the room and quickly closing the door. I closed my bedroom door behind me, crawled into bed, and quickly descended into a dreamless sleep.

I slept in until 8 o'clock the next morning, just in time for breakfast at the kitchen table. Sherry and Bruce were just starting to eat. The questions about Jason's condition started flying at me from both of them as soon as I walked through the door.

I started answering before sitting at the table. "Jason got through the surgery about two o'clock last night. The surgeon was comfortable that he was able to repair all of the damage the bullet caused. But Jason's having trouble breathing without a mechanical ventilator because of all the blood loss, so he'll be in the intensive care unit for a few days before we know he'll be OK for sure. I'll call the hospital for an update on his condition around lunch time; they should know a lot more by then."

Sherry took pity on me. "Have some breakfast, Roger. I can make bacon and eggs or we have toast and coffee. After that, I thought you'd want to look through the ledgers Jason and I found in Wally's safe last night."

The short night of sleep had left me hungry and craving caffeine. "Bacon, eggs, and a lot of coffee sounds good to me right now and I'd love to look at those ledgers over breakfast if that's OK. Considering what Jason's going through now, I hope they were worth getting shot for."

I sipped the first cup of coffee while waiting for the food and skimming the four ledgers. They were exactly what you'd expect from an ongoing business, lists of income and expenditures by item and date. Each entry included a few details about the specific transaction, with most of them coded by initials. Each ledger covered a period of three months, consistent with the business filing quarterly income tax returns.

"Do you have any first impressions?" asked Sherry as she put a plate in front of me and refilled the coffee cup.

Putting the ledgers aside to concentrate on bacon and eggs for the next couple of minutes, I replied, "Not yet. I'm just looking for patterns at this stage. The details will come later."

The next ten minutes were devoted to eggs, bacon, coffee, and getting back to the ledger entries, which I looked at a little more carefully on my second time through the oldest book in the pile. About halfway through the book I thought I noticed something unexpected.

Looking up from my reading, I asked, "Winemaking is a seasonal business, isn't it Sherry? When are the grapes usually harvested and made into wine, and when is the wine sold to whoever buys it from you?"

"We harvest grapes through the late summer and fall, depending on the particular varietal and the weather. They're crushed immediately and go into the tanks for fermentation as fast as we can. How long they're in the tanks depends on the varietal.

"Wine can stay in the tanks for different lengths of time depending on the varietal and the fermentation conditions. Then it goes into oak barrels for various lengths of time before it's bottled and sold. So we can sell wines at any time during the year. Some of our whites tend to move faster, with a lot less aging than the reds."

Sherry turned away to answer the doorbell when it rang. The deputy from last night walked in. "Sorry to bother you this early in the morning, Mrs. Fortune, but we've finished our investigation at the winery. We didn't find much of anything I'd refer to as a clue. But we were able to recover the bullet Mr. Culpepper was shot with.

"I called Clay Bedford and your brother-in-law Frank when I started my shift this morning to tell them not to come in to work today until they heard we were done here. Can you phone them to give them the all clear, please? I've got a lot to do and I'm already running late."

We heard a squeal of tires as the deputy sped out of the driveway.

Sherry turned to me. "Can I call Clay Bedford to tell him he can come to work now, Roger? Or do you want to check out the scene for clues the deputies might have missed now that it's bright daylight out before anybody else walks through there?"

"We should definitely look the crime scene over before anyone else tromps through it," I replied. "The shooter must have been watching the house. When he shot at you and Jason last night he had to improvise on the fly to get into position to shoot at you when he realized you went into the winery, and he had to leave in a hurry when he heard the deputy's car coming. That's when people make mistakes, when plans get changed in a hurry."

I put the ledgers away out of sight, just in case. Sherry, Bruce, and I walked over to the winery. There was a new hole in the wood surrounding the door with a big circle drawn in black ink around it where someone had dug something out of the entrance, presumably the bullet that had gone through Jason. But, looking more closely at the area around the door, I saw something missing.

"Sherry, can you stand as close to the exact spot where you were when Jason was shot, please?"

She stood a few feet out from the door and a little to the right of the doorway. Bruce nodded, saying, "I'll check it, Roger."

He walked over to the wall, peering closely at the wood and stucco alongside the door itself. He started about four feet up and closely scrutinized the surface.

"Got it!" he exclaimed. There was a click from his cell phone as he photographed the spot on the wall before he removed the bullet. Pulling out his pocketknife, he carefully dug out the bullet that had just missed Sherry the night before. He wrapped it carefully in his handkerchief before pocketing it and taking other photos of the wall with the new hole gouged in it, close-up and from a distance for perspective.

"Not that I don't think all overworked and underpaid deputy sheriffs in small rural areas do excellent police work at every crime scene they investigate, Bruce, but from what we've seen so far this one doesn't. Sherry told us it took less than a minute between her first hearing the siren from the deputy's car and when the killer's car started driving away. That means the murderer had to be shooting from a position very close to his car. If I were the shooter I'd have been prone for the most stable shooting position, lying just alongside where I'd parked my car. Let's take a walk over to where the shells should have been ejected and see what we can find," I suggested.

We walked away from the door along an imaginary line directly from Sherry's bullet hole toward the road, bypassing the driveway. After several hundred feet Sherry, Bruce, and I spread out a bit and started carefully scrutinizing the ground.

This was a slow, boring process, even with three of us searching. It was easy to see how a single deputy with too much else to do could quickly have become discouraged. We didn't see anything out of the ordinary for another hundred feet. Finally we spotted an area where the grass had been scrunched down a bit, as if something heavy, like a car, had been parked on it. We slowed and walked around the area searching the ground meticulously inside a large circle we avoided entering so as not to tramp over the dirt and grass.

On our third circuit around the compressed grass Bruce spotted the first shell lying on its side partially buried and almost completely invisible except at the perfect angle to catch a bit of reflected sunlight from it.

"You can pick that one up, Roger," he said. "I'll see if I can find any more."

"Click, click," and I had pictures on my phone of exactly where the shell had lain and what the ground looked like, and where the spot was in relation to the winery building and the road. I pocketed the shell. taking care not to touch the surface so as not to disturb any possible fingerprints the shooter may have left behind.

That was all we'd find here today. Ten minutes later we gave up the search. We'd found more than we hoped we would. It was time for us to head back to the house. Sherry called the winery manager as we walked back. She told Clay Bedford the deputy had come and gone so he could come to work now, suggesting Clay call Frank Fortune at his convenience.

Rummaging through the kitchen, I found a couple of plastic bags for the bullet and the shell. I carefully sealed both bags and labeled them with date, time, and details of where we found each of them by cross reference to the photos on Bruce's and my cell phones.

We were all sitting at the kitchen table watching me put evidence into bags. Sherry avoided interrupting until I finished preparing our evidence. "You were telling me what you thought was interesting about the ledgers when the deputy rang the doorbell, Roger," she reminded me. "Why don't we all sit down at the dining room table and have some coffee while you tell me. I had just made a fresh pot when the deputy got here."

'*Hmmm,*' I thought, not for the first time noting that Sherry was very sharp and really on top of things.

A few minutes later we were sipping coffee at a large oak table while I filled my client in on the investigation. "I don't know what's normal in the wine making business, but it surprised me to see how regular the income and expenditures were. Plus or minus a few percent, the cash flow in and out was constant from month to month. This is the sort of investigation Jason usually does for us, so I don't have any firsthand experience with the industry, but most businesses, especially seasonal ones, fluctuate a lot more than that."

Sherry carefully put her coffee cup down in its saucer. "So what will you do next?" she asked, idly playing with her coffee cup.

I studied the contents of a large antique breakfront filled with old serving pieces and elegant crystal glasses directly behind my client while thinking about the best answer to that question. "I'm not sure. I think it may be time to ask the Kaufman sisters for FBI help with this part. My gut tells me there's something wrong here, but I don't have access to the resources it'll take or the accounting background to do this kind of detailed financial investigation properly. Normally this is exactly the sort of thing I'd hand off to Jason."

I finished my coffee. "In the meantime, Bruce and I have a shooter to look for. And right now our only clues are in two plastic bags in my pocket. I think we need some FBI laboratory and database help with those samples. So it's probably the right time for me to call the hospital to get an update on Jason's condition. Then I'll try calling Gretchen Kaufman over her lunch break from the trial she's involved in to tell her what happened to Jason, who she knows quite well from his FBI agent days, and to update her on his condition."

I looked back at Sherry. "Can you call Francis and set up a meeting between you, me, and him as soon as possible, please?"

Picking up my cell phone I called my partner, Vincent Romero. "Vincent, I need some information from you as fast as you can get it. Jason was shot last night here at the winery. He's in intensive care at the university hospital in Sacramento. I'll get back to you as soon as I get an update on his condition.

"Now I need to know everything you can find out about the financial condition and background of the Fortune Winery in Winters, California. Please call me as soon as you get anything at all. I'll have a meeting with an attorney who handles the business part of things for the winery some time later today and I don't trust the man. I'd like to be able to do a reality check on everything he tells me."

87

I dialed the number Bridget had given me for the intensive care unit. Wonder of wonders, someone human answered the phone after only three rings. "ICU, Dr. Russell speaking."

"Can I get an update on the condition of one of your patients please, Jason Culpepper."

"And you are?" he asked.

"Roger Bowman."

I heard the click of computer keys. "OK, I see you listed here as a relative. I'm one of the pulmonary fellows on this service. You'll need to speak to the attending physician, Dr. Canyon, to get the information you're asking for. Please hold for a moment or two while I see if he can speak with you now."

In less than a minute a new voice came on the phone, "This is Dr. Canyon. You're calling about one of our patients, right?"

"Jason Culpepper," I answered. "He should have been admitted early this morning after emergency surgery for a gunshot wound. I was hoping for an update on his condition."

There was a perceptible pause. "Yes, I'm familiar with the case. Where are you now?"

"I'm calling from Winters."

The doctor paused again for a moment. "Tell me what the surgeon told you last night and I'll update it from there."

"He told me the surgery had gone very well but Jason was having trouble breathing on his own, which was what your unit specializes in."

"Good," replied Dr. Canyon. "The short answer is that's about where things are now. Mr. Culpepper is on mechanical ventilation here in the unit. The next 36 hours will be the critical time for him, but he's in the right place to be getting the best of care. He's young and strong so the prognosis is a lot better than for many of our patients here.

"If it's convenient for you to get here mid- to late-afternoon today I should have some time to talk to you and give you whatever details we have. Do you think you can make it here that soon?'

"I'll find the time," I said firmly. "Where do I go when I get to the hospital?"

"Call this number when you get here and someone can meet you at the main desk. We aren't easy to find if you're not familiar with the hospital layout."

"Thank you very much, Dr. Canyon. I'll see you later this afternoon."

Chapter 12. Lawyers and doctors

"Francis can see us in an hour," Sherry announced as she hung up her phone. "That's good timing for me. I want to get to Carmichael this afternoon so I can take care of my dogs."

I put down my empty coffee cup. "Good timing for me, too. I want to get over to the hospital to talk to Jason's doctor in person and see if I can connect with Gretchen and Barbara Kaufman somewhere downtown. Maybe I can hitch a ride with you?"

"Sure," she replied.

I called Vincent back. "We're scheduled to see the lawyer in an hour. Have you found anything for me yet?"

I heard the sound of paper rustling before he answered. "Based on public documents the winery makes a good bit of money. It has been around a while, so that's not too surprising. There was a big jump in gross and net income several years ago and they've stayed at the higher level since then.

"Claro. It's a privately held corporation so there aren't any SEC requirements for detailed financial information in annual reports. It's hard to find much more for you on short notice. I've requested credit reports from the usual databases but won't have any of that detailed information for a day or two. There's the same problem with the owner, A. Wallace Fortune and a couple of key employees, Fortune's brother and the winery manager, a guy named Bedford. I've requested all of their credit reports too.

He paused briefly. "Oh, and I checked out the client's first husband like you asked me to. He's still in jail, with at least one more year to serve before he's eligible for release. That's about it so far. How's Jason doing?"

"I'll get some real information about Jason's condition this afternoon, Vincent. In the meantime he's hanging in there."

****

Downtown Winters occupies a total of about four square blocks, so everything is easy to find. The biggest thing we drove past on the way were the hulking storage tanks and the factories of a large processing plant for the local nut cooperative, reminding me we were in the middle of California's, and therefore the entire United States', almond and walnut growth and processing industries.

We arrived at Francis Fortune's office, on the second floor of an old but well maintained building that might have been a wealthy family's private home a generation or two earlier, right on schedule. He greeted us cordially. My cynical internal voice reminded me Sherry was currently his biggest, and for all I knew his only, client.

After we were all seated, Francis behind a large old oak desk and Sherry and I on client chairs in front of the desk, we declined his offer of coffee. He turned to speak directly to Sherry, quite obviously choosing to ignore me. "What can I do for you today, Missy?"

As a very successful businesswoman in a male-dominated industry, she didn't need my help. But she got it anyway. Fortune really irritated me. It was about time to assert my claim to recognition as the alpha male here.

I slapped my hand sharply on the desk. Fortune instinctively turned to look at me. "I know how hard it must be to remember your sister-in-law's name, Francis, but you can address her as either Mrs. Fortune or Sherry. Anything else is disrespectful and totally inappropriate."

Something very nasty flashed in his eyes for just a fraction of a second, before he recovered his urbane poise.

Fortune turned back to Sherry. "My apologies, Mrs. Fortune. I meant no disrespect. What can I do for you today?"

"You may call me Sherry, Francis," she replied, twisting the knife just a little bit more. "I'm here today with Mr. Bowman to get an overview of the winery's financial picture and the disposition of Wallace's estate."

He shifted smoothly into his professional persona. "I know you were quite comfortable financially before you married my brother. You're now considerably wealthier. Except for some minor bequests to family, colleagues, and charities, you will beneficially inherit Wallace's entire estate, including the winery, the house, and other assets, which are substantial. There's a will with Wally's directions to me as his executor about disposition of all the assets. There's also a trust, of which you are the co-trustee, which owns the business and real estate. That means the estate doesn't have to go through probate and everything was yours the moment his body was formally identified.

"We can go through everything now if that is your wish, but if you'll allow me a couple of days to get everything organized for you first I can give you the relevant information a lot more efficiently. The way I set everything up for Wallace there aren't any estate or inheritance taxes that will be levied at this juncture. I hope you will let me maintain the current fiduciary relationship as the winery's and your personal attorney of record so I can set up the same sort of structures for your now multi-million dollar estate."

He handed her a piece of paper. "This is the current assessed value of the property: the winery, the land, and the house. I'll get an estimate of the fair market value, which will be considerably greater, from a couple of local realtors in the next day or two."

Sherry took a look, whistled appreciatively, and handed back the piece of paper. "Thank you, Francis. That's exactly what I wanted to know for now. Can we arrange for you to give me the more formal information the day after tomorrow?"

He made a production of checking his calendar. "How about 10 o'clock that morning?"

Everybody shook hands and we drove back to the house. Bruce and Juliet were out front playing fetch with a rubber dog toy.

"What are your plans for today?" I asked Bruce.

He threw the toy for Juliet to retrieve. "That's up to you, Roger. I can take Juliet for a walk over this entire property to get us both some much needed exercise, or I can drive back to L.A. to give Suzanne some much needed help caring for Robert and Romeo."

Juliet retrieved the toy, returning it to me to get me engaged in her game. I threw it as far as I could, tapping her head as a release to send her after it. "Why don't you take the exercise option for now, Bruce? You can probably plan on driving home tomorrow but I might need some help this evening, and for now at least you're it."

Going on into the house I joined Sherry in the front room and called Gretchen. She answered immediately. "It's Roger. I was hoping I could reach you, Gretchen. What does your schedule look like for today? Will you be tied up all day with your trial?"

"Probably. They seem to be letting us out around 4 o'clock. Why?"

I explained about Jason being shot and what little I knew about his current health status. "I'll know more after I connect with his doctor this afternoon. I also need some FBI-type help and was hoping you would volunteer. We recovered a shell and a bullet at the scene where Jason was shot and I don't trust the local law enforcement types to properly handle anything technical."

"Let's get together for dinner," she suggested. "We can get caught up on everything then. Which would be better for you, Sacramento or Winters?"

"Do you like roast duck?" I asked.

She answered immediately. "Love it. So does Barbara."

I was thinking of a place Suzanne had recommended. "Then let's meet for dinner at Seasons, in Davis. They have a regular Thursday night special of wood-oven roast duck, which is excellent. Suzanne suggested it if we had a chance to eat in Davis. Let's meet there at seven. The restaurant is on First and F Streets."

Gretchen agreed immediately. "Bring the evidence. I can arrange to have someone meet us at the restaurant and courier it back to the FBI lab in The City."

I turned back toward Sherry after breaking the connection. "I'm meeting the Kaufman sisters for dinner in Davis at seven. Would you like to join us?"

No hesitation this time. "Sure," she said brightly.

"In that case why don't we carpool to Sacramento like I suggested earlier? You can drop me in front of the hospital, head on home to Carmichael to do whatever you do with your dogs, and pick me up at the hospital whenever you're done. Don't worry about your schedule. I have plenty to do while I wait, and you should easily be able to figure out the best time to pick me up to get to Davis on time for dinner."

She thought a moment. "We should try to leave the UCD medical center before 6:30."

I carefully packed the ledgers in my attaché case along with my gun, a couple of clips of extra ammunition, and some paperwork I'd brought along to catch up on if I had an hour or two to kill.

Fifteen minutes later we were duplicating my drive from the night before, except at this hour of the day there was a lot more traffic sharing the highways with us. Sherry knew the back roads and was a good driver, so we were in front of the hospital about 45 minutes later.

Dropping me off in front of the main entrance she declared, "I'll pick you up back here at about six, maybe earlier. I'll call you when I leave Carmichael so you know when to be out here to meet and I won't have to find a place to park legally."

Most public buildings in California ban carrying guns on the premises even with a permit, so I locked my gun in the glove compartment before calling the ICU number. "ICU. Dr. Russell speaking," said a familiar voice.

"May I speak to Dr. Canyon, please? Tell him it's Roger Bowman here for our appointment."

"Where are you now?"

94

"At the main entrance."

"Wait there, somewhere near the information desk. I'll come down to get you. What do you look like?"

I described myself. Less than five minutes later Dr. Russell walked directly up to me. Tall, young to mid-thirties, dark hair cut longish, white coat, stethoscope, with a hospital-issued I.D. badge pinned to the coat. "Follow me," he said abruptly, turning to lead me to a bank of elevators in a corridor off the lobby.

"This wing is what we call 'the Tower' of the hospital," he said, pushing the button for the sixth floor. We were there, turning left off the elevator, in moments. We stopped in front of a locked door labeled MICU. Dr. Russell slipped his badge into a slot beside the door. It opened inward with a loud click.

"This is a twelve-bed unit. That may not sound like much, but we have upwards of thirty more intensive care beds we're responsible for throughout the hospital, and these are all critically ill patients who need a lot of one-on-one attention 24/7 from the senior staff. This MICU component is where our most acutely ill patients requiring highly skilled ventilator support are treated. It's also where sub-specialty Fellows like me are learning how to do this, eventually independently but currently under constant supervision."

He steered us to a corner of the small, crowded unit where there were several computers, a couple of desks, and a couple of chairs. He introduced me to Dr. Canyon, another doctor in a white coat, another stethoscope. A tall man with the stocky build of a former athlete getting soft, this doctor was a man in his mid-forties with light hair and a more expensive haircut. He offered a firm handshake and a friendly manner.

He looked me over thoroughly, sizing me up. "Do you have any training in human physiology?" he asked.

"A couple of undergraduate classes at UC San Diego, where I majored in chemistry," I answered.

"Good!" he said. "Mr. Culpepper is in the process of developing Acute Respiratory Distress Syndrome or ARDS, what used to be called shock lung during World War II and the Korean and Viet-Nam Wars. With a major traumatic injury and severe blood loss like Mr. Culpepper experienced, followed by successful resuscitation with fluids in the field and blood transfusions at the hospital, which he also experienced, we occasionally see a syndrome we now call ARDS. These days we can help him breathe with mechanical ventilation and supplemental oxygen therapy and we know how to add supportive care until his own body can take over breathing for him again.

"He's young and strong and we're good at what we do. If all goes well I'm confident we'll get him through this episode with just watchful vigilance and standard care. If he doesn't surprise us he should recover fully, even though it'll take longer than it would have without this unfortunate bump in the road. I'm on this service for the next week and a half, so he'll have consistent care available for longer than I anticipate he'll need ventilator support."

He paused for a moment to let me digest what he'd told me. "Do you have any questions yet, Mr. Bowman?"

"No, I think I understand everything you've told me so far. How long do you think it might be before he's conscious and I can see him?"

"Possibly a day or two, possibly longer. That's up to him."

"And how long before he'll be able to breathe without the ventilator?"

"Again, it's up to him and how fast he heals. My best guess, a week or so. Maybe less."

"And then what happens?"

"If all goes well a complete recovery after a lot of physical therapy for that shoulder. He had an excellent surgeon and he'll continue to have the best of care while he's here."

My gut was telling me Jason had lucked out in his choice of hospitals and doctors. "Thank you, Dr. Canyon. I appreciate your willingness to see me and to tell it to me like it is. I'll try not to bother you again if Jason's recovery follows the schedule you just laid out for him."

We shook hands. Dr. Canyon looked closely at me before continuing, "We try to keep things as clean and sterile in the unit as we possibly can to prevent infections in these patients. I can't offer to show you Mr. Culpepper's set-up now. But, if you have the time and you're interested I can show you the same type of ventilators and beds we use here in another unit where the patients aren't nearly as sick. That way you'll understand what's actually going on. Do you have time for that now?"

I said yes, earning a sterile cap, gown, and booties and an escorted tour courtesy of Dr. Russell through a Tower 7 unit where I saw patients on respirators and doctors tweaking the settings for the pressure and composition of the specific gas mixtures they were being administered with the aid of the machines.

96

Dr. Russell explained that with the sicker patients there were a lot more controls to adjust more or less continuously on the ventilators, especially remaining pressure at the end of the exhalation cycle, called Positive End Expiratory Pressure or PEEP. "That's part of what makes our job so complicated. As we control how the patients breathe, there are physiological changes in blood gases that can affect other tissues in the body. And, on top of that, too much ventilator pressure or too much oxygen can further damage the lungs. There's a lot going on in each patient we need to keep track of and regulate."

These were mostly older patients, I was told, who were not critically ill but for some reason had become chronically dependent on a mechanical ventilator and could not breathe without this support.

Half an hour later I was back in the lobby with a long wait ahead of me. I went back to reading the ledgers, much more carefully this time. This morning during breakfast I'd been looking for patterns in the entries. This time I looked at specific entries, especially the larger ones and the oft-repeated ones. I transcribed several of the most interesting entries to a new 'Word' file on my computer.

"Eureka!" I said to myself with eyesight blurring after an hour or two. *"There really was a pattern there and you spotted it! Now I know what we're looking for and I have the glimmerings of a theory about what we're seeing in these ledgers. And, by inference, why Jason was shot! But there's still the who to figure out, and that may be very, very difficult."*

The timing was perfect. Sherry called. She'd be here in less than fifteen minutes to pick me up. I was outside the main entrance waiting for her SUV in five.

Chapter 13. Up and about in Davis

The SUV turned left from X Street onto the curving driveway in front of the new 12-story hospital building. As soon as Sherry spotted me I trotted out to the big space behind the line of cars waiting to pick up discharged patients and visitors. In a minute or two she had unlocked the glove compartment and we were turning right onto Stockton Boulevard to pick up Highway 50 west to I-80, which would take us to downtown Davis, about 20 miles from the hospital.

"How's Jason doing?" she asked as soon as I was seated beside her in the vehicle.

I retrieved the gun, returning it to my attaché case. "He'll be listed in critical condition for the next few days, but the prognosis is generally optimistic if nothing else bad happens. He's getting what looks to me like the best of care here."

I checked my watch. It was almost four fifteen. "How long will it take us to drive to Davis?"

Sherry checked her speedometer. "There's lots of traffic, but we seem to be moving at about the speed limit. If it doesn't get any more congested than this, about 20 minutes. And it should get better as soon as we pass the I-5 on-ramp, a few miles ahead of us on the right."

"So we have two and a half hours, give or take, to kill in Davis. I've never been to the city before. What do you suggest we see when we get there?" I asked.

Sherry thought it over. "I think we should start with the UC Davis Arboretum and Putah Creek," she suggested. "It's a nice walk and we can both use some exercise. And maybe we can bounce some ideas back and forth about this case, just like you'd usually do with Suzanne."

We parked in a designated parking lot between E and F Streets reserved for customers of the copy service next to the lot. Removing the ledgers, I locked the attaché case containing my pistol in the trunk of the car. "Look at what's sitting there right in front of us," I told Sherry. "I have an idea."

We walked into the large Federal Express-Kinko store where a cheerful clerk, probably also a student at the university, greeted us immediately. "What can we do for you today, Sir?"

I pulled out my stack of four ledgers. "How long would it take you to scan all of these and make me a PDF file of each book plus four hard copies of everything?"

"About an hour, Sir."

"How late will you be open this evening for me to pick this order up?"

"Until 10 PM, Sir."

I left the ledgers. We cut over to E Street through the parking lot. Sherry guided us south through the downtown area to 1st Street. Passing lots of small shops and restaurants, a few office buildings, lots of pedestrians and even more bicyclists, and very few parking places, we came to a major intersection with an art gallery on the corner and a small mall across the street. We continued walking through the mall past a sushi restaurant before turning west through the parking lot. Small houses stood on tiny lots in front of us across a narrow street from the mini-mall. Another turn south brought us to the arboretum.

As we entered the tree-lined path beside a narrow creek, Sherry asked, "Are you ready to talk about the case now, Roger?"

****

Juliet was completely full of herself, prancing joyfully beside Bruce as they walked south from the house toward the winery. Halfway there he gave her the release command to let her run loose through the vineyard. Juliet followed her nose into a warm wind blowing gently from the northwest as she plunged into the densely packed grapes, then began quartering into the breeze to explore the huge field with her ground eating trot. Bruce followed her at a comfortable pace knowing she'd circle back frequently to check in with him and make sure he was still following her.

"You've been a little cooped up the last few days, haven't you?" he asked his canine companion as she trotted toward him.

Juliet circled around him and ran out in front as if to say, "I thought you'd never ask!"

Bruce navigated his way on the network of tractor-width paths that bisected the vineyard at frequent intervals. Juliet ducked, crashed, or jumped through the thick vines at the base of the meticulously pruned and shaped grapes between the paths.

Bruce picked a purple grape at random to taste. "Phooey!" he exclaimed as he spat out the bitter fruit. "I don't think you're ready for wine making yet," he told the grape vines as he threw the remainder of the grape as far away as he could.

"*What a great game*," thought Juliet as she ran out and retrieved the grape, carrying it delicately in her mouth until dropping it into Bruce's hand, no more damaged than it had been when she picked it up.

This time Bruce carefully let Juliet run off again before dropping the remains of the grape under one of the vines.

He'd covered almost a mile by his reckoning, which would translate to something like 3-4 miles for Juliet, when she suddenly locked onto a point and barked twice to alert Bruce.

"Uh, oh," he said aloud. "What have we here? Did you just find a wild pheasant, Juliet?" He headed west toward the mountains toward where he thought the barking had originated.

Bruce walked through several rows of vines before he found her, off to his left and pointing toward one of the grapevines planted on a mound of earth. He looked carefully for the bird, sighting along her nose to tail axis. "Where's the pheasant, Juliet?"

He made a wide circle around the dog searching for the bird to flush. A couple of minutes later he concluded there wasn't any bird. "We've got two choices now, Juliet. Old bird scent, but you know better than that. Or, someone has a lot of digging to do. I think I'll leave that part to the deputies."

Pulling his phone out of a pocket he dialed 911 to report finding another body at the Fortune winery. He introduced himself before explaining to the dispatcher. "I'm in the middle of the vineyard with my dog and no obvious landmarks."

He gave her the exact GPS coordinates where the deputies could find him. "I'll wait right here for the deputies."

Repeating the ritual with his flag marking the exact spot Juliet had pointed and the dog safely leashed, released from her point, and secured a safe distance away from the flagged spot, Bruce sat down beside Juliet. He offered her some well-earned treats, which she wolfed down.

"Now we wait and make sure nobody disturbs anything until the deputies get here," he told her, absent-mindedly scratching her ears.

Twenty minutes later he heard sirens. It took the deputies another ten minutes to get close enough to him to call out. He answered and carefully talked them over to his location by a route that wouldn't further compromise the crime scene. The lead deputy was the same one who'd been there just after Juliet found Wally Fortune's body and had been so impressed with her skills, so Bruce just told him what Juliet had found and his interpretation of what she was telling him.

"She went on point for a cadaver. Her body language told me it's been there for a long time and it's buried a whole lot deeper than the other one we found. I didn't want to do anything to mess up your crime scene so I just waited here for the experts to arrive. You guys have some serious digging to do right about there," he said, pointing to his flag in the ground directly where she had indicated.

The chief deputy directed the two other deputies who had arrived just behind him to get some shovels and start digging. "And bring another shovel for me," he ordered.

Twenty minutes later Bruce's flag had been returned to him and the hole was more than a foot deep, a couple of square feet across, and empty. The deputies were grumbling about how much work they had to do, and for what?

"Five bucks says there's nothing here," said one of the deputies. "Ten bucks you're right," mumbled the other.

"I've seen this guy's dog in action before, when we found Wally Fortune's body," replied the chief deputy. "I'll take both those bets!"

It took a couple of hours of digging in shifts and a lot more grumbling and complaining before they found the skeleton, buried about 6 feet deep. It was mostly intact, with some remaining hair and teeth. The deputies widened the hole to reveal the entire skeleton before climbing out to get stakes and crime scene tape from their cars to protect the scene from further intrusion. The body had clearly been buried here for a long time.

"Don't touch anything, but make sure nobody else does either until we get back" the chief deputy admonished Bruce as the cops headed back to their cars for tape and to radio in their finding.

Bruce took advantage of the few minutes they left him there alone to scamper down into the grave and remove a few disjointed bones from the ground with his handkerchief, which disappeared into his pocket. He checked the body carefully, quickly climbing out of the hole and assuming his previous position when he heard the deputies returning.

The chief deputy looked down into the grave, then at Juliet, shaking his head in disbelief. "What could she have smelled from a completely decomposed body completely covered by six or seven feet of dirt?" he asked.

"Some of the fluids from decomposition impregnate the soil and take a very long time to break down completely. The bones and teeth break down very slowly, but emit some gases while they're being decomposed. And, like I told you before, Juliet has a very special nose," Bruce answered quietly.

****

102

My phone buzzed. It was Bruce. "Juliet did it again, Roger. You get one guess what she found on our run through the vineyard today. I'll give you a little hint: This one was a lot deeper and had been there a lot longer."

'Was there any I.D. with this one?" I asked.

"Not that I saw. And it was just a skeleton. But knowing how crappy a job the sheriff's office will do on the investigation I took a couple of small bones as souvenirs for DNA analysis. I hope you can get the FBI to give the overworked deputies some help with this investigation."

"I'll see what I can do. We're having dinner with a couple of FBI agents in Davis tonight. They can swing by Winters on their way back to Sacramento to pick up the evidence, and maybe get some DNA swabs from Wally's body for comparison. You can figure we'll get there some time between nine and ten," I continued. "Now I have to look at some more trees and plants and debrief my client, so save anything else you have to tell me for later tonight."

****

"To answer your original question, Sherry, no, I'm not ready to discuss the case yet. We'll be talking all about it over dinner so I'd rather enjoy the flora and fauna here in the arboretum while we have the chance. According to the sign we just walked past, we're in the Australian Outback section now and I've never been there before."

****

After a quick stop at Kinko's, we walked back to the restaurant, on First and F Streets, just in time for our seven o'clock reservation. The hostess led us to a table set with four china plates, water and wine glasses, and good quality cutlery on a heavy white cotton table cloth, but no Kaufman sisters yet. A quick look around ascertained the restaurant was L-shaped, with the north-south axis parallel to a long bar occupying the back half of the inside wall. The east-west axis was filled with closely packed tables bisected by an aisle for access to the tables and an outside patio, which contained more tables.

Occupying pride of place in the center of the restaurant was a large wood-fired brick oven for cooking pizzas and ducks, with a long narrow kitchen behind the oven for the rest of the main courses and for the remainder of meal preparation. The place looked upscale and was filled with customers busily eating dinners, always a good sign.

The hostess told us all the wines on the menu were half price tonight, suggesting we order a bottle to tide us over while we waited for our friends. Sherry and I decided on an old-vine Zinfandel from a Sonoma County winery. Good choice!

We were on our second glasses when the FBI agents arrived, just in time to taste the wine and suggest a second bottle with dinner. "I ordered the house specialty, roast duck, for all of us when I made the reservation," I announced. "If anyone doesn't like duck there are plenty of other choices on the menu. Everything's supposed to be good, according to Suzanne."

Nobody said anything. The waiter came by for our choices. "We preordered four of the roasted duck halves and we'd like another bottle of your old-vine Zinfandel," I told him.

"Excellent choices. Does anyone want any appetizers?" Four heads shook 'no'.

He left each of us with a couple of long, narrow breadsticks and butter to staunch our hunger pangs until the ducks arrived.

"How's your trial going?" I asked Barbara.

She nibbled on a breadstick before answering, "Surprisingly quickly. They should be done with us tomorrow, so we're planning on driving back to The City after rush hour settles down. How is Jason doing?"

I updated his health status, emphasizing the positives and the quality of care he was receiving.

"How about your murder mystery?" she asked. "Our former colleague Jason getting shot made this into an FBI case as far as I'm concerned, so we're unofficially offering you our full cooperation."

"We've got lots of things to tell you. Let's start here," I said, reaching down to pick up one of several thick envelopes I was now carrying around with me.

I passed the yellow envelope to Barbara. "This is a photocopy of the entries in the four ledgers Jason and Sherry were taking from the winery when he was shot, collated and separated by individual ledgers. I think you need to let one of your agents with accounting skills look this over. I believe I'm seeing some interesting patterns in some of the numbers, but suspect an expert would find a lot more."

Barbara glanced inside the envelope before asking, "What should our agent be focusing on, Roger?"

"Maybe we should let him look this over with fresh eyes and no preconceived notions, Barbara. If he finds what I think I did, we'll all be more convinced you have a possible RICO case on your hands here."

She took the envelope, nodding her agreement.

I turned to Gretchen. "Bruce called me this afternoon. Juliet found another body buried in the vineyard. This second one has been there for a long time. Bruce shares my lack of confidence in the investigative skills of the local sheriff's office, so he very carefully grabbed a few loose bones for DNA analysis. We hope you can drive back to Sacramento by way of Sherry's house in Winters to pick up the new evidence, as well as taking some samples with Wally Fortune's DNA in them for comparison with the DNA pattern you find from the new body."

"We can do that," Gretchen agreed. "It's a good idea, even if it won't endear us with your friend the sheriff."

"Actually, it might. The deputies weren't very enthusiastic about the priorities or quality of the results they get from the State Police when they request laboratory work."

The duck was excellent and the wine was a perfect complement to the duck. We talked murder and motive over dinner. Then the Kaufman sisters followed us back to Winters.

****

Sitting at Sherry's brightly lit kitchen table, Barbara very carefully removed all of the pieces of bone from Bruce's handkerchief with a sterile tweezer, placing them in several specially prepared plastic evidence bags issued to FBI field agents for DNA sample collection. The bags were sealed, labeled, and placed in Barbara's bag.

Barbara turned to Sherry, who had been standing near Bruce watching the process by which the bones became evidence with a great deal of interest. "Do you still have your husband's personal items here in your house?"

"Yes, I do," she replied. "What do you need?"

"Do you still have his hairbrush or toothbrush somewhere?" the FBI agent replied.

"I haven't been ready yet to get Wally's personal things put away or disposed of," replied Sherry somberly. "Everything's right where he left it and nothing's been touched."

We all followed Sherry as she walked upstairs, turning left to the master bathroom next to the master bedroom. Barbara carefully removed hairs from Wally's hairbrush and bristles from Wally's toothbrush with another sterile tweezer, bagged and tagged the samples, and put them in her bag with the skeletal bone samples. "We should get all of this to the FBI lab tomorrow night," she declared.

We said goodnight to the sisters, who headed back to their hotel.

Chapter 14. A little family history

After Bruce and Juliet started their long drive to Los Angeles early the next morning I e-mailed a copy of the PDF file from Kinko's to my partner Vincent, asking him to analyze the entries in the ledgers from the perspective of a forensic accountant.

I'd thought quite a bit about how best to spend my day. "How well do you know your new neighbors here, Sherry?"

She looked surprised by my question. "Casually, but I've met most of them. Why are you asking?"

Sitting at the kitchen table sipping my coffee I asked, "I'm looking for an old-timer who's lived here forever, preferably a talkative and gossipy old timer. Do you have any suggestions?"

She sat quietly across from me and thought for a bit. "Our neighbors behind the vineyard, Trilby and Horace Cantwell, have lived here forever. They're probably over eighty, current retirees who grew up here in Winters as third or fourth generation farmers. If anyone knows the local history around here it'll be those two, and they still have good minds and excellent memories. They're always at home, so we can drop by anytime this morning."

Sherry thought some more. "This is a small town, Roger, with a small town way of thinking. They may not want to answer direct questions from strangers like you and me. What would you think if we went over there to find out more about the Fortune family history? After all, there were a lot of things Wally and I never had a chance to talk about. We just didn't have enough time together so I missed that part. And it'd be natural for you to join me if you were the former friend offering me emotional support in my time of need."

"I like it, Sherry. I didn't realize you were that devious and cunning. Guess I'll have to watch myself a bit more around you," I said with a smile.

"It's neither devious nor cunning," she said sadly. "It's the truth."

A short phone call and a short car ride later Trilby was pouring coffee for the four of us. My career in police work and as a detective taught me to always accept coffee or tea when it's offered. Interviews with witnesses or suspects tend to become less adversarial and go more smoothly with social lubricants. We were sitting comfortably in a small living room furnished with elegant old-fashioned pieces that had seen better days. Sherry introduced me as an old friend of her family.

107

"It's good to finally meet you, Sherry," Trilby spoke in hushed tones. "I'm sorry for your loss, and I'm sorry to be meeting you for the first time under these circumstances."

Sherry made her sales pitch. "I never really had a chance to talk to Wally about what it was like for him growing up here. I was hoping you two might fill in some of those blanks for me. I gather you watched him and his brother growing up from just about day one."

Horace cleared his throat. "I knew Wally's folks for most of their lives and watched those boys grow up literally from day one. They had some tough times. They lost their mom in a car accident when Francis was about nine or ten, which would have made Wally about four or five years old. She was driving home on a back road through the mountains in a big hurry when a tire blew out. They didn't find the car and the body for almost a week. Wally's dad had to raise the boys on his own, and he was too busy with the winery to give them much of his time. Francis did most of Wally's raising in those days."

He sipped some coffee before continuing his story. "When he wasn't being Wally's dad and mom, Francis was always reading books. He got good grades in school. Everybody knew he'd go on to college and some kind of professional career. Wally was a jock. He was good at any sport, played football and baseball in school, got OK grades. But mostly he loved farming and wine making. I don't know how much of that was an excuse to spend time with his dad, but he took to the farming from a real early age."

Horace stopped to drink some more coffee, holding his empty cup in the air while Trilby refilled it. Sherry thought a bit about what he'd said. "Can you tell me some more about Wally's dad and the winery?"

Horace stood up. "Sure I can. Come on outside with me so I can show you something."

Standing a few steps outside his front door, with a wide sweep of his arm, Horace declared, "Look all around you."

His all-encompassing gesture included his own house and the land it was built upon, the Fortune house and vineyard, the winery, and all the agricultural land as the foothills climbed into the coastal mountains. "Winters has been here as a town since the gold rush era. This was the place they stopped overnight on the main stagecoach route from San Francisco to Sacramento. That old hotel building the Buckhorn restaurant is in now goes back a long time. They had to rebuild it a couple of times after it burned down, but one way or another it has been an inn for more than 150 years.

"Farmers and ranchers have been growing things around the town for a lot longer than that. Putah Creek flowed by so they had a reliable supply of water for most of the year. A lot of the early settlers were from Spain, Basque sheep herders, cattle ranchers who grazed animals on the side of the mountains, and farmers who grew wine grapes, fruit, and nut trees, mostly almonds and walnuts. Prohibition gave the grape growers a bad name and no market for their grapes, so most of the vineyards turned into nut and fruit orchards. Somewhere about that time the Fortuna family, originally from Spain, became the Fortunes from California."

He paused to catch his breath. "When Prohibition was repealed Grandpa Fortune planted several acres of grapes to go along with alfalfa, which he could sell to the cattle farmers around here for winter feed while he put some nitrogen back into the soil. He made a lot of money from the alfalfa, and more money from the wine he started to make again.

"Fast forward to after World War II and the area started to grow. All those old walnut trees were fuel for wildfires. On top of that, walnut prices tended to be too low when the market was limited so all of a sudden that wasn't everybody's favorite crop anymore. People started thinking life would be easier in the cities and sold their land for whatever they could get. The Fortune land holdings got a whole lot bigger. Grandpa built the family winery about that time, and hired Clay Bedford's daddy Cal to manage the winery. Wally's father took over the family wine and grape business when he got out of high school but kept Cal, and later on Clay, Bedford on as day to day managers of the winery. Wally had the knack for growing good wine grapes and all that new land. Pretty soon the vineyards started growing to about half the size they are now. That other half used to be Cantwell farms before Francis and Wally bought out our property when I retired."

Horace stopped for a minute or two, apparently lost in his memories. "Grandpa Fortune died in a tractor accident so Wally's dad had to take over the entire farm. That's about when Francis and then Wally were born. Maybe 10 years after his grandpa died, give or take, Wally's mom died in the car accident. Wally was still in high school when his dad took off. No notes, no messages, no nothing. One day he was there and the next day he was gone. Nobody from around here ever saw him again. Francis took care of Wally till he graduated from high school, then Francis went off to college and law school in Sacramento and Wally married the farm and winery. And my throat's getting all dried out and needs another coffee. Let's head back to the kitchen now."

A few minutes later Sherry and I were in the car heading back to the house. "What did you think of Horace's story, Sherry?"

She pulled into the driveway. "Well, I learned a lot more about Wally and the Fortune family than Wally ever told me," she answered. "How about you?"

I chose my words carefully. "Two single vehicle deaths, a disappearance, and a murder in a small rural family like the Fortunes seem to be a lot more than coincidence. Let's call it food for thought."

"I assume you're guessing the skeleton in the vineyard will have a DNA match to Wally and we just solved the mystery of his father's sudden disappearance," Sherry mused aloud. "If you're right we're looking for a trans-generational serial killer. Do you think that's possible, Roger?"

"At this stage I don't know what to think, Sherry. But something very wrong is going on around here. Now you're the owner of a winery whose former owners had a lot of bad luck, or worse. I think we should be a lot more concerned about your safety than we've been until now."

Back at the house I called the hospital for an update on Jason's condition. He was still listed in critical condition, but Dr. Russell assured me Dr. Canyon was confident the news would be better in a day or two and Jason would completely recover.

I called my partner Vincent. "Did you get the files I sent you?"

"Yes," he answered. "I took a quick look. This is a job that'll take a lot of time to do right."

"I know, Vincent. The call is to ask you whether you can drop whatever you're doing in L.A. and bring your computer up here to Winters to bodyguard our client while I work on this case. All of a sudden we have multiple murders and I'm afraid Sherry may be the next name on our killer's list."

There was a short pause. "If you can wait until tonight for me to get there I can juggle the schedule to make this work," he answered.

"Thank you. Text me the flight number and arrival time and either Sherry or I will meet your flight."

I turned to my client. "You're grounded for the foreseeable future, Sherry. No leaving the house without Vincent or me with you until further notice. Better safe than sorry!"

I called Suzanne to give her an update on the case and to tell her I'd be staying here longer than I'd originally planned. I also let her know Bruce was on his way home, so she'd have some help.

"Now what?" Sherry asked.

"We seem to be on a roll with the whole family history thing. Why don't you ask your brother-in-law Francis some of the same questions? I'd love to hear how he spins the story Horace told us this morning. And, I'm looking forward to hearing his update on your financial status."

****

Sherry, Francis, and I met for lunch at The Putah Creek Cafe, directly across the street from The Buckhorn Restaurant.

"I heard you found another body in the vineyard. Has it been identified yet?" he asked as we sat down.

"No," Sherry replied. "That's going to take quite a while, if they ever succeed in identifying the remains. There wasn't much there besides a skeleton. In the meantime, we were hoping you could fill us in on the history of the winery and the Fortune family. I never really learned much from Wally about what his life was like before we met. There didn't ever seem to be enough time for us to just sit and talk about things like that. Now I want to know all I can find out about where Wally came from and what made him become the man I married."

Francis told us bits and pieces of history starting with he and Wally losing their mother and then growing up with their far too busy father, all of it consistent with what Horace remembered. He didn't know much about the business part of the winery until after he came back to Winters after college and law school and took on the winery as his first big client. He described preparing and filing the winery taxes and its business deals, especially land acquisitions, as a routine and stable source of income.

"I left growing grapes and making wine completely to Wally, and was quite content for him to own the winery and farm lock, stock, and barrel. I made a very nice living doing the paperwork and handling tax and real estate matters for a few dozen other regular clients I had in addition to whomever walked through the door.

"I never married, so building up a big estate isn't on my list of priorities. I was very happy to have a wealthy brother and even happier to see him finally get married to you, Sherry."

It was a perfect segue, so I asked Francis, "You were going to come up with a summary of Sherry's finances for her. Have you had a chance to get that done yet?"

He reached down under his chair, pulling up an old, well-worn attaché case. He pulled out a thin sheaf of papers, handing them to Sherry. "Here you go, Sherry. Why don't you take a quick look and tell me if this is what you were looking for?"

Sherry looked the pages over, nodded, and passed them on to me. I knew that much, if not most, of her work for the American Kennel Club involved dog show finances, so she'd know what she was looking at here. I assumed that Francis completely underestimated her level of financial and business sophistication, which was a potential advantage from my point of view.

The paperwork was rudimentary finances, right out of an entry-level accounting class at business school. Gross income, expenses, net income with no detailed breakdown of sources or recipients for categories labeled "winery operations", "farm operations", "investments", and "miscellaneous". "Winery" made a good positive net income, "investments" showed a nice gain, "farm operations" showed a modest loss, and "miscellaneous" showed another modest positive cash flow. All in all, Wally showed a total net income in the six figures for last year.

"I assume you have the details underlying all this for me somewhere?" Sherry asked the lawyer.

He handed her another, much thicker, sheaf of papers. "I expect you'll want to look these over after you get home, Sherry. They're kind of complicated in parts," he declared. "You may want to show them to your accountant first."

She smiled sweetly. "Fortunately, he'll be here tonight so I'll have plenty of help if I need it. Thank you, Francis."

I figured there'd be more than enough time later to look over the detailed paperwork, so didn't ask to see the thick stack over lunch.

We made small talk over the rest of the meal.

After lunch Sherry and I walked over to the Sheriff's office. A couple of deputies nodded to us, but didn't come over. I looked down the hall, noticing the door to the Sheriff's office was open. A middle-aged gentleman in a Sheriff's uniform was sitting behind an ornate desk. I asked one of the deputies whether we could see Sheriff Stuart. The deputy walked into the office, spoke to him for a moment then motioned us to come in, and introduced us.

"Howdy Mrs. Fortune," the Sheriff greeted Sherry heartily. "I'm always glad to see one of my local constituents when I'm here in Winters. What can I do for you today?"

I was being ignored. Nothing personal I assumed, just that I didn't vote in local elections and was unlikely to be a significant campaign donor.

"I was hoping you could update us on whatever progress your deputies have made in their investigation of Wally's death."

"I can't talk about details of an investigation in progress," he replied pompously as if he were an actor on a TV show reading the standard script.

"In other words, no progress of any sort, right Sheriff Stuart?" Sherry asked politely.

"I can't talk about details of an investigation in progress," he replied again, standing up to indicate our meeting was over.

I couldn't resist a little dig on the way out. "Is there anything you'd like Mrs. Fortune or me to tell the FBI agents on this case when we speak to them later today?"

"What FBI agents are you talking about?" the sheriff asked sternly.

"I'm sorry, but I can't talk about details of an investigation in progress," I replied politely as we turned around and left his office.

On our way out of the cop shop we passed a few deputies staring open-mouthed in surprise at Sheriff Stuart's office. They'd obviously heard everything through the open door.

The deputy who'd responded to Sherry's 911 emergency telephone call immediately after Jason was shot spoke softly, just to me. "I don't know why the sheriff is being so uncooperative about working with you, Mr. Bowman. He's usually into collaboration given how small and spread out the department is, not the territorial response you seem to be getting.

"I guess you must have just rubbed him wrong some way. I don't know if he's ever worked with a big city private eye before. Like I said, his nasty response to you is totally out of character. I'm sorry we seem to be on opposite sides in this case."

Chapter 15. Who will make the wine now?

With a couple of hours to kill and already being next door to the City Hall, I suggested a little bit of research. "You'll be safe here, Sherry. I want you to look at deeds, tax, and property records for the Fortune and Fortuna families, the Bedford family, and the Cantwells. Also birth and death certificates for all of these families. Make copies of anything interesting. Go back as far as there are records."

"What am I supposed to be looking for, Roger?"

"I don't know. Anything that corroborates what someone has told us or seems to be at odds with someone's story. Whatever else catches your interest or anything else that looks like interesting Winters history."

"And where will you be while I'm doing this?"

I smiled at her. "I'll be doing exactly the same thing at the local newspaper office archives. Wait for me here. I'll pick you up no later than 4:00."

It was more like 3:30 when I collected Sherry.

Downtown Winters, an area of about four square blocks, consisted of older brick buildings and once elegant, but now just old, Victorian houses. Deteriorating and empty older buildings stood side by side with flourishing and gentrified new shops and stores in remodeled older buildings. The downtown area had an overall small-town feeling.

It was a small town with a small newspaper, whose archives only went back to 2004. Older issues back to 1884 were kept in the Public Library on microfilm. The only thing I learned from the newspaper archives was that the city of Winters has been named for an early businessman, Thomas Winters, in return for a donation of 40 acres of land to the Vacaville and Clear Lake Railroad to start a town.

I made a mental note that a trip to the library's microfilm collection would be a good job for Sherry and Vincent if they needed something exciting to do in the next few days.

Sherry told me she hadn't found anything in the City records that looked like a clue, but she'd copied a lot of stuff I could look over at my convenience. She continued, "As far as property records go, the Fortune Winery and farm are both owned by Wally's trust with reasonable mortgages on both. Clay Bedford owns his house outright. Trilby and Horace Cantwell sold their farm to Wally several years ago, just like they said. Birth and death certificates are consistent with everything we've been told."

Our next stop was at the winery on the way to the house. No tour this time, just walk in and look around.

"Can I help you with anything, Mrs. Fortune?" came a voice from behind one of the large fermentation tanks. Clay Bedford, the winery manager, emerged with a large pipe wrench dangling from his hand by his right side.

"Roger had a couple of questions he wanted to ask you," Sherry replied. "Can we talk while you work?"

"Sure," he answered. "Come on over behind this tank while I try to get a balky hose fitting attached so it won't keep leaking. What can I help you with, Mr. Bowman?"

"Call me Roger, Clay. I haven't seen anything that looks like a tasting room here at the winery. Is it in one of those smaller buildings I haven't been in yet?"

"We don't have a tasting room here at the winery," he replied. "In point of fact, we don't have a tasting room anywhere. The room at the Old Sugar Mill where you had your first taste of a Fortune wine at the wedding was strictly temporary for that day, not a permanent tasting room. We sell all our wine through restaurants and local wine stores, mostly in the East Bay area.

"We get some additional sales by word of mouth after people taste the wine at one of several restaurants we sell directly to here in Winters, so we also stock the local wine shops and grocery stores to meet that need. And not having a tasting room was a business decision, so out of my job description. Frank could probably tell you why he and Wally made that choice."

That was probably enough small talk. It was time for me to get to the real questions. "Someone told me you sort of inherited the manager job here from your father. Is that true?"

"Yeah, that's about right. I worked here with my dad in a bunch of after-school and summer jobs since sixth grade so I learned everything there was to know about how a winery works by the time I graduated from high school. I have a knack for machinery, so switched over to full-time maintenance and part-time everything else when I graduated. When dad died, Wally and Frank offered me his old job and I jumped at the opportunity. Best decision I ever made in my whole life.

"Wally was best at growing grapes, handling all the viticulture parts of the job, and making decisions about when the wine was ready to come out of the tanks into barrels and out of the barrels into bottles. That made for a perfect distribution of labor between us. He supervised everything to do with getting the grapes grown and harvested and the wine made and bottled, while I made sure everything in the winery was there and working when it was needed. I designed most of the layout of the winery when we expanded it, and I make sure everything comes in and out on time. I hope you'll let me keep on doing this job for you, Mrs. Fortune. I promise that I won't ever disappoint you."

Sherry smiled, not saying anything in reply.

I guess that was Sherry's way of reminding me this was my idea. "How would you go about finding someone to take over Wally's part of the job, Clay? And how quickly does Sherry need someone else on board to keep the wine flowing from here?"

"You might want to check with the University's Viticulture and Enology Department, the local wineries, and the big wineries in Lodi and the Sonoma Valley whether anybody they know of who's qualified is looking for a viticulture and enologist's job. And you want to get them hired yesterday if you can! The workload never stops around here."

"Do you know of anyone, Clay?"

"No, I don't. But I'll ask around."

"Thank you," Sherry told him. "We'll talk some more about all of this and the future as soon as I get a little bit more up to speed on things around here. But I want you to know I'll be depending on you for a lot of help during this transition period."

We walked back to the house. It was a beautiful day, without any smoke or smog blocking the view thanks to a temporary shift in the wind direction. But we knew the wildfire was still out there across the mountain consuming vast amounts of trees and grasslands, continuing to threaten us here on this side of the coastal range were the wind to once again change its direction.

Sherry excused herself to start phoning people about how to find a new winemaker.

I called Gretchen, updating her on Jason's condition. "We met Sheriff Stuart for the first time today. It's a good thing the FBI is also looking into the killing here. He's a total jerk."

"Did any of your lab people have anything to tell you yet about the bones Bruce gave you?"

"Have a heart," she replied. "They've only had the sample for a few hours. The DNA work still takes a couple of days, even on a priority basis. But I can tell you this much pending the DNA analysis. Just looking at the bones under the microscope the technician could make an educated guess that the remains were male, middle aged or older, and had been buried for at least twenty years, probably longer."

"That fits with our current theory that the body was Wally Fortune's father who disappeared mysteriously when Wally was still a kid. The timing would work. The DNA analysis should be definitive if we're right. How about the forensic accounting with the ledgers?"

"Sorry Roger. That will have to wait its turn. My guess is it will take weeks to get any results from those ledgers unless this case moves a long way up on the FBI's priority list. And that would take evidence of a very a strong tie to organized crime to happen.

"But I do have one more very interesting thing to share. We found a couple of matches for the bullet that Bruce recovered from the winery wall after Jason was shot. One was from an unsolved killing in Lodi almost 20 years ago. The other was from an unsolved kidnapping and murder case in the Alexander Valley a year or two after that.

"And we finally got photomicrographs taken by the California State Crime Lab of a bullet recovered from Wally's body at autopsy. It was a perfect match for the second bullet shot at Jason and Sherry. We don't have the resources to follow up on any of the older cases, Roger, so I'll send you electronic copies of files for both of them and wish you the best of luck solving two very cold cases for us. And on that note I have to get back to work. Bye, Roger."

'*And thanks a lot for getting us involved, however peripherally, in another of your typical bizarre and convoluted murder cases, Roger,*' she thought with a rueful smile.

As I broke the connection my phone dinged. The text message told me Vincent would arrive in Sacramento on an 8:15 flight. I passed the word on to Sherry that we'd be driving to the airport together to meet his flight. We could stop somewhere for dinner after we picked him up.

Chapter 16. Warming up a couple of very cold cases

Two very large PDF case files arrived as attachments to the email Gretchen sent me. For want of anything better to do, I started reading the files. Two things were immediately apparent. Both cases had connections to wineries, involving medium-sized, privately owned operations similar to the Fortune winery. And, except for the matching bullets, the FBI was clueless, literally and figuratively, in both cases. I started reading very carefully.

In the Alexander Valley case someone kidnapped a winery owner before they shot and killed him. There was a ransom demand, but for some reason the victim was killed before arrangements could be made to pay the kidnappers. The body was found after an anonymous tip where the police should look for it. It faded away into the unsolved case files with little fanfare or follow-up.

The Lodi case should never have been an FBI investigation in the first place, as they had no reason for jurisdiction. Apparently somebody important knew somebody else and pulled some strings. A local homicide case, another shooting, was investigated by the FBI as well as by the local police. The victim was the owner of a local winery. Nobody solved the case and it too faded away.

Both locations were an hour or two drive away from Winters, in different directions. It looked like my next two days were going to be spent looking into these cases. Were the similarities between these crimes part of a larger pattern?

It was time to pick up Vincent at the airport. Sherry and I drove over, his flight arrived on time, and we had dinner at a good Mexican restaurant in Woodland on the way back. Vincent summarized his detailed analysis of the material in the ledgers. "I agree with your first impression, Roger. Something is peculiar. More money is coming in than I could account for from the wine sales. Something else is going on there. It's going to take a lot more information than I have to nail things down. Hopefully the FBI has the resources to do this right."

We agreed Sherry and Vincent would check out the newspaper archives on microfilm the next morning while I drove over to the Alexander Valley, on the other side of the coastal mountains, to see what I could find out about the former owner of the winery who was kidnapped and killed.

In the meantime Sherry started receiving applications for the job of winery manager via email and text messages. She explained, "I spoke to the owners of two of the larger wineries here in Winters and explained my problem. They both told me the same thing. I need to look for a UC Davis graduate with a viticulture and enology major. They will have training in both grapes and wines. Furthermore I should be looking for an applicant who's had experience as an assistant manager in a Central Valley or Napa Valley winery so they've learned how to make good wines on our scale.

"They both told me to use Clay Bedford to screen applicants for the necessary technical skills, but to use my own best judgment when it comes to finding someone I think can work with and is willing to work for me as an owner. That'll be my big project for tomorrow afternoon. I assume Vincent will babysit me just in case."

****

At ten o'clock the next morning I met with Clarissa Matthews, daughter of the kidnap-murder victim Harris Matthews, at her home, a small farmhouse not far from the winery in the Alexander Valley where she'd grown up. Several horses grazed contentedly in a paddock behind the house. The rest of the land was grassy so must have been irrigated, but seemed natural and suitable for grazing horses to enjoy. Clarissa was currently in her thirties and a fulltime wife and mother. She and her brother had sold the winery after the estate was settled.

The inside of the house seemed larger than I had guessed from the outside, with some elegant older pieces of wooden furniture and the skilled hand of a good designer apparent. I saw a formal dining room with a large oak table and a large bright kitchen containing ultra-modern, high end, appliances as Clarissa led me to a comfortable couch in the living room. She offered coffee, which I accepted, accompanied by homemade cookies, before sitting across from me on a straight-backed upholstered chair. I explained why I was here, to better understand the circumstances surrounding her father's death in relation to a current case I was working on with some similarities to it.

She repeated the same story I had gotten from the FBI file. When she finished I told her, "I got a lot of those facts from the FBI files. What I'm looking for from you is what's not in the files. What was your father like? Was the winery doing well at that time? Did anything else happen around then that may seem peculiar in retrospect?"

"That's funny," she replied. "Nobody asked me any of those questions when Dad died and everything was happening. Let me think."

"Take your time," I reassured her.

Clarissa nodded. "When my brother and I were growing up money was very tight around the house. Everything seemed to go into the winery. Then, kind of suddenly, about a year or so before my dad was kidnapped, things changed. We suddenly had money for new clothes and a new car. It was a great year. But dad seemed depressed instead of happy.

"Later on, when we sold the winery, we got an awful lot of money for it. Much more than I would have guessed it was worth, especially because there only seemed to be one person offering to buy it. And he was from Oakland or The City, not local.

I got the impression Mom didn't want to look a gift horse in the mouth so we sold the winery and got on with our lives. But something was wrong with that whole deal."

"Is anyone still around who would remember the financial details of the winery sale?" I asked.

"I don't think so," Clarissa replied. "My brother and I were just high school kids when all this happened. My Mom died a couple of years ago, and I think she handled all the financial stuff when we sold the winery."

"Do you remember the buyer's name?" I asked.

"Yes, I do. It was something or other Valducci. Enzo I think."

We talked for another half hour. I steered the conversation to her high school and college years but didn't learn anything else that might be relevant to the kidnap or murder.

****

On the way home I called the winery in Lodi to ask about surviving family or friends of the murdered owner from a decade before. The family had sold the winery and moved to Livermore. I got a phone number and reached Lavinia Monroe, widow of the victim, who agreed to see me that afternoon. So, I switched directions to get onto I-680 and headed south.

Lavinia was probably sixty-ish, well dressed and well preserved. Her house was big and expensive, in a gated community that smelled of money. She greeted me pleasantly but was obviously withholding judgment as to whether this was some sort of scam or whether I was what I said I was, a detective investigating a cold case.

I told her what I'd told Clarissa, that I'd read the FBI files and was looking for what wasn't in the files. "What was your husband like? Was the winery making money at that time? Did anything else happen around the time of the murder that may seem peculiar in retrospect?"

Her story was a lot like Clarissa's, but from the point of view of an adult at the time. "Wineries are money pits. In good years you make money, but reinvest it in new equipment or better grapes. In bad years you lose money hand over fist. It was a good thing I had a well paying steady job at the time. The year before Jacob was killed things changed. We had plenty of money. But for some reason Jacob didn't seem as happy about the business as I thought he'd be.

"When he died, I couldn't take over. I didn't know anything about running a commercial winery. It wasn't easy to sell, either. The wine industry was suffering from overplanting of too many grapes and a glut of low and moderately priced wines on the market. I finally got an offer from a lawyer representing an investment group that was half-again as much as I'd been told was the fair market value for the business. I took the money and ran, and here I am now living a much better life than I possibly could have if I'd stayed in Lodi."

"Do you remember the lawyer's name?" I asked.

"I think so. It was Ethan or Etan Frominger, if I remember correctly."

We talked a bit longer but all I learned was the police and FBI investigations had been perfunctory at best and Lavinia had long since moved on with her life. She asked why I was asking these questions now. I told her I was investigating a new case with some similarities to her husband's death. She wished me luck in my investigation but didn't ask me to stay in touch.

I headed home from there.

****

Sherry and Vincent were waiting for me in Sherry's comfortable kitchen. I poured myself a cup of coffee from the modern appliance on the counter between the sink and stove, joining them at the table. They had come back thoroughly bored and bleary eyed from a long and dusty morning at the public library. A thick pile of Xerox copies of old newspaper articles from the microfilm archives of the local press sat between them on the table. I'd asked them to copy whatever they found about any of the principals in our case. It was a small town, so the definition of news was just about anything about a Winters resident. They'd separated the big stack into several smaller piles, by individual or entity.

The largest pile, by far, was news about the Fortune winery. They were good at public relations, donating wine to most of the larger charitable events in Winters over a period of several decades. Each donation was dutifully noted in the media. Expansion of the winery was also newsworthy, as it was one of the bigger businesses in the small town. But there wasn't much of interest in any of this for me as I skimmed the copies and put them aside.

Much thinner piles documented key events in the lives of the individuals we were interested in. Two skimpy articles recounted the accident that killed Wally's mother, a single car crash into a tree at 1 AM in the morning. You could read between the lines that fatigue or alcohol might have contributed to the accident, but small town journalism did not allow for negative speculation or reporting of such lapses in judgment. The disappearance of Wally's father did not seem to merit even as much space as this. There weren't any articles to be found.

122

Pictures of Wally and Francis graduating from Winters High School, brief announcements of Francis graduating from college and law school, and pictures of Wally on the high school football team were the high points for the younger generation of the Fortune family. Similarly for the Bedfords, we found pictures of Clay on the high school football team and graduating as a classmate of Wally's. There were only two items for his father, Cal, an obituary when he died from natural causes and a photo of him donating a trophy deer head, antlers and all, to the Buckhorn Restaurant for its wall display.

For the moment, that was that, and it was a big disappointment. I called the hospital and got good news. Jason had been upgraded from critical to serious condition and I could actually visit with him if I came by this evening. He was still on a ventilator for now, so he couldn't talk, but he was awake and knew what was going on around him. They were going to try to wean him from the ventilator support tomorrow.

There were over a dozen applicants for the winery manger job, of which more than half appeared to be qualified. Sherry would start interviewing candidates tomorrow.

We discussed what I'd learned and what I guessed from today's interviews. The whole picture was slowly coming into focus. Something had happened to suddenly improve cash flow in two struggling wineries then the owners had misgivings. Finally the owners died suddenly. Buyers appeared as if by magic with generous offers, maybe too generous.

"This could be the tip of the iceberg," I commented. "These are just the cases that came to the FBI's attention because of the ballistic evidence matching our case. A normal routine murder case would never get to the FBI, just the local law enforcement authorities. There could be a whole lot of other wineries where murder or extortion took place following the same pattern. There is certainly the possibility that something like this went on at the Fortune winery, and could have been going on for a long time.

"Vincent, can you do an Internet search tonight for more winery owners from Northern California who died suspiciously over the last twenty or thirty years, while I visit Jason at the hospital? That would make a very nice group of cases for the FBI to begin collecting bullets and case files from to start figuring out how widespread this whole serial murder case may actually be."

****

Jason squeezed the hand I offered him. He lay on his back with lots of tubes and wires connected to machines at one end and him at the other. The ventilator made rhythmic clunking noises as it moved air in and out of his lungs. I felt clumsy in sterile disposable booties and coveralls, but Jason seemed pleased to see me. I thought he looked better, but still had a long way to go.

****

"I've got almost a dozen possible old cases for us to check out," Vincent told me when I got back to Winters that night. "It was too late to call the relevant law enforcement agencies by the time I collected my list. I also doubt they'll discuss what may still be open cases with us, so maybe you want to turf this job to one of the Kaufman sisters tomorrow morning."

****

I called Barbara at nine o'clock the next morning to update her on Jason's progress and to give her the list of possible murder victims and localities to check on for us. She immediately understood the possible importance of this line of inquiry and promised to get right on it. "If we get lucky there might still be ballistic evidence, bullets or shells, languishing around in some of these old case files. That might be all we need to get jurisdiction in these cases," she said excitedly.

"You might also want to light a fire under your forensic accountants, Barbara. Vincent analyzed those files in the ledgers much more carefully than I did and saw the same thing I thought after a quick look. There seems to be more money coming into the winery than can be accounted for from the wine sales. There may be a big money laundering operation going on there.

"If the same thing is happening at the other wineries on our list, we're talking millions of dollars a year for a lot of years, and a huge RICO case for the FBI to be investigating."

I called Bruce in Los Angeles. "Hey, Bruce, do you think there's any chance there could be more bodies buried in that vineyard? If there is, you may need to bring Juliet back here. I think we may be looking at a lot more dead bodies in this case."

Bruce chuckled audibly. "C'mon Roger, give me a little more credit than that. On my way back from the grave when the deputies dug up the skeleton I walked back to the house the long way. Juliet covered the entire field and didn't alert again. If there are any more bodies to be found under the grapevines they won't be as easy to discover as the first two were!"

Chapter 17. A pause in the action

A quick call to the hospital told me it would be OK to visit Jason again on my way to the airport. It was a quiet time in the investigation here while the FBI did its thing, so it was time for me to go home for a few days to my pregnant wife and a detective agency that needed to be managed. Sherry, however, had to remain in Winters to interview would-be winery managers.

Vincent assured me he could look after Sherry in my absence. "I do most of the bodyguard work for the agency in Los Angeles, Roger. Why not up here, too?"

Sherry, who didn't know Vincent as well as I did, wasn't so sure. So I explained, "Vincent spent most of his adult life as a CIA agent in deep cover in Chile. He survived because he was trained to sense danger and to do something about it before it happened. He's much better at body guarding than I'll ever be. You'll be perfectly safe with him watching out for your safety."

I made reservations for a flight south at an appropriate time. Vincent and Sherry would stay at the winery to interview candidates for the manager job, almost half a dozen of which had passed the initial screening steps, including Clay Bedford's vetting, and were ready to meet Sherry for formal interviews. I'd drive to the hospital and airport in one of Wally's extra cars, which I'd leave parked there in anticipation of returning in a couple of days to resume the investigation.

Jason had been extubated and was breathing on his own when I got there to visit. He was asleep, but starting to look like a normal Jason. Dr. Canyon promised he'd be out of the hospital and recovering within less than a week if nothing unexpected happened now that he was off mechanical ventilation.

****

Bruce and Robert met my flight and debriefed me on the trivia that I'd missed over the last few days.

The dinging of my cell phone announced a text message from Barbara Kaufman. It read simply, "One more bullet found thus far. It matched. There's another due to come tomorrow. You're probably right. A serial killer officially makes it FBI jurisdiction. Thanks for a juicy case!"

The next couple of days passed quickly. The second bullet sent to the FBI for analysis by the police in Lodi also matched the one that had barely missed Sherry. I thought about what this all meant and the significance of all of these bullets having been fired by the same weapon used to shoot at Jason and Sherry.

And, of course, the new bullets also matched the one used to shoot Wally, photomicrographs of which Barbara obtained from the California State Crime

Laboratory. And to also match the bullets used to kill several other Northern California winery owners through the years.

Gretchen Kaufman checked out the names I'd been given for the winery buyers of a decade ago in Lodi and the Alexander Valley. Neither of them matched the current owners and neither of them existed on paper other than in the records of the sales on file in the local jurisdictions. They were clearly phony, invented solely for the occasion, and reflected the lack of bureaucratic formality when the buyer paid cash for a piece of real estate.

I caught up on accumulated paper at work and paying proper attention to a very pregnant wife and the delightfully happy to see me son and dogs.

The phone rang just as we sat down to dinner on my first night home.

I answered. It was Connie Sherman, demanding an update on Jason's condition. *"Aha,"* I thought, *"We've created a monster!"*

"He's doing much better, Connie. Jason's got the best medical care available and he's a very strong guy. My best guess is he'll be able to talk on the phone in a couple of days and actually be able to come back to Los Angeles in a week or so. After that he'll have some serious rehabilitation to do for the shoulder, so won't be wrestling evildoers for a few months."

Time to change the subject. "How are you doing?"

I heard a couple of minutes of new mother-to-be complaints about her body and the Braxton-Hicks contractions, but everything seemed to be working out OK. "I finished the interviews and hired a nanny. His job will start the day the new baby is born. That'll give Victor, the nanny, a day or two to get the house organized before I'll be home with the newborn baby and need his help. Victor has a lot of experience and Bruce's blessings, so probably has a very good future ahead of him.

"Can I talk to Suzanne now, Roger?" Connie continued with a catch in her tone.

"Sure," I replied, handing the phone to my wife.

They talked to each other for another ten minutes.

I'd listened in to one side of the conversation. "What was all that about, Suzanne?" I asked.

She smiled at me. "Advanced pregnancy, hormones, and guilt, in more or less equal amounts," she answered. "Connie is convinced she's a black widow, and any man she's attracted to is destined to die a violent death. First it was her husband, Delbert. Now it's Jason."

"Well," I said hesitantly, "At least she likes Jason."

"That's the right way to think about it, Roger. I suspect she'll have to work through the guilt of being attracted to another man less than a year after losing her husband, but that's going to turn out a whole lot better in the long run than suppressing all those feelings for as long as it takes her to admit it's all right to find a cute male who's attractive to her."

I thought it over. "So, in summary, we have to wait for the baby to be born and the hormones to get back to normal, but we may have fixed two friends up with one another who both actually needed fixing up."

The night before I returned to Northern California, Connie called again. This time Suzanne answered the phone, which turned out to be a good thing from my point of view.

Connie was now on full alert for impending motherhood. Braxton-Hicks contractions were happening on an irregular basis. Her nominal due date was almost exactly one month from now. She had stopped going into the laboratory on a regular basis a week earlier, but she spent all afternoon, or more, every day writing manuscripts about completed studies or preparing grants about future studies in her home office.

She still drove into the campus on Friday mornings to debrief her research team on the past week's progress and to discuss any technical problems that had reared their ugly little heads. There were occasional conference calls with her deceased husband Delbert's clinical colleagues about nuances of his clinical trials that were now her formal responsibility as the co-investigator on his grants.

Connie was arguing with Suzanne on the phone. "Of course I'm coming up there to help with caring for Jason when he gets back. I can drive up once or twice a week, leaving late enough to miss the worst traffic. I have at least two more weeks before my obstetrician says I'm grounded. Even then, I just have to be within half an hour of the hospital unless he finds any indication my daughter is in a hurry to arrive."

Suzanne understood the futility of arguing, at least for the moment. "Let's see what kind of shape Jason is in when he gets here, Connie. My guess is he'll be stir crazy from all the time in the hospital and looking for excuses to get out of the house. Maybe we'll drive down there one or two of those times you two get together to accomplish all the same things without risking you getting stuck all alone in a freeway traffic jam when your water breaks. And stop bragging about having Braxton-Hicks contractions. You're not the only one having them!"

Eventually I'd learn there were a lot of phone calls for reassurance and amateur psychotherapy through the next week while I was up in Winters being a detective. For now, I found this the only even faintly amusing part about Jason stopping a bullet the hard way.

The next day I flew back to Sacramento early in the morning and drove back to Winters. If my thought process was correct, Sherry hiring a replacement manager for the winery rather than putting it up for sale was likely to precipitate some actions that could lead us to the killer.

Sherry had selected her new winery manager, an ideal candidate on paper who interviewed well. The manager was due to formally begin her new position in two weeks, but was going to be spending today at the vineyard and winery getting familiar with the setup. Francis had stayed in the background during the search for the manager, but was still responsible for the winery's legal and accounting work so would be reviewing the winery's finances later in the day with the new manager, Carol Marshall.

Sherry and Vincent had collected all the current bills and invoices from the winery under the pretext that Carol Marshall would need to review the cash flow before beginning her new job. Vincent had compared these numbers with Wally's data from the ledgers Jason was taking from the winery safe when he was shot. Vincent was even more certain now the books had been cooked to hide a sophisticated scheme for money laundering.

That left me with the problem of figuring out who was profiting from the funny money flowing in and out of the Fortune winery, and presumably several other wineries in the Northern California winemaking regions. I could follow the money trail from the bottom up or I could try guessing where the top of the pyramid was and start working down.

I called Gretchen, ostensibly to give her an update on Jason's condition. Then I asked her, "Who would have millions of dollars to launder and the organizational skills to hatch the kind of scheme I suspect took place a generation ago and is still ongoing?"

Gretchen hesitated a moment before she answered. "There are lots of possibilities, Roger. Organized crime in San Francisco, drug dealers in Oakland, Hell's Angels or other biker gangs selling drugs all over Northern California, street gangs like the Bloods and Crips in Stockton, and some of the crooked unions in the Bay Area. There are lots of possibilities and I only gave you a few of them."

Following the money trail up from the bottom suddenly looked like the better choice. And I knew just who to start with for this approach. I asked Sherry to call her brother-in-law to set up a meeting with her. "But it'll be a meeting with me,

128

not you," I explained. "It's about time we found out whose side Francis is on in this case."

Half an hour later I knocked gently on his door.

"Come on in, Sherry. It's open," came a disembodied voice from inside the office.

I went in.

Francis looked up from a pad of legal paper he was scribbling on. "I'm sorry, Roger, but I don't have time now. I'm expecting my sister-in-law."

I deliberately moved a chair to sit directly in front of him. "I'll be taking the appointment for her," I explained firmly. "She had a sudden emergency come up so sent me in her place."

Francis looked confused but seemed to believe me thus far. He put down his pen on the desk alongside the pad he'd been writing on. "What can I do for you then, Roger?"

I sat up straighter, putting a tone of command in my voice. "Just answer a few questions. You know more about the winery's history and finances than just about anyone else around here. A few things have come up that Sherry wants to understand a little better."

I was looking directly at his eyes. Something changed for a split second. I'd have missed it if I hadn't been looking directly at Francis, but it was there. I was pretty sure I was on the right track now.

I crossed my legs, sitting back on the chair in a more relaxed position. Now my body language said we were two buddies shooting the breeze. "It looks to Sherry like the winery is making a bigger profit than the sales receipts for the wines seem to indicate. What do you think it is that she's not understanding properly about the business?"

Francis decided to play it pompous. "Accounting and bookkeeping for a large business like the winery is complicated. That's why Wally always left those tasks to me. I'm sure Sherry doesn't have the right background and training to understand what she's actually looking at."

He obviously had me pegged for stupid muscle. Good! He was more likely to make a mistake as long as he underestimated me. "Actually, Francis, Sherry handles a lot of the American Kennel Club's finances for the western United States. That's a lot bigger business than the Fortune Winery. I'm pretty sure she knows what she's looking at when she examines the company's books."

Francis gave me a condescending look. "I think you may be giving Sherry too much credit, Roger. I'm a lawyer and it took me several years before I was comfortable handling the winery's finances. It's actually a very complicated operation."

It was time to pull the rug out from under his smug complacence. "Hmmm," I said. "Then you aren't worried the FBI will find anything wrong with the winery's books when their forensic accounting experts review the discrepancies Sherry thinks she's finding?"

"Who said anything about the FBI?" Francis asked, a look of alarm crossing his face.

"Initially I did," I answered. "But Sherry came around to my way of thinking when someone shot at her the other night. I thought you and I might have some straight talk today and save everyone a lot of grief over the long haul."

"I think this conversation is over," the lawyer said, standing up to indicate I was no longer welcome.

I stayed seated. "Come on, Francis. Play nice. I think you're going to need me on your side if you don't want to stand trial for murder when all of this shakes out."

There was a long pause as Francis digested the meaning of what I'd just said. He finally sat down again at the desk across from me. "Murder? What are you talking about?" he demanded.

Now it was my moment of decision. Was Francis dumb enough to have missed all the clues for most of his lifetime or was he putting on an act? I decided he was dumb enough to have missed the murder parts but had to be complicit in the money laundering at the Fortune winery. So I played it that way.

I sat up straight again, signaling we weren't buddies anymore. "I'm working closely with the FBI on this case. The best you can hope for is disbarment, a plea bargain, and a shorter prison term for a lifetime of money laundering if you cooperate with me now. If you don't, the offer is off the table and you'll be charged with capital murder. It's your call."

There was another long pause. Francis was most definitely not what you would call a quick study. "Exactly whom am I supposed to have murdered?" he eventually asked, getting back a small fraction of his bravado.

This time I was the one who took the long pause to build the pressure up. "Let's see," I mused out loud. "Your father, your mother, your brother, and at least four other victims we've identified so far. I suspect there will be several more when the investigation is complete."

Francis nervously rearranged the pen and pad of legal paper in front of him on his desk. This had obviously not been what he was expecting to hear. "What? My mother died in a car accident and my father disappeared. That's a far cry from murder!"

I tightened the screws a little bit more. "Your father reappeared as a skeleton in the vineyard last week. He was murdered and we can prove that."

Francis went from bluff and bluster to ashen with fear. "My father? Are you sure?"

I paused a few ticks to let him sweat a bit longer. "Yes," I lied.

He fell apart in front of me. "OK, I'll tell you everything I can about the money part. But that's all I know about. You've got to believe me!"

I raised a hand, signaling him to stop talking for a moment. "Wait a minute, Francis. I'm going to tape our conversation from here on just so we don't have any misunderstandings in the future." I pulled out my pocket tape recorder, switched it on, put it on the desk between us, and stated the date, time, and who was in the room.

The stage settings were ready for the next step, so I gestured for him to begin speaking again. "Tell me about the money part now, Francis."

He started slowly and haltingly, but did a lot better when he got into it. "A few years after I finished law school and came back to Winters, a couple of men in suits came by to make me an offer. They told me they were lawyers from The City and had a proposition for me. They knew it was a hard time for wineries in general and that ours was on the brink of bankruptcy. The lawyers wanted to buy into the winery as silent partners."

Francis stopped for a moment, pausing to look at the tape recorder in front of him on the desktop.

With an in for a penny, in for a pound expression and body language, he continued his story. "If we were willing to take several hundred thousand dollars of their money and run it through our business, we could keep 25% of the money as our fee for helping them out. It was a gift that saved us financially at the time, but of course we were making a bargain with the devil. I knew it, but it seemed like the only way out for us where we could keep the family winery."

He paused again, obviously calculating exactly what else he wanted to say. He seemed to be slowly regaining his initial confidence as he spoke. My internal lie detector went on red alert. "A few years later we were back in the black selling our wines, but there wasn't any way out of the deal. Twice a year they come by for their checks, withdrawing clean money from us as profits on their original investment. Every Christmas, we got a new infusion of dirty money to launder for them.

"At first my Dad and Wally didn't seem to understand what was going on, but Dad had to know. After Dad disappeared Wally got deeper into the finances and figured things out. I convinced him to go along with the arrangement. After all, we weren't hurting anyone and the extra money bought both of us a much better lifestyle than the winery could generate."

Like a wind-up toy that had wound down, he abruptly stopped talking.

I needed to get him started again. "And the names of the lawyers were?" I prompted.

Francis paused again, as if trying to remember from long ago while he invented a plausible answer. "The original lawyers were named Smith and Brown," he said, making air quotes as he spoke to let me know he understood those weren't their real names. "There are new ones every few years and nobody bothers with even the pretense of names anymore."

I pulled my chair closer to the desk so now we seemed to be two buddies just shooting the breeze. "How do they give you the dirty money?" I asked.

The answer was immediate, and probably true. "Cash, of course. There isn't any paper trail."

I thought about the logistics. "Did you ever follow them or get a license number?"

Francis gave another quick answer, which just might have been true. "No, I never did. I got the message they weren't people to be messed around with early in the relationship."

I changed the subject abruptly to shake him up a bit and get him off the prepared script. "Do you know of any other wineries around here with a similar arrangement?"

He hesitated for several moments, clearly trying to guess how much I really knew. "No, not directly. But it wouldn't surprise me if there were."

This was the time for the key question. "Do you have any idea at all who they are or who the source of the money is?"

There was another of those calculating pauses before he answered. "Maybe," he said cunningly. "What's in it for me if I do?"

I wasn't in any position to make specific offers in an FBI case, and he knew it. He was testing my sincerity. OK, I can be sincere if I have to be. "Bonus points for helping us out," I replied. "And trust me, you need all the bonus points you can get at this point."

Francis stood up to open a wall safe concealed behind a picture behind him then started to reach into it. I jumped up and grabbed his arm. "Very slowly and carefully, Frank. And there had better not be a gun in your hand when your arm comes out, or I'll break it."

He blanched. Out came a plastic bag with a metal letter opener shaped like a dull knife in it. "One of them was handling this letter opener I had on my desk last Christmas. I thought it might have his fingerprints on it, so I saved it just in case. This should be worth a few bonus points, right?"

"Maybe," I said. "It's a good start. Do you have any more clues to share?"

He looked everywhere except directly at me as he thought about his answer. "That's it," he said reluctantly. "Remember, you promised me a break if I talked to you."

We were in a too good a rhythm now for me to want to leave without one more very important line of inquiry satisfied. He was just answering my questions. There were fewer outright lies and less thinking, even if there were also some obvious evasions and only partial truths. All he wanted was for this to be over as quickly as it could happen.

There was another key question he might answer, especially if he didn't realize its significance. "One more thing, Francis," I added as if it were a meaningless afterthought. "Who else knew about this arrangement?"

"Wally, our father, Clay and Cal Bedford. That should be everyone who was ever responsible for actually ordering things for the winery or paying its bills."

I kept up the quick rhythm so he didn't have time to think. "Do you know how long the arrangement went on, Francis?"

"No, I don't. It started long before my time. My dad introduced me to the first pair of lawyers I told you about a couple of months after I got back from law school. I had the impression then that the deal had been going on for a while. Everyone seemed to know everyone else, and that included Cal Bedford as well as my dad."

Another quick follow-up kept him talking, not thinking. That's when he'd make mistakes. "But weren't there any names when you were being introduced?

"Like I told you before, Smith and Brown. But wait a minute. Now that I think about it, one of them was Larry and the other was Mitch or Mike, or maybe Mel or Mal." Francis looked like a partially trained dog waiting for a dog biscuit as a reward for remembering more than he had before.

It was time for another quick change of subject. "How about the other local wineries around here? Were any of them in on this deal?"

Francis leaned forward to convince me of his sincerity. He might just as well have announced an impeding prevarication. "I don't know. First my dad, then Wally, did all the schmoozing with the local winemakers since I've been living here. I was strictly allowed only to handle legal matters and taxes, nothing else, especially if it involved direct dealings with people. Actually, that was the way I liked it. I'm not really into all the social stuff, which is important if you're trying to sell wines to people."

He sat back, expecting the session to be over. "Who would know, Francis? Which of the local winery owners goes back the longest time?"

"I don't know," he whined. "I wasn't ever interested in that kind of thing. You'll have to ask someone else."

I thought about what we had both learned in law school, the importance of plausible deniability if you're involved in anything ethically or legally dubious. We had obviously reached a point of diminishing returns here. I stood up.

I stood directly in front of him, leaning over his desk and deliberately invading his personal space. No more Mr. Nice Guy! "I'll be back with some FBI agents to continue this discussion in the next day or two. In the meantime, I wouldn't try taking off or telling anyone about this conversation. Your friends seem to have a bad habit of killing anyone who doesn't cooperate with them when they ask."

Francis sat silently, looking crestfallen as he realized his world was about to come crashing down upon him.

"Do you have a passport in that safe, Francis?" I asked politely.

He nodded wordlessly.

"Please give it to me now," I demanded politely.

He did, and I left his office.

Chapter 18. Another trip back in time

Sitting with Sherry and Vincent at the kitchen table in her house, I pulled the plastic bag containing the letter opener, and perhaps a critical set of fingerprints, out of my pocket. My law school degree, police experience, and common sense were all telling me to open the bag and collect the prints. There was neither an established chain of custody for this piece of potential evidence nor a prayer of eventually being able to use whatever we found as evidence at a trial of someone who could afford to hire a decent criminal attorney. I motioned Vincent over to take a look.

"Did you bring a fingerprint kit with you on this trip, Vincent?" I asked.

"Claro! Of course I did. You know the agency motto, 'Don't leave home without it'," he replied with a smile.

He returned in a minute or two with a small leather case. In another moment he had donned a pair of latex gloves and was carefully removing the letter opener from the bag. Fine grey powder was applied with a small, fine brush. Like magic, fingerprints appeared on the metallic surface, clearly visible in the sunlight pouring through the kitchen window. Vincent carefully photographed the prints using a special App on his smart phone.

I gave him Barbara Kaufman's phone number, which he typed into the App. A brief e-mail added where the prints had come from and their significance, as well as suggesting a search of the San Francisco and Oakland police and the California Bar Association files in addition to the FBI's database. With a click the package was fully digitized and on its way to the FBI agent's cell phone.

I waited ten minutes before I called Barbara Kaufman to update her about the entire conversation I'd had with brother-in-law Francis, and my interpretation of what it really meant to our suddenly burgeoning racketeering and murder case. She promised to fast track identifying the fingerprints as well as she could.

"How about all of us walking over next door to visit Trilby and Horace Cantwell again. If anyone around here has the answers we're looking for about what happened in Winters a generation or two ago, it'll be them. At the very least, they should know which of the local winemakers likes to gossip about the good old days."

"Should I be nervous about getting shot at every time I go outside, Roger?" Sherry asked. She was completely serious, once again showing signs of the stress she'd been under since Wally's disappearance and the shooting at the winery.

"I think we're all safe in broad daylight, Sherry. But I'd be super careful where I went at night, and that includes staying away from the windows after dark if the lights are on in the room and the curtains aren't pulled tight. I have a pretty good idea of who shot Jason, so we can take some precautions, but I'm not going to lie to you about the dangers here."

"Who is it you suspect, Roger?" she asked immediately.

"Thinking I know who it is isn't the same as being able to prove it, Sherry. Until we have the proof we need to put our shooter in jail I'm not going to make any accusations I might come to regret later."

We walked quickly through the vineyard and field to the neighbors' house, Sherry and I walking close together, with Vincent on point looking for anything suspicious. Carefully avoiding the road so as to be less visible to passersby or anyone in the winery itself, we cut across the corner of the vineyard and the grassy field separating the Fortune property from its neighbor to the west.

Trilby answered the door when Sherry rang the bell. "This is a pleasant surprise," exclaimed Trilby. "What can I do you for?"

Sherry took the lead. "My friend Roger wants to ask you a couple more questions if you don't mind."

"Surely," she answered. "Come on in and rest your feet. Can I get anyone a cup of coffee?" she asked, leading us into her small, but functional, kitchen.

Sherry declined politely. "We won't be here that long."

I spoke directly to Trilby as we all sat down around her well-worn kitchen table, decorated with a makeshift vase that had previously been a Mason jar containing freshly picked wildflowers. "We're actually looking for someone who would be knowledgeable about the local wine industry in Winters back a while ago, when Wally was a kid growing up. Do you know anyone here in town who could tell us about some of the winery owners back then?"

"I'd like to help you myself," replied Trilby. "But those weren't the social and economic circles Howard and I were part of. You need a couple of the wealthier families here in town. Now let me think. Who would have been involved in wine making and the country club set back then?"

The old woman was lost in thought, perhaps reliving the long ago past, for a couple of minutes before she continued. "None of the bigger wineries in town except the Fortune's go back that far. The other big ones here now are either new in the last ten years or are owned by big corporations who bought up the old operations. You're probably looking for the descendants of a family who sold their winery a generation ago, even if it hasn't been making wines for a long time.

"Harold," she called. "Can you come in here please? I need your help."

Her husband shuffled in. He'd obviously been listening to the conversation from the next room, as he answered my question immediately. "You might want to check out Dr. Samuel Maunders, who has a practice over on Railroad Avenue. He's delivered and fixed babies and parents here in town for almost forty years. I think his daddy or his uncle owned a winery here in town in the old days."

"Thank you very much," I said sincerely. "That sounds exactly like what I'm looking for."

Harold stared shrewdly at me. "You are going to come back when you find out what you're looking for and tell us old coots what this is all about, aren't you, Son?"

"You have my promise, Sir." I replied.

I did a bit of magic on the Internet and dialed the office number for Dr. Maunders. His receptionist answered on the first ring. "Doctor's office. How may I help you?"

I gave my name and told her I wanted to see the doctor as soon as possible. She replied, "If you can get here in the next ten minutes he has an opening to see a patient."

We were there in eight minutes. The doctor's office was in an old brick building west of The Buckhorn, about halfway between the street corner and an old bridge, recently remodeled and widened, over Putah Creek. A small, but attractive, park was directly across the street, right next to a city parking lot where we left the car.

Vincent rang the doorbell. We walked into a large foyer with a staircase leading to the second floor on my right. The receptionist was sitting at her desk between the staircase and the doctor's office working on an appointment calendar. The remainder of the space was open, except for a couple of chairs and a table with old magazines scattered on the top for patients waiting for the doctor to see them.

The empty space created a narrow hall giving visitors access to the doctor's office. Access to the staircase was blocked off with a velvet rope suspended between the newel posts bearing a wooden placard saying 'residence'. A distinguished looking gentleman in his early sixties, about my height, with a full head of graying hair, wearing an old-fashioned white coat, greeted me with a handshake. "What can I do to help you today, Mr. Bowman?"

"I have a couple of questions you might be able to answer for me, Dr. Maunders. Do you have an office where we might sit down and talk for five or ten minutes, please?"

The doctor nodded, leading us into his small but comfortable office separated from the reception area by a set of French doors with privacy curtains hanging on the inside. A former living room had been converted to an examination room accessible by another set of curtained French doors on the right side of the office. Diplomas and family pictures decorated the office wall on the left side. The doctor sat behind his desk patiently waiting for me to explain why we were here. It took a moment while we found chairs.

"I'm a detective working with the FBI investigating the murder of Wally Fortune. The man with me is my colleague Vincent Romero. I don't know if you've met Sherry Fortune, Wally's widow, before, but this is her."

"I'm sorry for your loss, Mrs. Fortune," he said politely. "How may I help you, Mr. Bowman? I assume you chose me to interview for some particular reason."

My gut was telling me he was trustworthy and would be a lot more helpful if I told him the truth. "Our investigation of the murder is taking us back into the past. I understand you're descended from one of the early winemaking families here in Winters. I was hoping you might be completely frank with me today while I test out a theory of why Wally might have been killed. I'm not looking to assign blame to people for choices they made in a very different time, just to catch a murderer who killed his latest victim last week."

The doctor nodded again. I had the sense he knew what I'd be asking and was letting me know he'd give me at least some of the answers I was looking for.

It seemed like a good time to get back to the honest approach. "I assume as a physician you hear a lot of confidential information and are able to keep it to yourself?"

Maunders nodded affirmatively.

"We have evidence linking Wally's death to some previous unsolved killings. We also have evidence there was a criminal conspiracy that forced Wally's family into co-operating with some bad people in a large, and ongoing, money laundering scheme a long time ago. I need to know whether any of the other major wineries in Winters became involved in similar schemes with the same people, and who exactly these racketeers were and are."

Dr. Maunders looked thoughtful as he weighed the implications of what I told him. "You're trusting me a lot for a complete stranger, Mr. Bowman. Your faith in me gives me a strong feeling I can trust you as well. I think I can help you with some of what you're looking for, but not all of it.

"The publicly stated reason my father sold his winery was to be able to afford sending me to medical school. The real reason was he was tired of being cheated and threatened by the people who were running the same racket at the Fortune Winery, and at least two other small wineries here in town."

After a short pause he continued. "Wally's and my father imagined the Napa Valley model of all the winery owners co-operating to make the best possible wines to popularize the regional appellation might work here. The owners all met once a month at our house to discuss business and winemaking. That's how I know a couple of others, as well as the Fortune family, were involved in the scheme when I was still in my teens."

"Thank you. That's valuable information and confirms my theory," I said. "Do you know anything about who the criminals behind the money laundering scheme are, or were?"

The doctor was lost in his thoughts about the past for a moment before he answered. "I'm sorry, but I can't help you there. I never met any of them. They only dealt with my father, who passed away several years ago. And the other two small winery owners are long since out of business and moved away from Winters years ago. I'll give you their names but I don't know if either of them are still alive."

"I have only one more question for you, Doctor Maunders. Did your father, or any of the other winery owners, ever contact the police to ask for their help?"

"Yes, they did. The city of Winters has its own small police force. The Police Chief those days was Joshua Stewart, the current Sheriff's father. He wasn't at all helpful, and in fact accused my father of tax evasion and threatened to turn him in to the IRS if he ever came back to the police with his story. I think we had a crook in charge of the police force then, exactly the same as we do now that his son is the sheriff."

He scribbled a couple of names on a small piece of paper, which he handed to me. Then he stood and shook hands to indicate the interview was over.

I thanked him for his time before driving back to the house.

My phone dinged that a text message was waiting. Barbara had written, "Good get on the fingerprints, Roger. We found the fingers and are waiting for the necessary warrants before proceeding."

I called the hospital. Jason had been upgraded from serious to good condition. Dr. Canyon wanted to discuss logistics about his release with me at my convenience.

I asked Vincent to see if he could find out anything about the current whereabouts of the two former winery owners whose names Dr. Maunders had scribbled on his pad. "I'm going to drive to the hospital to see Jason and his doctor. Please stay here and keep an eye on Sherry while you try to track down those names we got from Dr. Maunders.

"When I get back I think we can celebrate having a new manager hired for the winery with a heart–to–heart talk with Clay Ballard. I've been putting this off until Sherry didn't need him here at the winery, just in case he decides to bolt after our talk. But he's not indispensable any more, so his temporary immunity isn't in force now."

I took the familiar drive to the medical center, parking in the garage alongside the main entrance. I had no trouble finding my way to the Medical Intensive Care Unit, where I found Dr. Canyon on duty.

"Hello, Roger," he greeted me with a handshake. "The news about your friend Jason's condition is definitely better today. If he continues to improve at this rate we should be able to release him to a regular hospital room this evening. I'd guess another day or two after that he'll be ready to go home. How does this plan sound to you?"

"That's the best news I've had all day, Doctor Canyon."

The doctor's facial expression changed from pleasant greeting mode to more serious as he looked me directly in the eye. "Of course, there are a few buts," he continued. "The first but is he lives in Los Angeles, right?"

"Yes," I replied.

"No flying allowed until the lungs have had a few more weeks to heal. He can travel home by train or car only. And he needs an adult companion with him at all times just in case something happens en route. I'd prefer he stay away from crowds and germs, so travel by car, especially a large, comfortable car, is preferred. Can you do this?"

"Yes, I can."

Canyon spoke slowly, for emphasis. "The second but is an adult companion with him at all times, 24/7, once he gets there. Can you arrange for nursing service or something like that at his home?"

I had a good answer ready for that one. "I can do better. He can stay with us. Bruce, the former EMT who kept him alive immediately after he was shot, is our son's live-in nanny. He can keep an eye on Jason, as can my wife and I when he needs a break."

142

Dr. Canyon smiled. "Only one more but to go, Roger. The third and last but is, he'll need some high tech follow-up in a week or two and in a month or two. If I refer you to my equivalent at UCLA will you promise to have Jason seen by him on a schedule I'll lay out for all the various tests?"

This was another easy one for me to answer. "Sure. We only live ten or fifteen minutes away from the UCLA Medical Center so can get there and back as many times as we have to. Plus, my wife is a Professor at the UCLA Medical School."

Dr. Canyon relaxed visibly. "Is she a physician?" he asked.

"No," I replied. "She's a biochemist."

He led me to Jason's bed, where the patient greeted me with a weak wave and a weaker smile. He clearly recognized who I was, and all the important parts seemed to be working. But he was clearly still very weak and on strong pain medications.

I updated Jason on where the case was and who I suspected to be the shooter. By then he was noticeably tired and starting to nod off. I left, promising to return the next day.

Chapter 19. Return to the winery

Back in the family room of the house I updated Sherry and Vincent on Jason's progress and the need for one of us to drive him down to Los Angeles in the next few days.

Vincent had tracked down the two small winery owners who'd left Winters a long time ago by pulling credit history reports for everyone with either of the names currently living anywhere in California who seemed to be the right age and had worked in a business related in some way to alcoholic beverages. He had a single match for each name that also included a previous residence or business address in Winters, California.

Vincent handed me a piece of paper with the names on it. "I'm pretty sure I've tracked down both of your missing small winery owners from the bad old days in Winters. Irwin Salas is presently living in Anaheim, where he makes a very good living from a retail wine and liquor store he owns there. Michael Felton is also making a very good living these days as the enologist at a winery in San Luis Obispo making high-end Pinot Noir wines. I've got their phone numbers if you want to call either or both of them. You may want to wait until this evening before you do that. I think I can reconstruct both of their histories in a lot more detail if you give me some more time on the Internet."

Walking into the kitchen, I grabbed a cup of coffee while I thought through the choices. "I'll give you a lot longer than that to nail down whatever you can about them Vincent. I think I'll be the one driving Jason back to L.A. in a couple of days. If I were either of the former winery owners you found I'm pretty sure they'd be a lot more willing to talk to me in person than over the phone. And please make sure you check whether there are any records of sales for either of those old wineries on the Internet or at the courthouse. The buyer's names on those might be very interesting."

I turned to Sherry. "Would you be comfortable driving down to L.A. with Jason and me, and staying there where I know you'll be safe until we clean up this mess here?"

"I'm sorry, Roger, but I just can't do that now," Sherry replied. "I have a new manager coming on board at the winery and a new crop of grapes to harvest and start making wine from. Even with Clay Ballard's help training the new manager, I have to be here to make business decisions both on the financial and the wine sides of things. There's no way I can leave this operation for a week or two, or even longer, at this time of the year and expect to come back to a financially viable business."

I considered the implications of Sherry's answer. "Then I guess it's time for me to rethink questioning Clay for now, or for the foreseeable future. I don't know

145

how much he could or would actually tell us about the winery back when his father was managing it, but maybe we can find out the same details from Salas and Fenton. I don't think we want to risk rocking his boat until your new manager is up to speed and can actually manage the winery on a day-to-day basis for you. If he decided to up and quit on you anytime before you have complete confidence in putting Carol Marshall in charge to run the show, you could have a major disaster on your hands."

I turned back to Vincent. "That means you have to stay here guarding the client's body and continuing the local investigation, Vincent, at least for the next week or so. Can you handle spending all of that time here rather than at home?"

Vincent smiled. "I'll have to make peace with my wife, but she's used to these kinds of things happening in our profession. Maybe she'd like to come up for a vacation, and a chance to see what Northern California looks like. Would that be OK with you, Sherry?"

"Of course," she replied. "The house is large enough to remodel into a Bed and Breakfast some day, and I must admit I've been thinking about doing that to generate a little more income from the place some time after all of this mess is over."

I called Barbara Kaufman to update her on Jason's condition and my plan to move him back to our house in Los Angeles for rest and recuperation. She listened politely until I had finished with my plans before switching the topic to the fingerprints on the letter opener.

She could barely hide the excitement in her tone. "Congratulations, Roger. You finally got the official attention of the FBI leadership in Washington in your case. The fingerprints belong to Harold Fong, a well-known local criminal attorney here in the City. His father, Victor Fong, has had his dirty fingers in every organized crime activity involving Chinese gangs in Oakland and The City for the past 50 years, especially drugs and prostitution. Grandpa Fong's record as the local Tong leader who organized the drug dealers in San Francisco's and Oakland's Chinatowns goes back 75 years.

"The FBI has been after the Fongs for most of those 75 years with nary a conviction for anything to show for thousands of hours of investigations. Your case has certainly attracted their attention."

"Hmmm," I thought aloud. "It's interesting that Francis didn't remember or comment on Smith and Brown's ethnicity when he was telling me about them. I suspect he probably prevaricated a little bit about the nature of the relationship. Do you think he might be dumb enough to see the FBI as a solution to his long-term entanglement with some very nasty people?"

"Anything is possible at this stage, Roger," she replied. "As of now, the FBI's interest is in a potential RICO case involving large scale extortion and money laundering by the largest gang on the West Coast dealing in drugs imported from Asia. Some of the higher-ups are already drooling over what's out there for the FBI to supplement their budget under the current asset forfeiture rules for cases like this. And some of the old-timers are drooling over the chance to drag the Fong family into court and tie them up in legal knots for the next few years."

I thought about the pros and cons, deciding not to clue Barbara into the possible witnesses living in Southern California, Salas and Fenton, who needed interviewing. At least not yet, not until I'd had the first chance to talk to each of them. I trusted the Kaufman sisters to treat us fairly and honestly, and our part of the case with respect. But, as soon as the FBI hierarchy in Washington, D.C. became involved, it would become much more difficult to tell the good guys from the bad guys. We'd be pushed out of the investigation while career bureaucrats grabbed whatever glory they could and control was fought over by agents more concerned about their careers than about justice for the victims.

"What's the FBI going to be doing now?" I asked. "I don't want to work at cross purposes to the agency."

'What do we usually do?" she answered. "We'll follow the money trail you so helpfully pointed us toward, probably mostly from here in San Francisco and Oakland and probably more top down than bottom up. For the near future, at least, the Winters part of the case is a good place for you to focus your investigation."

"I'll be driving Jason back to L.A. in a couple of days, but leaving Vincent Romero here to keep Sherry safe and to continue the historical parts of the investigation. I'll call and stay in touch if we learn anything else you should know, and would, of course, appreciate your keeping me in the loop."

We said good-byes and hung up.

I called Suzanne to update her on my plans and make sure everything was ready for Jason as a houseguest for an indeterminate time.

Then I grabbed a pad and sat down to do some serious thinking. I started by constructing a timeline of events, starting in Winters with Wally's birth.

It didn't take me too long to get bored. I decided to visit Francis again. Maybe he'd have some more answers for me.

I parked the car on the street several buildings down from Francis' before walking back and climbing the stairs to his second floor office. I checked and the door wasn't locked so walked right in, skipping the part where I was supposed to knock. Francis sat behind his desk, not looking at all surprised to see me enter. In fact, he looked downright pleased.

What didn't fit into this picture of a normal business day at the office were the two gorillas in slacks and sport jackets sitting on chairs against the wall at either side of the desk. Both at least my height, both outweighing me by at least fifty pounds, both Caucasian, both wearing the facial scars of professional boxers who had taken a lot of punches in their careers. I didn't see any telltale bulges of guns in shoulder holsters, so it looked like I was going to be taught a lesson with their fists today. Or else they carried their pistols in belt holsters, which would only be a threat after they stood up.

The setup screamed in my head, "*Attack immediately! They might have guns!*"

My legal training screamed back in my head, "*If you attack them, that's assault and battery, potentially a felony. Wait a bit and let one or both of them come to you and take the first swing. Then it's self-defense.*"

The tableau remained frozen for a long time. Or it seemed like a long time. It was probably only a few seconds. Long enough to plan my moves if it was just fists, and contingency countermoves if someone pulled a gun. So I was ready when the gorilla on the left stood up abruptly, his chair banging against the wall as he began to walk toward me. Obviously this was the part where I was supposed to start trembling in terror and pleading for mercy. Or it might have been that way in the movies. In real life I'd almost been looking forward to this chance to release some of my accumulated anger and frustration at some really not too bright criminals, including Sherry's brother-in-law Francis.

The gorilla continued approaching me slowly, savoring my imagined fear. He got close before swinging a big roundhouse right that would have put me down for the count if it had connected. It was painfully slow, making it all too apparent where those scars had come from. He clearly wasn't expecting any real resistance. I had a special surprise prepared for him, slipping the punch easily as I came up inside his guard. I made a judo half fist, hitting him as hard as I could in the solar plexus, a punch aimed at an imaginary target well behind him to ensure that the blow landed at full velocity.

As he started to fold over I snuck a look at the other gorilla on the right, still sitting in his chair not yet comprehending what was going on as he was screened from seeing my blow delivered. That meant I had plenty of time to hit the first gorilla again, this time with the edges of both my hands where they would do the most damage without risk of killing him, directly down onto the clavicle at the base of the neck breaking the bone in two places.

I disengaged quickly, starting to move toward the rapidly rising threat on my right. I was a lot faster than he was. We converged, with him just straightening up out of the chair as he reached behind his back for what I assumed was a gun. I couldn't think of any good reason to wait to find out. He got a karate kick directly at his left knee that dislocated the knee, causing him a great deal of pain while knocking him completely off balance. I followed up with a roundhouse kick to the side of his head that knocked him unconscious, presumably with a concussion to remember me by.

I stooped by the second thug and checked.

"What have we here?" I asked rhetorically for Francis' benefit, carefully removing and pocketing the 9mm pistol with a two-inch barrel using my handkerchief so as not to disturb any fingerprints present. I also removed his wallet putting it into another pocket for future reference. I went back to the softly moaning first thug and found the duplicate pistol still in its holster in the small of his back, borrowing his handkerchief to take and pocket his gun. Another wallet went into my now bulging pocket.

Then I sat down in front of Francis' desk. He looked stunned.

"I'm sorry to bother you, Francis, but it looks like you were expecting me so it can't be too much of a bother. I had a few more questions I wanted to ask you. Do you have a minute or two to answer them, please?"

He didn't answer. How rude!

"I was hoping you could give me a physical description of the two lawyers you told me about, Smith and Brown. I don't imagine these gentlemen on the floor are lawyers, are they? And if the cat's got your tongue and you don't answer I'll break your arm and swear you waved a pistol at me while I was disarming your friends who attacked me. Am I making myself clear?"

"How d-did you d-do that?" he stammered.

"That isn't what I asked you and I'm losing my patience. Last chance, Francis. What did Smith and Brown look like?"

Francis looked like he'd swallowed a frog. "T-they just l-looked like men in their t-thirties wearing s-suits and t-ties. They d-dressed like l-lawyers. That's all I c-can r-remember."

"Wrong answer, Francis. I'm sure Sherry will be embarrassed with a brother-in-law in jail. But that's your choice and you just made it. Have a good day."

"B-but what am I s-supposed to d-do with my t-two c-clients you just b-beat up on my f-floor?" he whined.

"I'd dial 911 and make up a story. They don't have any I.D. so you can tell Sheriff Stuart they're Smith and Brown. They sort of look like Smith and Brown in the fairy tale you told me, don't they?"

I left Francis' office and drove home, assuming the sheriff would find me there if he was stupid enough to try to arrest me based on whatever cock and bull story Francis was going to tell him.

Vincent carefully checked who rang the doorbell before letting me into the house. I quickly told him what had occurred at Francis' office. He and I put on Latex gloves before handling the evidence. We started with the two wallets, chock full of cash and I.D.s for Joseph Smith and William Jones. Not quite Smith and Brown, but close.

I speculated about whether there was any irony in the coincidence of Smiths here. After all, it's a common name. I finally decided Francis lacked the imagination and intellect to invent names on the spot and just picked the nearest hoodlum he knew to be the namesake for one of the mysterious lawyers.

Then we checked the guns. Both clean, not recently fired. Vincent got beautiful sets of fingerprints from both wallets and both guns. With the aid of his smart phone app the fingerprints were en route to Barbara Kaufman with a covering e-mail of explanation in less than ten minutes.

Just in time to hear the approaching sirens.

"Don't worry, Vincent. Sheriff Stuart didn't have nearly enough time to get a warrant and there aren't any exigent circumstances for an illegal entry or for an arrest. I hope we can just sit down and have a quiet chat after we put all the guns and wallets away."

Chapter 20. Sheriff Stuart

Sheriff Stuart apparently had read the eighth chapter in "Detecting for Dummies", the one that instructed use of loud, imperious, and demanding knocking on the door to terrorize suspects. He knocked loudly and long. I wasn't terrorized.

I opened the door just wide enough for us to see one another. Sheriff Stuart, backed by two of his biggest deputies, stood on my (well, Sherry's actually) doorstep, demanding entry.

"May I see your warrant, please?" I asked politely.

"Let us in! I don't need a warrant. You're under arrest!" he replied, notably less politely.

"In point of fact, you do need a warrant either to arrest me or to come into this house," I replied, still keeping my tone polite.

"If there's anything I hate worse than a big city private eye throwing his weight around in my town it's an amateur lawyer telling me what I can and can't do in my own jurisdiction," he blustered. "Now let us in voluntarily or we'll make you let us in."

I noted a certain lack of enthusiasm for the second option on the faces of the two deputies who had seen the carnage in Francis' office. At least they had a bit of common sense.

"I'm not an amateur lawyer," I corrected Sheriff Stuart, "In fact I'm a professionally licensed attorney in the State of California. Trust me on this: I know the relevant law here a lot better than you do. Unless you have a search warrant for the house or an arrest warrant for me, it's time for you to turn around and investigate any alleged crimes that might have occurred before you assume the liability that goes with falsely arresting people for those alleged crimes."

I was on a roll here so just before slamming the door in his face I told him. "After you've had a chance to come to speed on what actually happened today, you might want to telephone me with a polite invitation for a cup of coffee at one of the restaurants downtown. If you tell me what results you've obtained from your deputy's investigations of Wally Fortune's murder and Jason Culpepper's attempted murder, we might also discuss any concerns you have with my investigation."

It took a while, and some intense discussion with the two deputies, but Sheriff Stuart departed without any additional incidents.

Vincent and I got back to work. He started running the I.D. information for Smith and Jones through several online databases we had access to via our P.I.

licenses and a large annual fee. If either of the two gorillas had a criminal record anywhere in California, we'd know about it some time in the next hour or two.

It was a slow process, but we got hits on both of the hoodlums. Each of them had a long criminal record in various San Francisco Bay Area jurisdictions. Smith, who had been a professional boxer of no particular distinction, had most of his convictions in San Francisco and the South Bay cities. He spent some time in San Quentin after felony convictions for armed robbery and for assault with a deadly weapon (his fists, when he was still a professional boxer).

Jones, who seemed to have skipped professional boxing on his way to becoming a career criminal, had mostly gotten caught in Oakland or the East Bay court jurisdictions. He earned felony convictions for assault and manslaughter, both of which sent him to Folsom prison for his big time penitentiary experience before his twenty-first birthday.

Both worked their way up the criminal food chain to become small time muscle for the Fong Family enterprises after graduation from the California State Prison System. Smith and Jones had both been implicated as enforcers for Victor Fong. These allegations were never proven in a court of law thanks to the services of Harold Fong, who seemed to represent them for all of their arrests after they joined the Fong Family businesses.

****

After a brief discussion, Vincent and I decided to return the pistols I'd taken from Smith and Jones to the Sheriff. They were nice pistols, but the possibility existed they had been used in a crime so it wouldn't be a good idea for one of us to be caught carrying either of them.

Almost exactly two hours after he'd left the house Sheriff Stuart called with a polite invitation to me for coffee with him at the cafe across the street from The Buckhorn. He couched the invitation with a touch of humor. "Please join me for a cup of coffee. I promise not to try to arrest you again. In fact, I think I owe you an apology. The agenda will be updating each other on our respective investigations."

"Can I bring my partner, Vincent Romero, with me?" I asked to test the waters for his level of sincerity.

"Sure!" he replied pleasantly. "I'll even buy his cup of coffee, too."

****

I grabbed my gym bag containing exercise clothes, towels, and sneakers from the back of the car I'd just parked across Railroad Avenue from the Buckhorn Restaurant. Slipping the bag over my shoulder, I led Vincent across the street to the café, walking in front of the large outdoor pizza oven directly across the street from the Buckhorn.

We walked into the cafe, old booths against the wall on our right, a dining counter with stools on the left. A glass case with pies and desserts stood waist high just inside the door by the cash register against the wall in front of the counter. Lots of colors: red brick walls, varnished wood counters, pale tile floors, baby blue settees and pink tables in the booths. There were two additional rooms with tables and chairs in the back.

Jeb Stuart stood up just inside one of the additional rooms in back to shake hands as we entered the small cafe. "It's quieter back here and we won't have a big audience listening in," the sheriff explained.

I checked. There weren't any deputies lurking with machine guns and mortars, at least not that I could see in the cafe.

"What's in the bag?" asked the sheriff as I placed it on the seat beside me at our small table for four and sat down.

"Just my exercise stuff. I was hoping you could tell me if there's a good fitness place here in town or whether I have to drive all the way down to Davis to get a good workout."

Sheriff Stuart gave me a skeptical look, stood, and unzipped my bag as he asked, "May I?" He found exercise clothes and towels, of course. He sat down with a slightly less suspicious look on his face.

'Good camouflage,' I thought. 'Now he's ready to believe I'm just killing time on the client's dime since I haven't found anything in this investigation.'

We shook. No macho squeezes, just a normal handshake. A similar shake with Vincent while they introduced themselves followed. A waitress was hovering over our table before I had time to sit down.

"Can I get you gentlemen anything?" she asked.

Vincent and I ordered just coffee. The sheriff followed suit. We looked carefully at each other for a few seconds, deciding who was the predator and who was the prey here. Finally the sheriff broke the silence.

"I'm sorry for the attempted roust at the winery before. I was out of line."

"Good start," I thought. "No harm, no foul," I said. "What changed your mind about me?"

"I reacted to seeing a couple of severely damaged men being carted off on stretchers and Frank Fortune telling me you'd viciously attacked them with no provocation. After you educated me about the relevant law I did what I should have done at first, ran your name and the other two men's fingerprints through the state database. You beat the tar out of two very nasty dudes, Mr. Bowman. I assume in self-defense when you were provoked?"

"That sounds about right," I responded. "What are you planning on doing about Frank, the lawyer, who filed a false report among other misdemeanors he committed today?"

The sheriff smiled. "Not much of anything unless you want to press charges, Mr. Bowman. Frank's lived here in town a long time; none of you have."

I was being told, 'Forget it'. 'Not this time,' I thought.

This was a good time to get one of my agenda items completed. "That reminds me. I have two pistols I confiscated from those two convicted felons who will deny possession of the guns, which would be a felony. I've handled them carefully, so you'll find each of their fingerprints on their own guns, which will make any denial of ownership a lot less plausible when they go to trial or make their plea bargains. I'd appreciate your taking the guns off my hands when we go outside. You might want to test fire them and see if the bullets match any unsolved shootings in someone's jurisdiction."

"Hmmm," said the sheriff. "It sounds like you recognized those two men before you beat them senseless."

"Bad guess, Sheriff Stuart. I actually identified them and learned about their criminal pasts from the sets of fingerprints I sent to the FBI office in San Francisco after Vincent recovered them from the guns."

"There's that FBI connection again. Want to tell me about it?" the sheriff asked.

"Not now," I replied. "Maybe some other time."

The waitress refilled the cups with fresh coffee.

"What can you tell me about the activities of the Fong Family here in Winters over the last thirty or forty years?" I asked casually, more to see his reaction than expecting an answer.

He would be a lousy poker player, I observed. For several seconds he looked like he'd swallowed, or smelled, something very unpleasant.

154

Then he recovered. "Who? I don't think I know anybody named Fong. I don't guess I can tell you much of anything. Maybe it's time we went out and collected those guns you took."

Sheriff Stuart took the lead, clearly expecting us to follow him out of the cafe. It was time to do my magic trick with the gym bag. Shielding what I was doing from the other patrons and waitresses, I used my napkin to pick up the sheriff's coffee cup. Getting the cup safely wrapped, I put it in the bag with the convenient towels to cushion the china mug from impact. I took the cup out of the café and ultimately back to the house. With luck, it would come in handy when needed.

The sheriff walked over to an unmarked car parked directly in front of the side of the cafe where it faced Railroad Avenue and opened the trunk, removing a couple of large Ziploc bags and an attaché case. "Lead on," he commanded.

We walked across the street to our borrowed car. I popped the trunk and pointed to a plain brown paper bag in the right front corner by the spare tire. He looked into the bag, nodded, and picked it up. "I'll process these pieces of evidence when I get back to the station," he promised with highly questionable sincerity.

"There's just one more thing, Sheriff. You promised me an update on your investigations into Wally Fortune's murder and Jason Culpepper's attempted murder."

"Yes, I did, didn't I?" replied Sheriff Stuart contemplatively, if not grammatically. "We recovered a bullet from Fortune's body, which I sent to the State Police Laboratory in Sacramento. We're still waiting to hear back from them. My deputies recovered the bullet that went through your friend Culpepper from the door of the winery. That went to the State Lab about the same time as the other bullet. We're still waiting for those results too.

"Now you know what we know about both crimes. And you promised me an update on your investigations, Mr. Bowman. What are you going to tell me?"

That was easy. "I've been counting on your investigations to give us the answers we're looking for, Sheriff. I'm a little disappointed they seem to be going so slowly."

"There's just one more thing I wanted to ask you, too, Mr. Bowman," the sheriff responded. "You put two hardened criminals, one a former professional fighter, into the hospital with your bare hands. You say they attacked you. But I don't see a mark on you, even a little scratch. How did you do that little trick?"

"Just lucky, I guess," I answered with an insincere smile.

The Sheriff turned on his heel and drove off. Vincent and I drove back to the winery.

Sherry, who had locked herself securely into the house at my request with strict orders not to admit anyone until we got back, let us in. Leading us to the kitchen she offered coffee, which we both refused for a change. Our session with the sheriff had fully caffeinated both of us.

"Can you give me a ride over to one of the car rental agencies so I can rent a vehicle to drive Jason down to Los Angeles tomorrow morning?" I asked.

"Don't be silly, Roger. Pick the biggest and most comfortable car here and take it for your own use for as long as you need it. How long do you expect it to be before you get back?"

I made a quick calculation. "I'd guess three or four days, maybe a bit more. It depends how long it takes to get Jason set up in our place where I hope he can do the next stage of his recovery. I also have two possible witnesses to interview and each will take a day because they live in opposite directions from Los Angeles. And I need to give Suzanne and Bruce a break from childcare. Don't worry. Vincent can do everything necessary to keep this investigation moving until I get back."

Vincent and I discussed what he'd be doing in my absence. "Your first priority is keeping Sherry safe. From what I've seen so far, the biggest threat is a sniper with a rifle. You might want to make sure she gets in and out of cars inside the closed garage and keep her as far away from all the other obvious areas of vulnerability as you can. You should try to convince her to spend a few days at her other house in Carmichael, which would probably be safer than here.

"Otherwise, I think maybe you should continue reconstructing the history of the local wineries via the Internet. I'm convinced the answer to who killed Wally and shot Jason lies in the past. And if the killer ever comes to trial, we'll need to establish a motive. If anyone can dig that out of old records and newspaper stories, it's you."

I thought about contingencies and potential problems. "The trickiest part of protecting Sherry for you will be if she has to be here doing something at the winery. You probably have until the new manager takes over before that becomes an issue. I'll try to be back here before then."

I called Barbara Kaufman, who picked up on the first ring. After the pleasantries I explained why I'd called. "Two things, Barbara. First, I'll be checking Jason out of the hospital tomorrow morning and driving him down to our place where Bruce and Suzanne can take over nursing him. The other is Sheriff Stuart told me they found a bullet in Wally Fortune's body, which he says they sent to the California State Crime Lab where it's waiting for its turn in the queue for analysis. If he's telling the truth, maybe you want to offer the FBI's services to the state lab to help them with their backlog?"

She promised to follow up on this as soon as possible.

Chapter 21. The long drive south

I called the hospital at seven to ask about the checkout procedure for Jason.

"The attending physician, Dr. Canyon, has to examine him and check him out. He should be here at eight to start the process. Mr. Culpepper should be ready to go some time after that."

Foolish me! I got to fight the peak of commuter traffic down I-5 and across Route 50 to get there at 8:30. Driving directly into the parking garage beside the hospital entrance, I found a slot for the car in the crowded structure. The garage's exit by the cashier's cage was directly across the driveway from the main entrance to the new, clean, white 12-story University Hospital. I made my way to the information desk at the right rear of the lobby where I was told nothing had been done, but they could begin the patient discharge process immediately. The woman at the desk was polite, if not particularly helpful, and gave me a card containing the password to access the local WiFi. The only thing they let me do was approve the hospital bill on Jason's behalf.

I found a place to sit in a comfortably cushioned faux leather chair by the restrooms at the back of the lobby where I could plug in my computer, access the hospital's WiFi network, and address the backlogged e-mail and paperwork I'd accumulated over the last few days. At about 11:30 a friendly nurse told me to grab a quick lunch, pay the ransom to collect my car from the garage, and drive back around to the front of the hospital to pick up my passenger. "Buy some bottled water while you're getting lunch. And you can fill this prescription for painkillers at the hospital pharmacy in the lobby. He'll need to take some painkillers several times during your drive to Los Angeles. He should be there ready to actually go home by the time you get back."

I finally connected with Jason in a wheelchair, discharged and ready to go, at noon. The nurse who handed him off to me commented that was a fast-track discharge. The process usually took longer. The nurse handed me several pages of instructions for Jason's care outside of the hospital. "Your friend is strong and obviously takes care of himself. Nature will heal him. All you need to do is keep him as comfortable as you can during the healing process and get him started on physical therapy as soon as he's ready to do anything physical."

Having sat in his wheelchair for about an hour before he was finally delivered to the hospital entrance, Jason was exhausted when I finally got him settled in the shotgun seat.

"Do you need anything before we start driving, or are you hungry?" I asked him.

"No. I think a short nap will be just the thing. After that, let's talk about the case and the arrangements for me in Los Angeles. I have a lot to be brought up to date on."

I took Route 50 west a short distance to the 5 South, where I worked my way over to the carpool lane, heading toward home at a sedate 70 mph. Jason started snoring gently somewhere between the hospital and the freeway. He started to wake up from his short nap less than an hour later.

"I feel guilty as heck, Roger," Jason complained weakly as we drove through Stockton on our way south. "I was going to give Connie tons of help with her new baby when she was born and now I can't even take care of myself!"

I explained to Jason about Connie's new male nanny who would be available 24/7 to help out. "And she's looking forward to helping nurse you back to health, Jason. I'd play the wounded warrior card for all it's worth when you see her, which I've heard rumors may be fairly frequently for a week or two after we get back to L.A."

There were several minutes of silence in response to my suggestion, followed by the sound of gentle snoring again.

After another hour of silence except for light snores, Jason picked up the conversation where we'd left off at Stockton as we drove past a huge feedlot on the other side of I-5. "What's it like with a woman you care for when she's about to have a baby or right after? Do you remember what Suzanne was like during that part?"

I chuckled. "Suzanne's not Connie and vice-versa, Jason. Everybody's different. But I think I can generalize. Connie feels like she has to do everything by herself and needs a lot of support. Right now, she's hoping you'll be one of the supporting cast, so to speak, as she transitions from widow to mother. And I don't mean support as in holding her up or carrying groceries. I mean emotional support. She's wrestling with a lot of guilt now. First she was married to Delbert and he died. Now she's dated you a couple of times and you almost died. Can you imagine where her self-esteem is on a scale of one to ten?"

Jason mulled that over. "That's crazy, Roger. What happened to her husband isn't related to what happened to me."

"It may be crazy in the logical sense, Jason. But it makes some kind of emotional sense to a very confused and highly hormonal woman who's a lot smarter than either you or I are, so you need to try to understand what's going on in her head if you want to help her. I don't care how badly shot up you were or how weak you feel, you're going to have to be the strong one in this relationship if you want it to last."

This time Jason seemed to stay awake, but maybe dozed off a bit through the most boring part of the drive through the ancient oil rigs scattered in sandy soil that filled the southern part of the San Joaquin Valley. We lapsed back into silence for a couple of hours, until shortly before we'd begin the ascent of the grapevine where we'd leave the Central Valley to cross over the mountains at Cajon Pass.

"My shoulder is telling me I should take a couple of pills pretty soon, Roger. And I'd love to use a restroom. Can we make a quick pit stop at Buttonwillow before we head up the Grapevine?"

"Sure," I replied. "Can you walk from the parking lot to the restaurant or will I need to find a wheelchair for you?"

Jason laughed. "I've spent the last two days at the hospital proving I can walk on my own. They wouldn't let me out till I could make the round trip from one end of the corridor to the other end at least twice. I'd guess I'm good for several hundred feet on my own, about double that distance with your help or a rest break in between laps."

"Are you hungry?" I asked him.

"I'm not sure. We can try a burger and see how it feels. But let's buy it to go. I'm looking forward to a nice bed and some TLC and don't want to waste a lot of time here."

I glanced at my watch. It had taken just under four hours to drive this far. If we kept going we'd be in a carpool lane when we hit the worst of the rush hour commuter traffic through the San Fernando Valley, so it made sense to buy a few burgers and get back on the road as fast as we could.

We stopped at the least crowded burger chain restaurant we could find. I ordered two burgers to go, as well as a coffee for me. We used the facilities while we waited. Back at the car, a tired and sore Jason sat back slowly and carefully into his seat. I handed him his plastic pill container, a bottle of water, and the bag of food. We were back on the 5 and speeding south ten minutes later.

Up and over the Grapevine, through Tejon Pass, back downhill through Santa Clarita and the San Fernando Valley we made good time thanks to the intermittent carpool lane and driving the opposite direction from the bulk of commuter traffic. I munched my burger and sipped my coffee during the flat parts of the trip. Jason ate half of his, not bad considering. I filled him in on what we'd learned about the case while he was in the hospital, emphasizing the importance of the ledgers he'd removed from the winery as the key wedge in an unraveling tale of murder and greed.

We chose the 405 at the fork where it separated from the 5, then drove up another piece of mountain through Sepulveda Pass and on down into the Los Angeles basin. The poor man's imitation of the Tower of Pisa, a chain motel, marked the Sunset Boulevard exit where we exited and drove east to Beverly Hills and our house arriving in plenty of time for a real dinner.

Bruce and Juliet waited at the top of the driveway to help me bring Jason into the house. Juliet's tail, a manic metronome, flashed frantically in greeting as she remained on a heel command at Bruce's side. He gave her a release command. A liver-ticked white tornado with dark patches on her head and tail ran toward me at full speed. At the last possible second she skidded to a halt directly in front of me, the metronomic tail a beating blur, waiting for me to properly acknowledge her overture. Moments later Juliet with her ears ruffled, head rubbed, flanks patted, and belly scratched was convinced I still loved her and sat down directly onto one of my feet.

"Hi, Roger," Bruce greeted me. "Don't worry, you don't have to scratch my tummy unless you want to."

I didn't particularly want to. "Hello Bruce. Good to see you too."

Bruce helped me get Jason settled into one of our guest bedrooms. "Do you need any medic-type help with anything, Jason?" Bruce inquired politely.

"Not tonight, Bruce. I'd appreciate some help with the wound dressing tomorrow or the next day, but should be able to do everything else myself. And I have to figure out how to set up my physical therapy, but probably not for a week or so. I assume that means finding a place with vacancies in their schedule and getting appointments set up now. Which probably means I'll need help with transportation until I can drive myself safely."

Suzanne greeted me warmly. "Surprise!" she announced. "We have an additional dinner guest due to arrive shortly, Connie Sherman. She needs to see Jason alive and walking with her own two eyes before she'll believe he's really getting better. And she wants to give him some of the personal touch in healing."

Suzanne rolled her eyes. "I do believe we've created a monster, Roger."

The doorbell rang and a Force 5 hurricane came through! A very pregnant Connie said perfunctory hellos before asking if she could see Jason. Suzanne led Connie to the proper guest bedroom before discretely disappearing.

Bruce announced dinner about half an hour later. Connie and Jason appeared holding hands as if this were Senior Prom night. We sat the two of them down at the dining room table, one limping and the other waddling. It was easy to forget that both of them were in their thirties and Connie had been married for several years and was currently getting ready to give birth to her first child.

"Corny, but cute," I whispered to Suzanne, who nodded her agreement.

Dinner discussion was initially about Jason's health, but he bravely pretended to be perfectly comfortable while Connie sliced his beef for him and buttered his roll in deference to his having one arm immobilized in a sling.

Over dessert I filled everyone in on all the details of the case from start to finish. I spoke mainly to Suzanne, including the bits and pieces of what we had found out. I tried to put the story into chronological order as best as I could, not the random order in which we had learned the relevant details as we now knew them. That took a while. Somewhere during my narrative I noticed the two love birds getting tired and bored. Jason, with Connie following directly behind like a somewhat disoriented mother hen, excused himself to lie down shortly after finishing his dessert.

I continued my narrative. Suzanne has the most logical mind I've ever encountered. I had the feeling that if I constructed the complex story chronologically she would draw the same conclusions I did.

Suzanne began to have that 'Eureka' look when I told her about the first visit by Smith and Brown to Francis Fortune many years ago. She switched to her 'Aha' look when I told her about what we'd found out about Smith and Jones from their I.D.s and fingerprints during my next visit to Francis' office. The imaginary light bulb over her head positively glowed when I explained their linkage to the Fong Family.

"Do you think you know who shot Jason and Wally?" she asked when I stopped for breath.

"Yes, I think so. But I don't know how to prove it yet, at least to the level of a court of law finding the killer guilty beyond a reasonable doubt."

"I think I know who, too, and I see the problem with proving it. But, and it's a big but, maybe Bruce and Juliet can help you out one more time here. There's one key piece of evidence that links the killer with the crimes."

Suzanne looked directly at Bruce, who had been listening carefully to my monologue. "Hey, Bruce, I have a hypothetical situation for you. Are you ready to give me the answer I want to hear?"

Bruce nodded. "If I can."

"Roger needs to find the rifle that matches the bullets removed from multiple victims. The problem here is the killer has had several years to find a good hiding

163

place for the rifle, so a casual search is highly unlikely to find it. That's where Juliet comes in. She should be able to sniff it out if there's something unique about the rifle we can ask her to detect.

"My first thought was training her to find something the suspects had worn or handled, or to the individuals themselves. But that won't work. All of the suspects have spent time in and around the winery or been there to investigate the murder, so everything in the immediate area will have their scent on it. So, my hypothetical is whether each style of rifle has a unique odor we can train her to. We have the bullets and a used cartridge casing so we should be able to guess the kind of rifle it was fired from, right?"

It took Bruce less than thirty seconds to address her hypothetical question. "Sorry, Suzanne. Not right. This killer is a pro. The first thing he or she would have done after getting away from the scene of the crime was clean the rifle. The only thing it will smell like is solvent and gun oil."

I saw Suzanne's 'Aha' look just as I got it. "How many rifles and handguns would you guess there are at the winery and house, Roger?"

"I haven't seen any," I responded. "Wally doesn't seem to have been a collector and I haven't seen any gun racks or gun safes in the house. And I doubt they leave guns hanging on the walls of the winery with all the tourists coming through there."

Suzanne turned back to Bruce. "How long do you think it would take Juliet to look for something that smelled of gun oil at the winery, at Sherry's house, at Francis' house, at the Sheriff's house, and at anyone else's house we can think of who might be a suspect in this case. All we'd need then is a fired bullet for ballistic testing. And I suspect the FBI can come up with warrants for taking all the guns you find for testing.

"If I were a clever killer with a rifle that could be traced back to me I'd probably hide it, not display it on a gun rack. That's where Juliet comes in. She should be able to find any concealed weapons, no matter how cleverly they're hidden."

Bruce thought it all through. "I'm sorry to rain on your parade, Suzanne, but that idea can't possibly work. There must be dozens, or even hundreds, of brands of gun oil on the market, each with a different scent. How do you plan to guess which one you want to send Juliet out to find?"

"Actually, it can work, Bruce," Suzanne argued. "We're talking about a very small town. There's only one gun shop in Winters and that's the place everyone there uses for all things gun. Let's go with the odds. We can check out what brand or brands of gun oil they stock, buy a can or cans, and send Juliet out to look for a match with those brands of oil. At worst, it will only be a few brands she'll need to sort out. Remember, she can hunt pheasant, chukar, quail, and squirrel at the same time. She can remember a lot of different scents simultaneously while she's looking for all of them."

"Can I borrow Bruce and Juliet for three or four days, Suzanne?" I asked.

"I think I can keep up with Robert for that long. And it looks like Connie can and will handle all the nursing care for Jason. But you want to do this as soon as possible. Connie looks like she's almost ready to pop."

Chapter 22. Tying up a few loose ends

I called Barbara Kaufman, told her what we needed, and asked if she could get the necessary search warrants issued for when I got back to Northern California. She didn't even ask me why, simply replying, "Yes, I'm pretty sure I can."

There were still two witnesses from long ago I had to interview. I'd start with Irwin Salas, the former winery owner who now owned a liquor store in Anaheim. Vincent hadn't been able to find any more details about the sale of his winery a long time ago. I thought about the pros and cons of calling ahead, deciding that taking him by surprise with an unannounced visit might be worth the risk of driving down to Orange County and not finding him at the store. If he didn't have time to prepare his script he wouldn't be reading from the script when I got there.

Gritting my teeth I opted for the traffic-clogged freeway system and a 2-hour, 37-mile drive from Beverly Hills to Anaheim. There was more traffic on clogged streets, but eventually I found Salas Wines and Liquors on a busy avenue downtown in an older, but gradually gentrifying, neighborhood. A convenient parking lot on the next block helped improve my mood. I entered the store, almost empty at this hour of the morning. Two clerks stood behind the counter. One of them was a young man with long stringy hair in his twenties. The older man was probably Irwin.

I walked over to the older gentleman. "Is there something I can help you with?" he asked politely.

I looked around the store. It was moderately large, with most of the name brand liquors safely shelved behind the counter. The cheaper booze and twelve-packs of the standard mass-produced beers were available on shelves lining the three aisles and the back wall that filled the rest of the space. "I'm looking for Mr. Salas. Irwin Salas. Is that you?"

He looked me over carefully, apparently deciding I meant him no harm. The day-to-day nature of his business probably made him a good judge of things like that. He nodded in the affirmative.

I'd also looked him over carefully. He was in his 60s, about five eight, turning to fat, dressed casually in baggy slacks that needed ironing and an aging sport shirt, glasses, thinning grey hair. My snap judgment was to tell him an edited version of the truth.

I handed him my business card as an I.D. "I'm a private investigator from Los Angeles, Mr. Salas, working on a very complicated case. My client owns a winery in Yolo County. In fact it's the old Fortune Winery in Winters, which you probably remember from your time there."

A look of alarm crossed Salas' face then disappeared.

"It's OK, Mr. Salas," I said reassuringly. "All I want from you is a little information from a long time ago. Nobody knows I'm here, or that you're here either. And nobody else needs to know who and where you are."

Salas looked resigned to his fate. "I always knew this day would come," he said reluctantly. "Can I trust you to protect my new identity?"

"Yes, you can, Sir," I replied, looking him directly in the eyes to project sincerity. "And, if you tell me what I think you are going to, I can also promise you that the people you're afraid of will be one step closer to going to jail for a very, very long time. I'm working closely with the FBI on this case, so we have some powerful allies in our corner."

"I'm about ready for a break. Why don't we grab an early lunch, which you can pay for, at the restaurant across the street while I try to answer your questions?"

He turned to the other clerk. "I'll be back in half an hour or so, Lionel. You can grab your lunch when I get back. OK?"

"Sure," Lionel agreed.

The restaurant was Viet-Namese, not unusual in this part of Anaheim. "Can I order for both of us, Mr. Bowman?" Salas asked after a quick glance at the business card I'd given him.

"Why not?" I thought. *"It might help him with his self confidence."*

"Please do. I'm far from an expert on this style of food."

'Not true, but might help with building trust,' I thought.

Irwin Salas ordered several dishes for us. While we waited for the food to be served he asked, "What exactly do you want me to tell you about, Mr. Bowman?"

'He's asking me how much I know so he can decide what to say to me,' I thought to myself. *'That's easy. Imply we know everything and just want to confirm the facts.'*

I laid it all out for him. The facts as we knew them of what had happened long ago when the extortionists had forced their way into the local winery business in Winters, the murder of Wally's father and the suspicious death of his mother, the similar events in Lodi, and the apparent involvement of a major Chinese gang from the Bay Area.

I explained we needed to know whatever details he could give me about the people who had threatened him so we could identify exactly who was part of the plot. And I wanted to know if he'd gone to the local police for help and, if so, what happened.

He nodded, thought for a bit, and started talking. I had guessed correctly what would encourage him to open up.

"I was just a kid then, halfway through college when my father died. I inherited a winery and a full-time job. I had to take over; there wasn't anyone else, and my mother and sister depended on the winery for their support. It took a while but I figured things out and had things going well enough to start looking for a manager so I could get back to the university and finish my degree. That's when it all hit the fan."

He paused to allow the waiter to serve us. Then he continued. "A couple of very big men came by to tell me I had to either sell them the winery outright at a price they'd determine or take on a silent partner who'd handle all the finances for me. Initially I said I'd have to think about it. They gave me a week to make up my mind.

"In those days Winters was really a small town and everyone who did anything with wine or grapes knew everyone else. I talked to a few of the other winery owners and learned this was just one of the costs of doing business for a few of them who went along with the scheme. A couple of others told me these were very bad men and I should sell out for whatever price they'd give me and to consider moving as far away as I could. One of them told me he was selling out and I should too."

There was another pause while he adroitly ate some of today's special with his chopsticks. "To tell you the truth I wasn't enjoying the 24/7 life of the small winery owner very much. I was about 20 and wanted to have a life. I made up my mind that if they offered me enough to take care of my family I'd take their offer. But they took that decision out of my hands. My mother and sister were killed in a car accident during the week I was deciding. It was a single car accident, highly suspicious. The official finding by our local police force was 'driver error', as our Chief of Police, Chief Stuart, explained to me when I went to the cops.

"Chief Stuart also told me to keep my mouth shut and my opinions to myself or he'd arrest me for obstruction of justice or whatever charge he could think up. And that's when I decided discretion was the better part of valor. I sold the winery for a ridiculously low price, too low to allow me to finish college. I buried my family, and moved down here to start a new life."

I gave him a moment before asking my questions. "Chief Stuart was the father of the current sheriff, right?"

"I haven't ever looked back and have no idea what's happened in Winters since I left. Who's the current sheriff?" he replied.

"Jeb Stuart," I answered.

There was a little more chopstick action while Salas contemplated his reply. "Yes, the former police chief was his father. And Chief Stuart was corrupt, rotten to the core. He had to know what was going on at the wineries. And I'd guess his son was well aware of all this as well."

We took another minute to concentrate on eating. "Tell me about the men who threatened you. What can you remember about them?"

I finally got a big break. Irwin had an excellent memory for names and faces and a talent for sketching. He scrounged a couple of empty pages from the pocket-sized notebook I was scribbling notes into and drew me sketches of the hoodlums who'd shaken him down. He labeled one as John and the other Bob. Then he lobbed me what we detectives call a clue.

"These two came back to get me to sign a contract for the sale. They had someone else with them, who they called 'Boss'. I didn't get a name, but he was obviously Chinese. He was older than the hoods. They paid in cash, enough money to get me started with this store. There was enough left over to live on while I got the business started. And I've been here ever since."

We finished lunch. I paid for the check. "Thank you for talking to me today. You've been a big help. Please call me if you think of anything else I should know about that time," I said, shaking his hand.

It was 1:30 in Anaheim. If I started back now, I'd miss the worst of commuter traffic. That sounded like a great idea. I decided to head back by the 405. It was a few miles longer, but I'd avoid a lot of truck traffic and the drive was inherently prettier.

I was home before 3:30, with plenty of time to play with Robert and Suzanne before crashing on the couch before dinner. I was half sitting, half lying on the couch when a fifty-five pound stealth missile climbed surreptitiously up onto the couch next to me. Juliet's tongue darted in and out of her mouth, planting doggy kisses all over my face, with an emphasis on the tip of my nose.

After the formal greetings were completed, she snuggled with me. A German shorthaired pointer prefers the full body snuggle technique, where every square inch of dog is in contact with their person. Perhaps a better description would be she enveloped me. This isn't a breed that believes in token gestures; it's all in or not in at all!

The next morning I got an early start to beat the worst of the commuter crush. I left Beverly Hills for the four-hour drive north on the 101 to San Luis Obispo in a Pinot Noir growing region popularized by the movie "Sideways". Michael Felton worked there as an enologist at a high-end winery owned by an aging movie star from the 1950s and 60s, Hollywood's era of Grade B dark mysteries. The winery was called Hollywood Noir, a bad pun that made a popular line of good wines. As chief enologist, Felton was responsible for all aspects of planting, growing, and harvesting the grapes that went into the wines.

I made good time and was at the winery, a large single story wood building, before 10 o'clock. I didn't have any trouble finding the enologist standing in front of the empty tasting bar examining several bunches of grapes. Handing him my business card, I introduced myself.

"What can I do for you today?" he inquired politely after the pleasantries were over.

I told him pretty much what I'd said to Irwin Salas. "I'd like a little bit of your time, Sir. I'm a private investigator from Los Angeles, Mr. Felton, working on a very complicated case. My client currently owns the Fortune Winery in Winters, which you probably remember from your time there."

A look of curiosity crossed Felton' face, then disappeared.

"All I want from you today is a little information from a long time ago," I continued. He waited expectantly for me to continue.

This time my gut told me to adhere to the KISS principle of crime detection, 'Keep It Simple, Stupid'. "I was hoping you could tell me the circumstances surrounding your decision to sell your own winery and move down here to become the enologist for someone else's wine making business."

He surprised me. "Do you know the old expression 'It's an ill wind that blows no good', Mr. Bowman?

"Yes, I do indeed," I replied.

"The ill wind that blew through Winters and forced me to sell my winery was a group of thugs trying to strong-arm their way into the business. In my case their timing was perfect and did me a world of good. I learned pretty quickly after I bought the winery that I hated the business side of the wine industry. What I loved was growing grapes and making excellent wines from them. The industry was in a slump for several years and nobody wanted to buy me out.

"Then one day a couple of thugs arrived at my door. They offered me what they thought was a lowball price for the vineyard and winery. As far as I was concerned it was the best offer I'd be likely to see for at least five more years of overplanted California grapes and too much inexpensive, but good quality, Australian and Argentine wines on the market for prices to increase. So I accepted their offer, cashed their check, and moved down here. I had an excellent reputation for making good reasonably priced wines so was offered several jobs. I took this one. And here I am, still happy with the decision I made."

I showed him the sketches of the two thugs Irwin Salas had drawn for me. "Are these the two men who bought your vineyard and winery, Mr. Felton?"

He looked closely at the sketches. "Yes, I'm pretty sure they are. Where did these sketches come from?"

I pointedly didn't answer his question. Rather, I asked him one more. "Did you get any names to go with these two faces, Sir?"

"I honestly don't remember," he replied. "All of that was a long time ago and I've moved on with my life. Like I said, if I feel anything at all about the entire experience, it's gratitude to both of them for bailing me out of a job I hated and giving me the means to get a job I love."

I thanked him for his time. He handed me a bottle of his Pinot Noir wine saying, "Please try a bottle of our wine. I think you'll enjoy it."

We shook hands and I left him there with his grapes. I pointed the car north and drove to Winters via the 101, 680, and 80. This time the ride took 5 hours including a stop for lunch at a nice Mexican restaurant near San Juan Bautista.

As I drove north on the 101 through agricultural areas and forested wilderness, the smog and pollution of the South Coast Air Basin and the smoke and ash of the Winters wildfire were out of my nostrils and brain for the first time in weeks. It felt good to take a deep breath of air that smelled, well, like fresh air. Maybe a fortuitous wind direction change would bring some of this fresh air to rural Winters as well.

For the last couple of days I'd been thinking we were close to the endgame on this case. I thought I knew who did it, and why. I had a hazy idea of how to find the proof that might stand up in a court of law. It was nice to fantasize that if the bad guys were under arrest and awaiting trial the process of healing and rebirth would allow a small town to regain some of the innocence it lost when career criminals had substituted money laundering for winemaking as the primary product in the vineyards and wineries we'd investigated.

On my way to the winery I stopped at the small gun shop, the only one in Winters. Small was good for my purposes. I walked in and looked around while the old guy behind the counter discussed ammunition with a potential customer. Nobody was in any hurry. I found a rack that contained solvents for gun cleaning. Two choices: Hoppe's, which I had always used when I was on the Los Angeles Police Department's shooting team, and army surplus in a generic olive drab can. I picked up one of each and walked over to the counter, just as the clerk finished with his previous customer.

"Were you able to find what you wanted?" the clerk asked eyeing the cans.

"I think so. Is this all you have for cleaning my rifle?"

"That depends," answered the clerk. "Are you a serious marksman who hits his deer at 300 yards, or just a casual hunter and plinker? I carry a third line of gun oil, but it's quite a bit pricier and only the really dedicated shooters seem to buy it."

"I'll take one of the pricey ones, too, and do a little side by side comparison." I told him.

He reached under the counter and added a can to my small pile of purchases. It was half the size of the others and cost three times as much. He rang up the sale, gave me back a little bit of change from my $50 bill and a receipt, and instructed me to come back if I needed anything else.

After my quick stop at the gun store in Winters, it was back to the house where I found Sherry and Vincent waiting for me, sipping coffee at the kitchen table from a freshly made pot. I poured myself a cup and sat down with them.

"This is a nice place to talk freely," I said. "We can lower the wooden blinds covering the windows on the winery side of the kitchen, so we should be safe from prying eyes and ears here."

I brought them up to date on my interviews with the two former Winters winery owners and on Jason's new super nurse, Connie Sherman, hovering over him wherever he went. He didn't seem to be complaining about her attention either. "One more thing. Bruce and Juliet will be driving here tomorrow. Suzanne had an idea. I'll explain it to you when they get here.

"How about you two? Is there anything new on this end?"

Sherry looked at Vincent, who nodded back. "I've invited Clay Ballard and the new winery manager, Carol Marshall, over to dinner tomorrow night so we can all get to know one another socially rather than just as coworkers and owner. I also asked my brother-in-law Francis to come over. I hope you'll join us too, Roger. And Bruce. I'll be serving my legendary lasagna!"

"Of course I'll join you. That's a good idea, Sherry. How about you, Vincent? Is there anything new I need to hear about?"

"No, I don't think so. The good news is nothing has happened. Or maybe that's the bad news?"

"I think we'll put that in the good news category for now," I reflected.

Chapter 23. Another winery tour

Vincent's on-line research into the history of winery turnover in the north and west rural regions of Yolo County and on into neighboring Lake and Napa Counties came up with a couple of additional possibilities for us to check out. One was a family owned winery on the way to Napa selling Italian-style jug wines plus a few varietals, the other an old winery that had survived prohibition and was still in existence just off State route 128 a few miles after passing the dam.

We were sitting in the kitchen, redolent with the tantalizing odor of freshly brewed coffee. "Hey, Sherry, how would you like to get a break from cabin fever? I imagine that continuously being guarded in the house is getting old for both you and Vincent by now. If you two want to join me, I'd enjoy the company."

"Great idea," she replied. "I'll need less than five minutes to get ready."

Vincent, Sherry, and I piled into her car to check out the wineries. I programmed the car's GPS for the best routes to the two wineries, the nearer one first. As we pulled out on the highway, turning west on 128, I looked around seeing nothing suspicious. Checking the rearview mirror, I spotted a beat-up old pickup truck with peeling paint and lots of dents behind us, matching our speed. So were a lot of other cars, which made the pick-up truck noteworthy only because it was easy to recognize in the mirror.

"Do you know this area going up and over the pass on 128, Sherry?" I asked.

"Not really," she replied. "Wally was busy enough at the winery and me with my dog shows that we never just went exploring in this direction. When we went out it was usually to The City or to Sacramento."

"This is a first for me too, and I'm sure for Vincent. Let's just relax and have some fun. It should be a good excuse to taste some mediocre wines."

On the east side of the mountains we passed walnut and almond orchards stretching on and on alongside the gently curving narrow highway. Putah Creek on our left was largely invisible behind lush trees and shrubs that exulted in the year-long water supply running past as Lake Berryessa fed the creek with the water that sustained the region's nut and fruit trees. Traces of ash adhered to leaves and grass, but there wasn't any visible fire damage as the road climbed up from valley level to the pass through the mountains and the dam containing the lake on the west side. As we started climbing up the mountain frequent sharp curves became more and more pronounced.

Glancing at the rearview mirror I spotted a pick-up truck behind us that might have been the same beat-up old one I'd seen as we turned on to 128. A frisson ran up my spine as my warning systems kicked into high gear. Then reason kicked in. There wasn't anywhere else to go on 128 once we got west of Winters except up and over the pass, so any vehicle I spotted following us could be perfectly innocent. But, just in case, I mentioned it to Vincent.

I kept my voice low and calm for Sherry's benefit. "I may be overreacting, Vincent, but there's been a small truck behind us since we turned onto 128."

"Claro. I assume you mean the pick-up truck with all the rust that needs a new paint job," he replied. "I spotted it too."

"Keep your gun handy just in case, Vincent. But I don't expect anyone to make a move in broad daylight on a well used highway like this one."

The smell of smoke became more noticeable as we drove up the mountain road. With everything else going on I'd almost forgotten about the wildfire, which was still out there burning the drought desiccated trees and brush in the unpopulated forest reserves on the west side of the mountains. It had begun with a wayward lightning bolt or a careless camper before we first came to the winery; it would still be burning after we finally returned to our homes in Southern California.

I found myself thinking about the evil that had descended on the Fortune winery, and several others, a couple of generations ago. Families and local police institutions were corrupted over multiple generations. Once the rot was established it consumed people and families from the center outwards. The wildfire was almost a metaphor for the impact of the man-made evil that had struck this previously innocent community. I hoped it could also turn out to be a contributor to the complex process of cleansing that commenced with our investigation.

The devastation wreaked by the wildfire as we drove further west became shockingly more apparent. Two lanes of State Route 128 twisted and curved their way along the backside of the Blue Ridge Mountains en route to the Napa Valley. On one side of the road was a wall of rock and blackened ash where things had been growing a few weeks previously.

The other side of the highway featured steep drops into canyons devoid of life. An unbelievable landscape of death and desolation greeted us where previously there had been flora and fauna living in isolated preserves away from the urban encroachment a few miles away on the other side of the mountains. Charred areas of bushes, trees, and what used to be grassy scrublands covered with black ash and odds and ends of burned trees decorated what used to be forests and wild lands.

We made it to the Spallanzani vineyard with no incidents. The pickup continued going west on 128 after we turned off for the winery. Apparently it actually was just going in the same direction as we were on the narrow, well-traveled highway.

The winery was old, but had apparently been spared any damage from the fire. It consisted of several ramshackle buildings desperately needing a new paint job in a cleared area at the end of a dirt and gravel road, one with a sign proclaiming "Tasting Room". There was none of the architectural or landscaping elegance you might expect if your previous tasting experience included the big elegant wineries along The Silverado Trail in Napa. This operation stressed function, not form. At least, I hoped so.

We parked in a mostly empty small lot containing a couple of well-worn pickup trucks, and walked into the tasting room. There hadn't been any splurging on an architect or interior designer here either. A plain room with a tasting bar and lots of tourist junk for sale, not necessarily wine related, greeted us as we walked in. The tasting room smelled like spilled wine. Two people stood behind the bar pouring for the occasional tourists who found this place, which was most definitely off the grid. On the right was an attractive woman in her thirties who I imagined got most of the requests to pour.

On the left was an older gentleman, in his sixties or seventies, who'd obviously seen some hard living in his youth. He wore a stained apron over his jeans and lots of tattoos over his arms. I made a beeline straight to him.

"What can I pour for you folks to taste?" he asked cheerfully, tugging at the hem of his apron.

I rested an elbow on the bar and leaned toward him. "We don't know your wines at all. What would you recommend?" I answered for the three of us.

The old guy reached under the bar and pulled out a half-gallon jug of red wine, unscrewed the cap, and poured us three small glasses to taste. "We make jug wines to go with spaghetti that are surprisingly good, especially for the price we're charging. I think you might want to taste our Dago Red Blend before you draw any conclusions about how important the fancy labels and snooty varietal descriptions are for a good everyday table wine."

Vincent, Sherry, and I each sniffed, sipped, and considered. "This is just as good, or better, than the Chilean table wines we drank with dinner whenever there was a red sauce in the recipe," Vincent commented. "I like it."

Sherry and I agreed. Not elegant, not an explosion of fruit, tobacco, and shoe leather on the tongue, but a pleasant drinkable wine to accompany dinner. I bought a couple of jugs from the old man.

Now it was time to get down to business. "Thank you for the wine. It's really very good for the price. But we stopped by for another reason as well. May I introduce you to our friend Sherry Fortune, who has just become the owner of the

Fortune Winery in Winters. We're trying to get to know some of the other winery owners around here. Is the owner of this place around today?"

"You just met the owner," the old guy replied. "I'm Enzo Spallanzani, the third generation of Spallanzanis to run this winery." He reached over to shake Sherry's hand.

"You must be Wally's widow," he concluded. "I'm very sorry for your loss. And who are you two gentlemen?"

"I'm Roger Bowman and this is my colleague Vincent Romero," I said. "Could we sit somewhere or walk around the winery grounds and talk to you in private for a few minutes, please?"

Enzo took a long look at the three of us, made some sort of decision, and came around the bar to lead us to a table in the front corner of the room. "What's on your mind, Mr. Bowman?"

This was a man who'd do best with the truth, I decided. I told him Sherry had asked me to investigate the circumstances surrounding Wally's death. I was an old friend and a private detective. We had stumbled on evidence of organized crime activity going back a generation or two at some of the local wineries in Winters. I wondered whether anything like that might have happened to any of the wineries as far from Winters as his.

Enzo gave me a long look. He turned toward Sherry, asking, "Are you planning on selling the winery, Mrs. Fortune?"

"No," she answered, "I'm hoping to keep it as the owner. I've already hired a new manager to run the winery while I learn about the business parts of it, which I plan to take over as soon as I think I'm able to do it well."

"Good," he said. "You two are supposed to be detectives, eh?"

I nodded.

"Show me some I.D. that says you are, please."

Vincent and I pulled out our licenses and passed them to Enzo to look over. He studied them carefully before returning them to us. "OK, you're the real deal. And I want you, Mrs. Fortune, to feel free to come by or call me any time you need some help. I've been running this winery for more years than I'd like to admit to, so I'll answer your questions today."

"I really have only one question for you, Mr. Spallanzani. Did you, or more likely your father, ever get approached by some muscle from the Bay Area asking you to welcome them into becoming partners in this winery, or else bad things would happen? This would most likely have been twenty or thirty years ago."

Enzo scratched his head while he let out a low whistle. "It sounds like you boys have really done your homework. Yes, I was approached once. They threatened my family and the winery if we didn't go along. My wife had already called her uncles for help when she saw two nasty looking thugs walk in like they owned the place. In those days she had two uncles who served as the local deputy sheriffs. They kept the peace around here with a very direct approach, if you know what I mean.

"They came in quietly and got the drop on the thugs, who turned out to be carrying. Uncle Tom took their guns and very carefully made sure he had a nice set of the owner's fingerprints on each one before he explained the guns would be put away in a safe place. Then he handcuffed both of them, declaring this winery was off limits to either of them, or to their friends, for the rest of their lives. If he or Uncle Bob ever saw them again the guns with their fingerprints would be handed over to the sheriff. He guessed both were felons illegally in possession of a deadly weapon, which was a ten year minimum sentence if it went to trial in this county."

Enzo smiled, not a very nice smile. "They had that smug look career criminals have, thinking they were a whole lot smarter than we hicks were and would be coming back. Uncle Tom and Uncle Bob left the handcuffs on and gave them the worst beating they could this side of sending them to the hospital. Then my two uncles-in-law removed the cuffs, reminded the thugs things could, and would, be worse if they ever stopped here again, and sent them home.

"Is that what you wanted to know, Mr. Bowman?"

The old wine smell seemed stronger as I looked up at Enzo. "Yes, it is. Thank you very much. Can you describe the crooks or would anyone still have the guns your uncles took from them?"

Enzo thought a bit. "No, and it's not very likely. That all happened when I was a teenager and both the uncles died quite a while ago."

We thanked him for his help and shook hands to say good-bye. Sherry promised to stay in touch with him.

We drove further west on 128 to the second winery, going inside to taste wines. This was a slightly more tourist-oriented set-up, with two UC Davis co-eds in skimpy tops and short shorts pouring. The first wine they poured us was their top of the line Cabernet. Enzo's Dago Red tasted a lot better and had a great deal more complexity. I asked about seeing the owner.

One of the two wine pourers explained the owner was the CEO of a large conglomerate corporation out of Youngstown, Ohio, and never visited California as far as she knew.

We declined round two of the wine tasting and started our drive back to Winters. I spotted the pick-up truck with all the rust we'd been followed by earlier almost immediately. Vincent checked that I'd seen it, then relaxed and left the problem to me. We drove east at the speed limit. There was a lot less traffic than we'd had coming uphill, which was either good news or bad news depending on your perspective.

Sherry audibly sucked in a ragged breath. "Is this the part where I should start praying?" she asked in a frightened little voice.

"Claro. Don't worry," Vincent answered reassuringly. "We've both been in much tougher spots before and we're still here!"

The truck followed us at a discrete distance until we came to a steep stretch of ultra-curvy narrow two-lane highway just before the Spallanzani winery turnoff. There wasn't any traffic in sight in either direction. The rusty old pickup truck speeded up. I had expected this maneuver and floored the gas pedal, watching the speedometer pass 70 before easing off. The pick-up pursuing us continued to close the distance.

I had the advantage here of police training in high speed driving so kicked the throttle up another ten miles per hour, past 80. This was good strategy until we encountered a car in front of us going either direction; then it would quickly turn into a very bad strategy.

Vincent, sitting in the right front seat, very quietly said, "The next curve to the right let's see your panic stop. I should be lined up for the shot and be able to hit his engine block and take out the engine. I hope he's a good enough driver to stay on the road when that happens."

We did two more left curves at 80 mph before we saw a right curve in front of us. I eased off on the gas, but stayed away from the brake and the telltale red lights when I hit it. Halfway around the curve, sheer cliff to the right and deep canyon to the left, I hit the brake, hard, and wrestled the car to a stop broadside to the road. A second or two later I heard three well spaced shots and Vincent yelling, "Go, go, go!"

I went. There was a loud screech of brakes behind us followed by complete silence. I kept on to Winters. There wasn't anything to connect us to the pick-up truck no matter what sort of shape it might be in and I didn't trust Sheriff Stuart, whose county we were in, to dispense fair and even-handed justice were we to have killed anyone.

"Do you think all three rounds hit the engine block, Vincent?"

"Of course," he answered. "It was an easy shot."

"Good, now we don't have to worry about there being enough of any slug recovered to match your pistol. Let's go home. Are you all right, Sherry?"

She responded in a tiny, little girl voice. "Yes, I think so. But please don't do that again!"

Chapter 24. Juliet offers her three scents worth

Sherry got busy preparing her famous lasagna and the rest of dinner as soon as we got back to the house. Being busy was the best way for her to start forgetting the traumatic events of the day, so Vincent and I stayed out of her kitchen to discuss the case. Bruce and Juliet arrived at the winery late that afternoon. I had directed him to park on the side of the house away from the winery so neither his car nor Juliet would be visible from the winery or the road. Juliet immediately recognized where she was and ran off for a romp away from the winery through this end of the vineyard.

While we stood next to the far wall of the house watching Juliet running back and forth seeking interesting scents, we discussed the search to come. "I still don't get it, Roger. What makes you think our killer hid the rifle in or around the winery or the house? There must be a million other places he or she could hide a gun."

"Theoretically you're right Bruce. But as I thought about it I realized that somehow or other our killer spotted Jason and Sherry going into the winery and decided to act. He had what, less than ten minutes to go get his rifle, return, establish his position, and take his shots at them as they came out of the winery? The rifle has to be stashed somewhere close by or it just couldn't have happened that quickly.

"The odds favor the house, which he would have had free access to as soon as Sherry and Jason snuck out to the winery, or else one of the sheds or outbuildings next to the winery. It's also possible the rifle is securely buried somewhere in the area where it wouldn't turn up during whatever activities one does to grow grapes. We can probably rule out the winery itself because neither Jason nor Sherry heard anyone else in the building while they were searching Wally's office."

After letting Juliet work off the excess energy accumulated during eight hours of sitting in the car with just one or two brief stops en route, Bruce recalled her so we could get down to business.

Juliet sat down next to Bruce waiting for guidance as to whatever the next command might be while she hoped for a dog biscuit or two. She sat patiently beside Bruce while we continued our discussion.

"Do we have to do the search tonight when nobody is around, or do you want to let whoever it is see us and maybe paint a few bulls-eyes on our backs, Roger?"

"Good question, Bruce. Can you think of any other evidence besides the rifle our killer might remove or destroy if they know we're looking at them?"

"The usual: paperwork, computer files, letters, e-mails, or old phone bills. Anything else that links winemakers from Winters with Bay Area gangs. But I doubt we'll find any of those sorts of records hanging around, except maybe in a lawyer's safe deposit box if he thinks he might need insurance against the mob."

"I agree, Bruce. I think poking the snake with a stick is the right play for now. It gives us a Plan B if the rifle doesn't turn up. One good way to do that is to check the outbuildings and grounds surrounding them in plain sight first while we work Juliet back to the house. Can we do it that way in terms of the prevailing winds to optimize Juliet's search pattern?"

Bruce absent-mindedly scratched Juliet behind her ears and on the big patch on her rump. "That'll work, Roger. Let's start at the building closest to the winery and make a big loop toward the house. I can make a bit of a show of her searching the outside of the winery all around the building too if you'd like to lay it on thick."

I had been thinking about exactly the same thing. "The more I think about it the more I like the idea of painting a bulls-eye on our backs. Let's go whole hog and do a search of the inside of the winery too. If anyone asks what we're doing, we're searching for evidence. Nothing more specific than that."

Bruce reached down into his backpack, withdrawing three cans of gun cleaning solvent and several thick gauze pads, and three Zip-Lock bags numbered 1, 2, and 3. He poured several drops of oil from each can onto a gauze pad, which he placed into the corresponding plastic bag. One by one he offered each bag to Juliet to sniff the contents.

Juliet sniffed from bag #1, recoiled, and looked at the bag with an "it stinks" expression. Bag #2 elicited the identical response, with an added snort of displeasure.

Bag #3 got a resigned expression I'd interpret as 'at least that's the last one' followed by a 'now what?' look toward Bruce.

Bruce gave a "heel" command. Juliet walked about twenty yards beyond the far wall of the winery at his side before stopping next to him to wait for his next command. "Find", he said, tapping her twice on her head to release her.

Juliet trotted a few yards ahead of Bruce, then started quartering into the light breeze with her nose high in the air hoping to maybe find some bird scent as well as the 'icky' smells of the oil and solvents Bruce had asked her to look for. With Bruce's guidance she worked the width of the winery building plus about ten yards in either direction, working closer and closer to the building until she ran out of space.

He called her in to a heel position, walking her alongside the building on the near side, across the front of the winery, alongside the building on the far side, and on to the entrance where he sat the dog and waited for my instructions. Juliet hadn't shown any signs of alerting thus far. I nodded and we walked her at Bruce's heel through the winery itself, covering all the lanes and aisles we could find.

The staff looked aghast, but nobody challenged our right to be there. Juliet seemed to prefer the red wine odors, but I couldn't be sure because of potential overlaps with white wines aging in barrels along the walls.

Clay Ballard walked up to us. "Is there anything I can do to help?" he asked politely.

"I don't think so, Clay, but thanks for asking," I replied continuing to walk along.

"Are you finished now?" Clay asked a little while later as we came back almost to the front door.

"Just one more thing," I answered. "Where do you store the wine barrels for aging? Is there a cellar?"

"No, the local geology won't let us make a strong enough cellar to withstand the expansion and contraction of the clay soils here in rainy winters and dry summers. We store our wines for aging in several well-insulated temperature controlled buildings you can see between the winery and the house."

"Can we look around in those buildings?"

Ballard looked helpful. "Sure. Just be careful to close the doors tight going in and out. Keeping a constant temperature is critical for aging the wines evenly and properly."

"Are you sure you can trust me with that job?" I asked seriously.

"Yes, I am," he replied. "The whole system is alarmed. We'll know immediately if you screw up on door closure in any of the buildings."

We finished our human and canine winery tour and went on out to the road. Bruce repeated the process of guiding and orienting Juliet to search grounds, walls, and buildings for several storage buildings between the winery and the house, some of the buildings holding spare parts and old equipment, others neatly stacked barrels of wine separated by year of barreling and variety of wine.

The process was fascinating but uninformative from Juliet's point of view with no alerts. Bruce praised her thoroughly and slipped her a dog biscuit after each building was cleared, with all of us eventually ending up at the house itself.

We rang the bell. Vincent checked us out through a convenient window before opening the door to let us in. I explained what we were doing and asked Sherry if Juliet could do her thing here in the house. She said, "Sure."

The layout was two stories, master bedroom, guest bedrooms and bathrooms upstairs with another bathroom, family room, living room, study, kitchen, and dining room downstairs. Bruce and Juliet checked the upstairs, finding nothing.

"Is there an attic up there, Sherry?" I asked.

"Yes, but you have to climb a pull-down ladder and enter via a ceiling panel," she replied.

A few moments later, Bruce reached up grabbing the loop hanging down from the ceiling. Down came the ladder, allowing him to climb up into the low attic above the second floor. He took a quick look around. "I'll need to borrow a flashlight to see anything," he observed.

Sherry found an old-fashioned two-cell flashlight, which she passed up to Bruce. He flashed it around for less than a minute. "Now I can see a whole lot of things up here, but it's too dark to see what they are," he complained.

There was a long pause before Bruce stuck his head out of the trapdoor. "It's worth the effort to get Juliet up here for a thorough search, Roger," he declared.

"Stay there," I suggested to Bruce. "I think I know how we can do this."

I picked up Juliet and placed her front paws on the third rung of the ladder, with her hind paws firmly on the ground. That was pretty easy; she trusted me enough to assume I knew what I was doing. Bruce gave her a 'come' command. She walked up the ladder a step at a time until her front paws were over the sill, then scampered into the attic. I was willing to bet the killer hadn't anticipated Juliet could easily climb up a ladder, so maybe she'd actually find something there.

Juliet handled herself exceedingly well. With an expression Bruce read as saying *'you guys must be crazy but I can do this if it will make you happy, Bruce'* she stepped gingerly forward till she was in the heel position. She accepted the two biscuits he handed her appreciatively, but with dignity. There was a short pause after he said, "Find". She quickly worked out how to travel in the attic, joist by joist.

The lack of wind was a problem until Sherry remembered the switch controlling the attic fan, which exhausted house air to the outside, bringing in fresh, presumably cool, air through open windows on the second floor. At the lowest setting, it created a perfect breeze for Juliet to work.

Less than three minutes later she went on alert. Bruce called down, "We have an alert! Please bring me my backpack, which I left on the floor in the living room downstairs."

Sherry ran downstairs, returning in less than a minute with Bruce's backpack. I climbed the ladder, handing the pack to him while standing on one of the rungs with my head and shoulders sticking up into the attic itself. He carefully withdrew a pair of latex gloves followed by a couple of 25-gallon black plastic garbage bags and a small, high-intensity, LED flashlight from the pack.

He handed me the larger flashlight. "Get as much light as you can over by where Juliet is standing, please, Roger."

I circled the beam across the attic until I spotted Juliet, not easy with her dark patches and ticked coat standing motionless at a classic point posture in the gloom. The reflective collar she wore at all times made the difference. I held the beam as steadily as I could on the area directly in front of her while Bruce carefully maneuvered over to her joist by joist.

I could see a lot more when Bruce turned on his high intensity beam and aimed it at the spot Juliet was pointing toward. A layer of pink fiberglass insulation filled the space between two joists. Without the dog it would have looked exactly like the rest of the floor of a very large attic. With the dog we knew exactly where to look. Bruce carefully lifted the insulation, pulling the entire batten over the joist to reveal what was hidden under it.

BINGO! There was a leather case the right size to hold a rifle and several boxes of ammunition in the cache under the fiberglass. Bruce carefully put all the items in one of the garbage bags, which he sealed with a bag tie and carefully carried back to pass it to me.

"Don't start celebrating yet, Roger. There's still a lot of attic for Juliet to search."

Bruce worked his way back to Juliet, who stood still marking the spot. He carefully probed all around where he'd found the gun and ammunition, finding nothing else. He restored the fiberglass to its previous position, removed any other traces of his having visited the cache, and gave Juliet another "Find" command followed by a release.

Juliet worked the attic systematically left and right, front and back. It took ten minutes this time before she locked on to another point. Bruce repeated the search process, finding another buried treasure. This time it was a dark plastic box containing a pistol and several more boxes of ammunition that presumably went with the handgun. Another garbage bag was filled and sealed and another cache was restored to its former pristine state. Juliet got a biscuit and a third "Find" command. This time she finished her search of the attic with no more goodies to be found.

We got the two plastic garbage bags and Juliet out of the attic and safely down the ladder without any mishaps. Neither Bruce nor I expected to find anything else, but he and Juliet thoroughly searched the downstairs of the house and the grounds around it. Neither of us was surprised when the search of the grounds came up empty.

"If anyone is watching us they'll have seen us come up empty. That may give us some time before we get those bulls-eyes on our backs," Bruce observed. "That may be an advantage for us. Is there anything else you had in mind for Juliet and I to do while we're here, Roger?"

"Yes, but now after all Juliet just found in the attic, maybe not. What's the current status of those search warrants for our various suspects' houses, Vincent?"

"Still pending, Roger. One judge wanted more probable cause, another balked at the lack of any physical evidence linking any of the suspects to any of the murders."

I thought about the pros and cons. "I think the best way to play this is for you to drive home tonight, Bruce. That'll get you and Juliet out of harm's way. Until we get the forensic and fingerprint evidence on today's haul we really don't have any good justification for searching elsewhere. If we have the rifle that matches Jason's bullet, we have the foundation for a murder case and should be able to turn this over to the FBI to do all the detailed investigation it's going to take to build a case for a jury to hear."

Bruce smiled as if he had just remembered a good joke. "OK, Roger, if you let me do just one thing with the evidence first."

"Sure, go ahead," I replied. "You and Juliet found it."

Bruce put on a pair of latex gloves before removing the pistol case from its bag. He eased the lid up and looked inside. Then he laughed. "As usual, Suzanne was right. It's the same brand of gun cleaning solvent as the expensive can you bought at the local gun store."

He returned the box to the plastic bag, which he resealed. "Nice job, Juliet!"

Her tail wagging rapidly back and forth like a metronome set on allegro, Juliet barked twice and sat down to wait for her biscuit. Bruce obliged her, patting her behind the ears and telling her what a good dog she was.

I called Barbara Kaufman. She answered her cell phone on the third ring. "Hello, Roger. You caught me at a busy time. Can you make this quick, please?'

"Sure. We just found a rifle. It might be the rifle! Could you drive up here tonight to pick it up or should I plan on bringing it to you?"

After a brief pause Barbara came back on line. "We're all up to our eyeballs in alligators, and it's partly your fault. Based on your leads back to the Fong Family we suddenly have a chance to make a case against some very bad people the FBI's been trying to put away for more than twenty years. There's a lot of paper to go through, but at least we have an idea of what it is we're looking for this time.

"Gretchen and I expect to be home after eight tonight, so you should plan on driving to The City after dinner when traffic has gotten a little less insane than during the evening rush hour. Do you have our address? It's a new one since last year."

I worked out the times and distances. "I think we're going to send Bruce and Juliet home to Los Angeles tonight. Please give me your new address. Either Bruce or I will swing by around nine or ten to drop a couple of bags of evidence we found off with you. Do you have fingerprints or DNA for all of our local suspects in Winters or should we be trying to get samples for you?"

Barbara told me who we needed samples from. I promised to start collecting them immediately. I could email fingerprints but we'd have to deliver any samples I could find for DNA analysis the old fashioned way.

"You could leave now and be back in L.A. about one o'clock, Bruce, or you could deliver these guns to the Kaufman sisters and get home by four or five AM, just in time to miss the L.A. rush hour tomorrow morning. What's your pleasure?"

"Juliet and I can do the San Francisco run and save you the trip, Roger. I won't need more than ten or fifteen minutes to get organized and ready to go right after dinner."

"Great. Thank you Bruce. That'll give me plenty of time to seal those garbage bags properly and get them labeled to establish the chain of custody on them if they turn out to be useful as evidence."

Chapter 25. Evidence and clues

Looking for something that would go well with coffee, I did a quick run to a local bakery for dessert, selecting an apple pie. Sherry scrounged several bottles of wine, both white and red, from her winery. Tonight's lasagna would be served French style, with two styles of wine glass. White wine would accompany the salad, served after the lasagna. Red wine would be served with the lasagna. I coached Sherry in the proper serving technique for a private detective, handling the wine glasses only by their stems as she cleared the table and handling the coffee cups only by their saucers.

Coffee (regular or decaf) would be served in the designated cups on their saucers with dessert. Separate places in the kitchen were set aside for the cups and glasses for our special guests.

"Just in case our killer is starting to get nervous, Sherry, why don't you plan on making an announcement during dinner that you plan to stay on here running the winery for good. Maybe we can encourage somebody to do something stupid and catch them at it."

"I'm not sure how I feel about being a target," she answered. "But I'll do it."

I looked her straight in the eye. "If what we believe has been going on here for two generations or longer is correct, that bulls-eye was painted on your back the moment you said, 'I do' to Wally. And the longer we wait to smoke the killer out, the more the advantage shifts from us to him. There's no way Vincent, Jason, or I can protect you indefinitely so we need to lure him out into the open while we're here and ready for him."

Everyone had been invited for six. We added Bruce to the guest list for tonight's dinner party. As much as we all loved Juliet, she didn't get a place at the dinner table. Missing the worst of the traffic at the Oakland Bay Bridge would get them into The City quite a bit faster, so Bruce wouldn't lose much time getting fed before he started the long drive with Juliet.

The bell rang promptly at six. Clay Ballard and Carol Marshall were punctual, not so difficult since they only had a short walk from the winery to the house. We only had time to introduce everyone when the doorbell rang again to signal brother-in-law Francis' arrival. Another round of introductions and we were all sipping a sparkling wine in the family room courtesy of a bottle of Two Buck Chuck sparkling wine Francis had brought with him. The wine was very Francis, mediocre or worse in a fancy bottle with a fancy label. We all made small talk for fifteen minutes of pretending we liked one another before Sherry announced dinner was ready to eat.

Shrimp cocktails for an appetizer served with the white wine started us off, followed by Sherry's lasagna with the red wine, accompanied by garlic toast and sautéed zucchini. The dinner conversation centered on Carol's first impressions of the winery, the grapes, and the wines. As a UC Davis graduate she knew Winters well, especially The Buckhorn's steaks and the tapas restaurant across the street from the steakhouse.

After a sip of wine Carol shared her opinion of the grapes. "Your husband did a very good job of selecting grape varietals and growing them here. That part of the winery can run on autopilot until the harvest. Clay and I have been discussing making some blends with the smaller plots of grapes to cut down on the number of different varietals we're marketing. For the red wines we have a lot of Cabernet Sauvignon, Petite Syrah, Tempranillo, and Merlot, and relatively small amounts of Cabernet Franc, Granache, Tannat, and Malbec grapes. For the whites, lots of Chardonnay and Viognier, with less Albarino and Roussanne.

"We could easily make quite a few varieties of meritages to produce lower priced wines that would allow us to handle fluctuations in varietal yields from year to year a lot more efficiently. Clay has a good handle on how much of what we have this year; what do you think, Clay?"

He thought about Carol's suggestion for a few seconds. "Mostly I think I'm very glad someone besides me is making the business decisions. I love the problem solving and technical parts of winemaking but I hate having to make the decisions where success or failure running a profitable business is concerned," he replied.

Clay took a large sip of wine before continuing. "Yes, I think we've done everything the same way for a long time here and shaking things up a bit is a good idea. It'll obviously be easier having fewer fermentations of small batches of grapes to worry about, and not having to keeping track of lots of small batches of different wines during barrel aging. And blended wines are becoming popular with younger customers who don't want to worry about whether the wine they liked at a party was a Cabernet Sauvignon or a Cabernet Franc."

"*Interesting,*" I thought. As far as I could tell he was being completely honest unless he was a really fine actor. "*If I'm reading Clay correctly, we can rule out his wanting Wally's job as a possible motive for the killing.*"

Francis had been silent during this exchange. I guess he must have felt a social obligation to join in and contribute some small talk. Or maybe he just wanted to steer the conversation away from the business part of winemaking. "Have you ever been to Yolo County before, Vincent, or are you a true Southern Californian who didn't realize most of the state is north of the Los Angeles suburbs?"

Vincent laughed. "Like most L.A. residents I'm from somewhere else," he declared. "I was born in Wisconsin and lived in Northern Chile for a while. This is my first trip to the Sacramento area, but I've been to San Francisco before."

Francis took a large bite of Sherry's famous lasagna before continuing. "What do you think of our nice little community here?" Francis asked. "Clay and I have lived here all our lives."

Vincent patted his lips with a napkin and replied. "I really haven't had a chance to see much of it. What I've seen is great. I like the open space and the vineyards remind me of Chile. The only thing I don't like is the air quality, which is almost as bad as Los Angeles. I assume it's usually a lot better when you don't have all that smoke and ash from the forest fires blowing over you."

That precipitated a discussion of global warming and its likely impact on grape growing in the Central Valley, which took us through the main part of dinner and on to dessert. Sherry had decorated the apple pie with cheddar cheese slices and vanilla ice cream, as well as serving coffee to everyone without asking who wanted what. Over dessert Sherry got into the discussion about the future of winemaking at the Fortune Winery, making it clear that she planned to permanently move into the house and act like a winery owner.

Sherry helped herself to another big scoop of ice cream and a thick slice of cheese for her pie. "I'm looking forward to the grape harvest and starting to learn how everything is done around here," she exclaimed. "We'll put a few kennel runs out back of the house and I'll move my dog breeding operation out here so I don't have to go back and forth to Sacramento all the time."

I glanced over at Francis. He briefly looked like he'd bitten into something that disagreed with him, but recovered quickly into his usual bland lawyerly image.

Sherry offered wine or brandy after dinner but there weren't any takers. The party broke up and people headed home. Bruce, Juliet, and what would become two large bags of evidence after a bit of further preparation were almost ready to start the long drive to Los Angeles via San Francisco.

Vincent, Bruce, and I followed Sherry back into the kitchen, where our little treasure trove of glasses and cups, in two separate clusters, awaited us. Sherry pointed to one of the clusters. "Those are the ones Francis used. The other group is from Clay."

Vincent donned a pair of latex gloves before he picked up two glasses from each cluster and examined them carefully under the bright fluorescent light. "All four of the glasses have what I think will be nice fingerprints on them, and almost certainly will have plenty of DNA on the rims. You might as well take these with you for the FBI to play with, Bruce."

Vincent wrapped each glass separately into a fluffy dishtowel along with a slip of paper inserted into each glass with the user's name, then carefully packed the wineglass collection into a paper bag with additional towels for padding. He handed the prize to Bruce. "Handle with care. We could lose some of those prints if any of these glasses break en route."

On his way out the door Bruce remarked, "I took another peek into the pistol case before I sealed the plastic bag, Roger. The rifle ammo was stored there. They were custom hand loads, the kind of ammunition a pro would use. Be careful. He may have another rifle or two squirreled away somewhere else!"

We went back to the kitchen to play a little more over the dinner dishes. Vincent came up with his handy fingerprinting supplies and carefully brushed powder over the surface of the two cups we were interested in.

"Voila!" he announced. "Now we get to play with these guy's records too. I can't think of any reason why the FBI should have all the fun."

"Just a minute, Vincent, I have another cup for you to have fun with."

I retrieved the cup decorated with Sheriff Stuart's fingerprints I'd liberated from the cafe when we'd had coffee together. Vincent repeated the process and found another good set of prints for us to use. He photographed all the prints with his cellphone and went off somewhere to email them to his laptop. Just for chuckles I took a couple of swabs from the cup, up at the top rim where the DNA should be, just in case we might want the samples later.

Armed with photographs of three sets of fingerprints from three coffee cups, Vincent went off to play on his computer. I spent a little time thinking about what everybody had said and done over dinner before calling Suzanne to give her an update on today's activities and a heads-up on Bruce and Juliet's planned arrival very early next morning.

****

An hour later we were sitting together in the family room, killing time until the local TV News got to the updated weather and wildfire report. This evening's sunset had been spectacular, another reminder of the major wildfire lurking somewhere out of sight to the northwest, but never out of mind. The sun itself was an orange ball surrounded by a sea of pastel colors in concentric circles around the smoldering brilliance of the central orb. An air of menace radiated out from the palette of pigmented beauty, as if menace lurked within the veil of color. I shivered unconsciously at the premonition of more evil still to come.

Vincent was saying, "I don't know what it means Roger, but we got a hit on one of those sets of fingerprints we collected. Twenty-five years ago or so, one of our coffee drinkers, along with two Asian males, was arrested in Contra Costa County for assault and battery on a storekeeper. There aren't any follow-ups on the arrest so somebody must have pulled some strings to get the three alleged assaulters sprung from the local sheriff's custody."

"What made this arrest special, Vincent? And whose fingerprints were they?"

Vincent looked thoughtfully at me. "The prints belong to Sheriff Jeb Stuart. Had he gone on to trial I don't think he would have been considered sheriff material, so that was certainly a lucky break for him. Maybe his father, the police chief, got Jeb his get out of jail free card as a professional courtesy. Sheriff Stuart would have been about the right age to be a college student in those days.

"But there's another, even more interesting, possibility here. One of the other alleged assaulters was named Harold Fong. Remember that Oakland is in Contra Costa County, so Grandpa Fong probably had plenty of juice with the local law even that far back. It looks like we have a direct link established between the Fong Family and the current sheriff here in Yolo County, and perhaps between the Fongs and the sheriff's father, the former Chief of Police in Winters. As they say in the old British mystery novels, the plot thickens!"

I spent a little time digesting this piece of the puzzle. "It looks like we finally have a good motive for one of our suspects in the killings here, Vincent. Nice work!"

It suddenly seemed a little more dangerous here. "Can you give me a hand here please. I think it's probably time Sherry was killed. Don't you?"

"What do you have in mind, Roger?"

"Close all the windows and pull the blinds or drapes so nobody can see inside clearly. Then let's fix the lighting so Sherry's silhouette is visible through the covering on one of those front windows."

"Don't you think we should wait for her check for our services to clear before we kill her off?" Vincent asked facetiously.

Sherry chimed in. "Do I get a vote in this election?"

"No, I don't think so, Sherry. But you could get me something shaped like a woman's head we could put in this chair here so the visitor I expect later tonight has something to shoot at. Do you have a big doll we can use, or a pillow we can make into the shape of a head?"

"Let me look around," she replied. "I really don't know what's in most of the upstairs rooms in this house."

Sherry was back downstairs in less than ten minutes. "Look what I found," she said proudly. She had a large stuffed Panda Bear, a woman's wig, and a large pair of scissors. Moving over to a wastebasket she gave the wig a quick haircut to approximate the length and style she was currently wearing.

Placing the wig over the Panda's head and sitting the stuffed animal upright in a chair, she asked, "How do I look?"

"Let's see," I answered, turning off lights except for one reading lamp strategically placed to cast a shadow from the Panda to the window shade, and leaving the flickering TV on.

Like magic, a woman's silhouette and the outline of the chair appeared on the shade.

"Not bad," said Vincent. "Not bad at all!"

He turned to me. "Where do you want me, Roger? Outside where we guess he'll take his shot from or upstairs at a window with a pistol?"

"I think the odds of getting him will be a lot better if you're outside. Why don't we plan on that? I'll stay with Sherry, but not here in this room!"

Two hours later, Sherry and I were sitting in one of the second floor bedrooms enjoying a companionable silence when the loud crack of a rifle shot rang out in the night. No silencer this time. The silence was broken a few seconds later by the sound of four pistol shots, evenly spaced, that were most likely from Vincent's 9mm.

We waited. Sherry looked worried. "What just happened, Roger?"

"The first shot you heard was someone shooting you with a rifle. Or at least they shot a stuffed panda that looked like you silhouetted on the blind. The rest of the shots were from Vincent, who guessed where the rifleman would shoot from and set himself up to be able to shoot back."

Sherry still looked worried. "Didn't you let Vincent take a terrible risk out there, in the dark, with a killer?"

"Not really, Sherry. Vincent is a lot better trained than our killer for this kind of night fighting in the dark. As I've told you before, he spent most of his adult life before we got together as a CIA agent in deep cover in Chile doing this sort of thing, so he's very good at it. It wasn't much of a risk for him. On the other hand, it was probably the first time anyone ever shot back at the rifleman, so I'd guess he ran as fast as he could to get away and isn't in any hurry to come back."

196

Eventually the doorbell sounded, its loud clang echoing through the silent house. I whispered to Sherry she should stay put and headed downstairs, my 9mm handgun at the ready. I waited at the door.

"It's OK Roger, it's me," came Vincent's voice.

A quick look assured me Vincent was alone and in good shape. I let him in and called Sherry to come downstairs.

We all sat down at the kitchen table. The kitchen didn't have any windows without tightly closed blinds facing the front where the shot had come from. The old CIA training kicked in. Vincent reloaded the clip on his pistol just in case he might need it again tonight on short notice.

"Did you get a look at him, Vincent?" I asked.

He returned his pistol to its holster. "No, it was much too dark for me to see anything except his muzzle flash. I just shot at where I guessed he was. By the time I was on the move toward him I heard a car start up and head out of here without any lights so I didn't see the car either. The good news is I'm pretty sure I winged him. I found some blood spots on the ground close to the area he probably took his shot from."

I checked my watch, which told me it was getting late. "I think we can be pretty sure he won't be back tonight. Let's get some sleep and try to sort things out tomorrow morning when it'll be light enough to see."

Vincent looked uncomfortable. "Shouldn't we be calling the cops? I suspect it's a crime in Winters not to report an attempted murder."

"I don't think so. That shooter could have been the sheriff. I think we should just leave things as they are for now and see what happens next."

Sherry joined us as we walked into the family room to check the damage, turning on the lights as she came into the room. She walked over to look more closely at the Panda. The poor bear had taken a direct head shot that quite literally knocked the stuffing out of him. Bits and pieces of fiber fill littered the floor. The top half of the stuffed animal was unrecognizable.

Sherry looked ruefully at the Panda, obviously visualizing herself splattered all over the floor had it been her in the chair. A look of doubt crossed her face as she considered the question of whether she should ever have gotten all of us involved in whatever this violence was all about. She quite noticeably pulled herself together before turning back to look at Vincent and me.

"I'm very, very glad that wasn't me sitting there," exclaimed Sherry. "Thank you Roger. And thank you too, Vincent. You really did guess exactly what our unknown shooter was going to do. What do you plan on doing now?"

I checked my watch again. "Going to bed and getting some sleep. I'm pretty sure we're safe for now. That's probably the first time any of his would-be victims shot back. I doubt he liked the feeling at all. We can discuss what comes next at breakfast tomorrow after Vincent and I look around to see if we can find the bullet our killer shot the Panda with."

"I don't know about that sleep part for me," Sherry replied. "I'm thinking more about nightmares for me than sweet dreams tonight. Don't let the lights in my room interfere with your sleep, but I don't think I'll be comfortable in any dark rooms for a while."

Chapter 26. Starting to put it all together

An obviously still shaken Sherry occupied herself scrambling eggs and frying bacon while Vincent and I searched for a bullet hole in the wall. We took a guess at where the shot had come from and assumed he'd shot from the prone position. Based on guesswork and crude triangulation, we started looking near the top of the wall on the left side of the large room. It took fifteen minutes and several times across the same stretch of wall, but Vincent eventually found the hole, partially obscured by the crown molding.

I found a step stool in the kitchen. "I've got this one," Vincent declared. He took a quick photo with his cell phone to document the location of the bullet and climbed up on the wobbly steps until his arms were parallel to the hole.

Out came a pocketknife. With the utmost care he worked around the outside of the hole with the smallest and sharpest blade.

"Got it!" he exclaimed triumphantly, showing me the lethal looking slug, only slightly flattened out, in his hand. He quickly put it in a plastic baggie, which he sealed and marked with his initials, the date, and the location where it was found. Another photo of the now empty bullet hole completed the process of documentation.

Despite its impact with the Panda and the wallboard the slug was in very good shape. It should make for some interesting ballistic comparisons.

Sherry called us in to eat. We sat down for breakfast while I speed dialed Barbara Kaufman. I quickly filled her in on the attempt on Sherry's life and our recovery of the bullet.

"If you can get away today and bring those search warrants with you, we have a pretty good chance of putting a would-be killer with a rifle together with the bullet he used to shoot and kill a Panda Bear that looked a lot like Sherry in the dark.

"How are your search warrants written, Barbara? Specifically by name of the alleged shooter or as John Doe warrants so you can search anywhere?"

"Specifically by name, Roger. For Francis Fortune and Clay Ballard, just as we discussed."

"You need to add one more to the list, our local Sheriff, Jeb Stuart. Vincent ran a fingerprint check on him through a pretty thorough list of databases he has access to. It turns out our sheriff was arrested for assault as a young adult in the East Bay, along with a couple of other young hoodlums including Victor Fong. That's an interesting connection, isn't it?"

There was a long pause on the phone line. I could almost hear the wheels going around as she digested everything I'd said. "I'll be there as soon as I can, Roger, probably by mid-afternoon. I should have the results of the ballistic and fingerprint analyses on the guns Bruce dropped off with us last night by then."

I couldn't help noting that until now the Kaufman sisters had been only too happy to have us running a proxy investigation on the FBI's behalf. Now we were starting to get the personal touch. It probably said a great deal about the Feds' new high level of enthusiasm for this case.

Barbara continued, "If the rifle Bruce gave me is really the gun that shot Jason and the others we matched it up to by ballistic analysis, it had to have been a different rifle last night. And I'll want to hear more about this connection Vincent found between Sheriff Stuart and the Fong Family."

I debated with myself whether I should share my current train of thought with my friend from the FBI. Why not? "Barbara, have you thought about the possibility it was not only a different rifle, but also a different shooter, maybe a copycat taking advantage of the opportunity to kill Sherry and not be blamed?"

"Hmmmm," she replied, just before hanging up the phone. "That's an interesting idea, Roger. I'll see you later today."

Ten minutes later we'd finished breakfast and were out front trying to guess exactly where last night's uninvited guest had taken his shot from. We crudely triangulated from where we'd found the bullet and our assumption the shooter had fired from the prone position. Given how dark it was, Vincent could only guess where he'd been when he fired back at the shooter. Now we were looking for the intersection of two triangles, which narrowed the potentially huge search area down considerably. We walked two sets of grids across the area of interest. I took a north to south transect while Vincent took east to west.

We were looking for a small cartridge case in a large area of grass, dirt, and asphalt road, not quite a needle in a haystack but close. The grass had not been recently mowed given everything else going on here, so had grown long and shaggy, more than enough cover to make a small piece of metal invisible from above. The road surface was easy to scan except at the edges, where grass creeping over the sides gave a convenient hiding place for something as small as we were looking for. The area of dirt contained small patches of weeds scattered at random against a dark soil rich in clay, affording perfect camouflage for the missing cartridge case.

It was slow, boring work, which required being careful, methodical, and lucky to find what we were looking for. About half an hour later lucky won. Vincent spotted a reflection in the grassy area at the end of a random beam of sunlight and we had an ejected cartridge casing carefully picked up with a pencil and transferred to a plastic baggie. The shell gave us the caliber of the rifle we were looking for, a .30-.30. With luck, maybe the FBI could find at least a partial fingerprint on it.

I imagined the shooter in the prone position, lying out as indicated by the location of the ejected shell. "Let's see if he used a tripod to steady the gun," I thought out loud.

We both looked just in front of the imaginary prone shooter's position and a little to each side. It took another five minutes, but the telltale divots were there.

"It looks like this guy's a pro, or at least a serious hunter using pro equipment," said Vincent. "I guessed as much when he hit the doll dead center in the head on a dark night from almost two hundred feet away."

"One last question for you, Vincent. If you actually winged him, where would you guess the wound would be?"

"Well," he mused, "I would have been over there somewhere," he said pointing back over his shoulder.

"The shooter was on the ground, just about perpendicular to me. I'd say the right arm or shoulder, more likely the upper arm."

"It'll be interesting to see if any of our suspects have a sore arm when we look for their rifles," I said. "Would you like to make a bet who'll wince when I squeeze his shoulder?"

"No, not particularly, Roger. But I did like Uncle Bob's and Uncle Tom's approach if he resists service on the warrant."

****

Barbara Kaufman drove up to the house around two o'clock with a surprise companion. Her sister Gretchen had come along for the ride. Knowing Gretchen's busy schedule I realized she assumed we were coming into the end game here and wanted to be part of it. We all sat down in the living room, the most comfortable room in the house.

I handed the two plastic baggies containing the cartridge case and bullet we'd found this morning, each now tagged and sealed, to Barbara, sitting next to her sister on the couch. "A little more evidence for this case. They're souvenirs the man who shot at Sherry last night left behind when he departed in a hurry. We didn't want to contaminate anything so we didn't look for fingerprints. They're all yours."

I also told the two FBI agents about our trip to the wineries on route 128.

Barbara shifted around on the couch to look directly at me. "Thank you, Roger. And I owe you an update on FBI forensics and the overall investigation. The rifle Juliet and Bruce found in the attic fired the bullets you and we have collected from Jason's attempted murder and the older killings, including Wally Fortune's, which also matched Jason's bullet. The outside of the rifle was wiped clean and thoroughly oiled: No fingerprints, no other forensic evidence.

"We found a couple of partials on the magazine. None of the partials had enough points for an absolutely positive I.D., but if we arrest a suspect we can link him to the rifle with statistical odds of better than 1,000:1 if we get a match to the partials. In a town the size of Winters, that's probably good enough. We did get a match with one of the sets of fingerprints you sent us but like I said, that won't hold up as a definitive I.D. in a trial. Would you like to guess who?"

"Not yet, Barbara. I'm pretty sure I know who it is but I'd like to hear what else you found out first."

"The box from the attic contained a 9mm pistol, ammo for it and the rifle, and a small can of an expensive premium gun cleaning solvent. Everything was cleaned and oiled so no fingerprints there. We're running a few bullets we test fired with the pistol through the system to see if they match any bullets from unsolved cases in our files or the California State collection. That can take a while, but I put a priority on it."

Gretchen looked a little more closely at the baggies containing the bullet and cartridge case I'd handed to her sister. "Barbara got all the fun parts of this investigation," Gretchen began, "while I got to direct a few agents on a paper chase. I put a couple of our best agents to work backtracking the paper trail Vincent found linking the Fongs and your winery killings. I used to think the FBI had more and better databases to search and that our agents are better trained than any private eye. Maybe it's time for me to rethink that idea. Somehow or other, Vincent got most of what we found. But we did find a few more tidbits I can share with you.

"Wallace Fortune, his winery manager Clay Ballard, and the local sheriff, Jeb Stuart are all the same age. In fact they played together on the Winters high school football team for three years, as well as junior varsity during their time together in junior high school. They probably played organized football together half their lives until they graduated from high school and went their various ways. All three of their fathers' lives were also linked together by growing up at about the same time in what was then a very small town."

Gretchen smiled. "And, for any trivia buffs among us, the Winters High School football field was featured in the 1973 TV movie "Blood Sport", probably the major claim to fame for Winters after railroads and cars made stagecoach travel obsolete."

"OK," I started to summarize. "Two of our suspects in Winters grew up together and were probably good friends with each other and with the victim. Both of the suspects also grew up with the current sheriff, who has a link to the Fongs. We have the murder weapon, but no complete fingerprints or DNA to link it to any of our suspects. Our killer also seems to have murdered several other people connected with local wineries. We have links between a major gang run by the Fong Family in the East Bay and an extortion and money-laundering scheme involving several local wineries for at least two generations. We have direct evidence for a link between the victim's brother Francis and the Fongs."

After a short pause for dramatic effect, I continued, "We also have an attempted murder of Sherry Fortune. The shooter used a different rifle than the one we found hidden in the attic of this house that we know was used for several killings, including Wally Fortune's and the attempt on Jason's life. It could have been the same killer with a different rifle, which is what we'll be searching for today, or it could be a copycat trying to literally get away with murder. I think our next step should be serving these three warrants and trying to collect a few rifles."

Gretchen nodded. "I agree, Roger. But there's a real risk that whoever we start with will notify the others and the weapon will be hidden out of reach by the time we get through three searches."

I thought about the various combinations and permutations possible here. "You're right, Gretchen. We can't all be in three places at once. And tactically speaking we have only two police officers that can legally execute a search warrant in our little group here. It sounds like one of those puzzles we used to have to work out as kids. How do you get the fox, the rat, and the chicken across the river one at a time without some animal eating the other? In this case I think we have to split up and do all of the three searches simultaneously.

"I'd suggest the toughest of the three suspects and therefore the most dangerous situation will be Sheriff Stuart, who will certainly be armed. How about Barbara and Vincent doing that search. We have Barbara there to guarantee the search is legal if there's ever a trial and Vincent can easily handle the sheriff if he objects too strenuously."

Gretchen frowned. "That's the easy one, relatively speaking. But that still leaves two searches with only one law official, me."

I nodded. "That was an interesting choice of words, Gretchen. You actually came up with the solution to both of our problems with your subconscious choice. The second search will be you, by yourself, searching Clay Ballard's property. There's some risk there but you'll be prepared beforehand so it should be OK if you detain and handcuff him first thing. That's a little dubious legally, but you can argue exigent circumstances and make it stick if it gets that far. Especially with the evidence we have that the sheriff is dirty so you couldn't trust the local law for backup."

I shifted my glance to Sherry, who'd been sitting on one of the comfortable chairs listening to our conversation. "I don't feel comfortable leaving Sherry unprotected since there may be other bad guys floating around or we might be wrong in our theories, so she'll go with me to search Francis Fortune's properties, office, car, and home. The law on this one is fuzzy enough to make a good argument it was a legal search if we find anything linking him to the murders since Francis is technically an employee of the Fortune Winery, which Sherry owns. I don't expect any resistance there since Francis had a chance to watch a demonstration of my martial arts skills and is a physical coward."

Barbara stood up decisively. "It sounds like it's time to move," suggested Barbara. "Give us the addresses where each of us has to be and let's get started.

Vincent texted the pertinent addresses for GPS guidance to each of us. "Everything is close together here. If we all start out at the same time we should be at our search sites within a minute or two of each other. So we should be able to skip synchronizing watches and all the usual nonsense we see on TV."

Vincent and I strapped on pistols under our jackets, the Kaufman sisters checked their guns, and we all started out.

Chapter 27. Three searches

It was a weekday but things were slow at the winery so there was a fair chance Clay Ballard would be at home. Gretchen Kaufman knocked on his door. Less than a minute later he opened the door, not recognizing the FBI agent. "Good afternoon. What can I do for you?" he asked politely.

Gretchen flashed her badge and credentials at him. "I need to come in and search the premises for the objects specified in this search warrant," she recited, handing him the warrant.

He just glanced at the legal document, stepping back to let her enter. "What's this all about?" Ballard asked.

"Please just sit down and get back to the game you were watching on TV and let me do my thing here," Gretchen said firmly. "I'll explain what you should know after I complete my search. I'll try to be as careful as possible with your things. In the meantime you can speed things up if you can tell me whether you have any firearms here in the house."

"Should I be calling Sheriff Stuart?" he asked. "I can't imagine what legal right you have to show up unannounced and start searching my house."

"Please sit down, Sir," replied the FBI agent. "My legal right is spelled out in the search warrant I gave you to read. If you attempt to interfere with my search or to telephone anybody until we're finished here I'll put you under arrest and handcuff you. And you'll be liable for a felony, interfering with a police officer performing their duty. Am I making myself clear?"

Ballard sat down in front of the TV in the family room after Gretchen carefully searched him and the room, including under the chair cushions, for any concealed weapons. Nothing turned up. She walked back over to where Ballard sat sullenly and cuffed his hands behind his back. "I'm sorry about the discomfort, Sir, but I think we'll both feel a lot safer this way."

She started searching on the first floor of his two-story house, keeping an eye on him. The kitchen, bathroom, and dining room were devoid of guns. In this part of California houses were built on concrete slabs to accommodate rainy and dry seasonal expansion and contraction of soils rich in clay, so she didn't need to worry about basements or crawl spaces. The living room featured a large gun cabinet, which was locked.

"Where do you keep the keys for the gun cabinet?" Gretchen asked the now surly Clay Ballard.

He remained silent.

"Bad choice," she called out, breaking into the case with the aid of a large screwdriver she'd brought into the house. Three long guns, two rifles and a 12-guage shotgun, stood on their cushioned butts in custom crafted racks. Gretchen donned latex gloves and carefully carried all three guns to the trunk of her car.

Returning to the gun cabinet she checked out several drawers and racks, finding ammunition, cleaning oil and solvents, and a larger locked drawer. She broke into the locked drawer with the screwdriver to find a small collection of handguns, collecting and bagging each pistol and revolver and the gun cleaning supplies to add to her collection in the car trunk.

She quickly but thoroughly searched the rest of the living room and the single bedroom on the lower floor. Gretchen ordered Ballard to lead the way upstairs and accompany her in the room-to-room search of three bedrooms and a master bathroom, then to stand in plain sight while she searched the attic. The prize was in the attic, partially hidden under the fiberglass batting insulation between two joists. Gretchen climbed down from the attic dangling a pair of military issue night vision goggles. The goggles were bagged, tagged, and added to the treasure trove in the trunk of the car.

****

Meanwhile, Barbara and Vincent knocked on Sheriff Stuart's door. He answered immediately, dressed in his sheriff's uniform with his gun at his hip, but in obvious need of a shave. "What do you want Mr. Romero? And who is this lovely lady with you?" he asked cheerfully.

Barbara flashed her badge and I.D. at him, pulling out her gun and casually holding it pointing downward at some point between her and the sheriff. "I have a warrant to search the premises, Sheriff. Would you please take your gun out of the holster very slowly and carefully with just your thumb and one other finger and hand it to my colleague here?"

"I'll need to see your warrant first," he blustered.

"No, we'll do it my way," Barbara insisted. "And if you make us take your gun away from you I'll let Vincent do the job and won't be able to guarantee that all your parts will be intact when he's finished. Now, slowly take the gun out and hand it to my partner or he'll take it from you by force. I won't ask again."

Stuart looked like he was ready to go for a gunfight. Suddenly Vincent's pistol materialized in his hand out of thin air, pointing at the sheriff's head. The sheriff shook his head in disbelief at the fast draw, but it seemed to take all the fight out of him. He ever so slowly withdrew his weapon and silently handed it to

206

Vincent, who had already donned his latex gloves. The sheriff's handgun disappeared into a large baggie, tagged as potential evidence.

"May I see your warrant now?" he asked Barbara in a subdued tone.

Wordlessly she handed it to him.

He scanned it quickly, then more carefully. There was a flash of fear in his expression, just for an instant. Then his poker face returned.

"This isn't legal, you know? You're in my jurisdiction and you didn't consult with the local law enforcement agency before serving this warrant. Anything you find won't be admissible in a court of law."

"I'll be the judge of that," Barbara said firmly. "But, for the moment, I'll interpret your comments as indicative of a lack of cooperation. Please put these handcuffs on him, Vincent, and cuff him around one of the larger pipes in the bathroom so he can't exercise his lack of cooperation more forcefully. And check for any other weapons under his boots or in any of the usual places."

A small semi-automatic pistol with a two-inch barrel came out of an ankle holster and a small, but sinister, stiletto came out of a scabbard on his back, just under his neck. Two more baggies of possible evidence were added to their collection.

Barbara and Vincent performed a fast, but methodical, search of the old house. They found an unlocked gun cabinet in the living room containing space for four rifles or shotguns, with only two rifles and a shotgun occupying three of the spaces. There was a lot of ammunition in various calibers and several handguns, both revolvers and pistols, of various larger calibers. The garage had a scale and press for loading cartridges in various calibers, with boxes of fired shells, resized shells, and newly cast bullets on the rack directly above the equipment. They did lots more bagging and tagging before several additional items went into the trunk of Barbara's car.

Barbara led the way back into the house. A search of the second floor and the attic did not unearth any more items related to those specified in the search warrant. Just for fun Barbara cloned the entire contents of Sheriff Stuart's computer onto a flash drive she had in her pocket. She also picked up a flash drive and a backup external hard drive from the back of the desk top, handing them to Vincent.

"I'm not allowed to browse here and take evidence not specified in the warrant but there aren't any restrictions on a civilian like you doing so if you were invited into the house and they were in plain sight, Vincent. I distinctly remember the sheriff asking you to step inside before I served the warrant. Please let me know what you find on them."

They walked back into the first floor bathroom where the sheriff, seething with anger, was still handcuffed to a pipe. "You'll both pay for this," he growled through tightly clenched teeth.

"Play nice or we'll just leave you here in handcuffs and call it into the deputies to release you," Barbara responded. "That's not the image you want to portray, is it Jeb?" Barbara deliberately used the first name, not the title, as a gesture of disrespect to let him know she wasn't intimidated.

After a slow count of ten he managed to say, "I'm sorry. Would you please remove these handcuffs?"

Barbara did.

"Now, may I have my service sidearm back?"

"I'm afraid not," the FBI agent replied. "I'll be taking it, along with all of the firearms we've found here today, back to the FBI laboratory in San Francisco for testing. We'll let you know when you can drive to The City and reclaim your property as soon as we've finished the tests we plan to perform unless any of it is impounded as evidence in a criminal case."

"How do you expect me to perform my duties as the Sheriff of Yolo County without a gun?" he asked rhetorically.

"I don't think that'll be a problem for long," she replied cheerfully as we left the house. "And please don't try to do anything stupid. I can have the State Police and an FBI SWAT team from Sacramento here in force in less than twenty minutes if any of us start feeling threatened."

****

Sherry stood behind me as I knocked on Francis Fortune's front door. No answer. Nor was there a car under the Porte Cochere at the end of the driveway alongside the house. The only possible threat I could see was a large black sedan with tinted windows, dark enough to make it impossible to see inside the car, parked half way up the street. The license plate holder extolled the virtues of a car dealer in Oakland. The odds were good the car contained a couple of Fong Gang hoods, watching over the house to keep track of Francis. Maybe he was late on a payment?

I considered the odds. Even if there were a couple of Fong goons in the car they were probably tasked only with surveillance, not action. With three different searches going on simultaneously, there wouldn't be any secret we'd searched the house after we finished. So the only risk here was they might intervene, but I was pretty sure I could handle that contingency with my fists or the gun I was wearing if it occurred.

I rang the bell. There was still no answer. Pulling a small case out of my pocket I had the lock picked in just under two minutes. We entered the house, stopping to listen just inside the door. The house looked and felt deserted. I checked to make sure the entire downstairs was empty. It was. I locked the front door and found a sheltered spot for Sherry to stand watch that nobody came down the stairs or to the front door unannounced to avoid any unexpected surprises.

I walked quickly through the apparently deserted house to get a feel for the layout. In this part of rural Northern California many of the men were hunters and/or fishermen. I looked for the gun case or rack that he would use to keep shotguns for bird hunting and rifles for deer. It turned out to be a rack screwed into the back wall in one of the bedroom closets, hidden by the clothes hanging in front of the closet until you moved lots of suits, slacks, and jackets aside.

I collected a rifle, an old-fashioned model .30-.30 Winchester lever action he probably used once a season for deer hunting, and a 12-gauge shotgun good for duck, pheasant and maybe deer when loaded with buckshot or slugs. I packed the ammo for each and the gun cleaning kits. All of this was piled by the door for when we were ready to go back to the car, parked out of sight further up the street.

I checked upstairs. Nobody was there either. Then I did a careful search, looking for additional hidden guns, papers, or computer records. Twenty minutes later I concluded there wasn't anything interesting on either floor or in the attic. It was time to go. Transferring everything we would take with us outside to the porch I locked the door on our way out.

I handed Sherry a pair of latex gloves. Together we carried all the firearms back to Sherry's car and stuffed them into the trunk. We drove off to our next stop, Francis' office. Looking in my rear view mirror I noted the black car remained where it had been parked, not following us. I found a parking spot half a block from the building we wanted. A large black sedan, identical to the one I'd spotted parked outside Francis' house, stood in a parking space almost half a block on the other side of Francis' office from where we'd parked. It had the same tinted windows as the first sedan so it was impossible to tell whether it was occupied.

Sherry and I walked into the building. "Stay behind me and be ready to run if there's anybody in the office besides your least favorite lawyer, Sherry. There's a car parked further up the street that looks like he may have some additional clients visiting."

I tried the door to the office, which turned out to be unlocked. We entered quietly and carefully. Francis was there, sitting alone at his desk. I explained it had been a long day and I didn't want to have to beat the tar out of him, so he was to just sit at his desk while I executed a valid search warrant.

He didn't offer any resistance. I went through the office, checking his safe. No guns were hidden anywhere. I rifled the papers in and on his desk, finding nothing special. The computer and hard drive took several minutes to copy onto a flash drive from my pocket. And that was that, at least as far as searching his office. Now the problem was extricating our selves from what might be a dicey predicament with Sherry at risk.

"There's still the possibility of our meeting whoever was parked in the car I saw on the street, Sherry. If we do, I doubt they'll greet us pleasantly. Follow my instructions immediately. Don't ask me any questions and I think everything will be fine. For starters, stay behind me and wait for instructions if we meet anyone between here and our car."

"OK, I understand," she replied.

I opened the door quickly, immediately checking the staircase. Two large Asian men were climbing the stairs, about halfway up the flight. I had the advantage here, so took it. I drew my pistol before either man could react while shouting, "Freeze. Police."

They saw the gun pointing at them and froze.

"These guys look like pros," I thought to myself. "Assume the position!"

Both men turned toward the wall, putting their hands on the wall above their heads and carefully stepping back so their weight was on their hands while they leaned forward.

"Stay where you are Sherry," I ordered as I walked over to a position behind the goon on the upper step. Covering his partner on the lower step, I quickly frisked him. I found one 9mm gun in a hip holster, which I took and slipped through my belt, as well as a smaller semi-automatic pistol in an ankle holster, which I left alone for now, and a stiletto in a neck scabbard which I took and slipped into my jacket pocket. I also took his wallet and pocketed it.

I took a step down and repeated the process on the second hoodlum, this time netting one large and one small pistol, a wallet, and another knife. It was safe now for me to reach up and remove the remaining pistol from the first hoodlum's ankle holster.

"You can pick up your guns and knives at Sheriff Stuart's office when you're ready to leave town," I told them in my most reasonable tone. "In the meantime don't stick your heads out of the front door for five minutes or you'll lose a body part you really don't want to lose."

I had my own pistol in my right hand, one of the 9mm pistols donated by the hoodlums in my left hand, and the two smaller pistols, the other 9mm pistol, two wallets, and two knives distributed in various pockets or in my belt. I stood directly behind the two men, a gun pressing hard against one kidney of each, leaving enough space for Sherry to pass behind me.

"You can come down now, Sherry. Walk slowly and carefully behind me and past us down to the front door. Wait for me there."

Sherry said, "OK" softly when she reached the door.

"If either of you moves back from the wall until we're gone you'll get a bullet in a kneecap," I told them pleasantly. I walked carefully down the stairs keeping an eye on the two men hugging the wall, joining Sherry at the door. I cracked the door open far enough to check the black sedan. It was still parked where I'd first seen it, with nobody who looked big and Chinese anywhere in sight.

"Take the car keys, Sherry. Get the car started and drive slowly down the block to the big black sedan parked six or seven cars further down the street. You'll pick me up there. If anything goes wrong just hit the gas and get as far away from here as you can, preferably somewhere across the river in Sacramento County."

I trotted over to the black sedan, keeping an eye on the front door of Francis' office building. Nobody stuck a head out. I took one of the razor sharp stilettos out of its scabbard and stabbed all four tires on the sedan. The sound of compressed air escaping seemed very loud as Sherry pulled up and I jumped into the car's passenger seat.

We drove back to the house to meet the others and transfer everything we'd come up with in our searches to the FBI car. I told Gretchen what had happened while bagging and tagging the six weapons and two wallets I'd just liberated from the hoodlums at Francis' office and added them to the piles. I hadn't removed my latex gloves when leaving the lawyer's office so everything should still be pristine and uncontaminated with innocent fingerprints or DNA.

"I thought you told those two gangsters you'd leave their guns for them with Sheriff Stuart, Roger," Sherry reminded me.

"I did. But they knew I was just yanking their chains. I'm sure they both have criminal records, so it would be admitting to a felony if they claimed any of those weapons belonged to them, especially to the sheriff. There's a possibility one or more of those guns might have been used in a crime and left a bullet behind. The FBI ballistics tests will check that possibility out.

"In the meantime I'm sure Victor Fong won't be happy when two more of his gang return home with some sort of fairy tale about losing their weapons, and it's always fun to stir the pot a little bit to see what happens."

Now there'd be a long period of waiting while a team of FBI agents sorted through all the paper and computerized records. Vincent was able to copy the various flash drives we collected from the suspects' computers so he'd have something to do while we waited for results from the FBI investigation.

It would take a lot less time while an FBI forensics team shot test bullets and compared ballistics between all of the guns we recovered and the bullet someone shot at Sherry's Panda doll. That would be the FBI's highest priority. If we got a hit on any of the seized rifles that would be grounds for arrest of a suspect, setting into motion a chain of investigations into their motives and associates that would be vastly more thorough than anything the Kaufman sisters by themselves or we could do with our limited resources. Pending the outcome of these tests the FBI would keep all three suspects under 24/7 surveillance, so nobody would be in a position to commit illegal flight to avoid prosecution.

It was time for us to go home to Los Angeles while we waited. It was easy to convince Sherry to join us in Southern California as a well-protected houseguest until an arrest was made and the FBI could guarantee her safety. Sherry gave me permission to share my complete report, when I finished preparing it, with Barbara Kaufman so there wouldn't be any missing details from our pattern of hit or miss communication over the last few weeks.

Checking the local newspaper and the TV news since we got back from our exciting ride from the wineries, Vincent hadn't found any mention of a car crash on Route 128. Whoever it was in the pick-up truck seemed to have survived and found a quiet solution to being stranded in the middle of nowhere on a narrow road with a completely dysfunctional vehicle. What the men who followed us lacked in subtle skills tailing cars they apparently made up for with improvisation skills under pressure.

Chapter 28. One of our suspects goes ballistic

It took a couple of days but the FBI ballistic specialists came up with a hit.

Barbara called me in Los Angeles. "The bullet Vincent recovered from the wall after it went through the Panda doll's head was a .30-.30. It matched perfectly the comparison bullets fired from Francis Fortune's lever action Winchester. And we found a partial fingerprint on the cartridge case you found. Not enough for conclusive evidence in a trial, but also a match to Francis. We're working on the arrest warrant now.

"And thank you for your investigative report you sent us yesterday. The timing is perfect. The rifle gave us means and your report gives us plenty of motivation and a lot of information we can use to threaten him with prosecution for more than taking a shot at a doll. Opportunity isn't at issue. He's got a long time in jail waiting for him after we go through the plea bargaining stage of the process. I take it you're not too surprised he's the one who took the shot. You warned us this could be a copycat from the beginning."

"Yeah," I replied, "I'm not surprised. But I think I speak for Sherry when I say she's not out for revenge here. If you can convince Francis he's looking at life in prison without parole when you try him for all the murders, I think he'll crack and spill all he knows about the Fong Family and their involvement in the previous killings and money laundering. This may be the lever you need to start getting everyone trying to rat out the others so you can catch a much bigger prize, our serial killer, not just a sniveling coward like Francis.

"But I'd be real careful he doesn't get out on bail or mix with the general prison population while all this is going on. I wouldn't give a plugged nickel for his life expectancy after the Fong Family learns you have him in custody where he can trade a confession for a lighter sentence, or even your federal witness protection program."

"Point taken, Roger. He should be safe in Federal custody. The Fong gang tends to be incarcerated in the State of California prison system when we catch them, not our federal lockups, so their influence is minimal. Bail's trickier. We need the right judge who'll listen when we explain what's at stake here. I'd give that one less than a 50-50 chance."

I thought about the possibilities here. "If I can catch a flight to The City this afternoon, would you be able to get me a crack at questioning Francis without his lawyer present? Remember, I'm just a private citizen here."

"Good question. I can try. I'll get back to you within the hour."

It turned out to be forty-five minutes. In that time I typed out everything we knew about Francis' past, in chronological order, and everything criminal I guessed or suspected he was involved in. It was a long list.

No small talk this time. Barbara told me my flight number and departure time.

"The FBI will pay for your travel. Someone will meet your flight and bring you here. You'll be monitored and taped during your questioning of Francis, but nobody else will have to be in the room with you. I need your promise not to touch or threaten him."

This was much more than I expected. "You've got my promise. Thank you very much for this chance to get some more information."

Three hours later Special Agent Sanderson, who'd pulled me aside as I exited the plane, delivered me to San Francisco's Federal Detention Center. I was hustled into a dismal looking little interrogation room where I sat for twenty minutes before Francis was settled into a metal chair and handcuffed to the table.

"He's all yours, Sir," said the uniformed guard deferentially. "Just push the button by the door when you're finished questioning the suspect."

I waited for the door to close behind the guard. "Hello again, Francis. It looks like you're in a heck of a mess this time."

"I haven't any idea what you're talking about, Mr. Bowman. I want my lawyer."

I looked around us at the interrogation room. Four unadorned walls painted an institutional yuck color, a small table in the middle, bright ceiling lights shining on the suspect so the video images would be sharp, and a one-way mirror on the wall behind me so interrogations could be observed at all times. "Given I'm not a cop, you haven't any right to a lawyer, Francis. You can answer my questions or not as you see fit, but unless you convince me your worthless life is worth saving I don't think you're going to find many advocates around here.

"I also think you've underestimated what we've already learned. Why don't we start by my telling you some of the things I know before you plead ignorance about everything that was going on at the Fortune Winery."

I paused, but Francis didn't seem to have anything to say. I walked over to him and patted him firmly on the shoulder to reassure him, then returned to my seat.

"We know the bullet fired at your sister-in-law a few nights ago came from your rifle. Based on how you winced when I touched your shoulder just then you have a bullet crease in your upper arm. You may be able to find a lawyer who'll argue you were wounded in a hunting accident, but that begs the questions of why you didn't report the incident and where you had a hunting accident in California out of the legal hunting season for deer.

"I have an operative who shot at the gunman the other night outside of Sherry's house who'll swear under oath he thought he winged the shooter in the same arm you seem to have a wound in."

Francis remained silent.

I looked him straight in the eye and went for my most sincere tone. "You're a lawyer, Francis. Not a very good one, but a walking, talking demonstration of a little knowledge being a dangerous thing. You're thinking the worst the FBI can get you for is attempted murder, with a plea bargain down to assault with a deadly weapon or felonious assault.

"I don't think Sherry or I ever mentioned it to you, Francis, but I'm a lawyer too. I went to a good law school so I know a lot more about criminal law than you do. The real problem you're facing is that the attempted murder is icing on the cake. You're going to be charged with your brother's murder, which will include the 'lying in wait' Special Circumstance. That means the death penalty if you're convicted in California, with at best a plea bargain to life in prison without parole if you plead guilty."

This time I saw Francis flinch. I was getting to him. "There's a lot more than that for you to worry about, Francis. The bullet that killed Wally came from the same rifle that killed at least three other people. And guess where we found that rifle? That's right. In your brother's house, which only Sherry and you had access to at any time. So if you're charged in Wally's death, you get three more murder charges hung on you as a bonus."

I paused for effect. "Then there's your long term relationship with the Fong Family. We can prove you were part of a criminal conspiracy involving them. That's not necessary to put you away for life, as I've explained to you. But put yourself in Victor Fong's shoes. Would you let somebody who knows as much as you do about his criminal activities live long enough to testify once your arrest becomes common knowledge?

"And, by the way, the lawyer you wanted here. Was it Harold Fong? If so, what side do you think he'll be on if it's you or his father going to jail for life?"

Somewhere between Murder with Special Circumstances and Harold Fong's divided loyalties I got through to Francis. I saw him folding, literally and figuratively, right in front of my eyes.

He started to cry. His body was wracked with sobs. It took five minutes before he was composed enough to ask to talk to the FBI agent in charge of his case.

Gretchen and Barbara came into the room, telling me it was time to go. They'd keep me in the loop as to what they learned, but I didn't need to jeopardize the admissibility of the coming confession by appearing on the tape with the FBI agents and Francis. As I walked out of the door I heard them advising Francis about his right to have an attorney present or to decline the lawyer. I was pretty sure he'd opt for the latter choice at this point.

Special Agent Sanderson took me back in tow, immediately driving me to the airport so I would have time to catch a Southwest shuttle flight home in time for dinner.

Suzanne, Sherry, Bruce, and I discussed the case over dinner. I concluded my description of interrogating Sherry's brother-in-law Francis by summarizing, "He's out of your life for the next few decades of prison time he'll have to serve. I suspect the threat to your life is less now that he's in custody, Sherry, but I'm not sure you're completely safe yet either.

"That leaves us with only two real suspects for our serial killer: Sheriff Jeb Stuart or Clay Ballard, the winery manager. Or maybe it's both of them in collusion. And at least for the moment I'm stumped as to how we'll be able to smoke out which one it is."

Suzanne looked thoughtful. "Two of the little details you and Vincent found when you were trying to backtrack the history of the winery extortion scheme sort of stuck in my mind. I wonder if either of them is worth following up on. The first was a picture of Clay Bedford's dad with a trophy deer he shot and donated the head and rack of antlers to a local restaurant. That makes him either very lucky or an excellent marksman. I wonder if Clay is also a crack shot, just like our serial killer almost has to be.

"The other detail that sticks in my mind is the arrest of Jeb Stuart before he was the sheriff, along with a couple of the Fong gang, having Harold Fong as his lawyer. I wonder if there's a paper trail that links Jeb's father to Victor Fong or his father, Ching Fong, or that links Jeb Stuart to Harold Fong after that episode. Maybe going over the computer records you liberated from Clay's and Jeb's houses might be enlightening on one or both of these issues."

"Both of these are good suggestions, Suzanne. I'll get to work on them immediately."

"In the meantime, Roger, could you maybe drive some kind of wedge between Bedford and Stuart and see what happens if each one thinks the other one is talking to the FBI?"

"Good idea, but I don't think it'll work here. They've known each other all their lives. It wouldn't be easy to start that kind of wedge between two long-term buddies. Stuart may not be particularly bright but he's a tough old bird who would turn physical long before he'd start planning how to out-think somebody. And if Bedford is our serial killer he's a sociopath who's spent an entire lifetime building up his uncompetitive nice guy persona, which means he's a superb planner, schemer, and actor. There's no way he's going to fall for some variant of a cliché like good cop-bad cop. And as long as Stuart remains the county sheriff, we can't risk doing anything illegal without having a big hammer fall potentially on whoever they catch."

Suzanne took a small spoonful of something chocolate and decadent Bruce had made for desert. "On a happier topic, I assume you noticed Jason isn't having dinner with us tonight. He's a quick healer and surprisingly strong. It took only a couple of days before he was taking walks around the block with Connie. A couple of days ago he officially moved in with her for the next stage of his recuperation. I hear they walk a mile or so twice a day, which should be good for her pregnancy and his recovery. He's starting to make noises about coming back to work if you're OK with him telecommuting from Irvine."

I smiled a happy smile. "Good to hear. And he enjoys paperwork a lot more than I do. I suspect telecommunication will be discussed tomorrow, along with our progress on the case."

I spent an hour that night indexing and organizing the various computer files. I'd spend most of tomorrow doing keyword searches of documents and e-mails searching for the links Suzanne suggested might already be there right in front of us.

Chapter 29. Following a lead

The next day Vincent and I spent a lot of time on our computers doing keyword searches on copied computer files, as well as catching up with large piles of accumulated routine work piled high in our in-boxes. Hopefully, the FBI was doing the same thing with all the paper and electronic files they had accumulated, as well as interrogating Francis Fortune.

Just before lunch Suzanne called. Connie was in labor and had been admitted to the UC Irvine Hospital to deliver her baby. Jason was providing moral support and Lamaze breathing instructions, based on a pamphlet he'd read a few times. Suzanne was driving down to see if she could help and would get back to me after she had a better idea of when the baby would be born and how Jason was doing as a birth coach.

Later that afternoon Gretchen Kaufman called. "Just a quick update for you Roger. Nothing new yet from our analysis of the computer files, but we're getting through the various copied hard drives. Barbara's interrogation of Francis Fortune is going slowly. His lawyerly instincts have kicked in and he only wants to play 'let's make a deal' before he gives us anything juicy. It's clear he knew what was going on with the money laundering and extortion and was involved with the Fong gang as their point of contact at the Fortune Winery, at least since his father was killed.

"It isn't clear whether he was leading or following in all the crimes he may have committed through the years. My best guess would be some of each. He's worked it out that he's at risk from his former associates so is happy to be in custody where he's safe for now. I'm afraid this is going to take a while to play out. We're also taking a good hard look at Sheriff Stuart, who is probably the second generation of corrupt law enforcement officials in his family to profit from the whole winery extortion scheme. He had to know what was going on."

I remained silent for a minute while processing this information. Not much there, at least not yet. "How about Clay Ballard? Did you find out anything new about him we should know about?"

"Not really," Gretchen replied. "He seems to have spent his entire life after high school in Winters, working at the winery. He has a good credit rating, owns his own home, which he inherited, and never seems to have gotten in trouble with the law. On the other hand, we did find something interesting about his father, Cal. Cal was the right age for Viet Nam, so was drafted and served in the army. He saw combat in the war and was honorably discharged.

"Now come the good parts. His specialty was being trained as a sniper and getting medals for his marksmanship and for bravery in action. And, one of the members of his unit, which was mostly made up of draftees from Northern

California, turns out to be an older brother of Victor Fong. The brother was killed in a gang-related shooting in Oakland a dozen years after he got out of the army."

"What's the brother's name, Gretchen? He sounds like an interesting possible connection to check out."

"His name was Winston, Winston Fong. And I have one other tidbit for you, Roger. The California Highway Patrol got a report from a gas station and garage outside of Winters called "Gary's Garage" that a wrecked pickup truck they towed in had a few bullets in the engine block. The pickup, which was an old junker, had been reported as stolen from a farm in the middle of a lot of other farms between Woodland and Winters.

"The garage owner, Gary, didn't know anything about whose car it was. They got a request to pick it up from a dirt road going nowhere off 128 and tow it in. The client, who was very unmemorable, asked them to arrange for it be junked. The client paid cash in advance and used a false I.D. He left an address that turned out to be an empty lot in Woodland. And the garage stood to make some money out of the deal so didn't ask too many questions. So that lead is a dead end."

"Thanks for the update, Gretchen. There are a few leads there we can check out."

I hung up and thought about what the FBI agent had told me. It sounded like I had another trip to Winters ahead of me. Between the lines I assumed she was hoping to use me to recheck the garage and see if Gary might be a bit more able to remember his mysterious customer if he was offered a little cash to jar his memory.

A few minutes later Suzanne called. "False alarm, Roger. Connie is back home for now. Jason handled everything like a pro so I can relax and come home. If I leave now I should be there in time for dinner."

****

Over dinner I told Suzanne and Sherry I'd be going back to Winters for at least a day or two, asking, "Do you have any reason you need to go back and check things out, Sherry? I'm still not comfortable you'll be safe there, even if we have taken Francis out of the equation, at least for now."

Sherry thought about the logistics. "Thank you, Roger. I admit it would feel a little spooky going back to the winery after almost being shot there two different times. If you can find time to check whether I have any mail at the Winters address or at my Sacramento house, I think I'll be fine just staying here where I can feel safe. But please take my house keys so you can stay someplace comfortable while you're there.

"I've been calling Carmichael every day to make sure my dogs and house are safe. So far everything's been fine. But with me still alive and safely out of the area I'm afraid that could be a place where I'm still vulnerable to the killer using them as leverage to make me do whatever he wants with the winery. Is there any way you can arrange to have the dogs moved to a safe place where somebody trustworthy can look after them until this is all over and I'm back to Winters?"

So that's how I ended up flying back north by myself and driving a rental car from Sacramento Airport to Winters. On the flight from Los Angeles I went over my notes from Gretchen's call and thought long and hard about crime, the time lines, and a bible passage about 'sin'. And about a lot of chance meetings between people that might have set all the events at the winery into motion.

I carefully considered whether I was risking my life wandering around Winters by myself with a hostile sheriff there potentially looking for an excuse to do something bad to me. It was an absolutely minimal risk as long as I was invisible driving around in a rental car nobody would recognize, I decided. And my apparent FBI connection had, at least until now, given Sheriff Stuart good cause to exercise restraint. As had my demonstrated ability to win any fight I was pushed into.

I found Gary's Garage with a lot of help from my smart phone navigation app. It had apparently been there for a long time, featuring an old-fashioned style with several gas pumps in front of a large garage bay where two cars were up on hydraulic lifts being serviced. Several other cars stood around the station waiting their turn for repairs or an oil change.

All of the cars I could see were at least ten years old, harking back to an era when car repairs were done with screwdrivers, wrenches, and mechanics with grease-stained coveralls, not computers and new motherboards. The original building was pre-World War II vintage, looking almost exactly like the Hollywood version of a dingy service station in the movie "The Big Sleep".

I pulled into the facility, parking off to the side of the garage bay away from the gas pumps. Walking into the service bay I asked a mechanic whether Gary was around. The mechanic, a short and skinny old guy in greasy blue coveralls that had been around for several years, took his time answering as he sized me up. A wad of tobacco swelled his cheek. He spat carefully into an old coffee can, obviously reserved for this purpose, on a table next to him.

Then he asked, "You a cop?"

"No," I replied. "But I am looking for the answers to a few questions."

"Time's valuable around here," he said cagily.

"Fair enough," I responded, nodding in agreement.

He considered his next comment for a while before spitting into the can again. "I'm Gary," he admitted.

I'd already figured that out. I'm a detective. His name was written in red thread script on top of the coverall's breast pocket. "I'm here because of an old pickup truck that got towed to your station a few days ago."

Gary nodded, chewing his tobacco like a cow with a particularly tasty cud. "I figured that was it. Is it worth fifty dollars to you to find out what I know?"

"More like twenty," I replied, pulling out a couple of ten-dollar bills I'd put in my pocket for just this moment. The implication was clear. 'Take this or you get nothing!'

He told me the same story he'd told the Highway Patrol. "Good," I said handing him one of the ten-dollar bills. "You can have the other bill if you describe the guy who came in, or twice that amount if you can I.D. him for me."

"You look like a cop," he said pensively. "Have you ever been one?"

"Yeah," I admitted. "Down south of here, in L.A."

He chewed some more tobacco, spitting the results into the can. "OK, let me see a little more cash."

I pulled out another ten. "Here you go, but this is for an I.D."

He paused for a count of ten. "The guy was a couple of inches shorter than you are, weightlifter's build so I'd guess twenty or thirty pounds heavier. Dark hair, acne scars on his face like a guy who's been taking 'roids. Big muscles, usually wears jeans and a muscle shirt. He hangs out at a biker bar called 'Mother's' a few miles up the highway from here. You can usually find him there guzzling beer and shooting pool with his gang this time of day. They call him 'Soto'. And I wouldn't go there alone if I was you. Soto's plenty tough and his gang would love to stomp you silly after Soto finishes beating you senseless."

I handed him another twenty dollars wordlessly. I nodded my thanks and headed back to my rental car, driving it up the highway a few miles before I came to 'Mother's'. The parking lot was two-thirds fancy bike, one-third pickup trucks with Easy Rider gun racks in the cabs and NRA stickers on the bumpers. I had the only car visible in the lot, which I parked carefully behind a tree facing in the correct direction for a fast exit. Then I walked into the bar.

Unless Gary had Soto on speed dial the odds were pretty good nobody had called ahead to warn him I was coming. Still, I stood out like a sore thumb in this bar. I was the square dude in the suit in a biker bar. I took a few steps into the bar, stopped to let my eyes adjust to the gloom, and waited to see what might happen next.

I spotted a muscle-bound weightlifter at the pool table that had to be Soto. He matched Gary's description perfectly. He was one of a quartet of players at the table. One of the others, a young punk dressed in the standard issue biker uniform of jeans, t-shirt, and black leather vest with his gang name, Vaquero, on it, strutted over exuding cockiness and testosterone with every step.

He deliberately violated my personal space before coming to a halt, staring up at me before asking, "Are you looking for somebody here or did you just make a wrong turn on the road and get lost?"

His acolyte audience laughed at that piece of stoned biker humor, which encouraged him to escalate his rude greeting to me. "We don't take kindly to strangers coming into our bar uninvited, pendejo!"

I ignored him, walking on over to Soto's pool table. "I'm looking for a gentleman named Soto. I'd like to ask him a few questions."

Vaquero came running up to a point midway between Soto and me. "Don't worry Soto. I'll take care of this cabron."

He took a slow swing at my face that would have taken my head off if it landed. It didn't. I slipped inside the punch, blocked it, and hit him very hard with a half fist in his solar plexus, stepping aside as he fell to the floor.

"I'm still looking for Soto," I announced to the table.

This time the guy I assumed to be the real Soto walked slowly around the table. I noted he was still holding the pool cue in his right hand, clenched tightly in his fist. Subtle, he wasn't.

"You found me," he said tersely, continuing to advance to what he considered to be the ideal striking position.

I had two problems immediately ahead of me. Soto and his pool cue, which didn't bother me at all, and how I would get Soto out of here for a private chat without having to fight his whole gang en route. I worked out the strategy and spacing, keeping my eye on Soto's shoulder for the telltale tensing that would announce he was about to lift and swing the pool cue at me.

He got about half of the cue's length from me and made his move. It was a roundhouse swing with the leaded butt end directed at my head. I stepped inside the blow, pivoted, and caught his wrist with my left hand. My right hand got his

223

right arm just above the elbow. I simultaneously pulled with my right hand, pushed with my left, and twisted with the momentum of my body. Something had to give. In this case it was Soto's elbow, which dislocated painfully with a loud pop.

I continued the move until I had his useless right arm in front of me and had slid my left hand down to grasp his right hand and twisted it back half way to his arm to apply a come-along grip. I now stood slightly behind him pulling his wrist back to the arm, which inflicted a good deal of pain and effectively ended our brief fight. I pulled the wrist just a bit tighter for emphasis, quietly telling him to order his gang to stay inside the bar and not interfere while we went out to the parking lot for a chat. Subtle doesn't usually work with gang bangers like Soto. So, I increased the pressure on his wrist just enough to increase the pain level, but not the damage, at least not yet.

Soto did exactly as I asked. "Stay calm, muchachos. The gringo and I are going out into the parking lot, just to talk. You can watch us through the windows. But I want all of you to stay in the bar unless I call you out or unless this cabron pulls out a gun."

I started walking him out, pointing him toward the door. Halfway to the door I stopped him briefly to repeat the orders he'd given his men, again increasing the pressure on his wrist to remind him of all he had at stake here. He did exactly as I asked.

Finally, and uneventfully, we stood next to the tree I'd parked behind so the men in the bar could see he was safe through the windows. "Will you behave and answer my questions if I let go of your arm?"

Soto nodded yes. With the continuing pain in his elbow and wrist a constant reminder I could do it again, I believed him.

I quickly shifted my grip to his good hand and bent back the little finger. "Now we're going to play a little game, Soto," I explained. "I'll ask a question. You'll answer it, completely and honestly. Then I'll ask some other questions. If you answer properly I'll be happy. If I'm happy, you'll be happy. If you don't answer, or lie to me, I'll dislocate your fingers one by one. If you think your elbow hurts now, let me warn you, the dislocated fingers hurt more.

"Are you ready for my first question?"

Soto nodded sullenly.

I increased the pressure on his little finger to remind him of the rules of our little game. "A few days ago someone hired you to steal a pickup truck and follow my friends and me from Winters up and down route 128. Who hired you?"

"I don't know what you're talking about," he muttered through tightly gritted teeth.

I jerked the finger back, with a loud pop as it dislocated. He stifled a scream.

I shifted my grip to the next finger over, the ring finger. "I'll ask you again Soto, a few days ago someone hired you to steal a pickup truck and follow my friends and me from Winters up and down route 128. Who hired you?"

I'll give him credit. He was tough. "I don't know what you're talking about," he repeated.

I jerked the ring finger back, dislocating it. The pain must have been extreme. I shifted my grip to the next finger. He sobbed in pain and frustration. "OK, OK, I'll talk. No more fingers."

"I'm listening," I said.

"I don't know any names. It was two Chinese guys I never saw before. They paid cash, a lot of cash."

Interesting! I thought a bit before deciding on my next question. "How did they find you?"

"They told me the sheriff had sent them. That I shouldn't worry, the sheriff would cover for me afterward."

Even more interesting! "What exactly were you supposed to do with us that the sheriff would cover up for you?"

"We were supposed to ram your car on the steepest part of the road going downhill. There was a bonus promised if you went all the way over the edge and down into the canyon."

"Describe the Chinese guys."

"Nothing special. Just Chinese. Well dressed. They paid good money."

I thought a little more. He was badly broken, with little or no resistance left in him. With his size this may have been the first time he'd ever been on the taking end of a painful fight. "Is that all of it or is there more you should tell me?"

"You've got it all. Can you let go of my finger now?"

I bent the finger back just a bit to remind him of what else could happen. "I'll let you go in just a minute. You're welcome to go back into the bar and join your friends. But I want to make sure you understand the rules before I let you go. You need a doctor and an emergency room or you might never have the full use of your hand and arm again. Get one of your buddies to drive you to the hospital.

"When you get enough painkillers in you you're going to start thinking about what you and your gang will do to me the next time. Bad idea. Remember, you tried to kill me a couple of times now. The next time you try to attack me you'll learn what real pain is like and what it feels like to be completely broken. Do you understand me?"

Soto nodded mutely. "I don't ever want to see you again."

The odds were very good to excellent Soto would come up with a further show of resistance to try to save face with his gang. I needed a head start so he couldn't.

Chapter 30. Visiting some suspects

A strategic retreat was in order and I still had a damaged, but potentially deadly, Soto to deal with. I kicked his legs out from under him steering him into a fall on his bad arm with the dislocated elbow and on the other hand with the dislocated fingers. He screamed in pain as I dashed around the tree and started my car, flooring the gas pedal. I could see Soto's gang streaming into the parking lot in my rearview mirror. Tires screeching, I beat a strategic retreat back to the winery.

The two-lane road was still curvy, with the Blue Ridge Mountains a central feature. The air was smoggy, with hints of irritants and ash to remind me of the ever-present wildfire lurking somewhere out of sight to the northwest, an existential threat to erupt again nearby should the wind direction change.

Everything looked like it had a few days earlier when I left Winters. The house stood silent and empty. The winery looked busy, with several of the employees' cars parked in front. The apparent activity reminded me that catching the killer was long overdue, as Sherry was at risk for as long as the murderer remained free to try to kill another winery owner. It was definitely time to stir things up and try to provoke a mistake. Hopefully a mistake that wouldn't get me killed in the process.

I checked Sherry's mail. There wasn't any.

My next step in an emerging plan was to visit Sheriff Stuart and rattle the bars in his cage a bit. I drove over to the Sheriff's office, parked in a visitor-only space, and walked straight through to Sheriff Stuart's office in back of the building without wasting any time. I wanted to have the advantage of surprise so I skipped the step where I was supposed to check in with the deputy guarding the sanctuary. I walked quickly past his desk into the corridor leading to Stuart's office.

Needless to say the deputy, impotently sitting at his desk in front of the station, was upset and called out to me, "You can't just go back there, Sir. We have procedures here."

By then I was at the sheriff's office door. I ignored the deputy, knocked softly, and walked right on in. "Good afternoon, Sheriff Stuart," I said politely.

He looked up from some papers on his desk. "You again," he sputtered. "How did you get back here?"

Uninvited, I pulled up a chair and sat down in front of the sheriff, on my side of the desk. "I walked," I answered innocently.

227

He obviously didn't appreciate my sense of humor. I didn't take that personally. A lot of people don't seem to find me funny, especially people who didn't like me. "What do you want? I'm busy," he practically snarled at me.

I smiled and tried to look innocent. "Well, first of all I was hoping you could update me on your investigation of Wallace Fortune's murder and Jason Culpepper's shooting."

The Sheriff smiled back at me, not nicely. "No, I'm not at liberty to comment on either of those two investigations at this time. Is that everything you want to know?"

I did my best to match his not so nice smile. "How about a comment on your previous and ongoing relationship with Victor Fong?" I tried.

"This interview is over," he said evenly. "Please leave my office now. You're trespassing!"

I took my time, looking at the office walls. There were lots of photos of the Sheriff with local celebrities and people in uniform. A framed diploma told me Jeb Stuart had graduated from a California State College in the Bay Area. However, there wasn't any diploma from a Law School hanging on the wall.

"There's that amateur lawyer routine of yours again, Jeb," I said, using his name rather than title to irritate him a little more. "As a member of the public, I can't trespass in an office in a public building that technically belongs to us taxpayers. Remember, the door wasn't locked when I knocked and walked in."

The sheriff's face turned red as he leaned over the desk to emphasize his threat. "Get out of here right now before I arrest you for being an obnoxious jerk, or maybe shoot you because you threatened me."

I noted that he'd found a large revolver somewhere to strap on his hip since the FBI seized all of the guns at his house. Perhaps he kept a spare gun or two at the office?

I kept the nasty smile on my face. "It might be harder than you think to get your gun out of that fancy holster faster than I can get mine out of my holster, Sheriff. And I doubt you've ever had a face-to-face gunfight with handguns at close quarters. I have. And they usually don't end well for either participant!"

We remained frozen in this tableau for ten or fifteen seconds. One more poke with a stick and I'd have completely accomplished what I set out to do. "Somehow, Sheriff Stuart, I see you as being a whole lot more comfortable shooting someone in the back from a couple hundred yards away with a rifle than up close and personal with a pistol. Frankly, I doubt you have the guts to try.

"And, let me give you a word of warning. If you try to come after me with a bunch of deputies and without a warrant I'll take my chances on a verdict of self-defense rather than letting you arrest me illegally and shoot me trying to escape. I'll be leaving you now. And, by the way, your buddy Soto sends his regards."

I carefully backed out of the room so as not to give the sheriff an inviting target, got in my car, and drove off. Checking the rearview mirror, I assured myself I wasn't being followed. I stayed under the speed limit until I got out of Yolo County on my way to Sacramento.

Crossing the causeway and bridge over the Sacramento River I called Gretchen Kaufman and quickly filled her in on my meeting with Gary, at the garage named after him, and my chat with Soto. "There's another link between the Fong family and the local law in Winters. Don't you think this might be a good time to arrest Sheriff Stuart and see how well he stands up to interrogation? Or at least to see if his attorney of choice is named Harold Fong?"

I switched lanes and sped up to pass a truck rumbling along at forty miles per hour in the fast lane. "Oh, I probably should also mention my visit to the sheriff." I told her how that discussion went, not leaving anything out. "That's another good reason for you to arrest him, Gretchen. If he comes after me before you put him in jail, you're going to have a badly broken or dead sheriff rather than a healthy witness against the Fong Family.

"One last thing, Gretchen. I assume Francis Fortune is still in FBI custody?"

"Yes, he is," she replied.

"May I interview him today if I drive to San Francisco after I finish my business here in Sacramento?"

She agreed immediately. "I think that can be arranged."

When I eventually got to Sacramento on the 5, I headed east on route 50 to Sherry's house in Carmichael, a large post-World War II vintage bungalow updated with modern additions and a couple of major remodels. The kennel manager taking care of her dogs, a heavy-set woman in her upper forties named Lydia, reported everything was fine and she was enjoying the 24-hours per day amenities of the house. She led me to two piles of mail for Sherry, labeled possibly important and junk. I took each pile in a separate large envelope and locked them in my attaché case in the car trunk.

Accompanied by Lydia I went out back to the dog runs, concrete pads with galvanized steel wire fencing and built in dog houses for shelter, running from the back of the house out into the large dirt and grass back yard. I paid my respects to

Juliet's extended family, with an extra scratch behind the ears for Hercules, Juliet's nephew, who remembered me from the time he impersonated Vincent's hunting dog during another case.

"He's a lovely dog, isn't he Mr. Bowman?" asked Lydia. "He seems to know you."

"Yes, he does," I answered. "He stayed at our house for a while and we own his cousin."

As we slowly walked back to the house I turned to Lydia. "Sherry's going to stay with us in Los Angeles for a while. She's a little bit worried about how safe you and the dogs will be here at her house until she gets back. Do you know of any good boarding kennels where we can leave her dogs until she gets back?"

Lydia looked thoughtful. "I knew there was something wrong when Sherry made these arrangements with me and started calling every day to make sure the dogs were OK. She usually isn't into bugging me that often. She knows I've been around dogs all my life and trusts me to look after them for her.

"So," she thought out loud, "we need a place where the dogs and I can't be found by anyone out to damage the animals as a way to hurt Sherry.

"That's easy. I have all kinds of dogs and kennel runs at my place in Rio Linda. There's no way anybody besides me or Sherry would be able to pick Sherry's dogs out of the mix. I'll be glad to look after her dogs there for the same amount she's paying me here. She knows my number so can contact me anytime she needs to. I can pack everything up and have the dogs on the way to my place in less than half an hour. There's plenty of room in my van for all the dogs and their food so I can do this in one trip. Just to make sure we're safe, can you stay until we get on the road?"

I helped Lydia load her suitcase, several weeks worth of dog food, and several GSPs into her van. We checked the house was completely locked up, with a few bathroom windows that were too small to climb through cracked open to let the house cool off at night. Lydia drove off while I watched carefully to make sure nobody was following her.

A short walk back to my car and I was driving west on 50, followed by I-80 to San Francisco. It took more than two hours with heavy traffic in the Bay Area, but I finally met Gretchen at the Federal Detention Center. Less than half an hour later we were sitting together in the same interrogation room as the last time across the table from Francis. His short time in prison had already affected Sherry's brother-in-law. He'd lost weight, his complexion was more sallow, and he carried himself with a posture of defeat. The outward appearance of arrogance had totally disappeared.

Gretchen recited the usual formula: date, time, the occasion being an interrogation of a suspect, Francis Fortune, and who was present in the room.

"What do you want from me now?" he asked us.

"I want to lay out a scenario for you we've constructed, Francis. Some of it can be proven, but some is still speculation. You can confirm some of those sketchier parts of it for us. That could help at your trial for attempted murder if Gretchen testifies you cooperated with us. If you're willing to testify as a witness against the Fongs at their racketeering and corruption trial, I believe Gretchen could also arrange immunity from prosecution for your part in their crimes."

Gretchen nodded her agreement.

Francis looked sullen. His body language was clearly saying none of this was going to happen. He remained silent.

I continued. "Hear me out, please. You don't have to say or do anything, just listen. I'm pretty sure we know a lot more about the past than you think we do, and maybe we're even a little more sympathetic about the part you played in all of this than you realize. If you're willing to discuss this, or have anything to add to what I'm saying, feel free to interrupt me at any time."

Francis continued just sitting there without responding.

I glanced at a sheet of paper on which I'd outlined the timeline while I was waiting for Francis to appear. "The story begins a long time ago, before you were born. A gangster from Oakland named Ching Fong had a bright idea. The local wineries in Winters and Lodi could be used as money laundering machines for organized crime in the East Bay. He was able to coerce your father, and several other local winery owners, into making him a silent partner in their wineries. All went well for a long time, perhaps because the infusion of mob money into the wineries rescued them from severe financial stress at a time when the industry was in a downturn and investment in a winery was extremely risky.

"I think what eventually went wrong was the local winery owners, led by your father, started communicating with one another. They had sons and daughters they wanted to bring into the family winery business. All of a sudden the deal with the gangsters didn't look or feel as good. The owners tried to convince their silent partners they were no longer welcome. The gangsters responded with intimidation, and worse, to force the owners to either sell them their wineries or continue the status quo without complaint. Several owners sold their wineries, while others were killed. One of the murdered owners was your own father, and very likely also your mother."

I could see Francis was jolted by that suggestion. He was uncomfortably looking at the same world he'd lived in all his life with the facts slightly rearranged. All of a sudden this whole world was turned upside down. It was time for me to press the advantage. A little poetic license was in order here.

The walls were still painted institutional yucky and the overhead light was still harsh. Francis seemed to be shrinking into himself as I continued. "By that time you were old enough to be in charge of things at the Fortune Winery and had your younger brother to look after. It's easy to see how you went along with the Fongs to protect your brother all those early years. I don't know if you were ever tempted to go to the law, but it's an open secret that Jeb Stuart and his father Joshua were both in the Fong's pocket, so that wouldn't have helped. Because nobody did anything, a second generation of gangster control of the local wineries just happened, which ultimately led to your brother's murder when he got married, which threatened the status quo.

"The FBI is currently putting together the evidence to prosecute the Fong gang for racketeering and worse in connection with their extortion and money laundering activities at the wineries. If you just told your own story of what it was like growing up in that world, and what the demands were the gang put on you as you became the winery's Chief Financial Officer, it would be a big help in proving that case."

I watched Francis process what I'd been saying. Seducing a hostile witness is a complex dance. This was a good place to stop and let him work things out on his own, not try to apply more pressure. "Thanks for hearing me out, Francis. We know a lot more I can't tell you about now, but you have the outlines of the story plus your own personal knowledge of the history and the characters. Gretchen Kaufman here is in charge of the Task Force working on the Fong case and will be happy to work with you if you decide to cooperate. After all the damage the Fongs have done to you and your family, I think you're lucky to have this chance to even the score a little bit."

Ten minutes later Gretchen and I were sitting in her office discussing the interview with Francis. "You did a great job there, Roger. You gave him just enough information to draw him in, not hard sell that would have turned him off. I'll keep you posted if he contacts me or wants to talk to you again. I suspect he may feel a bond to you at this point, which we might want to take advantage of."

I picked up a letter opener from her desk and played with it so I had something to do with my hands. "We still have a crooked sheriff to deal with here, Gretchen. Do you think you have enough evidence to make a case yet? If not, Francis might be willing to make a deal to testify against Jeb Stuart in return for an FBI guarantee of a minimum security prison to serve his sentence in."

"It's worth a try, Roger. I see Francis every day while we dance around how we can use one another. I'll bounce your suggestion off him tomorrow."

I thought for a bit. "And, we still have a professional killer to catch. I'm pretty sure I know who it is, but I haven't any idea how to prove it beyond a reasonable doubt unless you can play let's make a deal with one of the Fongs for their testimony. Do you have any suggestions?"

Gretchen answered, "We're still trying to untangle the Fong finances. That might help, especially if we see large regular payments to one of our suspects that we can match to the dates of the killings we know about. On the other hand, if his going price is $9,999.99 or less per hit we'd never see it. The banks only have to report deposits and withdrawals of $10,000 or more."

I thought about it all a little longer while I fidgeted some more with the letter opener. "Do you think there's any way to get some member of the Fong gang to testify about who was the gang's designated hit man in Winters in return for immunity from prosecution on the racketeering charges?"

Gretchen unconsciously copied me doing the routine with another letter opener. "No, Roger, I think that's going to be impossible. Nobody would dare testify against Vincent Fong for fear of it costing them, and their families, their lives."

Chapter 31. A big breakthrough from an unexpected source

Gretchen called as I was driving through the heavy traffic near Berkeley on my way back to the Sacramento airport to catch a flight home. "Can you come back here now, Roger? Francis Fortune says he wants to do some serious horse trading and he'll only do it with you."

I exited I-80 at University Avenue and turned around to head back to the City. "I'll be there in an hour or so, traffic permitting."

It took more like an hour and a half, but I got there. "I'm sorry to have dragged you all the way back here on a glorified hunch, but I'm hoping it'll turn out to be worth it, Roger. Francis wouldn't tell me what he wanted or what was being offered in exchange, but I think he's for real."

Half an hour later I was sitting in the now all-too familiar interrogation room across the table from Francis Fortune. Earlier he had looked much the worse for wear after just a short time in prison, but tonight he seemed much more energized than previously, a good sign.

"Thank you for coming, Mr. Bowman," he began.

If he was really ready to open up about his criminal activities, my best move was to be less adversarial, more engaged with him. Starting with he prefers Frank to Francis. "You can call me Roger, Frank. Most people do."

"The reason I wanted to talk with you, Roger, is I think I have some information you need, and I think you have some influence with the FBI you can use in return."

I tried to look sincere. "Tell me in general terms what you have and what it is you want, Frank, and I'll give you an honest answer whether I believe we can get buy-in from the FBI."

"I've done a lot of stupid things in my life. One of them was to totally underestimate you. When you showed up after Wally's disappearance I assumed you were Sherry's former boyfriend, not a serious detective. When you started figuring things out, I assumed a few words with Victor Fong would be all it would take to make you disappear. You seem to not only be awfully persistent and very clever, but maybe even tougher than Victor. That's a rare combination.

"On top of that, you seem to have a great deal of influence with the Special Agent-in-Charge here at the FBI. She seems to listen to you. I sense I'll be a whole lot better off with you negotiating my terms of surrender than if I hired a criminal defense lawyer off the street to do it. Or even worse, if I put my fate in Harold Fong's hands."

He hesitated as he considered what to say at this stage. I could see the wheels going around and his lawyerly reluctance to make the first move and give something away before being paid in advance. Francis slouched in his chair, avoiding any direct eye contact. He needed a push.

"I appreciate the flattery, Frank. But I've got a plane to catch tonight and you're going to have to give me something now to convince me I should be sitting here trying to help you out."

His body language suddenly said he made a decision as he sat up straighter and looked me in the eye. "You know I handle all the legal and financial work for the winery and have done so for a very long time. That's not my sole source of earning money. I get very busy around income tax time, doing the returns for a lot of people in Winters, not just the winery. That lets me see a lot about people's private lives. At this stage of the game I don't think I have to worry about the ethics of breaching a client's confidence in this area."

He paused for a while, waiting for me to respond. I didn't. It's a mistake to break the rhythm by interrupting when they start talking. Finally, he began again. "As far as quid pro quo, as lawyers like to say, I've come to accept the certainty that I'll be going to jail. The logical thing for me to ask is how can I make the experience as safe and comfortable as possible. Why don't we plan on using that goal as a guideline for negotiation?"

I considered what he might have to offer. The mantra for a private detective on a tough case is 'Follow the money'. Francis seemed to be hinting he had the financial details to incriminate someone in something. The odds were good he might have been preparing and filing income tax returns for a local professional hit man.

I'd already discussed the FBI recommending routing Francis to a minimum-security prison to serve his sentence with Gretchen and she'd indicated this was feasible. I couldn't see any downside in going forward in this conversation, with a huge potential upside.

"OK, Frank. One of us has to start putting their cards on the table. I think I can assure you that what you're asking for is not unreasonable under the circumstances. I'm confident the FBI would cooperate if you give us not only the name of whose tax forms had the incriminating information but a promise to testify about this information if they come to trial. I'd recommend that we invite Special Agent-in-Charge Kaufman to join us at that stage of our discussion so she can speak for herself and the FBI about any specific offer."

He thought about what I'd just said to him. No, it was more than that. He studied the words and the syntax, the way lawyers do when they're looking for lies underneath apparent truths. "I'm impressed, Roger. No fancy parsing of words, just a reasonable quo for my quid. I guess it's my turn to put a few cards on the table. Like I said, I see a lot of details about people's cash flow. For example, without naming any names at this point, one of my tax clients receives a regular monthly stipend from a dummy corporation owned by Victor Fong. I presume that's in return for miscellaneous services rendered. I think you would be quite surprised if I told you who."

I nodded and smiled. "Sheriff Jeb Stuart, I assume. We already know he's dirty. Your testimony against him would have some value as the FBI builds its case against him. But not enough value, by itself, to get you a free ticket to a federal prison for white collar criminals."

A look of surprise crossed Francis' face. He broke eye contact as he prepared to dissemble. "What would it take to buy me that kind of ticket, Roger? I've told you quite a bit for nothing more than just a vague promise."

He needed another push. "It would take you telling me something I didn't already know, not just that the sheriff is crooked and on the take. Or that his father, the Chief of Police, was the role model he learned how to be a crooked cop from as he was growing up."

"You really are good, Roger. And your assumption about Chief Stuart is also correct. But Sheriff Stuart is just my little fish, sort of an appetizer for you before the main course.

"One of my other clients has his regular income supplemented by five monthly payments of $9,000 each, followed by a sixth payment of $5,000 the last month of the sequence. That's $50,000 paid out in installments below the IRS reporting requirements for a bank transaction. Now what do you think someone has to do to earn that kind of money, paid in that fashion, every year or two?"

I nodded and smiled again. "May I assume the money originates from the same dummy corporation the Fongs use to pay off the sheriff?"

Francis hesitated for a long time before answering. He straightened up again and looked me in the eye. "Yes, you can, Roger. And I think that's a lot for me to tell you without getting anything back from you in return."

I thought about the best way to let him know I already knew everything and all we really needed from him was his testimony. "So I guess my next question should be whether your income tax preparation business goes back far enough so you can implicate Cal, as well as Clay, Bedford in the murder for hire business? And the Fong Family as one of the major clients they worked for?"

Francis let out a long, slow whistle of surprise. "How the heck did you figure that out? There's no way anybody told you about Clay or Cal."

"I'm the one asking the questions here, Francis, not you. If you're ready to make a written statement about all of this we've talked about and to guarantee your testimony from the statement at several trials, I'll call Special Agent-in-Charge Kaufman into the room and we can see if she's willing to formalize an agreement on the part of the FBI as to where you'll serve your prison term."

Francis looked a lot less cocky than he had a minute or two previously. "Yes, Roger, I can implicate both Clay and his father as professional killers, the money did come from Victor Fong by way of a dummy corporation he controlled, and I am willing to sign a statement about this testimony if the FBI gives me the guarantees I want in writing."

****

We were back in Gretchen's office as she updated me. "I've got the icing on the cake for you. One of my agents called a while ago from Sacramento, where he arrested Soto for suspicion of felonious assault at the Emergency room of the Medical Center based on his admission to you that he tried to kill you on the highway. After Soto was splinted and fixed by the trauma doctors there the agent got him downtown to the FBI offices where he was questioned.

"You made quite an impression on Soto. He respects you for what you did to him and your lack of fear of him and his gang. Our agent was able to get a signed statement from Soto, who admitted that two men he didn't know hired him for the job. Soto's willing to try to identify those two men for us from mug shots. More importantly, he implicated the sheriff in the attempted murder based upon what the two men told him. He's willing to help us get the men who hired him and the sheriff who lied about protecting him in return for immunity from prosecution for the attempt on your life. I think that's a pretty good deal.

"Very good," I said. "That is indeed icing on this evening's cake. What do you plan to do now?"

Gretchen organized the piles of paper on her desk, pointing to a large pile in the middle. "Based on what we have here I'm ordering an FBI SWAT team and a few agents to arrest Sheriff Stuart tonight in Winters and to charge him with conspiracy to commit murder and multiple violations of the RICO statutes. That should keep him in jail for at least five days with the weekend coming, which should be plenty of time to search his bank accounts and safe deposit boxes for the kind of evidence that'll hold up in a major trial. And, if we can convince a judge there's enough evidence to try him on the conspiracy to commit murder charges and he's a flight risk, we have a shot at no bail until his trial.

238

"We'll also give Soto a chance to look at mug shots of all the Fong gang members we have any pictures of to see if he can pick out one or two of them we can arrest and interrogate. With the threat of a major felony trial in Yolo County, where Victor Fong doesn't have influence over DA's and judges, we might get someone to talk."

Gretchen excused herself for a couple of minutes as she called several people and made the complicated arrangements to start the cumbersome wheels of justice moving in the right direction.

Then she turned back to me. "My compliments to you once again, Roger. That was a superbly orchestrated interrogation you performed on Francis Fortune. You used exactly the right mixture of carrots and sticks to get just what you wanted from him. But tell me something. Were you just guessing about Cal Bedford's involvement in the murder for hire business, or did I miss a key piece of evidence along the way?"

"I pretty much knew it all along, Gretchen. Vincent found an innocuous looking puff piece in the local newspaper from a long time ago showing Cal with a trophy deer head he'd killed, so I knew he was a crack shot. Clay would have been a little kid when Wally's father was murdered, suggesting we had two killers at work with the same rifle over a period of decades. I also knew Cal was a marksman when it was a human target from his military record as a sniper in Korea. And he was connected with the Fong Family via his wartime buddy, Victor Fong's older brother, so it all fit. Francis also told me Cal was in on the payoffs and that Clay knew about them when I interrogated him in his office after I beat up the two hoodlums he tried to sic on me. It's all on the tape recording I gave you from that interrogation."

Gretchen looked thoughtful. "All three of them, Francis Fortune, Clay Bedford, and Jeb Stuart had ties to Victor or Harold Fong. If we could get them all to talk, we could get Victor arrested here in Yolo County, where he doesn't have the political clout, for conspiracy to commit murder. If he spent a few months in prison awaiting trial, his gang would fall apart without him running things on a day-to-day basis. And the resulting vacuum would permanently destroy his criminal network in the East Bay when the other ethnic gangs rushed in to grab their pieces of the pie."

I got up to go. "You've still got a lot of work to do and I have to get home and spend a little quality time with Suzanne while I still can. Let's be sure to stay in touch."

Chapter 32. Dinner in Los Angeles, a few days later

The Kaufman sisters were in L.A. on FBI business. Suzanne and I invited them to dinner at our house so we could catch up on what had been happening since I said good-bye to Winters and San Francisco after questioning Francis Fortune for the last time. Also on our guest list were a much healthier Jason Culpepper; Vincent Romero; Bruce, when he wasn't serving; Sherry Wyne, who was in town supervising a big dog show before returning to Winters now that it was safe for her to begin actively running the winery without 24/7 bodyguards; and Juliet, the unsung heroine of our recent case.

Eight of us sat at the table in our large dining room while the ninth lay contentedly curled up under the table with her rump in contact with Suzanne's feet and most of the rest of her draped over Bruce's feet. Each time Bruce got up to serve something Juliet rearranged her body to maximize her contact between Suzanne and me, until Bruce came back to his chair and sat down. If anyone dropped a morsel of food, the bonus made her position under the table so much the better.

Bruce got us organized with an appetizer of asparagus spears wrapped in prosciutto accompanied by large shrimp stuffed with fresh Dungeness crabmeat. A Sonoma Chardonnay was poured with the course for everybody except for Suzanne, who had to make do with grape juice prepared from Welch's grapes. The mood was festive, almost celebratory.

I tasted the asparagus and Chardonnay, both of which were excellent. "None of the news from Winters or Oakland makes it into our media down here, so maybe Barbara or Gretchen would like to fill us in on what's happened since I left."

Barbara laid down her fork, seemingly somewhat reluctantly, and began, "Lots. I'll try to update you on my parts of this while Gretchen eats. Soto, who looks a lot better as a potential witness cleaned up and dressed in a suit and tie, turned out to be surprisingly observant. He had no trouble picking out his two employers from a mug book, or later on from a police lineup. I got approval for Soto's immunity from prosecution for the attempt on your lives in return for his testimony against the men who hired him for the attempted murder.

"We arrested both of the men who hired Soto. They had long criminal records and were both known members of the Fong gang. They were most unhappy when they were jailed in Yolo County and informed they'd be arraigned before a Federal judge in Sacramento County. I don't know if you've ever seen the Yolo County jail, which is in Woodland, just off I-5. It's pretty depressing. All concrete with narrow slits for windows and overcrowded. Right next door to an animal shelter, which gives it a certain ambiance."

Barbara sipped some wine before continuing. "They were even less happy when Harold Fong refused to defend them and they were appointed public defenders for their arraignments. So, we had two very nasty, but also experienced, hoodlums asking to see me to talk plea bargains and deals. Long story short, things are beginning to fall apart for Victor Fong. Both of the hoodlums will testify they were following Victor Fong's orders and paying his money when they hired Soto. And both of them will testify Fong also assured them that Sheriff Stuart would protect Soto, so no blame could come back to them.

"What do you think they asked for in return for this testimony, folks?"

Suzanne, chewing on a large piece of her shrimp, quickly said, "Let me guess."

Barbara nodded to her.

"They both asked to be allowed to serve their prison time as far away from Oakland and Victor Fong as they could get. I'd guess that would be Hawaii or Florida if they also wanted good weather. Since they're Chinese-American, I'd guess Hawaii."

"Give that girl a big cigar," announced Barbara, "You're exactly right. And for bonus points, why did Harold Fong refuse to defend these miscreants?"

"That's harder," mused Suzanne. "It's either he's discovered ethics and morality late in life and wants to distance himself from Daddy and Grandpa while he can, or he followed Daddy's orders for whatever reason Victor might have had. Maybe Victor wanted to punish his hoodlums for failure to complete the assigned task. I think I'll go with ethics and morality, at least as a lawyer like Harold might define those terms."

"Wow, you are good at gangster trivia, Suzanne. But we already knew that."

"Now we come to Jeb Stuart and Clay Ballard," Barbara continued, sipping a little of her wine while she spoke. "Gretchen's raiding party arrested Sheriff Stuart with no resistance. He's still in jail, appealing a denial of bail based on the seriousness of the charges and the flight risk. We did find the money trail linking him to the regular payments from Victor Fong's dummy corporation, so I don't think we'll see Sheriff Stuart out of prison for at least twenty years or so. And I think he'll be Mr. Stuart pretty soon. There's already a recall petition circulating in Yolo County requesting a special election for his successor next November. And the former Chief Deputy is officially serving as the acting sheriff until then.

"Stuart's not talking, but I don't think anyone much cares. We have him dead to rights and he really doesn't have any information we don't already have to bargain with. Now let me think. Is there anything else? Yes. The State authorities announced the wildfire was finally completely contained the same day we arrested Stuart and Ballard. It also rained the next day in the area of the fire so the wildfire is officially out." And so saying she went back to eating dinner.

Bruce cleared the plates and moved us on to the main course, a large piece of fish poached with an olive and herb mixture cooked down to a flavorful sauce in the Italian Provincial style. Fresh vegetables complemented the fish. A second bottle of Chardonnay appeared, this time from the Fortune Winery in Yolo County, courtesy of Sherry.

Gretchen put down her wine glass after a sip. "Our investigation of the Fong finances is going slowly, but it looks like we have all we need for an arrest and prosecution of Victor on multiple counts of racketeering, and probably tax evasion. I think this is going to be a big win for the FBI in its ongoing war against organized crime."

She looked nostalgically at the empty bottle of Sonoma Chardonnay. The message was clear. "Francis is cooperating fully with us and giving us a lot of background information that will make him a convincing witness at the trial. We arrested Clay Bedford the same night we picked up Jeb Stuart. Clay's in jail charged with multiple murders. They don't allow bail in those cases. He's refusing to say anything but we've got him cold based on his gun firing the bullets that killed at least five people we know about.

"We have several FBI experts who've examined the photo of Cal Bedford with his trophy deer who can swear it's the same make and model of rifle in the photo as the murder weapon we recovered thanks to Juliet. And, we have a paper trail of cash flow to the Bedfords in the right amounts at the right times to coincide with several of the killings paid by the same dummy corporation that made payments to the sheriff."

Everybody involved in the investigation had something to celebrate. We all took a few minutes to eat, drink the second bottle of wine, and try to begin to forget about serial killers. The wine wasn't bad, but it certainly wasn't as good as the Sonoma Chardonnay we'd started with, a wine made from grapes grown one or two valleys to the west over the coastal range.

'Hey, Jason, what's happening with Connie? " I asked. Everyone else at the table looked at me strangely, with a 'where have you been for the last two weeks?' expression.

"You mean Suzanne didn't tell you yet, Roger?" Jason asked incredulously.

I was beginning to get it. I wondered if I'd missed my chance at a cigar. "Tell me what?"

"Connie's a mom and I'm a godfather to a beautiful little girl, Suzanne Delbert Sherman, 6 pounds, 15 ounces. Everybody's healthy!"

"Things were pretty hectic for me the last week or two, Jason. I seem to have missed all the news since the last time I was back in L.A. What else hasn't anyone told me?"

Jason thought quickly. "I'm back to work on a fairly regular basis, commuting from Irvine. The doctors have signed off on me as getting better. Now it's up to me and the physical therapists in terms of getting back all my strength in the shoulder that got shot. Connie and I are seeing each other a lot. This might be the real thing for me, but we'll have to see while Connie adjusts to being a single mother.

"Thanks a lot for that very unsubtle introduction at your barbeque last month. Suzanne seems to have finally paired me off with the right person."

He sipped a bit of wine before continuing with a thoughtful expression. "And thanks for catching the guy that shot me. Given Clay's track record I'm feeling very lucky to be alive. Especially now, with so much to look forward to."

Suzanne added, with a twinkle in her eye, "You can also look forward to Connie getting a new job offer from UCLA as an assistant professor on the tenure track some time in the next few months. It will be completely flexible about the timing of the move, but you won't have to commute between Irvine and L.A. after she decides to take the offer and switches to UCLA."

Vincent raised his wineglass in a toast. "Claro. To Jason, welcome back; to Connie, for making Jason a godfather; and to Juliet, our newest recruit to the detective agency."

I was still trying to catch up. An awful lot seemed to have happened while I was in Northern California. "What else did I miss, Vincent?"

"Not too much new here. I found some interesting news articles from the past that might shed more light on the extent of the Fong Family's involvement in the wine industry. I think we just scratched the surface of a lot of crime and corruption in wineries all over the Central Valley in our investigation. I'll send you copies of everything for your files, Barbara."

Sherry, who was beginning to look like her former self-confident and capable self again, raised her glass in the next toast. "Thank you all for keeping me alive and for bringing me some closure after Wally's murder. I can't thank you enough."

Her eyes misted up, but she continued, "I've been spending a lot of time on the phone with my new manager, Carol Marshall. She's full of ideas about how to modernize and improve the Fortune Winery. More importantly, perhaps, she's calculated how the balance sheets will look after our silent partner Victor Fong stops draining money from the operation and my brother-in-law Francis is completely off the books. I can already handle everything he did with the taxes and financial parts of running the winery. Quite frankly, he didn't really do much more than input data into computer programs and print out the results.

"The bottom line: the winery can practically run itself under Carol and the present staff after we hire Clay Bedford's replacement, and it will make a whole lot of money for us in the process. I'll need to explore the legalities, but think we can organize a profit sharing plan where the employees get stock in the company as an incentive to stay on and as bonuses for helping grow sales and new products. I'll be moving my kennel operation over to the winery in the next couple of weeks and keep my current job with the AKC, at least until I get tired of all the travel. I'll also probably keep the Carmichael house as a rental property. It has a lot of sentimental value to me since I grew up there."

Suzanne turned to Bruce, who'd just served dessert and sat down again at the table. "What is Juliet's next big surprise for us likely to be?"

Bruce reached under the table to scratch the dog behind her ears. "I haven't figured that one out yet. But, if she keeps finding buried bodies, my guess is Roger will have to give her a full-time job as a detective."

Suzanne raised her half-empty glass of grape juice, pantomiming a final toast. "How about you, Roger? Do you have any final comments on this strange case?"

I took some time to think about it before answering. Half a glass of wine helped too. "I'm sorry for your loss, Sherry. From what little time I spent with your husband, Wally, he seemed like a good man. But he was apparently doomed by the past and there wasn't anything you could have done about it. The whole case played out like a classic Greek tragedy.

"A couple of generations ago three boys grew up at about the same time in Winters, which should have been a bucolic childhood for all of them. For whatever reason, all three independently made a few bad decisions about their lives, which ultimately doomed each of their first-born sons to repeat the cycle of bad decisions and evil. And it's probably not too much of a stretch to say Grandpa Fong in Oakland did the same thing to his son Victor when he chose the wrong path in life."

I sipped the rest of my wine. This was all much more philosophical than I normally let myself be about cases I investigated. "Actually, it's all right out of the bible, which accurately describes both ends of this sorry affair, Winters and Oakland. I'm thinking of the quotation, 'the sins of the fathers are visited upon the sons' as being all too apropos here for all four of the families at the middle of this case."

Epilogue

Winters, where agricultural development of the Sacramento Valley began, was first settled in 1842, seven years before the Gold Rush. Vegetables, fruits, nuts, and grape vines were cultivated in the area by these early pioneers. Cattle grazed the foothills of the Blue Ridge Range while the land below boasted rich soils and abundant water from Putah Creek. With the coming of the railroad in 1875, the town of Winters was established.

Wallace Fortune's Great-Grandfather, also named Wallace, came to Winters on one of those trains in 1899 as a returning veteran from the Spanish-American War. Land was cheap in those days. He bought a small farm that grew into the current Fortune property through the years. Wallace Fortuna planted cherry trees, grapes, and alfalfa. His farm prospered.

Grandfather Fortune steered the farm through the Prohibition years, maintaining the grapevines by selling grape juice instead of wines. The local cattle commanded premium prices during the World War II years and the farm's alfalfa became highly profitable. The profits were reinvested into expansion of the farm, especially during the immediate post-war years.

Wally's father, Peter Fortune, born in 1930, was too young to serve in World War II. Shortly after graduating from the UC Davis College of Agriculture in 1952, he inherited the family farm, which earned him an occupational deferment from the Korean War draft. Peter immediately recognized the potential of those old grapes and built a small winery on the property. The Spanish style table wines sold well locally. The family grew and prospered. Wallace was born in 1970, Francis several years earlier.

Alas, farming and winemaking are cyclic industries, featuring periods of both boom and bust. Peter's fateful decision was made in the 1960s, during one of those periods of bust.

It all seemed innocent enough at the time. An investment firm representing a group of Chinese businessmen from Oakland was looking to invest in a small winery. The infusion of capital could finance rapid growth of the winery and a good return on their money. Peter desperately needed money to keep up with the payments on the mortgaged recent land acquisitions and the increasing costs of making and selling his wines.

Ching Fong and two of his colleagues had telephoned ahead for an appointment before pulling up to the house in an expensive Cadillac to discuss their offer with Peter. After much bowing and handshaking as everyone introduced himself they went into the house for coffee and to talk business.

Ching, tall for a Chinese and broad shouldered, was fluent in English, but spoke with a strong Chinese accent. The others were younger Chinese-Americans and spoke perfect English. All wore expensive business suits and looked the part of investment bankers. Peter looked the part of a farmer in overalls and boots.

The two younger "bankers" were deferential to Ching Fong, who spoke for the group. "It is a pleasure to meet you, Mr. Fortune. You have a beautiful farm here. I hope we can see your winery too after we discuss our business."

"Of course, Mr. Fong," Peter replied. "Would you like to see our winery now?"

"I don't think that will be necessary. We invest in people, not things, so taking a little time now over your very good coffee to get to know one another is most important to us.

"As we discussed over the telephone, we represent a group of successful businessmen from the East Bay area who seek to diversify their investment portfolios. We see a very profitable future for the California wine industry as the world comes to better appreciate the quality of its wines, and several advantages to making our investments here in the Central Valley rather than in the already overpriced companies in the Napa and Sonoma Valleys. We believe an adequate investment in your winery to allow for expansion and more distribution channels for your wines could be highly profitable for all concerned."

Peter took a greedy sip of his coffee to satisfy his dry mouth. "Of all the wineries you might have chosen in this region, why did you select me for your investment, Mr. Fong?" Peter inquired politely.

"You are not the only winery we selected, Mr. Fortune," Ching responded equally politely. "We are talking about making very substantial investments in several of the local wineries. As I said, we believe the industry is ready to sustain very rapid growth, which we want to participate in."

Peter relaxed visibly. He was a very bad poker player sitting at the table with one of the best. "What would you expect to receive in return for your investment, Mr. Fong?"

"Ah, you are very direct, Mr. Fortune. I like that in a business colleague. I shall be equally direct with you. We would be silent partners. We have no interest in running a winery. Our interest is in sharing in a relatively small percentage of the profits of the joint venture and benefitting from a portion of the tax benefits of depreciation of the winery and its equipment. We would also hope to be able to explore the potential profitability of marketing your wines through several restaurants our group owns or otherwise does business with."

Peter took another sip of coffee. "As long as we are being direct, Mr. Fong, may I ask how large the percentage would be and how much money you are offering to invest in the Fortune Winery?"

Ching smiled. If Peter had been more alert, or more sophisticated, he might have noticed the smile stopped at his mouth. Fong's eyes remained extremely serious. "The percentage would vary with the amount of the investment. Perhaps it would be an excellent idea for us to look at your winery now. We can return to this discussion as soon as we have had a chance to estimate the proper amount for us to invest here."

The small group walked over to the winery, just to the north of the house. A man of Peter's age, who was introduced as Cal Bedford, greeted them immediately. "Can you take a few minutes to guide us on a tour of the winery, Cal?" Peter inquired politely.

Cal looked quizzically at the small group. "Sure, Peter."

After Peter performed introductions, they all walked through the fermentation and bottling areas with Bedford answering questions about the capacity of the equipment, its condition, and what newer equipment might mean in terms of economies of scale.

Peter noted with surprise that nobody asked about the wines themself except to ask how many total bottles of wine were being produced there. Even more surprising, perhaps, was that nobody asked to taste any of the wines. At the end of the tour, Fong suggested they return to the house to finish their discussion.

They sat at the table with fresh cups of coffee. Ching pulled a small notebook out of his pocket. "Will you please excuse me while I do a few calculations?" he asked.

Less than three minutes later Fong nodded, sipped a bit of coffee, and turned back to Peter. "We would be prepared to put $225,000, payable in three annual installments of $75,000, into your winery expansion in return for 25% of the additional profits you will make and a pro rata share of the tax benefits in perpetuity.

"In addition, in any years the winery loses money we will guarantee to reimburse you whatever it takes to break even, so you will not have any additional personal financial risk due to the expansion. This is, I believe, a very generous offer."

Peter thought quickly. 'The bank is breathing down my neck. They're threatening to foreclose on everything at the moment. He's offering me a new lease on life. How can I say no to all of this?'

"Thank you, Mr. Fong. If you can have your lawyers draw up all the legal papers I can have my banker and lawyer look the offer over and we can move forward on this."

"That won't be necessary, Mr. Fortune," replied Fong. "I prefer to do business with my partners by a handshake. If you want to proceed I can have a cashier's check in your hands by Friday afternoon."

He offered his hand. Peter hesitated a second, then shook on the deal. He had the check deposited in the bank and no financial worries by the end of the week. Life was good!

Ching Fong hadn't gotten to the top of the highly competitive and incredibly brutal gangland career ladder in Oakland, California by blindly trusting his colleagues, or in fact by trusting anybody. Less than a week before his meeting with Peter Fortune he had arranged the first of what were to be several meetings with Cal Bedford. He already knew of Cal as a friend of his son, who had served with him in the Korean War. Bedford was only too happy to receive an annual substantial off-the-books salary supplement in return for being Fong's eyes and ears in Yolo County, a legacy he passed on to Clay when the proper time came to do so.

In Cal's initial job interview, Ching feigned ignorance about Cal's past, asking about his history and hobbies. Cal explained to him he was a former army sniper who had seen combat in Korea with Ching's older son, and an avid deer hunter. Ching Fong carefully filed away this information for possible future use, noting he could have a lot of use for a man with that particular skill set, especially a greedy man who would betray his friends for money.

Less than a decade later Peter's wife would have died in a car accident and Peter himself would have disappeared under suspicious circumstances. Cal Bedford, and later his son Clay, managed the winery competently and profitably while Francis and Wally grew up, so the Fortune Farm and Winery remained in the family.

After Wallace graduated from UC Davis with a degree in Viticulture and Enology, he focused on farming and winemaking while Francis handled all things financial for Fortune Farms and the Fortune Winery. Working together, Wallace and Francis expanded the winery and bought even more land on which to grow grapes. Francis had graduated from law school several years previously and was now handling all the business affairs of the winery so nobody saw any immediate reason to tell Wally about the winery's silent partners.

***********THE END**********

From the Author

I hope you enjoyed this Roger and Suzanne mystery novel. Please consider writing a brief book review for posting on the novel's Amazon Book Page. It will help future buyers decide if this is the right book for them. A few sentences and a star rating is enough to allow most browsers to decide if they want to read a book. Book reviews also help an author sell their books, and are appreciated. Thank you very much.

Special Offer: If you post a review of this book on Amazon, message me on Facebook [https://www.facebook.com/RogerAndSuzanneMysteries] with your e-mail address, the preferred format for your e-book reader, and the name you used to "sign" the review. I'll send you a free copy of a short story featuring the series characters. Thank you.

About the series: The Roger and Suzanne mystery series currently consists of thirteen earlier books and the present novel. All except "The Body in the Alpaca Pasture" are published on Amazon KDP (all Amazon outlets worldwide, in English) and are currently available FREE if you belong to Kindle Unlimited. You can download all eight novels free right now if you are a KU member, and will have some very pleasant reading ahead for the next month or two.

I've tried to keep the book prices as low as possible for the entire series. In chronological order, they are:

1. The Ambivalent Corpse. The dismembered body of a young woman is discovered in Montevideo, Uruguay. Who did the brutal murder, and why? Meet several of the recurring characters in their first appearance in this series. $2.99. http://www.amazon.com/Ambivalent-Corpse-Crime-Meant-ebook/dp/B0060ZFRQG

2. The Surreal Killer. What motivates a serial killer? The answer to this question is the "whydunit" that leads Roger Bowman and Suzanne Foster to "whodunit", the solution to a series of brutal murders in Peru, Chile, and Bolivia. This tightly written mystery story will keep you guessing all the way to the thrilling conclusion. An Indie Book of the Day Award Winning psychological thriller. $3.99. http://www.amazon.com/The-Surreal-Killer-ebook/dp/B007H21EFO

3. The Body in the Parking Structure. A hard-boiled mystery novella featuring characters from the author's popular South American mystery novel series, including Bruce the nanny's debut, working on a murder case at home in Los Angeles. The clues are all there: Can you figure out whodunit before Roger does? $0.99 http://www.amazon.com/Body-Parking-Structure-ebook/dp/B008PDV9WC

4. The Matador Murders. This mystery novel, set in exotic Montevideo, Uruguay and Santiago, Chile, is a fast paced romp with lots of action and a suspenseful whodunit storyline reminiscent of Dashiell Hammett's Red Harvest. $3.99. http://www.amazon.com/Matador-Murders-American-Mystery-ebook/dp/B008QD4BJE

5. The Body in the Bed. An international whodunit novella that brings Roger and Suzanne back to Montevideo, Uruguay where another bloody murder mystery needs to be solved. $0.99. http://www.amazon.com/South-American-Mystery-Series-ebook/dp/B00A1PZZ86

6. Five Quickies for Roger and Suzanne. An anthology of three short stories: The Haunted Gymnasium, The Dog With No Name, and Someone Did It To The Butler, plus two longer novellas, The Body in the Parking Structure (see Book #3) and a completely re-edited, shortened, and improved version of The Empanada Affair (originally the first novel in the series, where Roger meets Suzanne). Together, the collection of five stories is the length of a traditional novel. All five of the stories feature characters from the series. The Haunted Gymnasium (Fortaleza, Brazil) and The Empanada Affair (Salta, Argentina) are set in South America, while the other three stories take place in Southern California. $3.99. http://www.amazon.com/Quickies-Roger-Suzanne-Mysteries-ebook/dp/B00F7VRMKS

7. The Deadly Dog Show. Roger and Bruce are hired to go undercover impersonating the owner and handler of a Champion German Shorthaired Pointer named Juliet. There's murder and miscellaneous other crimes occurring at California dog shows, and who better to solve them? The reviewers are enthusiastic about this book, which should appeal to mystery readers, dog lovers, and anyone else looking for a fast paced, entertaining novel. $3.99.
US: http://www.amazon.com/Deadly-Roger-Suzanne-Mysteries-ebook/dp/B00E25BM3I
UK: http://www.amazon.co.uk/Deadly-Roger-Suzanne-Mysteries-ebook/dp/B00E25BM3I
CA: http://www.amazon.ca/Deadly-Roger-Suzanne-Mysteries-ebook/dp/B00E25BM3I
Paperback version: https://www.createspace.com/6414558

8. The Origin of Murder. Roger and Suzanne are back in South America. This time, the couple are on a luxury cruise through the Galapagos Islands when

Suzanne finds a woman's body with a couple of bullet holes in it floating in the Pacific Ocean. There's a ship full of suspects, including a shady DEA agent and two nubile sisters from San Francisco, and more dead bodies to come. The supporting cast includes Bruce the Nanny, Eduardo Gomez, and a few new characters that will be featured in subsequent books in the series. Join our detectives on a visit to the Galapagos Islands as Charles Darwin might have seen them on his historical voyage on HMS Beagle, and visit the ancient capital of Ecuador, Quito, high in South America's Andes Mountains. $3.99. http://www.amazon.com/Origin-Murder-Suzanne-American-Mystery-ebook/dp/B00K4KDL3O

9. Unbearably Deadly For a change, the butler didn't do it; a bear did. Or did it? Roger and Suzanne visit Alaska to find out the circumstances surrounding their friends' deaths. The FBI investigation concludes the cause of death was a tragic accident. With nothing more than a gut feeling that something is amiss, our sleuths head to Alaska to search for the truth. The vast expanse of Denali National Park creates a 6-million acre locked room murder case for our sleuths to solve. There are no suspects, no clues, and little help available. Conspiracies abound and the truth is much more complicated than it appears. Can the detective couple solve their most difficult case to date? Can be read as a series entry or a standalone mystery novel. $3.99.
http://www.amazon.com/dp/B00RAOVJWW
CA: http://www.amazon.ca/dp/B00RAOVJWW

10. Science Can Be Murder. Are Suzanne's talents as a professor of biochemistry wasted in the Roger and Suzanne South American mysteries? No! Science Can Be Murder combines three books from the series, two full-length novels and a novella, into one omnibus volume. The unifying theme of these three stories is Suzanne's scientific skills and knowledge, which are important elements of their plots. In "The Ambivalent Corpse", the first book in the series, Suzanne brings Roger to South America to collect plants and botanicals for her research on new drugs to treat cancer. "The Origin of Murder", set on a cruise ship traveling around Ecuador's Galapagos Islands, gives Suzanne an opportunity to start developing her son Robert's interests in science on the right track. Suzanne's interest in anti-cancer drugs and Vincent Romero's early career as a professor of chemistry in Chile play prominent roles in "The Body in the Parking Structure". With a combined price for the three books individually of $7.97, this omnibus volume is a terrific bargain at $4.99 (an almost 40% discount from buying the three books individually).
http://www.amazon.com/dp/B00TVIM31Q

11. The Body in the Alpaca Pasture. Roger and Suzanne celebrate their third wedding anniversary solving a baffling murder case in their newest South American mystery. Set in the small town of Molinos, high in the Andes Mountains separating Argentina from Chile, the story features an exotic setting, a complex murder case, and a traditional cozy whodunit. The novella is available from various retailers including Amazon, Smashwords, Barnes and Noble, Kobo, Apple, and iBooks.
http://www.amazon.com/gp/product/B0176JLHFY

12. Hunter Down. A high-powered rifle shot rings out in California's early morning stillness launching Roger, Suzanne, and German shorthaired pointer Juliet into another suspenseful mystery thriller. In a complex whodunit set against a backdrop of pointing dogs and canine hunt tests, private detective Roger Bowman has to solve a murder case with no clues, no suspects, and no apparent motive. There's lots of action as the dogs hunt for birds while the humans hunt for a cold-blooded killer. Free from Kindle Unlimited.
US: http://www.amazon.com/gp/product/B016V4GQGA
UK: http://www.amazon.co.uk/gp/product/B016V4GQGA
CA: http://www.amazon.ca/gp/product/B016V4GQGA
Paperback version: https://www.createspace.com/6462804

13. Rum, Cigars, and Corpses. After more than half a century U.S. citizens can once again take a cruise ship or a scheduled airline flight to Cuba. What's Cuba really like? Enjoy this exciting international thriller while you get a good look at contemporary Cuba as described by an author who has recently been there.
US: http://www.amazon.com/Cigars-Corpses-Roger-Suzanne-mystery-ebook/dp/B01EZBDCRC
UK: http://www.amazon.co.uk/Cigars-Corpses-Roger-Suzanne-mystery-ebook/dp/B01EZBDCRC
CA: http://www.amazon.ca/Cigars-Corpses-Roger-Suzanne-mystery-ebook/dp/B01EZBDCRC
Paperback version: https://www.createspace.com/6491954

Made in the USA
Columbia, SC
09 November 2020

24217312R00139